P. 32, 43, 58, 105/9.

THE FINGERED CITY

Who shall doubt 'the secret hid
Under Cheops' pyramid'
Was that the Contractor did
    Cheops out of several millions?
Or that Joseph's sudden rise
To Comptroller of Supplies
Was a fraud of monstrous size
    On King Pharaoh's smart Civilians?

Thus, the artless songs I sing
Do not deal with anything
    New or never said before.
As it was in the beginning
Is to-day official sinning,
    And shall be for evermore.

RUDYARD KIPLING

The Fingered City

DENISON HATCH

NEW ENGLISH LIBRARY
TIMES MIRROR

For Peggy

First published in the USA by Paul S. Eriksson, Inc. New York in 1973
First published in Great Britain by New English Library in 1975
© by Denison Hatch 1973

*

FIRST NEL PAPERBACK EDITION MARCH 1976

*

*NEL Books are published by The New English Library Limited from Barnard's Inn,
Holborn, London EC1. Made and printed in Great Britain by C. Nicholls & Company Ltd*

45002760 0

Chapter 1

The rain began coming down harder, sweeping in waves up the avenue. It beat with a ceaseless din against the sidewalks, adding grimly to the whining cacophony of rush-hour traffic crawling north. The wet wind whipped around corners to race down the dingy side streets, where it flung the lids of waiting garbage cans high in the air and sent them clattering down the sidewalk toward Broadway. The soggy brown bags of garbage, left on the sidewalk beside the overflowing corner trash bins, were washing over the kerb into the gutter where they clogged the drains with their contents, causing floods at the crosswalks. In the city, April is a cruel month, stirring dull turds with spring rain; by July the smell of dogs would be everywhere.

Devereaux Page picked his way slowly through the storm along Columbus Avenue. Even though he stayed close to the buildings, rainwater sprayed off his hat and down the back of his neck; his coat was soaked through. At the corner of 100th Street, the light turned green, and a pickup truck spurted by kicking up a wall of garbagey water which sloshed against his knees and drained down into his shoes. He could have ducked under an awning to wait out the worst of the storm as many others were doing, but he pressed on. It was important to make this appointment – whatever it was – and be done with it quickly so he wouldn't miss his plane. The bastards had promised to leave him his weekends; without the horse show circuit, he'd be nothing and they knew that. But when the call comes, and they want to see you, you go. And you hope to hell they aren't late as usual; he'd already changed his flight twice, and if that 6.30 left Newark without him, he'd miss the dinner party in Cincinnati. Nuts.

His destination was the corner of 101st Street, the Showboat Lounge, where he'd never been before. Through the window he could see it was the usual – a dim, carpeted emporium with wood panelling and no customers. Any place those people touched was like this, smelling of failure. At least it was a place where he could get out of the rain and have a drink while waiting. Page went inside and stood for a moment blinking at the bright lights from the cigarette machine, trying to get accustomed to the darkness.

'Mr Page?'

He looked up. Instantly, two men stepped from the shadows and pinioned his arms. Instinct told him not to resist; these were obvious experts.

'Come with us.' It was a clear baritone voice from behind him. They had him in a double hammerlock, each with a fierce grip on his upper arm, and he was hustled along through the side hall past the crappers and telephones into the kitchen. The men were behind him, and he couldn't see what they looked like. In seconds he was out the back door into the rain again. At the kerb was a waiting black sedan. Beside the car was a short man in a trench coat holding an umbrella against the downpour. On seeing the trio emerge, he reached for the handle of the rear door and opened it. Seconds later, Page found himself squeezed between his two captors in the back seat; the short one who had been waiting with the umbrella got in next to the driver. 'Okay, Jimmy, let's go,' the short one said, and the car pulled away at a very sedate pace west toward Broadway.

Page still hadn't got a good look at the two men who had pinned his arms and carted him off. The windows were tinted, and it was dark in the car. The driver – Jimmy they called him – was so short his head couldn't be seen above the high front seat. Was he a midget? Was he tall enough to see over the wheel?

In the back seat, Page sat wedged between the two men who had grabbed him, both of whom sat staring stonily ahead. The car was air-conditioned, so all the windows were up; the only sound was the schuss of the wheels on the wet street outside and the splatter of rain on the roof when they stopped for a red light. It was an American car, a Buick or Oldsmobile, but with custom upholstery of soft dark leather that smelled like the cars of the very rich.

Page began to be afraid. He felt as though a football were being blown up inside his gut, getting bigger and bigger. From the rear vent, cold air was blowing on the back of his neck and wet shoulders. He hated these men. Blind, raging anger suddenly coursed through him. He wanted to fight, taking on the whole ugly crew of bullies, and beat them to a bloody pulp. But as he leaned forward slightly, he felt the men on either side of him tense, pressing on him more with the understated power of their steel-hard bodies. To resist would be hopeless. He slumped back, and the football in his gut grew bigger. His chest hurt and there was a throbbing his head. Looking down, he saw his hands were shaking.

At 96th Street, they turned west again. After passing the big complex of parking garages on the right, they went under the Riverside Drive bridge and circled around to the southbound side of the Henry Hudson Parkway. To the right was the grey ruffled Hudson River, shrouded in a misty rain. The high banks of the Palisades on the other side were bare silhouettes in the fog.

Suddenly Page felt terribly menaced, as though all the things he'd ever believed in were threatened. There was no way he knew of to cope with this crew of goons. The famous Devereaux Page charm, the quick wit, the pixie half-smile that women loved – none of it would go here. He was had. The trembling in his hands became more pronounced, and his mouth was dry. You can't have a casual relationship with these people; he knew that now. But it was too late. And besides, without the business they funnelled into him, he wouldn't have a life at all. Why was he here? Were they going to kill him? Perhaps death would be better than going on with the lie he had been living. Page shrugged, and instantly the big bodies tensed on either side of him. Any attempt at freedom would be useless, so he sat still.

The car picked up speed. Just as Page started to let his mind go blank, the short dark man next to the driver turned and stared at him. He was olive complexioned with close-cropped hair and a tight, thin mouth. The memorable thing about him was his eyes, which were black and which bore into his own with almost hypnotic intensity. Page felt that layer after layer of himself was being stripped away until nothing remained but the cold core of his being, dancing naked and embarrassed in a spotlight. Page had never seen eyes like these; they kept staring at him for minutes on end as the car silently travelled south in the rain. There was no getting away from them. He tried to look away, nonchalant, down at his lap, out the window, but there was always the presence of those eyes. Then without a word the man turned around and faced front. He couldn't have been more than thirty.

At 40th Street, they started down the exit ramp, and Page realized they had passed the Americana Hotel where he had planned to catch a cab for Newark Airport. 'I guess I won't be making my plane for Cincinnati,' he said glumly.

The man with the eyes swivelled around. 'That's right.'

'I'm expected for dinner; I'd like to let the people know I'm not coming.'

'They already know.'

'My hostess is Mrs George Phipps. She ought to –'

'Mrs Phipps knows you won't be there,' the man in the front seat said firmly. He had a flat voice and spoke in a clipped staccato.

'Don't worry, Mr Page,' the one on his right said with a broad grin. 'Mark called her up, didn't you, Mark?'

'That's right,' the young man with eyes retorted.

'Mark thinks of everything.'

Page took a deep breath. 'Well then, what about my suitcase? It's back there in the Americana where I checked it.'

'We've got it in the trunk of the car,' Mark said and turned around, leaving Page speechless.

These men had not only come into his life, they had taken it over. Were they going to kill him? Probably. Mark must be the killer who had been studying his captive and wondering how he would take death. There were times when the long sleep rather appealed to Page; what an easy way out. At other times death had its terrors. At this point, he was simply numb with disbelief and very frightened. Through the windshield he could see the obscene dark underbelly of the West Side Highway with its dirty steel legs between which they drove in silence.

They came to the West Side Heliport at 30th Street. Sitting on the rain-swept concrete apron was a small Bell Jetranger, its buglike windowed cabin painted red and white with a thin band of green encircling it. Ten feet overhead, the long thin rotor blades were stilled and bent slightly from their own weight. A pilot was waiting at the controls.

When the sedan came to a stop, the two men in the back seat

quickly got out and ordered their captive to do likewise. Standing in the rain, it was then he got his first good look at one of the men from the back seat. He had a very Irish face with a well-chiselled nose and a set of magnificently even white teeth; if he were ever able to cut loose from this crew, Page thought, he could make a hell of a living doing toothpaste commercials. Mark, the young man with the eyes, called over to them: 'P.J., you get Mr Page aboard. Nick and I will be right along with his suitcase.'

'Okay, Mark,' P.J. nodded good-naturedly and turned to Page. 'Come on, Mr Page,' he said, flashing a wide grin, 'let's you and me get out of the rain.'

They headed for the little helicopter. Just beyond the landing pad was the Hudson River. Should he make a break for it? A quick dash for the edge would certainly take P.J. by surprise. A plunge overboard, and he could swim to freedom. He wouldn't have time to shed his coat or shoes, but he could make it. And he was a good swimmer. The pilot reached behind and opened the door for them. They were at the steps of the Jetranger. It was now or never. Heart pounding wildly, he paused. Did he dare make a break for it by jumping over the side and staying under water for a while? Surface slowly next to the dock and then go under quickly again. Since he didn't smoke, his breath was in good shape. Hell, they'd never find him in that dirty water.

'Go ahead, Mr Page,' P.J. prodded. 'Get right aboard.'

He climbed into the tiny cabin obediently. If he had played John Wayne and managed a daring escape, they'd only find him again and be more careful next time. And more pissed off. The hell with it. Besides, he thought, who'd want to jump into that stinking, filthy river? He'd probably die from disease. P.J. climbed in next to him. 'You did the smart thing, Mr Page.'

'What's that?'

'Not trying to make a break for it.'

'What do you mean?'

'I used to be a Green Beret. We had to do the hundred-yard dash with full pack in ten seconds flat and swim a hundred meters in one minute.'

Page was afraid again. He slumped in the narrow seat behind the pilot and looked out at the rainy city through the scratched plexiglass of the windshield.

'Cigarette?' P.J. was offering him a Lucky Strike.

'Don't smoke, thanks.'

P.J. put the cigarettes away. 'I don't smoke either. I just carry these around to offer people. This pack must be a year old.'

The sedan with the little chauffeur drove off. Mark was coming toward the helicopter. The third man, Nick, followed, carrying the suitcase. He shoved it into the baggage compartment with a thump and slammed the hatch door.

Moments later they were airborne, strapped into the little crate which rattled and shook. Page watched the ground drop away as they headed out over the river toward the far shore.

'Is this thing safe in weather like this?' Mark shouted over the whine of the engine to the blond pilot with big ears who was next to him.

'It's the safest time of all; nothing else is flying.'

'Should we blindfold our passenger?'

'What for?'

'So he won't know where he's going.'

'Look, friend,' the pilot shouted, 'it'll be all I can do to find where *I'm* going in this weather! Don't you worry about him!'

They flew at about 200 feet, staying just off the Jersey shoreline over the river. It was cramped in the tiny cabin. In the distance the New York skyline had become massive shapes in the haze. After passing Jersey City, they saw the Statue of Liberty in the mist to the left. Ahead was the Verrazano-Narrows Bridge, slender and magnificent, stretching across the open bay. The pilot flew under it and, as the bridge went by overhead, Mark turned and winked at Page; it was the first sign of humanity he had detected in the young man with the eyes.

They flew for close to an hour, bumping along in the storm at low altitude, going south along the coastline with its deserted beaches, summer houses, and ricky-tick towns. Then suddenly they darted inland and dropped out of the sky for a landing on to the rolling green lawn in front of a huge white stucco mansion with a pink tile roof. To one side was the swimming pool, empty still from winter, with dark patches showing through where the bright green paint had peeled. Beside it were two pool houses joined by a verandah. The main house itself was immense, its flagstone terraces superbly landscaped with neatly trimmed bushes and hedges.

The helicopter motor remained idling while the four passengers ducked out on to the smooth lawn. Mark ordered P.J. and the captive to accompany him into the house, telling Nick to follow with the suitcase. As they reached the terrace by the house, the engine of the little flying machine revved up full, and the three paused in the rain to watch it take off again sending swirls of water in every direction before disappearing into the overcast.

'Follow me,' Mark commanded and they went inside.

It was a sunless, murky house with big rooms and small windows. Judging by the high ceilings and dark wood panelling, it was probably built in the late 1920s. The furniture, too, was of the same period, heavy carved oak tables and chairs. All the upholstered pieces were oversized and adorned with white anti-macassars. But the rugs! All over the dark, highly polished wood floors were richly coloured Persian rugs, their designs and hues seeming to glow from within, creating their own opalescent light in the dimness of the house. There were rugs everywhere – runners the length of the narrow hallways, huge multicoloured oval rugs, rectangular rugs, tiny rugs under the small pieces of furniture. As they walked along the main hallway, Mark in the lead with P.J. following, Page caught sight of the dining room on his right, with a long wood table and high-backed medieval chairs; it was entirely wood panelled, with a white ceiling; yet a rose colour filled the room, radiating from a vast Persian carpet that created light like a stained glass window.

Page's room upstairs, overlooking the rainy lawn on which they had landed in the helicopter, was large and pleasant, with a white shag rug and blue curtains tied back from the windows. In the distance were two good-sized white houses, each with its own expanse of lawn joining that of the main house. Surrounding the entire property was a high stucco wall; beyond it Page could see a strip of beach and the ocean.

Nick, the other abductor, opened the suitcase and began unpacking it. He was huge and looked to be the toughest of the three, with a square, rock-hard body, bull neck and pug nose. Unlike P.J., whose handsome Irish face betrayed his every mood, Nick had a perpetually vacant look. His cheeks and neck were pockmarked, and running down the left side of his pitted face from ear to chin was a thin scar that followed the line of his jaw. He moved mechanically, his dull eyes seemingly unseeing, his skin oily as though from the overflow of too much lubricating fluid in his robot works. Nick seldom spoke.

In the room, Mark was all business. He seemed to have a mind like a System 360 computer that hummed and whirred. He was very short, barely taller than five feet, five inches, with closely trimmed dark hair and a strong jaw that tensed as he ground his teeth with impatience. In moments of anxiety, his thin lips tightened, making his mouth a straight slit, and his dark eyes brooded fire.

'Okay,' he said with abbreviated gestures. 'Bedroom here, bathroom in there. Don't try anything funny, because there are always guards on duty and the place is rigged with electronics. So watch it.'

Page crumpled on to one of the beds where he sat looking at Mark. 'What are you going to do with me?'

'We're going to keep you very busy, if you want to know.' Mark was pacing back and forth in front of the window. 'There are a lot of tests you're going to be taking, a lot of people for you to meet. We might even get some fun in over the course of the next few days.'

'How long are you going to keep me?'

'Look, friend, just stop asking questions.' Mark glared at him. 'We're trying to put this thing together, and we haven't much time, so all I ask is your cooperation. No backtalk, no bullshit. Okay?'

Page stared moodily ahead. 'Okay.'

There was a brief silence. Nick's gargantuan physique filled the mirror on the opened bathroom door as he silently laid out Page's shaving gear next to the sink. Mark whirled on Page and pointed a finger at him. 'Is there anything in your past that you could be held responsible for that could have serious consequences later on?'

'What the hell is this – the Inquisition?'

'Answer me!' Mark was looking at him with the jackhammer eyes. 'Is there anything in your past that could cause your downfall?'

'My downfall?' Page smiled his little half smile. 'Been down so long it all looks up to me.'

'I'm serious, Mr Page.'

'So am I.'

'Let me rephrase the question.' Mark was sounding like a lawyer. 'Apart from a rather messy divorce from your wife, Kay, is there anyone who could walk in out of your past and cause you embarrassment? In other words, if you suddenly got to be famous, and your name got in the papers a lot, is there somebody – anybody – who could call up the *Times* and say he could prove you committed a felony – murder, rape, robbery, cheated on your income tax – that kind of thing?'

'Apart from Kay and the divorce?'

'Apart from Kay and the seventeen-year-old girl in Berryville.'

'Jesus, how'd you find out about her?'

'Answer the question, Mr Page.'

'How about some of my shady new customers at the firm – the ones with all the cash to invest? Somebody could blow the whistle on me for that.'

'Apart from that.' Mark was shaking his head impatiently.

Page cast his mind backward and forward across his memory disc, letting the needle fall at various random points in his life . . . Exeter . . . Princeton . . . Olympic Games . . . Kay . . . brokerage business . . . horse show. Horse Show. He'd travelled a good deal around the country, officiating at local horse shows, judging occasionally. He'd been offered a couple of bribes from over-zealous parents to let little Suzie or William get a ribbon, but he had turned them down flat; in fact, he purposely did not give an award to one of those kids, even though it might have been deserved, just to teach the parents a lesson. It had happened twice, and both times after the show he'd had to go out back and throw up; but he had been right.

When travelling, he'd stayed at some very good houses where the wife or daughter had occasionally come to his bed in the night, but had crept out again by morning. Mostly they were horsey types in the boondocks, to whom it was something to have made it with the president of the National Horse Show Association. He had obliged them, and the next day they seemed terribly grateful. A smile crossed his lips as he remembered one really naughty wench – a slender, vivacious woman who said to him as he was leaving to catch the plane to New York, 'It's been so nice having you.' She extended her hand and smiled radiantly. 'You must come again very soon, Mr Page . . .'

'What the hell are you smirking at?'

Page looked up. Mark and Nick were watching him intently. 'I was trying to remember if there was anybody who could get me in trouble.'

'And –?'

'I don't think so.'

'Are you sure?'

'As sure as I can be.'

'Because if you're lying, Page, we'll kill you,' Mark announced gently. Nick, who was leaning in the bathroom doorway, shifted his weight uneasily from one foot to the other. 'Do you understand that?'

Page nodded.

'We'll kill you,' Mark repeated. 'And it might take a few weeks, so you'll have plenty of time to think about it.'

'Would you guys mind telling me what this is all about?' There was an edge of anger to Page's voice now; these men were trying to play God with him, and they at least owed him an explanation.

'Are you going to tell him?' P.J. asked.

Mark nodded. 'Mr Devereaux Page, how would you like to be the next mayor of New York City?'

'The *what?*'

'Given a little luck and a little cooperation on your part, you're going to be the next mayor of the City of New York.'

In disbelief, Page looked at the three men, letting his eyes travel from face to blank face. There was a pause. A scene tumbled through his head – the year the Lindsays had been his guests in the president's box at the National Horse Show and the party afterward at Gracie Mansion, with its wood floors and high ceilings. He sucked in his breath and let it out again. Turning to Mark, he said, 'Could I ask you one small question?'

'Shoot.'

'Are you out of your fucking mind?'

Chapter 2

Mark Altschul burst out laughing. It was a rare explosion of emotion for one who had been tagged the Little Computer by his classmates at NYU Law School.

'Mayor of New York?' Page asked again. 'Me?'

'Why not?'

'What do I know about politics?'

'Don't worry about it.'

'But nobody's even ever heard of me!'

'With mass media, you could be a household word in 72 hours if we cared to spend the money.'

'But the mayor . . . Isn't he in charge of the police? Sanitation? Fire? I don't know anything about that.'

'Neither did Lindsay when he took office; he was just a little congressman from the East Side.'

'And look what he did to the city.'

'Don't worry about it,' Mark restated firmly. 'We'll teach you. I'm going to teach you everything.'

'What do you know about city government?'

'I was in it for five years.'

P.J. broke into his toothpaste smile. 'There's hardly a department Mark hasn't worked in.'

'I know New York City government, and I'll tell you something. It's a mess. It's crippled by welfare. People are afraid to walk the streets. The air is terrible – rated unsatisfactory by the Department of Air Resources four days out of every five. The subways are dangerous to human life. Traffic can't move.' Mark was pacing up and down. 'You know why? You know why New York is a mess?'

'Why?'

'Labour. Labour has got New York by the balls. If you're in city government, you can't do anything. You can't move. The

Police Benevolent Association . . . DeLury with his Sanitation Union . . . Vic Gotbaum and his Civil Service people . . . Shanker and the teachers . . . They've got the city tied up in knots!'

There was a momentary silence in the room. Nick Gigante, the big pockmarked goon standing in the doorway of the john, shifted his weight again and sucked his teeth.

'And you expect me – a nobody – coming out of nowhere – to become mayor of New York City?'

'You'll have behind you the most efficient organization the world has ever seen.'

'What do you mean?'

Mark brought his face within inches of Page's and stared at him with those mile-deep eyes. 'Don't you know who we are?'

'I know who you are very well.'

Mark sat back on the other bed. His tone changed, to one of lethal reasonableness. 'There'll be no narcotics problem, because we are narcotics. There'll be no crime problem, because we are crime. There'll be no labour problems, because we know about labour, about unions, about strikes and strike busting. There'll be no police corruption, because we are the corruptors and know where the bones are buried. There'll be no welfare problem, because we'll figure out ways to get money to pay for it. And we have no qualms about beating the crap out of people who are on welfare and shouldn't be, and the social workers who put them on and are getting kickbacks. Or beating the crap out of anybody, for that matter, who keeps the city from being a decent place to live in. And that goes for congressmen and city officials right on down to the guy who sweeps the streets and takes too long a coffee break.'

Page shook his head, trying to let the whole bizarre idea sink in.

'The only way to cope with violence and corruption is to put into power an organization that truly understands violence and corruption – and in fact was built on it. We're the only power that can take the entrenched bureaucracy and make it work. And I'll tell you something else. Mr Page,' Mark was spitting the words out with precision; if he could speak in rhyme, it would have been pure Gilbert and Sullivan, in a grotesque and twisted way. 'I'll tell you something else. If the people of New York ever found out who was really behind your candidacy – and they won't find out, because it will be a closely guarded secret, even from key people in the campaign – but if the voters were to find out you were really our candidate, you know something? They'd flock to the voting booths to elect you. You know why? Because the people are sick of the way things are being run today.'

'You mean once *you*, Devereaux Page, are in office.'

'Once I'm in – once the city is in the hands of the – the –'

'Careful what you say,' Nick grunted.

'Once the city's in the hands of this Organization, it's going to be plundered and raped and looted and bled white like the days of the Tweed Ring. Worse. Within a year, you guys will have pulled the plug and Manhattan will have sunk into the East River.'

'Bullshit.'

'No bullshit. I know you guys!' Page stood up. 'You get into somebody's life and you milk him until he's squeezed dry, and then you leave him by the wayside. And you'll do it to the City of New York and, frankly, I don't want any part of it.' He was shouting. 'No, I'm not your whore, your front man, your patsy, your pimp – I won't go down in history as the man who killed New York!'

'The professional politicans and the unions have already done all of those things,' Mark said quietly.

'Go fuck yourself!'

Mark gave a barely perceptible nod to P.J. who stepped forward and sent Page sprawling across the bed and on to the floor. It was a soft blow, dealt across the chin with the back of P.J.'s lightning-fast hands. Page was more stunned than hurt. He sat on the white shag rug rubbing his jaw, confused.

'There's more where that came from,' Mark said icily.

'You can't scare me with those kind of tactics. You might be able to force a man to do a lot of things against his will, but running for mayor of New York City isn't one of them. The whole thing is nuts. You're all nuts!'

'Wouldn't you like to be mayor?'

'I don't know. I never thought about it until now.'

'Well, think about it.'

'What if I don't feel I can handle it?'

'Mr Page, you got kids?' Nick asked. Page looked up. The huge goon had moved across the room and was standing over him like a colossus. The end of a toothpick danced crazily in his mouth.

'I have two little girls. Why?'

'Because, Mr Page, if you don't do what we want, each kid might have two broken legs – or worse.' With that, Nick extracted the toothpick from his mouth and broke it between his fingers. The tiny cracking sound seemed to fill the room.

Page's gut suddenly wrenched, and he threw up all over the white shag rug, just missing himself and Nick's shoes. P.J. and Nick picked him up and rushed him into the bathroom and held his head over the toilet.

Mark sat tight-lipped on the bed. The room smelled of vomit. At length he picked up the receiver of the white phone on the bedside table and called for the upstairs maid to come take out the rug and get it cleaned. Then he crossed the room and raised the window wide. As he stood looking out over the wet green lawns and the grey ocean beyond, the fresh sea air washed into his nostrils and lungs, while the patter of rain muted the sounds coming from the bathroom. Moments later there was a knock at the door; it was the chambermaid, a wisp of an Italian girl just off the boat. Two gardeners were with her, and they began to struggle with the beds and roll up the rug. Mark turned his back to the scene and stared out the window.

Here was the eighth applicant in as many weeks. Mark smiled to himself at the word applicant, since none had actually applied, except for Rafael LoCicero, the peppery, pint-sized state senator from the Bronx who had openly wept when he was told one Sunday night he wasn't being considered for the slot.

If Mark Altschul and his scouts couldn't come up with a mayoral candidate quick, it would be too late. It was already April; the election was only seven months away.

Mark turned from the window. The maid and her two helpers were just taking the long rug out the door. 'Could you come back to clean up the bathroom, please?'

'*Si, signor*,' she curtsied and disappeared into the hall. She was a little thing, dark haired with a cheeky behind that was delineated by her tight black uniform.

Page was put into a hot shower, and afterward, wearing only a bathrobe, he stretched out on one of the beds. He seemed totally spent. 'I'm sorry,' he said weakly. 'Right now I was supposed to be on a plane for Cincinnati. Instead I was kidnapped and for the last hour and a half I thought you were going to kill me. And then – when Nick said that about breaking the kids' legs . . . I'm sorry. I just couldn't take it.'

P.J. brought him a foaming white drink which Page regarded with suspicion. 'Come on, Mr Page,' P.J. reassured him, 'it's only a Bromo.' He handed Page three yellow-and-green Librium capsules to take with the drink. A few minutes later, the little maid arrived with a tray of *pasta in brodo* – that clear chicken broth with tiny pasta bits sprinkled on top with grated parmesan cheese which Page always associated with his first trip to Italy – fluffy white buttered bread and a small pot of tea. 'Can't let you face the cameras on an empty stomach,' Mark said.

'What cameras?'

'We're having a press conference in an hour.'

'A *what*?'

'Don't worry about it. You'll do fine.'

'But I can't –'

'Eat.'

When he had finished eating, P.J. lowered the venetian blinds. After cautioning him that Nick would be just outside the door if he needed anything, they left, and he was alone in the semi-darkened room. The Librium began to work, and the scenes of the preceding hours drifted dreamlike through his mind in slow motion. His mind seemed to be floating outside himself, looking down at the figure on the bed. Being manipulated by the Mob wasn't so bad. As long as they left the kids alone, he'd go along with their screwy idea of running for mayor. Wouldn't it be a hoot to wake up one morning and find yourself in Gracie Mansion? Think of what it would do to that bitch he'd been married to for 14 years – and how it would shake up her stuffy friends in Brookville! Page began to chuckle aloud, and as he did so, Mark and P.J. trooped in. They had been gone exactly an hour.

'Up and at 'em, soldier!' Mark said jovially. 'How do you feel?' He crossed the room and raised the blinds.

'Better. Much better.'

'Good, because you have a hell of a tough schedule.'

Page sat up and let his bare feet touch the polished wood floor where the shag rug had been. 'What have you got in store for me?'

'Press conference. Physical exam. Cattels, Rorschachs, Kuder Preferences, and a few others.'

'What are you talking about?'

'Tests, Mr Page. We're certainly not going to spend ten million dollars on a mayoral campaign only to find halfway through that our candidate has the I.Q. of a moron or has rampant homosexual proclivities.'

'What if I flunk?'

'We'll look for somebody else. And if you ever breathe so much as a word of what we're doing *to anybody*, you'll be dead in 24 hours.'

Page swallowed hard and nodded. 'You promise not to touch the kids.'

'If you cooperate, we won't go near your kids. You have our solemn promise of that. You will have absolutely nothing to worry about in the next seven months except winning this election.'

Big oily-faced Nick suddenly filled the open door of the bedroom; he was massive enough to fill any door – barn, garage, even an airplane hangar door. He was carrying Page's grey suit, the one he was wearing earlier when he had been abducted. It had been freshly pressed. Under Nick's arm was a big Saks Fifth Avenue box containing six shirts and three bright striped ties. Page shaved and dressed quickly, luxuriating in the feel of the new shirt; it was light blue with a long narrow collar and the letters D L P – for Devereaux LeGrand Page – embroidered on the pocket. These guys thought of everything. As he was knotting one of the new ties, a blue and white rep, he asked, 'Who's going to be at the press conference? The *Times*, I suppose, will send a guy. They cover everything.'

P.J. and Nick both turned to Mark, who was buried in thought by the window. All at once he surfaced and began talking in his machine-gun monologue style. 'Okay. This isn't a real press conference. There'll be cameras and lights and questions but it's more a screen test than a real press conference. We want to see how you look on the screen and how much work you'll need.'

'What'll I talk about?'

'It doesn't matter. We just want to get a look at you. Talk about yourself – where you went to college, the horse show business – anything.' Page started to run a comb through his hair. 'Don't worry about how you look,' Mark snapped. 'A makeup man will take care of that.'

P.J. helped Page on with his jacket, and the four of them went the length of the hallway to the servants' quarters and descended the narrow wooden back stairs to the basement two floors below. To the right of the stairs was a small, well-lighted room where Page was put into a barber's chair; huge mirrors on opposite walls gave him the illusion of looking down a corridor of mirrors that zinged out to infinity. As soon as he sat down, a curly-haired, very precise young man named Vin covered his neck and body with a barber's cloth and began studying him from various angles. P.J. and Nick left the room, and Mark started a rapid-fire barrage of instructions. Page watched him in the mirror.

'Do you know about television?'

'What do you mean?'

'How to behave in front of the camera?'

'Act natural, I guess,' he replied with a shrug. 'Is that it?'

'Success on television depends on achieving a low-pressure, low-key style. It's an intimate medium, demanding understatement, gentle wit, irony if you can do it. You don't make a speech to the camera; you talk to it like you were having a quiet conversation together. Even with a roomful of people shouting questions at you, your answers should be directed straight to the camera, as though it were a person – in fact, the only person in the room. Do you understand that?'

Page nodded. Vin began dabbing on pancake makeup. Mark continued talking. In the mirrors Page watched him pacing restlessly up and down, hands jammed deep in his pockets. 'On television you are coming into a person's living room or bedroom. You are a guest in the house. Never shout at them, or you'll turn them off, and they'll turn you off.'

Vin's expert hands were dusting powder on Page's face, in the crevices of his ears, and under his chin.

'It's crucial that you play it cool. Speak clearly, but not too loud. The audio guys will compensate. Be nonchalant. Not smart-ass nonchalant, but easy going, and casual. You're a charming guy. Just be yourself.'

'What do I talk about?'

Mark paused. 'Okay. Here's what to expect. We've set up a lectern at one end of the ping-pong room. There'll be a lot of lights on you, so you won't be able to see too much out front. The little red lights mean the cameras are on. Try and talk to the little red lights. Even if a question comes from the side of the room, concentrate on the red lights. It'll be confusing at first, but just remember the little red lights are good friends of yours and you're talking to them in the quiet of your living room.'

Vin was running a comb through Page's hair. Then, using one hand to shield the face, he applied a coat of hair lacquer from a spray can.

'Do you want me to talk first, and then people will ask me questions, or what?'

'Hell, you give talks at these horse show dinners, don't you?'

'Constantly.'

'Give one of those.'

With that, Vin swirled the barber cloth away from Page like a bullfighter performing a *rebolera* with the cape, and the candidate stepped from the chair. 'How long before I go on?'

P.J. popped his head into the room. 'They're ready out front. Are you?'

'As ready as we'll ever be,' Mark said. 'Come on, Mr Page.'

Chapter 3

Roberto DeStefano walked alone along the edge of the indoor pool. He was a short, wiry man with a big Adam's apple and thin face, crowned with a neatly shaped mop of brown hair that he was constantly brushing out of his eyes. His skeletal, almost sickly outward appearance belied the fact that he was a Black Belt and carried a gun with nine notches on it. Actually the notches were symbolic. His favourite method of execution was the garrote – not the current Spanish practice of placing a tight leather collar on a prisoner and strangling the life away by a slow twisting of the wooden peg, but the classic garrote, used when the unsuspecting victim was walking from one room to another and the executioner – in this case Bobby DeStefano – would jump him from behind with a jungle cry, encircling the neck with a steel wire held cross-handed in a loop. His knee stuck in his victim's mid-back, and with a twisting pulling motion of the wire, Bobby would nip the life out of the victim as the body came crashing down on top of him with a gurgling strangled cry, after which he would perform a finishing twist, leaping out of the way just before the sphincters relaxed to drench the corpse in urine and shit.

Not that the youngest son of Joe DeStefano had to engage in such spectacular antics to gain and keep his place in the Organization. A simple squeeze of the trigger against one victim who could have been held and blindfolded for him would have assured him a high place in the councils. But very early on, there was one precept he had heard and lived by: if you're the son of the Boss, you had to be better and tougher and smarter than everybody else. Each member of the Organization had to know why Bobby was on top, and that reason was not because he was the son of the Boss. In the act of murder, witnesses noticed Bobby's own blue eyes shone, and his lips parted in a boyish grin with what an Army psychologist once called his 'sunny brutality.'

Bobby let himself into the ping-pong room and looked around, letting his hand nervously brush back the brown forelock that constantly got in his eyes. The tables he'd played on as a boy had been folded and stacked against the far wall, and the room had been turned into a miniature studio. There were two sets: the lectern, where the candidate would first appear to make a statement and answer a few questions; and a small interview corner with two swivel chairs, where close-up shots would be taken during an informal talk. In front of both sets were banks of hot floodlights; overhead were scoop lights on a scaffold of steel pipes. The combined wattage could light up the room like daylight. The events coming up were to be recorded in three ways: a pair of 35-mm Nikons would be shooting stills in black-and-white and colour; there was a 16-mm Auricon with 400-foot film magazines that resembled giant Mickey Mouse ears; and a closed-circuit Sony Videorover II TV system. It was admittedly crude, but here were the rudiments necessary to see a candidate and how he related on mass media. The television tape could be rerun instantly, and if it seemed worth it, the film would be flown by helicopter to New York where an all-night lab would have it processed by morning.

The young Boss settled into a chair in the darkness at the back of the room and fingered his West Point ring. In front of him, the last-minute preparations were going on – the adjusting of lights, focusing of the various cameras, and work on the sound system. One of his *capos*, Johnny DiSantis, was acting as cameraman and director. For years Bobby had kidded the tall, dour Johnny about his hobby of photography, needling him in council meetings that he'd make more money if he spent less time with his cameras. But big Johnny, who stood over six feet and had a long John Carradine face with a crew cut, used to smile and say, 'Someday you'll be glad I know how to operate a camera. I swear on my father's grave.' And he had been right. The camera work and sound were flawless, and, more importantly, Bobby didn't have to hire an outsider at these early stages when the whole scheme might well be aborted; the fewer people who knew, the better.

Actually, he had been pleased all along that Johnny DiSantis was good with cameras. It had become almost a fetish with Bobby that every member of his Family, including himself, could hold down some kind of legitimate job to help justify his expenditures.

Another of Bobby's hard rules was that no member of his Family – either his own blood relations or his official Family – could get their names in the papers. Success in this business meant keeping a low profile at all times.

Bobby's own father, old Joe DeStefano, had spent too many days in court and too many months up the river for his perpetual fights with the law to be either meaningful or profitable. As long as Bobby was Boss, no member of his Family would put a tiny child through the torture of an hysterical good-bye to Daddy who was going away for a long time, as his father had done to him when he was little. No amount of money was worth that, or the months in a household headed by moody Latin women who would be pistol-whipped by a brother-in-law if they so much as looked at another man.

The last time Joe DeStefano had been jailed (perjury before a federal grand jury), his older son, Joe Jr., had become head of the Family, and for a time it looked as though things would be done the old way – the perpetual scrapes with the law, bloody gangland assassinations, soldiers being arrested for everything from gambling and extortion to morals and narcotics. But six years ago Joe Jr. had been blasted through the roof of his Cadillac convertible by a fulminate of mercury bomb wired to the starter. Roberto had been charged with picking up the fallen standard; things were going to be different. Gradually he eased out the old crowd, retiring them with good incomes to Florida, the Bahamas, or back to Sicily, with strict orders on penalty of a contract to stay out of any and all action. Then he brought up the brighter younger ones – those who were American born and well spoken – schooling them carefully in the workings of society and law enforcement, so that now the DeStefanos went virtually unnoticed. From the Department of Justice right on down to the New Jersey state and local cops, the heat was off; the law was concentrating on Sam the Plumber DiCavalcante and the gang wars across the river resulting from the shootings of Joe Colombo and Crazy Joey Gallo.

Bobby turned to look around the ping-pong room. It was almost time to begin. Others had drifted into the room to get a first (and perhaps last) look at the applicant. Old Joe DeStefano, titular head of the Family and now in semi-retirement, was ensconced in a leather armchair across the room; he and Bobby nodded to each other, as much out of respect as mutual love. P.J. was acting as a stand-in by the microphones as Johnny DiSantis made a final check of the cameras. Nick lumbered around the set, moving baby spotlights which Johnny was monitoring with a light meter. P.J. and Nick always worked together. Where P.J. was lightning fast – as a result of his training in the Green Berets and the jungles of Vietnam – Nick was slower, but he had such tremendous size and strength that he and P.J. were an unbeatable team. As hit men they were unmatched anywhere in the Organization, especially with Johnny DiSantis acting as fingerman. In the 16 years of his employ with the DeStefanos, the whole face of the enterprise had changed, moving from old-fashioned violence – bank heists, extortion, and gangland killings – into legitimate business such as restaurants, trucking corporations, refuse hauling, and now politics.

Nick Gigante wasn't part of the inner councils of the DeStefano Family, but he never questioned his assignments, nor the sums of money he was paid to carry them out. His earning these days approached $60,000 a year, always in tax-free cash, which he continued to keep in safe deposit boxes, but under joint access with his wife, so that in case anything happened to him, she would be taken care of. But this political thing was new.

Nick remembered that February night, with icy winds blowing off the ocean, when Bobby DeStefano had summoned his aides to the big white clapboard house at the far end of the compound, and in a rare moment had invited them into his panelled, carpeted study for a brandy. It was a motley group that had crunched across the glistening snow of the compound and were now arranged around the Boss, relaxing and sipping Grand Armagnac before the blazing fire. In descending order of size, there was the vast Nick Gigante, muscled like a washboard; Johnny DiSantis, nearly as tall but so thin as to be almost cadaverous; and P.J. with his dark Irish good looks and compact frame that could move with the speed of a coiled rattlesnake. The two little guys were there too: Tony the Elf Mauro, the former jockey, with his pointed ears and pixie mouth; and the driver, Jimmy the Dwarf, whom Nick had brought into the Organization fourteen years ago when Bobby mentioned he couldn't find a decent driver who knew his way around the New York area.

They had never before been privileged to share a drink with the Boss, except, of course, during the holidays; but those occasions were perfunctory. This time they had been invited into his study for a chat; something big must be in the wind. Bobby sat with his feet up on the big curved desk across the room and frequently ran his fingers through his long, tousled mop of brown hair as he talked in his reedy, New York accented voice. The thrust of the Organization was changing, he said, and new areas of involvement were being explored. One of the new possible profit centres was the computer business. The great robberies of the future weren't going to be spectacular bank holdups, with guns in the face and wild escapes in a waiting getaway car; Bonnie and Clyde were dead. Instead, a technician familiar with the computer installation of that same bank was going to insert an IBM card into a stack of other IBM cards. The result would be the transfer of two million dollars to someone's account in another city which would then be drawn out by writing a check. If there was any question about it, why it would simply be called a key punch error – an extra two zeros had been punched in by mistake. The moneylending business was still pretty good and counted for forty per cent of their current income. There was some question about how long gambling would remain profitable, what with the success of Off-Track Betting in New York, and the legislatures of many states looking into legalized casino-type gambling as a way of raising much needed revenues. Of course there would always be bookmakers, because bookmakers could extend credit where government would not. But otherwise the cities and states, with their desperate need for money, might well turn to gambling, simply because the populace was sick to death with ever increasing taxes and less services and protection to show for it. The day was coming when Coney Island or Atlantic City might become a Las Vegas East; it was being discussed in the state legislatures right now.

Nick listened attentively, sipping the brandy which he didn't much like, and trying to understand the various things the Boss was saying. Surely there would always be room in the Syndicate for someone with Nick's abilities, so he wondered what all this was leading up to. Suddenly Bobby was on his feet pacing the room and talking very quickly. 'A guy came to see me last week,' he said, 'a lawyer who used to work in the Lindsay Administration, who said that with enough money and a halfway decent candidate, we could elect a mayor of New York. He outlined a plan how we could do it – put our own guy in Gracie Mansion.'

'Why buy when you can rent?'

Bobby looked up and saw it was Tony the Elf who had asked the question.

'And why New York rather than Jersey City or Newark?' asked Johnny DiSantis. 'They're easier. We own them already.'

'Because New York's the big apple. Because they guy who came to me knows New York City like the back of his hand and it's a fantastic plan he's come up with. And because if we can get the city this year, we'll go after the state legislature and the governorship next year. Then the presidency in seventy-six or eighty!'

'But why buy when you can rent?' repeated Tony the Elf.

Bobby turned to face the former jockey. 'Which do you think is more profitable: owning the entire business or shaking down the head man until he spills everything to the police and we all go to jail?'

'Owning the whole business.'

'You're fucking-a right. And what's more, we'll not only own the business, we'll own the police and jails as well.'

Bobby resumed his placing. Not much taller than Tony the Elf, his sinewy frame moved pantherlike around the room. He talked about how he had dismissed the whole idea at first, but the more he thought about it, the more he began to believe the Organization could run the city better than the city was being run now. 'We could cut the running expenses in half, keep a quarter of the savings, give the taxpayers back a quarter, and everybody would be happy. Right?'

There was silence in the room.

'Does anybody here doubt we could run the city better than it's currently being run?'

Nobody said anything.

'Well, for Crissakes,' Bobby shouted with exasperation, 'what do you think of the idea?'

'Why ask us?' Nick shrugged. 'If you want to take over the city, we'll help you take over the city. You don't have to ask nobody's opinion.'

Bobby's mouth twitched. Or was it a flicker of light from the fire? 'Here's why I have to ask you guys,' he explained. 'Because you're going to be the keys to the whole fucking thing, that's why.'

'What do you mean?' Jimmy the Dwarf was leaning forward, his grotesque hump silhouetted against the blazing logs in the hearth.

'You guys are a team,' Bobby said. 'You're the best in the entire Confederation; you're the best in the country and perhaps even in the world. And you've got one thing going for you that nobody else has. Nobody. Do you know what that is?'

Silence.

'Not one of you has ever been arrested, fingerprinted, or mugged. The cops don't know you. The newspapers don't know you. So if we go into this thing, you five guys are going to have to be my representatives in the campaign. Nobody else in this Family can show his face, or he'll turn up in the newspapers and blow the whole thing. You guys are it. What do you think of that?'

'Tell us what you want us to do, and we'll do it,' Johnny Di-Santis said simply.

'It'll mean a lot of work,' Bobby said. 'Long hours from now till November. You'll be lucky to see your families once a week, if that. But it's a hell of a challenge. It'll be the biggest thing any of us has ever done.'

'So let's do it,' Johnny DiSantis said.

'I'll drink to that,' P.J. echoed.

'Me, too.'

'Why not?'

They raised their glasses and downed the last of the brandy. 'Nothing's definite yet,' Bobby warned them. 'We've got to find a candidate first, and then decide whether we want to go ahead. But I've authorized $100,000 to be charged against R & D to look into the possibility.'

None of the five knew what R & D was, Nick thought, but nobody was going to ask and look stupid.

'Needless to say, I'll keep you all informed every step of the way,' the Boss said formally, concluding the meeting. But as they filed out the door, he exclaimed, 'You know, it's a fucking exciting idea!'

P.J. was now at the microphone saying, 'One . . . two . . . three . . . testing.' Others buzzed around the room in frantic last-minute preparations. Reading the VU meter on the Nagra IV tape recorder and various cameras was the best audio man in the east, Tony the Elf Mauro, a former jockey who stood four-foot-eleven in elevator shoes and weighed 98 pounds soaking wet. Nearby, sitting alone on a folding bridge chair, was Bobby's only child, his lithe, black-haired daughter Mia, wearing tan stretch pants and a beige silk blouse that outlined her sumptuous breasts with their out-sized nipples. For Mia, horses were her whole life; she was expert in the saddle, and Bobby wished he could relax his stand on no publicity in order that she could compete in shows and perhaps go on to Madison Square Garden. But he couldn't have his daughter's picture all over the *New York Times* sports pages, or the wrong people might start asking what young Bobby DeStefano was doing these days. Apart from not being allowed to compete in horse shows, Mia had a good life, with her own cottage in the compound and a stable of five magnificent show horses. In the fall when she reached nineteen, she would be marrying young Paulie Coppola of Buffalo, thus uniting two great Families. Meanwhile, he wished to Christ she would wear underwear. He had overheard some bawdy speculations on the part of his soldiers that had infuriated him, even though he knew it had been just talk. No one would dare touch her, or Bobby himself would garrote the violator; it would not be the usual quick garrote at which Bobby had become so expert, but one that took perhaps a half day, while someone else did the same thing to his balls. Even the thought of little Paulie Coppola pawing over Mia on their wedding night riled Bobby, but he couldn't keep her chained to the compound forever.

Suddenly all the photographic lights went on at once, flooding the front of the room with brilliant light and causing the ten or fifteen people assembled in the back to blink in the reflected glare. Instantly the room went silent with anticipation. The red lights were on in front of the two cameras, and big Johnny DiSantis loped over to the lectern with a black-and-white striped take-board on which was written in chalk: DEVEREAUX PAGE – TAKE 1. He clapped the slapstick down and darted back behind the cameras. 'You're on, P.J.,' he called.

P.J. Costello stepped up to the podium to make a short statement. If anyone in the Organization had the raw talent for the cameras it was P.J., who flashed his smile and started talking. It was Mark's idea to use P.J. because he was so damn good looking with his square jaw and white, perfect teeth. P.J. was also completely at ease before cameras, so it was possible to judge the performance – either good or bad – of anyone who followed. P.J. wasn't smart enough to keep up the front for long, and he knew that. But for a few brief moments there appeared on screen a personality every bit as attractive as John V. Lindsay. P.J. talked for a minute, winding up with 'and so as all of you know, this is not a formal press conference, but a chance to meet the candidate and see what kind of a guy he is. So I give you now the president of the National Horse Show, Devereaux Page.'

The side door opened, and Page came out, followed by Mark, There was a hollow patter of applause from the few people in the room led by P.J., who relinquished the microphone. Page stepped up to the lectern and smiled as the applause continued. P.J. and Mark were on either side, out of the camera's range, clapping loudly and gesturing for the others in the room to do likewise.

Page was interesting to look at, with his sandy red hair coming down to a widow's peak and a triangular face, its straightness broken by high cheekbones that were most in evidence when he smiled. His grey suit was without a wrinkle, and his blue-and-white tie shone in the lights. Above all, he seemed relaxed, and even though he blinked and squinted in the garish lights, there was a great deal of confidence about him as he waited for the little ovation to cease. Then P.J. and Mark stood to one side, and everyone strained to hear what he would say.

Page began by clearing his throat, and the sound cracked over the loud speaker like a pistol shot, causing a ripple of laughter among the onlookers. Then he began to speak in a firm, resonant voice; here at least was a man who was used to making speeches:

P.J., thank you for that generous introduction, and I'm delighted to be here with you ladies and gentlemen this evening. Actually my title is president of the National Horse Show *Association*, which is far older than the horse show itself. I certainly don't want anyone to confuse an old reprobate such as myself with my distinguished colleague William Joshua Barney, Jr., who is president of the National Horse Show itself, or my esteemed friend, Albert E. Hart Jr., who is president of the American Horse Show Association.

What followed was an inane talk, all about the history of the National Horse Show Association which was founded shortly after the War of 1812 and went into virtual eclipse during the Civil War on up to the 1880s when it was revived again in conjunction with the National Horse Show.

Actually the National Horse Show Association *sponsors* the Horse Show in Madison Square Garden every year, just as the American Horse Show Association *sponsors* all the shows around the country where riders must compete to get to the Garden. Of course, I haven't been on a horse for years, and the real reason they keep me on year after year is that nobody else wants the job.   Ha-ha-ha.

Page stood there with a smug, shiteating grin on his face, jaw extended, eyes closed waiting for the laughter which never came. He was dreadful. There was all the confidence in the world about the man – so much so that he was positively offensive. What was worse, while the native timbre of his voice was good, the tone was nasal with one of those eastern society accents caused by pushing his jaw forward and never moving it when he spoke; it was the classic Locust Valley Lockjaw accent.

In all seriousness [he continued] my real work with this organization is not all just administrative and ceremonial. Actually I'm responsible for all the advertising in the horse show programme. Ha-ha-ha.

There it was again, that stupid grin and laugh. Mark winced. Bobby DeStefano pivoted in his chair and crossed his legs. Old Joe DeStefano got up to leave, accidently kicking over a tool box whose contents landed with a clatter òn the terrazzo floor; this was followed, all the way to the door, by a stream of Italian oaths. At the podium, Page stood with that smile on his face, squinting to see what was going on beyond the blinding lights and waiting for quiet in the studio so he could continue. At length he went on with a few stories about the horse show business and ended up by saying how wonderful it was for children to grow up with horses because it taught them responsibility and schooled them in a tradition of sportsmanship and fair play which originated with the knights of the Middle Ages, changing and growing until it reached full flower at the end of the nineteenth century.

My rewards in this job [he concluded] come from helping to carry on this great tradition, to create an atmosphere of formality and discipline which is so important to the development of young people, and which is often lost in this age of permissiveness, violence, and drugs in which they are growing up.

It's up to all of us here in this room to continue this tradition so that our kids will have the background to be the future leaders of this country – to come forth like knights on horseback, as it were, to lead the American people out of the Dark Ages we seem to be in. In the words of Rudyard Kipling:

> Since first the White Horse Banner blew free,
>   By Hengist's horde unfurled,
> Nothing has changed on land or sea
>   Of the things that steer the world.

Thank you all very much.

Page stood there nodding slightly, eyes half closed, in cocksure anticipation of the round of applause that always followed this little talk.

Bobby DeStefano let out a raspberry cheer which reverberated through the room. Everybody was convulsed except for Deveraux Page who suddenly looked puzzled and hurt. 'What's the matter?' he wanted to know. The cameras were still recording the scene. 'What's wrong? Is something wrong?'

'You're a fucking snot!' Bobby snarled, and hurled himself from his chair to the front of the room where he knocked over the lectern and cracked Page across the face, sending him back against the panelled wall with a thud. The candidate's legs went out from under him, and he slid limply to the floor. A moment later his nostrils turned bright red as a cascade of blood rolled down to his mouth and chin and dripped onto his clothes. Bobby, his eyes flashing hatred, fists clenched in a helpless rage, began kicking

the downed man in the side and thighs. P.J. sprang between
them, pulling Bobby off and pinning him against the wall until
the Boss had calmed down. 'He's a fucking snot!' Bobby screamed
'I'll kill the sonofabitch! I'll kill him!'

'Take it easy, Lieutenant,' P.J. said with deadly calm. It was
only in times of great stress that P.J. addressed his former
commanding officer by his Army rank.

Nick grabbed Page under the arms and dragged him from the
room; on the way out Mark dabbed at the bloodied nose with a
handkerchief.

Bobby continued to tremble a few moments longer and then
relaxed. 'It's okay, P.J.,' he said quietly. 'I'm okay now, thanks.'
P.J. stepped aside, allowing Bobby to stand alone by the toppled
lectern in the lights that made the whole scene seem brighter than
life. Bobby looked up and squinted into the lights. 'I'm sorry
about that,' he announced to the still horrified onlookers. 'That
guy's accent just pissed me off. I once went to a party full of
people like that, and they all talked with the same snotty society
accent. I finally asked the guy I was with why everybody talked
with their teeth clenched, and he said it was the only way they
could keep the shit from pouring out.'

P.J. burst out laughing as did everyone else in the room. Mark
Altschul steamed out of the dressing room. 'What the hell's so
funny?' he demanded. 'You've just busted up my candidate but
good!'

'Your candidate,' snapped Bobby, '*my ass!*'

'No, wait,' Mark contradicted, 'give him a chance.'

'Get rid of him.'

'Bobby, we can't screw around forever looking for a guy.'

'Can you imagine that smug WASP asshole trying to talk to the
voters in Brooklyn or the Bronx? They'd boo him out of the boroughs. And I'd come off looking like the biggest jerk since Joe
Colombo. And that's not easy.'

'He can learn.'

'Bullshit he can learn! He's terrible!'

'Jack Kennedy was terrible when he started, and he got
elected. So was Bobby Kennedy and Harry Truman.'

'The answer is no.'

'Bobby, we've got the cameras set up. Let me finish the screen tests. We're paying a doctor, so we can give him a physical, and some intelligence tests, and make up our minds on Sunday.'

Bobby stared coldly at Mark. 'Do what the fuck you want.' And he stalked out.

Chapter 4

Back in the dressing room the barber chair was tilted all the way back with Devereaux Page stretched out in it. Vin, the makeup man, was working on the bloody nose like a prizefighter's second. 'What'd you do to the guy?' he kept asking. 'What happened?'

Vin gingerly probed the area around Page's nose and cheeks. 'That hurt?' he asked. P.J. was massaging Page's shoulders.

'Does what hurt?' The Librium was still working; Page only felt numb. He closed his eyes and breathed through his mouth. Somebody applied ice, and the bleeding subsided. Mark Altschul came in.

'What'd you do to the guy?' Vin asked again.

'How is he?' Mark wanted to know. The lights in the room were very bright. Page's head was swathed in bloodstained towels; with two men working over him, the whole scene had a morgue-like aura.

'He'll be all right,' Vin reported. 'No broken bones anyway.'

'What happened?' Page mumbled from under the towels. His accent was all nasal because his nose was clamped shut and covered with ice. 'What'd I do wrong?'

'Your first lesson in politics, Mr Page. Never give the wrong speech to the wrong audience.'

'What do you mean? You said you wanted me to say a few words so you could see how I looked on television.'

'I know that.' Mark was grinding his teeth between sentences. 'But they were the wrong words for these people.'

'Why?'

'Maybe it was because you came on like a rich society guy – to the manner born with a silver spoon in your mouth – and you were talking to a bunch of people whose parents came over on a cattle boat and had to scrape their way to the top. I don't know. But you pissed them off plenty.'

'What's going to happen to me?'

'We're going to finish the screen tests, and go on with the programme as though nothing happened.'

'It won't do any good.'

Mark turned to Vin. 'I'd let him rest for a half hour or so and he'll be all right.'

'I'm not your candidate, Mark,' Page protested plaintively. 'If I make people that mad . . .'

'Let me be the judge.' Mark flicked out all but one small light. 'Come on, Vin.'

'Mark, I don't think I want any part of this.'

'Until it's finally decided, you'll do as we say.'

An hour later, Devereaux Page, wearing a clean blue shirt and rep tie, was ready for the cameras. Just before he went on, Mark said to him. 'Do you remember what I told you about how to act?'

'Treat the camera as if it were a person, and I am talking to it alone.'

'Right.'

'That's what I tried to do before.'

'You gave a stuffy, pompous after-dinner talk to a stuffy, pompous horse show dinner party, and you're lucky your balls aren't in your throat.'

'But I always give that talk. And it always goes over.'

'*It's the wrong talk for this crowd!* How many times do I have to tell you?'

'Okay, Mark.' Page looked down on the shorter man with a patronizing smile and said gently, 'Tell me exactly what you want, and I will try my best to do it.'

'Don't get smart-ass with me.'

'I'm not being smart-ass.'

'Keep this up, and we'll break your kid's legs and your head. Don't you forget that.'

Page shuddered. Apparently that was the only reminder he needed. 'Okay,' he said. 'what'll I talk about this time?'

'When you get in front of the camera, we're going to ask you questions. Answer them simply and honestly. And when you do, remember three things.'

'What three things?'

'Those two cameras with the little red lights are like two people – the most important two people in the world. You talk quietly to them and to nobody else.' Mark smiled. 'Don't take your eyes off those cameras, or they'll sneak out of the room when you're not looking and go bust your kid's legs.'

'That's not funny.'

'The second thing to remember,' Mark continued, ignoring him, 'is that you want to be mayor of New York City so bad you can taste it, and you've got to convince those two cameras that you're the man for the job.'

'And third?'

'And third, you are a dumb rich schmuck who doesn't know shit about being mayor or making a speech or about anything, but you're going to learn. Otherwise, you're going to get your balls ripped off and your kid's legs will be broken.' Mark marched up to the podium and called for quiet on the set. 'Once the cameras are running, I don't want anybody to move. If you have a question, ask it from where you are sitting. Ask it loud and clear. But I repeat, don't move, or you'll cause Mr Page to shift his eyes. Okay? Let's roll 'em!'

It was a different Devereaux Page who went before the cameras the second time around. He was cool, humble, and honest. Why did he want to be mayor of New York, came a question from the floor. 'The city is in terrible shape, and I would like to try to make it a decent place to live again.' What made him think he could do a better job than the present administration? 'I sure as hell couldn't do any worse,' he laughed; it was a natural, honest laugh this time, as opposed to that smug cackle earlier. More questions came from the floor, and somehow Page remembered to talk only to the cameras. After twenty minutes, somebody yelled 'Cut!' and the bright floodlights went out, making the room seem terribly dark. Of the original fifteen people who had witnessed the first fiasco, only about seven remained, and they all left the candidate in the front of the room to crowd around the tiny playback deck for a replay on the miniature screen in black and white only. Primitive though the system was, it gave an indication of the applicant's raw qualities as a performer, and he didn't look all that bad. Midway through the replay, Mark ordered Johnny DiSantis to set up his equipment in front of the other set, where the candidate could be interviewed in much more intimate circumstances. In a half hour they were ready to go again.

Mark Altschul stood with Page to one side. 'Okay, this is a different approach. Totally intimate. I'm going to be sitting in one chair and you'll be in the other. I'll ask some questions, or maybe we'll just talk. But the important thing here is the cameras are going to be over my shoulders and set for extreme close-ups. Your face is going to fill the entire screen, understand?'

'Why so close? That's not natural.'

'If you can come across in extreme close-ups, you'll be all right in medium and long shots. Call this one the shit detector test; if you're full of shit, we're going to know it.'

They sat down opposite one another in the floodlighted corner. As Tony the Elf adjusted microphones around the participants' necks, Mark continued giving instructions. 'Again, remember, you're not talking to me. You're talking to the red light over my shoulder. Low key. Low, low key. Speak clearly; speak positively; but play the whole thing with quiet confidence.'

Page cleared his throat. Johnny DiSantis rolled the cameras in tight – one over each of Mark's shoulders, until the candidate's face filled the viewfinders. 'You've got to keep your head very still, Mr Page,' Johnny DiSantis cautioned.

'And your voice at a conversational level,' added Tony the Elf. 'Now say something.'

'This whole thing is crazy,' Page said. 'I have to believe everyone in this room is out of his tree.'

'That's good!' Tony the Elf called.

'He's got to play it to one camera or the other, Mark,' DiSantis explained. 'When you're in this tight, a shifting of the eyes looks really lousy.'

Mark swivelled around, almost bumping his head on the Auricon camera lens. 'Play it to this one, Mr Page,' Mark said touching the side of the small Sony Videorover II camera that was mounted on a simple tripod. 'This is the television camera, and this is going to be a television campaign.' He spun around to face the candidate who was starting to concentrate on the small camera just over Mark's shoulder.

'Now don't mug or make funny faces, Mr Page. Don't be self-conscious. Pretend you're going into the living rooms of thousands of people all over the city of New York, and you want to be like John Kennedy rather than Hubert Humphrey. You're a guest in people's homes. The most important quality in a candidate is honesty; once you learn to fake that, you've got it made.'

'Okay.'

'Are you ready?'

'Am I ready to be mayor of New York City? No.'

'One step at a time, Mr Page. Are you ready to go on camera?'

'I guess so.'

'Okay, Johnny, roll 'em.'

The two red lights went on, and Johnny DiSantis almost took off Page's nose as he clapped the black-and-white board down on the take. Everybody laughed, and then Mark started asking questions.

The interview apparently went well. Page had always been at his best in small groups. His was a very mobile face, one that could register change in tiny ways – the raising of one eyebrow, the slight purse of the lips just before saying something, the barely perceptible smile when he was amused, and half a hundred little facial mannerisms that had fascinated people at dinner parties or small gatherings; he was a superb listener and had a quick wit that enabled him to turn ideas back at you with a new twist, sending the conversation off on a different tangent. The horsey set in which Page travelled the most was not known for its intellect or depth of understanding of the human condition, but Dev Page was well liked everywhere by both men and women because – well, because he was fun to talk to. He had almost total recall, able to remember every story and every person he had ever met, and he was able to call them back from memory as they had been when he had first known them, whether yesterday or twenty years back. All this came out in the conversation with Mark before the cameras. They talked of his boyhood, of his parents, of school, moving from Princeton where he had been captain of the debating team to the stock market where he'd spent most of his working life as a broker, and back to his first days with the horse show; he had been captain of the Princeton equestrian team and a member of the United States team in the 1956 Olympics in Melbourne – and they talked about that, too.

Sitting opposite Page was Mark Altschul, reading from his typed script in a precise style which was exactly the opposite of Page's. But Mark wasn't on camera, so it didn't matter; it was Page's show, and he was doing fine. At the end of twenty minutes Mark terminated the conversation, and the cameras were turned off. It was fiercely hot under the spotlights, and Mark's face glistened with perspiration; Page's makeup had kept his face smooth and dry, even though his underwear and shirt were soaked through. The bright lights remained on, and the candidate slumped in his chair; he was tired, and his side was bruised and tender where he had been kicked earlier by an angry Bobby DeStefano.

He was sitting alone now. The others had repaired to the Sony monitor where they stood in a knot waiting for the tape to be rewound and played back. Mia DeStefano came to the front of the room and sat down opposite Page in the chair Mark had used for the interview. 'Mr Page?' she said softly. He looked up to find two enormous black pools of eyes searching his. 'I thought you were very good.'

'Who are you?'

'My name is Mia. I'm afraid my father was the one who hit you earlier.'

'A lovely man,' Page growled. She had a narrow face with finely chiselled features and long black hair drawn back in a pony tail.

'Mr Page, I ride horses. I have a stable here with five horses and I ride every day. When the horse show comes to Madison Square Garden I go to all the events – every night and every day.' The words kept tumbling out, almost as though she'd had no one to talk to for weeks. 'I'm probably the only person here who has ever heard of you, and I just feel awful about what's happening to you. If there's anything I can do to help . . .' She looked away, her face crinkled in bewilderment. Page noticed she wasn't wearing a bra beneath her beige silk blouse and saw her nipples were the size of his thumb tips. She looked at him and said, 'The only thing I hate to see mistreated more than another human being is a horse.'

'Mia!' Bobby DeStefano's voice thundered from the darkness beyond the bright lights under which they were sitting. 'Get the hell out of here and leave Mr Page alone!' Wordlessly the girl rose and left the room.

A moment later the lights were extinguished, and Page sat in the darkness. P.J. came up to him. 'Will you follow me, Mr Page? We're going to give you a physical.'

'How'd the interviews come out? Did I do all right?'

'I really couldn't say, Mr Page. I do know they're sending the film into New York to be developed tonight. Beyond that, it's anybody's guess. Meanwhile, I've got orders to keep you on schedule.'

P.J. Costello regarded the eighth applicant for the job of mayor of New York City. Devereaux Page was standing on a scale wearing only his white jockey briefs and a pair of paper hospital slippers, while a young doctor with long blond hair and watery blue eyes recorded Page's weight and height. It wasn't a bad body, P.J. thought; there was a little roll of excess fat around the middle, but that would come off with some exercise and a decent diet. P.J. looked around the small gym with its massage tables, reducing machine, and workout equipment. Through the open door was Joe DeStefano's indoor pool; behind him the steam room. Nearby were the punching bags, a 200-pound stuffed cylinder and the little leather one, just the size of a human head, mounted at eye level. Until the physical examination was over, there was nothing to do but kill time. P.J. was better at killing people than time. He sent his fist into the big punching bag with a satisfying smack; it was a short punch, travelling no more than four inches, and he could feel its power all the way up his arm and in to his muscular shoulders. He'd never let his body go stale. Keeping in shape was almost a religion with him. Who could tell what he'd be asked to do next . . . a hard tail on a fast walker . . . rough somebody up . . . kill . . . or abduct another candidate if this one didn't work out.

There was a hissing sound, and he looked over at Devereaux Page who was sitting on the edge of the massage table having his blood pressure taken. P.J. thought they had a real chance with this one, if he was smart enough and could learn to deliver a speech. Mark had been insistent the candidate have plenty of grey matter, and had built in all kinds of tests to run throughout the weekend to measure his intelligence under stress. Four weeks ago the applicant was turned down because he couldn't think straight when he was tired. Mark had blackballed him. But then Mark was Jewish, and smarts mean a lot to Jews.

At the conclusion of the physical examination, the candidate dressed and P.J. marched him down the hall to Mark's office, a cluttered little room in the basement at the other end of the indoor swimming pool. There was just space for two desks, some file cabinets, a maroon leather couch, and some chairs. On the floor was one of those thick, iridescent Persian rugs that were to be found in almost every room of the house. This one was blue and gold with a red-and-black filigree design. The walls were panelled in blond wood.

As P.J. and the candidate came in, Mark looked up from his desk and told them to sit down. Page sprawled on the maroon couch, letting his head loll back to stare at the ceiling. Exhausted, he closed his eyes and tried to believe this wasn't happening to him. P.J. stood at ease by the door, legs slightly apart, hands clasped behind him. P.J. was ready. He was always ready. Four years in the jungles of Vietnam had taught him never to take anything for granted.

Mark continued to scribble on a yellow pad at his desk. The only sound in the room was the quiet rasp of the pencil. Suddenly Mark dove into the bottom drawer of his desk and pulled out a white booklet. 'Give Mr Page the first test in here,' he said to P.J. 'He can work at the other desk. He has eight minutes, and I'll be finished with what I'm doing by then.'

P.J. took the test booklet and gestured for Page to sit at the second desk facing Mark. 'We'll be giving you parts of this test throughout the weekend,' Mark said abruptly. 'We want to see if you can think rationally under pressure and when you're tired.'

'Don't worry about my intelligence,' Page assured him. 'I do the *Times* puzzle every Sunday.'

'So do I,' Mark retorted. 'In ink.'

P.J. handed the candidate a sheet of paper titled:

CATTELL INTELLIGENCE TESTS
PRACTISE TEST
(time allowed: 5 minutes)

On it were a series of unnumbered questions. They were very simple:

Good is the opposite of (*big, poor, bad*)
Up is the opposite of (*tall, down, less*)

Page scanned it and began to work. In one minute he had finished.

'Even I could get through that one,' P.J. said. 'Now here's the real one.' He tossed a booklet on the desk in front of the candidate. The white cover was filled with paragraphs of instructions in small type. There was a headline which read:

AMERICAN MENSA SELECTION AGENCY
CATTELL INTELLIGENCE TESTS
GROUP AND INDIVIDUAL

'Skip the stuff on the front,' Mark said without looking up. 'Break the seal and take the first test. Time him, P.J. He has eight minutes.'

Page broke the seal and folded back the page to TEST 1 – SYNONYMS. There were twenty, and they were all relatively easy:

Prohibit means the same as (*contradict, hinder, forbid, restrain, defend*)
Belief means the same as (*sincerity, faith, honesty, credit, ignorance*)

In four minutes Page had completed the twenty questions. After glancing over his work, he closed the booklet and sat back.

'You've got four more minutes,' P.J. reminded him.

'I finished.'

'Holy mackerel!' P. J. enunciated each syllable. 'A live one!'

There was a knock at the door. P.J. opened it a fraction. The young doctor was standing outside, his black suitcase packed. Mark looked up. 'Is he okay?'

'Seems healthy as a horse. I'll run the urine and blood samples through the lab.'

'We'll do the chest X-ray Sunday morning and fly it in to you to look at.' Mark handed him a white envelope. 'Don't spend it all in one place.'

The young doctor nodded and left.

'So what do you think?' Mark asked Page.

'Think about what?'

'About the possibility of being mayor of New York?'

Page shook his head. 'I don't know. I don't know. What do I know about the issues?' he said. 'Nothing.'

'Don't worry about that, Mr Page,' Mark answered. 'This will be government by mini-memo.'

'What?'

'Every issue can be reduced to one page of information – a mini-memo. Eisenhower governed that way. Reagan runs California via the mini-memo. On that single page is all the background you'll need on a specific issue, the current facts and figures, the most persuasive arguments for and against it, and finally your position on it. When you get the mini-memo on a subject, it will be presented to you by an expert in that field who will fully explain it to you. You can ask questions and take notes'

'Who's the expert?'

Mark's mouth went into a tight little automatic smile. 'We'll have experts, Mr Page. Part of my job as campaign manager is to put together the finest research staff ever assembled in a political campaign, and we'll keep them on in the government once you're elected.'

'You mean *if* I'm elected.'

'There's no *if* about it, Mr Page. Our candidate will be elected. The only question is whether we want to run you or someone else, and whether it's this year and this election.' Mark looked up at P.J. 'Get Mr Page to finish this intelligence test. Take him into the ping-pong room. Then give him a good workout in the gym. Let's really simulate the pressures of a campaign.'

'Come on, Mr Page,' P.J. said, jerking his thumb toward the door. 'Let's go see how smart you really are.'

'And, Mr Page –'

The candidate turned back to face Mark.

'If you're selected to be the candidate, don't worry about it. Marlon Brando once said about acting that we all carry the seeds in us of any character we might play. The same is true of politics. Somewhere inside you are the seeds of the mayor of New York City. It's my job to make them grow and flourish.'

'It's going to take an awful lot of manure,' Page said as he walked out of the room.

Chapter 5

Mark Altschul watched P.J. take the candidate into the hall. Then he sat back in his messy little panelled office with the rich carpeting and began to massage his teeth with a pencil eraser. He had come a long way in politics from that balmy May evening when he went to the Roosevelt Hotel with a lawyer colleague to meet a young congressman from Manhattan's east side who was going to make a run for mayor – John V. Lindsay.

It had been late afternoon when they climbed aboard the crowded subway at Wall Street and stood pressed amid the swaying, pushing people rattling north to midtown. It was a stinking city, Mark thought then, filled with violence, dirt, and poverty; yet it was the capital of the world – the big apple. To make it at all in New York meant you could make it big anywhere else on earth.

Although it was not yet official, Mark had known that Congressman Lindsay was going to announce for mayor. Lindsay's twin brother was a partner of the Wall Street law firm where Mark had been working since December, and word had been circulated that any and all help in the campaign would be appreciated. Already several of the young lawyers had journeyed north to the Roosevelt to sign on as campaign aides; politics was a way to meet people and get your face known around town.

At that point in his life, Mark had the average citizen's disdain for politics. He had voted because it was his duty; but he never felt his vote did much good. It seemed to him that the basic political system was like a cesspool, with hundreds of turds bouncing against each other causing little pieces to come off; the strongest and biggest ones eventually got jostled to the top, and you found floating on the surface the Richard Nixons and the Lyndon Johnsons and the Robert Wagners. Beneath were the hundreds of little stinkers – the bosses, ward heelers, com-mittee men and women, and the whole unheavenly host of minor functionaries who took a piece of you in return for giving you a little bounce upward. What made it interesting was the occasional flush in the pan that sent a Barry Goldwater or a Robert Kennedy swishing to the top to make their splash, only to sink back down to their proper level. As he reached the Hotel Roosevelt that evening in May 1965, Mark wrinkled his nose. To be in politics was to be in a toilet bowl.

John Lindsay turned out to be the most attractive man Mark had ever met. If anyone could bring back the Kennedy magic to politics and maybe save New York, it would be this immensely tall, angular-faced young congressman with the thatch of unruly blond hair and the piercing blue eyes. As they were introduced, Lindsay looked down and smiled. 'Thank you for coming,' he said simply. 'We're going to need all the help we can get.'

'Glad to be here, Mr Congressman,' Mark had mumbled, and was promptly put to work overseeing a roomful of young volunteers copying telephone numbers on to voter cards.

Mark began going up to the Roosevelt every evening after work and clocking in long hours, often not leaving until well after midnight. But there was purpose; there was excitement. At first he knew nothing of the political process, or how to get people out to vote for a candidate. But he learned fast. Soon he gained the reputation around campaign headquarters of being a guy to whom you could give any kind of stinking job, and it would get done. He came in contact with Bob Price, the peripatetic, balding campaign manager, one of the rudest, most brilliant men Mark had ever met. It was Price who talked about the wholesale and retail phase of the campaign and for the first time in any election made extensive use of computers.

A week later, Lindsay declared, causing a flurry in the press and a huge increase in invitations to speak. As a result, more stops were added to the candidate's schedule, and Mark was tapped to be an advance man. It became his job to arrive an hour before a scheduled appearance and make sure the crowd was there and ready. He had to call into headquarters to learn if the candidate was on time (which he never was), and then soothe the person in charge until the Lindsay party got there. As an advance man, there were for Mark long, dreary subway rides to the outlands, to dingy local Republican clubs in Queens and Brooklyn, with their retinues of seedy little hangers-on and the windy district leaders who wouldn't relinquish the microphone, causing the candidate to fall further and further behind schedule. This was the wholesale phase of the campaign – selling the candidate to a selected few, who in turn would themselves go out and sell him to the masses. Lindsay needed the backing of these clubs to get elected. He needed their building captains and election district captains to ring the doorbells, give out literature, and bring out the voters on election day. Once the wholesaling was complete, the retail phase would begin; this was the incredibly complex task of selling Lindsay to the entire electorate, a polyglot collection of over three million voters covering 320 square miles.

For six months Mark travelled to the boroughs. Week nights he advanced one or two stops; more on the weekends. However grim and lonely it was, often riding for an hour or more on subways and buses to reach some dark corner of the city, Mark was learning. This was the guts of politics – getting out to the people. As well as the stinking stops in the boroughs, there were the occasional goodies, like advancing the East Side Young Republican Club meeting at Delmonico's on Park Avenue and staying for the party after the candidate had gone on to another function, or hooking a lift back from Brooklyn with Lindsay's party after the last stop and being invited to go along for a drink at Toots Shor's where Toots himself came over and let fly with some colourful political wisdom. Too, there were the strategy meetings with the other advance men, chaired by Lindsay himself or Bob Price, or one of his aides like the hulking Richard Aurelio, on loan from Senator Javits, or David Garth, the cherubic television producer who was to mastermind the candidate's television appearances. Every night and several times a weekend Mark was able to observe the candidate in action, watch him grow as an orator, as 'The Speech' became more polished, the timing more precise in terms of getting laughs and relating directly to his listeners. Each speech was tailored to the audience – to a group of Jews, Lindsay would use a line of Yiddish; at Garfield Bobo's all Negro club in Brooklyn, he would quote Martin Luther King – all with stunning effect. And he would know the problems of the

neighbourhoods and offer solutions directly pertaining to each
new audience. At first Lindsay appeared superhuman in his
knowledge and perception of city affairs; a little later, Mark was
to realize that behind every good candidate was a great research
office grinding out the facts, the figures, the statistics, and the
speeches. In the car between stops Lindsay would be prepped by
his close advisers, the muscular Sid Davidoff or Barry Ghotterer,
a lawyer working with the campaign team full time. As the
campaign began to roll, it became evident that few of the
Republican clubs were to be of any help; the old-time clubhouse
politics was dead in New York. So, starting from scratch, Bob
Price and the team built up an organization which was to have
over 120 storefront headquarters, at least one in each of the city's
68 assembly districts, with a minimum of twenty-five volunteers
(many of them disenchanted Democrats) who were to keep
them open until 11.00 p.m. every night of the week. The candidate's schedule picked up to a frantic pace as he covered every
section of the city over and over again during the following weeks
and months. 'There is no party behind us,' Lindsay would say.
'No organization. No machine. Nothing between us and the
people!'

Mark considered quitting the law firm or taking a leave of
absence for the duration of the campaign, but he had no money
and the campaign coffers were not that full. So he kept on at the
job; but his heart was in the campaign. The world of politics had
seized him and wouldn't let go.

Lindsay had made a miserable mayor. Mark knew this first
hand, because he had joined the administration, serving first as a
deputy in the old Housing Administration, later being shifted
around into several of the new superagencies that Lindsay had
consolidated from the myriad little departments and agencies,
many of which were doing the very same jobs. For one who
thrived on excellence – indeed wouldn't let go of a thing until
he was sure it was as perfect as he could make it – Mark learned
to settle for mediocrity in New York City government. Its
budget was smaller in size only than that of the federal government, California, and New York State. And voting in a handsome, liberal congressman who had never had any administrative
responsibility whatsoever (other than overseeing a small staff

of aides in Washington and New York) was akin to taking a used car salesman off the lot and making him chief executive officer of General Motors. It simply could not work.

Surrounding Lindsay was his own Palace Guard – a crew of tough, toadying young sycophants, feeding like jackals on the power of the mayor, competing with each other to see who spent the most amount of time in his presence. There was Sid Davidoff, a scowling weight lifter who never left Lindsay's side; the rotund Barry Ghotterer who was Davidoff's alter ego; little Jay Kriegel who, weighing in at barely 100 pounds, could only be described as an arch brat; and a smashing redhead divorcée with green eyes named Enid Feist who loved to keep important visitors waiting in the outer office while she monopolized her boss with prattle about a new dress or where she was having her hair done these days. There were others, including Jeff Katzenberg, the son of a very rich Lindsay backer. In the eighth grade Jeff had begun to hang around City Hall running errands; by the age of fourteen, 'Squirt' Katzenberg was a full-fledged power broker, holding whispered conferences in the corridors, snarling at callers, and summoning city commissioners or ordering old ladies off of elevators. Squirt's hold on his job was the stock tips to Davidoff and others in the Palace Guard, courtesy of his father, a partner in a Wall Street brokerage house. As former Nixon aide Richard J. Whalen has suggested, no potential danger is more ominous in a free society than the secret leaching away of authority from the man the people chose to the men he chooses. Fiercely loyal, these members of the inner circle were everything Lindsay wasn't. Where he had class, they were crass. Not only did they keep Lindsay isolated from the electorate, but from his own commissioners as well. To a man, this Palace Guard delighted in playing the bully – telephoning people in every layer of government from garbage men on the street or the cop on the beat right on up to top city officials, ordering them to perform some silly favour or other in the name of the mayor, until the best, most dedicated, hardest-working members of the administration threw up their hands and got out.

As re-election time rolled around, the city was a shambles. One out of every seven New Yorkers was on welfare; one in twelve had a police record. The streets were dirtier, the blacks were angrier, crime was up 92 per cent, and the city was again bankrupt. Yet Lindsay managed to squeak through for another term.

Shortly after the 1969 election, Mark got out – John Lindsay's future was behind him. Mark had met enough people in his years with the city to land a good job in one of the top law firms at $25,000 a year to start. He was set, specializing in real estate law. For the first time in Mark's rather ascetic life, he began to enjoy the amenities of big city living on a big income. He moved out of his mother's house in Queens to a modern one-bedroom apartment on the upper east side. It was a high-rise building with huge picture windows looking east and south over the city. He began acquiring things – a Fisher stereo, modern furniture from Bloomingdale's and Bon Marché, lithographs from the little galleries along Madison Avenue where he would spend his Saturday mornings, and books which for the first time in his busy life he found time to read – for enjoyment, not study.

Though he gained more confidence in himself, Mark never lost that tight-lipped driving quality, that grim energy that made him a dynamo, a truly superb inside man who could grind out masses of work and oversee the production of much more. Within seven months he was made a junior associate of the firm and was throwing himself into law and living in New York with zeal.

Although he was outside city government, he remained in touch with many of his former co-workers who had stayed on. He could look on the struggles within City Hall as a bemused bystander. Although he missed the drama of government and the excitement of being close to the seat of power, he realized more and more that too many people hated Lindsay for him to be an effective mayor. From a consummate politician, sensitive to all the nuances and trends and power blocs in the city, the mayor had let his Palace Guard get between him and what was happening. The man in power is like the Greek giant Antaeus whose strength was invincible as long as he remained in contact with his mother Earth; Lindsay, like LBJ and Richard Nixon, did not. More and more it became government by press release, issued by press secretary Tom Morgan, a real greenhorn who replaced the superb Harry O'Donnel.

Then one night Mark watched a rookie policeman get shot right in front of his building; the boy was only nineteen years old.

The next morning he awoke angry. The city was ungovernable. It stank. He went out for breakfast in a rage, and by the first cup of coffee was so depressed he didn't want to go back to his apartment. Over the days and weeks that followed, he became a brooder, more tight and bitter than any of his friends could remember. Jesus, he'd like to make the city livable again. He knew a lot about governing and about running a campaign, from raising cash to the nitty-gritty of getting out the vote. God, if there were only a candidate, maybe he could change things. No question about it, politics was once again in his blood.

Chapter 6

Dev Page lay in bed staring into the blackness of his room. From out the opened window came the sound of the ocean in the distance as it rolled and washed on to the beach. It had been very late the night before – well after midnight – when P.J. had finally led him back to his room and let him go to bed. He had been sore from the various beatings, and bone tired from workouts in the gym and a seemingly endless series of tests. Tonight, lying there in his own pyjamas between the coolness of clean sheets, he tried to sort out his thoughts. It had been a long, wild two days, brutal at times and almost surreal, like a Kafka story or a Fellini film. Only the whole thing had really happened. Of that he was sure . . .

For three hours he had worked over the Cattell Intelligence Tests, a mishmash of words and symbols:

Umbrella is to *raindrops* as *army* is to (*enemy, warfare, invasion, country, general*)
Season is to *rhythm* as *day* is to (*sun, interval, monotony, repetition, succession*)

It was probably the most difficult, mind-bending, frustrating exercise he had ever been through – worse than the *Times* Double-Crostic, tougher even than the *New York* magazine puzzles which he did regularly. Some of it was impossible: curious analogies and syllogisms; strange words and ideas, long paragraphs to be read and questions about them to be answered; maddening problems in logic – Do you ask the blind man or the deaf man or the mute man?; formulas to learn and unlearn; and math problems that set his brain whirling in confusion. None of the tests had much to do with how much he knew about history or math or English, but rather with problem-solving and thought processes. At the end of three hours of solid concentration, he was exhausted, drained of all will to go on to anything. He craved sleep, or just a chance to lie down for a few minutes.

Realizing Page was too tired to function, Mark dismissed him for the night, with the warning that there was a full day scheduled for tomorrow, starting early. P.J. led him upstairs to his room, he stumbled out of his clothes, P.J. hung them up for him, putting his soiled shirt and underwear in the bathroom hamper. He mumbled thanks as he fell into bed, and P.J. turned out the lights before he left. The last man-made sound Page heard was the key turning in the lock. Then there was only the ocean out the opened window. A few minutes later, sleep came.

About an hour passed, and Page was gradually awakened by a pulling on his pyjamas. He surfaced reluctantly from a deep sleep to find he was not alone in bed; he was being French-kissed in the ear. 'What the hell!' A hand was clapped over his mouth. 'Shhhh, Mr Page,' came a whisper, 'just relax and enjoy it.'

The French kiss in his ear ceased as the wet tongue began to travel down his chin to his chest, his stomach, and beyond. The deep musky smell of perfume was everywhere. Just before the moment of truth, Page picked up the bed covers and called down in a hoarse, desperate whisper, 'Are you male or female, for Chrissake?'

'Very, very female.'

'Thank God for small favours,' he muttered and felt himself beginning to stir. After a moment, he said 'Hey, come back up here.' The action ceased as his new partner slithered up alongside him and put her face next to his. It was too dark to see what she looked like, but he stroked the long hair and felt her lean, warm body beside him. The natural move would be a tender embrace, but Page was hesitant to kiss a perfect stranger who had just had a cock in her mouth, even though it had been his. 'Who the hell are you?' he whispered.

'Mia.'

'Mia?'

'Mia DeStefano. We met downstairs earlier when you finished making the movie. Remember?'

'You're the girl with the horses.'

'That's right.'

'And the nipples.'

Mia let out a squealing giggle which sliced through the darkness. A frozen silence followed as they lay listening for footsteps and the sound of the key in the lock. No one came, and they were alone. Page let his lips brush her eyes, and with his hand touching her cheek, guided her mouth to his and with his tongue began exploring the wet places inside. He could not remember a more responsive woman as she rolled and twisted next to him, seeming to demand that his hands encircle her and find their way all over her little body. The more places he touched, the more sensitive she became, with little writhes and cries in his ear. Page wanted those nipples, and pushing her away slightly, ran his hand from her firm thighs along the soft front of her torso to her breast where his fingers closed around the giant rubbery tip. Gently he felt it, then prying his mouth loose from hers, brought his lips and tongue down on the biggest mouthful of nipple he'd ever tasted; for the first time in his life, Page wished he had two heads and six cocks so he could keep going for a week.

Mia cradled his head in both her arms, uttering little moans and cries in the blackness. Not good. Noisy women are great, but not when your room may be wired for sound and the lady in question happens to be the granddaughter of the host, whose colleagues of an earlier era perpetrated the St Valentine's Day massacre. Reluctantly, Page brought his head next to hers and tried to offer whispered reassurances which would, he hoped, quiet her down. But she lay there moaning, moving her head from side to side saying, 'Take me . . . take me now . . . take me.' Page put his lips to hers and felt his tongue sucked from his mouth while her body rippled and twitched uncontrollably beside him. It was all too fast. She was like a caged animal in heat. Only men were supposed to get that excited that quickly; women took some doing. But then, he'd never had an Italian; in fact, he didn't even know many.

'I want you in me,' she kept repeating. 'I want you in me.'

On the horse show circuit, Dev Page was generally regarded as an excellent bed partner, not so much for size (which was only average) but for endurance; besides that, he was president of the association, and a member of the '56 Olympic equestrian team, which was a big deal to those horsey women in the boonies. But he had never had anything like this. As Mia rolled and pitched wildly beneath him, the decibel level of her groaning grew louder, until Page had to muffle it by fastening his mouth to hers. Now he was locked at both ends in some kind of great machine not unlike one of those motorized reducing horses that go faster and faster as you turn the handle. Suddenly at the climactic moment, she pulled her mouth away from his and shouted at the top of her lungs, 'Oh My God, Mr Page!'

'Call me Dev!'

Within moments there was a key in the lock, and the lights snapped on. Standing in the opened doorway was big oily-faced Nick. 'Jesus Christ, you all right, Mr Page?'

The candidate blinked in the sudden light. He was alone in bed. 'I was having terrible dreams,' he said, looking confused. 'I'm sorry if I disturbed anybody.'

'I was on duty down the hall and heard this noise.' Nick was wearing black chino pants and a tee shirt; all over his muscled arms were gaudy Oriental tattoos. 'Would youse like a sleeping pill or something?' He seemed genuinely concerned.

'No. No, thanks. I'll get back to sleep all right.'

'That bed's all rumpled up, Mr Page,' He took a step toward the candidate. 'Let me help you straighten it up.'

'It's all right,' Page said quickly, holding up his hand. Like a trained dog, Nick stopped in his tracks.

'Ya sure I can't –'

Page's heart was pounding. 'It's okay, Nick, really,' he protested. 'I – I appreciate your coming in. And now, if you'll just go away, I'll get back to sleep.'

Nick stood swaying in the middle of the room between the doorway and the bed; he looked confused. For the first time, Page noticed Nick's balding head was absolutely flat on top, and going across his face just above the eyes and nose was one thick evil eyebrow. 'Really, Nick – I'm okay. I often have bad dreams. And today I was under a lot of pressure.'

'Ya sure I can't get you a pill or something?'

'Just go away, Nick. Please.'

There was a long, sickening pause as the big man stood staring at Page. Where was the girl? Was it all a dream? Christ, no; he was sitting in a pool of Mia's cream and the bed reeked of her musky perfume. 'Really, Nick, you can go now.' Page clenched his fist beside him. 'Please go. I'll be all right.'

After an interminable moment, the big man took a step backward and then another. Finally he turned and lumbered toward the door where he stood, hand on the light switch, staring dumbly at the candidate. 'You're sure?'

'It's all right now, Nick. Thank you very much for coming. I'm delighted to know there's somebody nearby.'

'Okay, Mr Page,' he nodded at length. 'If you want anything, I'll be right outside in the hall.' The light snapped off and the door closed. The key turned in the lock. Page sat motionless in the blackness. Sweat was pouring down him. Minutes passed. Finally he heard Mia crawl out from under the bed and watched her black silhouette as she stepped into a pair of stretch pants and pulled on a sweater. He whispered across the room to her, 'How will you get out of here?'

'The way I came in – through the window.'

She sat on the edge of the bed and pulled on her boots. 'I came down the fire rope from the third floor. They have fire ropes with harnesses, and you slide down. I used to play on them when I was little. My grandfather is terrified of fire, so he put them in 40 years ago when he bought the house.'

He began to massage her back and she moved gratefully against his hand. 'How safe is a 40-year-old fire rope?'

'It's okay. He gets new ropes every year. I mean he really has a thing about fires. Worries about it all the time.'

'But it's a stone house. Or stucco anyway. Does stucco burn?'

'He's crazy,' she said matter-of-factly. 'My whole family's crazy.' She put her hand on Page's cheek. 'I've got to go,' she said and kissed him. 'Mr Page, thank you.'

'Call me Dev.'

'Dev, thank you.'

'I hope we can do it again.'

'We will.' She crossed the room and climbed through the open window, where she sat and pulled the harness over her head and arms.

'What would your father say if he knew you'd been here?'

'He wouldn't say anything.'

'Nothing at all?'

'I'd be dead in three minutes, and you'd be dead in three hours.'
Page swallowed hard. 'What?'

'He'd probably cut your genitals off slowly, stick them in your mouth, and let you bleed to death.'

'I've had more threats to my genitals in the past two days than in the last 36 years.'

'We Italians have a thing for genitals.' Mia reached down and, tweaking the end of the candidate's limp, sticky limb, hiked herself out of the window in the harness.

'For Christ's sake, be careful,' Page called in a whisper.

'You be careful, Dev.' Mia grabbed the rope and pushed herself off. In a moment she was gone. Page leaned out the window and watched her descend to the ground where she got out of the harness and disappeared around the side of the house What about the rope? What if it's found hanging outside the house going past his bedroom window tomorrow morning? Panic seized him for a moment, and then he figured, the hell with it. He really didn't care any more – about anything. Back in bed he lay down on the dry top sheet, and pulling the blanket over him, slept again.

Chapter 7

On the evening of the third day, the helicopter was bumping through the darkness. Below, the lights of Atlantic Highlands twinkled at the edge of the blackness that was the ocean; inside the craft the luminous dials of the instrument panel glowed an eerie lavender. Mark Altschul rode next to the pilot. Two men occupied the back seat, an exhilarated Devereaux Page and Nick Gigante. In the hold were Page's suitcase and the packet containing the undeveloped film from his final appearances of the weekend. It was a wonderfully clear night, and in the far distance they could make out the lights of the Verrazano-Narrows Bridge, a span sixty feet longer than the Golden Gate, stretching like a jewelled necklace across the inky sky from shore to shore. Finally Page broke the silence. 'So what do you think?' he called to Mark over the throb of the whirling rotor.

Mark's head snapped around. 'I think you should go back to your apartment and resume a normal life as if nothing happened.'

'As if nothing happened? Jesus!'

Mark cracked one of his infrequent smiles. Later, as the tiny craft made its way along the Hudson River, Mark turned to Page and with a gesture toward the vast array of lights and streets and structures that were the city, announced, 'Think of it, Mr Page. By November, all this might be yours!'

'What are my chances?'

'Of running or winning?'

'Either.'

'If we decide to go with you, we'll win.'

'When will you decide on a candidate?'

'In a week or two. Maybe longer. There're a couple of other applicants we may want to look at. Compare the films, test results, that kind of thing.'

Page sat back as they came in for a landing at the West Side

Heliport. Jimmy the Dwarf was there to meet them in the black sedan which had been the kidnap vehicle Friday night. The pilot remained in the craft while the three passengers alighted, keeping their heads low under the idling rotor. Nick put the candidate's suitcase in the trunk of the car and handed the film packets to Jimmy the Dwarf who put them in the front seat.

'A word of advice, Mr Page,' Mark shouted over the noise of of the chopper engine. '*Omerta!*'

'What?'

'*Omerta*,' Mark repeated and put his finger to his lips. 'The Sicilian word for silence. Not a word of what happened this weekend *to anybody*. Or you've got real troubles.'

'When can I expect to hear?'

'Maybe in a week. Maybe never.'

'For Chrissake, let me know one way or the other!'

'You sound eager to run.'

'I think I am, dammit.'

'Well, don't get your hopes up.' Mark reached out and they shook hands. 'And don't call us. We'll call you.'

Mark and Nick reboarded the helicopter, which, with a howl from its engine and gale winds of its own creation, lifted from the pad and vanished into the night, leaving Page and Jimmy the Dwarf in the silence that was broken by an occasional automobile whizzing along the West Side Highway that loomed above on giant black stilts. Slowly Page made his way to the sedan where where the little hunchbacked driver held open a rear door, and then closed it behind him.

Jimmy the Dwarf let Page off in front of his apartment building on East 57th Street, and the doorman came out to take the suitcase to the elevator. It was a modern high-rise of white bricks with a pissy little fountain and plastic flowers in the lobby. When the split with Kay had become irreconcilable, he had moved to the city, deciding at once not to spend a lot of money for a big apartment; at the same time he needed a proper address, commensurate with his position as president of the National Horse Show Association. So, for $300 a month, he found this studio efficiency – one smallish room with kitchenette and bath. He had furnished it with a Castro convertible sofa, two low bureaus, a wall unit of bookshelves on which he kept his stereo and portable television, and on the floor a thick yellow carpet, wall to wall, which Kay had given him when she redecorated the Brookville house. He also managed to salvage some of his mother's good china and some plated silverware. He had felt a bit peculiar at the time he rented the place, with his mother and soon-to-be-ex-wife worrying about his linens and draperies, as though he were going away to school and about to be alone in the world for the first time in his life. That was the year he was thirty-five. But he became acclimatized quickly to his new way of living, finding life without Kay and the two girls very pleasant.

Obviously this meagre abode was no place to entertain (except, of course, when a lady had a sleepover date), and as a result, none of his friends or associates had any idea how far down in class he'd dropped from Kay's sprawling fifty acres in Brookville, with its vast stone mansion and courtyards and six-car garage, its swimming pool, outbuildings, tennis court, stables, and endless stretches of manicured lawns and fields, all bordered with white rail fences. Even his two daughters had never seen Daddy's New York apartment; Page preferred to squire them about the city on visiting day, taking them to lunch at Sardi's and to a matinée. The girls were nine and thirteen and might not understand his modest surroundings.

During his marriage to Kay, Page was a full-fledged partner in a small brokerage house and produced a great deal of business, virtually all of it from the management of his wife's account. When they were divorced, Kay took her business elsewhere and the equity in the firm along with it, leaving Page without a partnership and minus his major client.

That first year without Kay he joined Harris-Hutton, an immense firm with offices all over the country. The market was bullish, so he managed to gross himself almost thirty thousand, which was pretty good, considering how little time he spent brokering and how much he spent on the Horse Show Association. But then came the down-turn, when everyone was afraid to buy or sell, and his income nosedived to less than twelve. It was time, he decided, to actually tally up his expenses, and he found that what with travel almost every weekend – plane fares, rented cars, hotels when he couldn't stay with friends – his horse show activities cost him eighteen thousand a year in cash outlays.

When the horse show was at Madison Square Garden in November, his bill for the week was close to six thousand dollars by the time he got through paying for the president's box and giving dinner parties at a private suite at the Waldorf for all those who had entertained him throughout the country over the past year. Prior to this, Kay had always picked up the tab, and with all that juicy Mellon money behind her, his own income could go for his wardrobe and presents for Kay and the girls. He even managed to save a few thousand. To his astonishment, he found that his horse show expenses weren't even tax deductible; it was a hobby, with no way he could earn any income from the activities. There were two choices left to him: call Kay for money, or resign as president of the Horse Show Association. Without that affiliation, Devereaux Page would be nothing – just another divorced stockbroker living in Manhattan, trying to scratch out a bare living from the bear market. Christ, they'd probably take him out of *Who's Who in the East*.

So he called Kay for money. After exchanging a few pleasantries, he stammered through a prepared speech about how broke he was, what with all his expenses travelling around the country and the horse show coming up at the Garden in a couple of months. Could she let him have some money? There was silence on the other end of the telephone, followed by peals of laughter, Kay's husky voice guffawing cruelly into his ear. Could she *lend* him some money then? It would only be until the market picked up. More hoots of laughter. What would the children think, he asked, if he had to give up the horse show? Suddenly she was serious, her voice snarling out of the earpiece. 'Did you think of the children when you were rolling around in the hay with that teenager in the Byrds' stables in Berryville? Fuck you, Devereaux Page. Fuck you! Fuck you! Fuck you!' And the line went dead.

Page slowly replaced the receiver in its cradle. His world had crumbled. He felt his manhood begin to vanish, the years of his adult life dropping away until he was again a boy of five, exuberant and happy at the children's Christmas table, when suddenly G-Ma arose from the adult table across the room and announced he was too loud and ordered him to his room. Those sobs of defeat and disappointment thirty years ago were the same sobs that racked Dev Page after the abortive phone call to Kay.

But now, instead of a seige lasting hours, as it had when he was a boy, Page lost control for only a few minutes. Then, completely relaxed, he slept.

To most men, such a scene would be a sign to themselves of weakness. Instead of letting their frustration come out in a big blast of tears and trauma, the pain is kept bottled inside, eased only by alcohol, cigarettes, or pills. So instead of waking with a ghastly hangover and smoker's cough, Dev Page, after one of these attacks, would awaken completely refreshed and clear of mind. The cork had blown, the juices overflowed, and once again all was tranquil.

Within a week after Kay had turned him down, Page had made the necessary connections to bring his income well over his needs. To be sure, he felt guilty at first about going in to the laundry business – taking dirty money and cleaning it up through legitimate transactions. Sometimes he dealt with stolen securities, but more often it was in gigantic amounts of cash that had come from God knows what illicit sources that he put through the stock purchases. Further, he hated these new clients, immaculately dressed and manicured, faceless behind their dark glasses, and crude of speech and gesture. But through them his income rose again, and he was able to continue with the horse show circuit. And they promised to leave him alone on weekends, seeming to understand the importance of his avocation to his position in business. The illusion was created that his travels around the country on behalf of the Horse Show brought Devereaux Page into contact with a lot of wealthy people who became his clients, and enabled him to pick up some good stock tips as well. This was basically true, although Page never exploited the horsey crowd for himself. He was a shy person, and what's more the stock market bored him. Horses were his real love. He was a broker only because his father before him was a broker. While married to Kay, he kept the Wall Street job just to maintain the respectability of gainful employment; after the divorce he was damn glad to have it.

This past Friday was the first time his contacts had ever intruded themselves into a weekend. And what a weekend it had been! He went to his little bar in the big wooden wall unit to pour some Wild Turkey bourbon into a cordial glass, and then returned to the couch. Did it all really happen, or was he on some wild fantasy, the result of a hash party with the stewardesses down the hall? It was real all right; the scenes were too vivid to him . . . the kidnap . . . the tests . . . the beatings from which he still ached . . . being roused at four on Sunday morning to be driven to the deserted hospital for chest X rays . . . the helicopter . . . Mia . . . A smile crossed his face. Mia. Would he ever see that wild cunt again? He poured another Wild Turkey and sipped it, letting the mellow fire singe his tongue and trickle down his throat. He was relaxed at last, trying to imagine himself as the mayor of New York. Quite a jump from the horse show. A jump from the horse show. Would he have the horse sense to do the job? Maybe he would be the mare of New York. Wasn't that better than being the mare of Philadelphia? Or the mare of filly? After another sip of whiskey he closed his eyes and, fully dressed, with the lights in his tiny one-room world burning brightly, Devereaux Page slept, like the dead.

Two hours later he struggled awake to the frantic buzzing of his doorbell. In a half stupor he lurched from the couch and threw open the door of his apartment. There, attired in a white trench coat and yellow ski glasses, wearing a mischievous half smile, stood Mia DeStefano.

Chapter 8

They had been following the car for about a half mile, ever since it turned out of the long, tree-lined driveway and proceeded briskly along the winding two-lane country road. For Jimmy the Dwarf it was an easy tail, a big old Oldsmobile station wagon in broad daylight with no traffic. Next to Jimmy the Dwarf sat Nick Gigante, massive and immutable, his sullen eyes staring straight out over the oily pits and hollows of his cheeks, his bare flat head brushing the plush lining of the roof. Every thirty seconds or so Nick's big right hand slipped into the open flap of his trench coat past his chest to feel the checkered walnut butt of the Colt .38 Detective Special nestled in the shoulder holster under his left arm. Until he went to work for the DeStefanos, Nick had never held a gun in his life; now, sixteen years later, he was expert in its use, and was always reassured by the bulge of it next to his side.

A straight stretch of road about a mile in length opened up before them. 'Okay, Jimmy, take her,' came a nasal growl from the back seat. Before the order was out of Bobby DeStefano's mouth, Jimmy the Dwarf had punched the accelerator to the floor, and the black Chrysler shot forward, hurling Bobby against the custom leather upholstery of the back seat. At the same time, Nick placed a high-intensity flashing red light on the dashboard by the windshield, and with horn blaring, they swiftly overtook their quarry, forcing the other vehicle off the road and coming to rest at an angle in front of it. Instantly Bobby DeStefano, donning a pair of wrap-around dark glasses, was out of the car and standing by the opened window of the station wagon. The lone occupant, a woman in her mid thirties with faded blonde fair and a thin, hard little mouth, looked out at him. There was hurt confusion in her eyes. 'Officer, I don't think I was speeding.'

'Are you Mrs Devereaux Page?' Bobby inquired politely.

'Why yes, I . . .'

He opened the door for her. 'Would you mind getting into the back seat of my car? I'd like to talk to you.' Bobby smiled and held the car door open. She was wearing brown slacks and a tan sweater over her crisp white blouse, a gold circle pin on the collar.

'Just who the hell do you think you are?' she snapped.

Without warning she was looking down the business end of a tiny Erma automatic pistol which Bobby was holding inches from her face. 'Get out of that car, lady,' he spat, 'or I'll blow your fucking brains out!'

Kay's arrogance withered. She stepped from the car. 'Are you going to hurt me?'

'Just move it, lady. I haven't got all day.' Bobby enjoyed doing his Humphrey Bogart bit, especially knowing that in real life Bogart was a coward and a drunk while he, Bobby, was tough as hell. Kay walked quickly to Bobby's black sedan and climbed into the back seat with Bobby following. He ordered Nick to follow them in Kay's car, and then instructed Jimmy the Dwarf to get on the Long Island Expressway heading toward eastern Long Island. They drove in silence, with Bobby hunched in the corner of the back seat studying Kay, who sat stiffly facing front. All the windows were up, and the only sound was the soft whoosh of the air conditioner. Once on the six-lane Expressway, Bobby relaxed. Five car lengths behind was Nick in Kay's red station wagon.

'So you're Mrs Devereaux Page,' Bobby said with a smile.

'Mrs Mellon Page,' she retorted. 'We're divorced.'

Bobby slipped the little Erma pistol into his jacket pocket. It was the perfect weapon for him, weighing only 21 ounces with six .32-calibre cartridges, and having an overall length of just six and a half inches. With his slight frame and perfectly cut $400 suits from Dunhill Tailors, anything bigger would be impossible to conceal on his person; he was content to leave the heavy artillery to the big boys. 'All the doors and windows in this car are locked and controlled by the driver,' he announced quietly, 'and I have a Black Belt in karate, so don't try anything funny, okay?'

'Just who are you and what do you want?' She continued to stare straight ahead.

'I'm a friend of Mr Page's, and I want to talk to you.'

'I had no idea Dev had sunk so low.'

Any thought Bobby DeStefano and Mark Altschul had about a reunion between Kay and the candidate for the sake of the campaign were fast disintegrating. The woman was a spoiled bitch with a sharp tongue who could really ruin things. Page had told them the marriage was over, but Bobby had wanted to see for himself, in the hopes that Kay might be a Mary Lindsay type, stable and homely, who could make occasional appearances with him and be hostess at teas and kaffeeklatches. But there was no way with this babe.

'Where were you going when we stopped you?'

'To play bridge at the club.'

'You'll be twenty minutes late. Now listen to me.' Bobby spoke in a flat monotone, barely audible over the sound of the car's air conditioner. 'Something very big may be happening to Mr Page.'

'What are you talking about?' Her interest was finally piqued enough to look at him.

'I can't tell you now, because nothing is definite. If it happens, you'll read about it in the papers.'

'Give me a hint.'

'Shut up and listen.'

Kay turned away from the man in the dark glasses; she was not in the habit of being spoken to that way.

'When a man takes a big step up in his career, it's usually a good thing for everybody concerned if he has a wife and family. So I wanted to talk to you to see if there was any chance of reconciliation.'

'With that little bastard?' she laughed. 'Not a chance.'

'Don't worry, lady, I wouldn't have you around on a bet.'

'What?'

'If I were Mr Page, I'd have dumped you years ago.'

Kay turned on him, suddenly furious. 'Just who the hell do you think you are!'

The back of Bobby's hand cracked like lightning against Kay's face. 'That's who I am for openers,' he snarled. 'And there's lots more where that came from.'

They were tooling down the Long Island Expressway at a sedate fifty miles per hour. Cars and trucks continuously overtook and passed them, oblivious to what was going on behind the closed, tinted windows of the black sedan. 'I don't like to get rough,' Bobby said quietly, 'but sometimes people don't understand.'

Kay was too startled to reply. She cowered in the corner of the back seat, rubbing her mouth and jaw where Bobby had connected.

'Now then, Mr Page tells me you might be going to Europe with your two little girls this summer. Is that right?'

She nodded.

'We may want you out of the country sooner. Like next week.'

'Impossible. The girls are still in school.'

'Put them in school over there.'

'With only two months left in the school year? You're crazy. I won't do it.'

Bobby spoke through clenched teeth. 'Mrs Page, if we tell you to get out of the country, you'll get out. Understand?'

Kay was confused. 'But you – you can't just order people around.'

Bobby smiled and sank slowly back into the dark leather cushioning which moulded to the contours of his body. 'Mrs Page, your daughters. How old are they?'

'Nine and thirteen.'

'Okay, I'll give you a choice: take them to Europe next week, or wait till they get out of the hospital.'

'Out of the hospital?'

'With their arms and legs broken.'

Her face contorted. 'You wouldn't – '

'Wanna bet?'

'But – but they're – *little girls!*'

'Think it over, Mrs Page.' He leaned forward to tell the driver to get off at the next exit so they could give Mrs Page back her car. Then he sat back and turned to the woman across from him. 'One more thing, Mrs Page. You don't mention this to anyone, understand. *Not to anyone.* Not Mr Page, not your lawyer, not any of your friends at the club, not the police.' As he talked he was shaking his head in the negative. 'No one. Understand?' Bobby's voice was acid calm and precise, as though he were talking to an imbecile. He moved toward her in a confidential manner, causing her to draw back. Her sense of disgust must have been compounded as he curled back his upper lip and sucked his teeth which were very white, contrasting with the black gash of his sleek wraparound glasses. 'We may decide not to go ahead with this, in which case you'll never hear from us again. But if the call comes, your bags better be packed.'

Kay was frightened now. With her hand still against her hurt jaw she sat slumped and shaken. The car slowed and eased off the Expressway onto the service road at the Jericho-Westbury exit. Nick in the red station wagon was following. As they came to a stop, Bobby turned to her again. 'Like I said, it may never happen. But if we tell you to get out of the country, you do it. We'll pay for it.'

'I don't need your money.'

'And if you should find Mr Page's name suddenly appearing in the papers, you don't say anything to anybody. If somebody calls you up for a quote or an interview . . . well, you'll be out of the country anyway, so you can't say anything.'

The locks clicked open, and Nick, who was standing outside, opened Kay's door. 'Remember, Mrs Page, do as we say,' Bobby counselled. 'And don't blab to anyone, because we'll know about it and your little girls' arms and legs will be broken.' He smiled again. 'And you might find yourself being fitted for a pair of cement shoes.'

'Can I go now?'

'By all means,' Bobby said with a wave of his hand. 'And I hope you enjoy your bridge game at the club.'

Kay stepped unsteadily from the darkened car into the bright sunlight. She was crying. Nick helped her back to the red Olds. When he returned to the car, Jimmy the Dwarf sped off, heading to catch the Northern State Parkway back to New York. With a flick of a button under the dashboard, the two phoney New York license plates spun on their mountings, and it was once again a Delaware car. It was a device Bobby had first seen in a James Bond movie, and he'd had Tony the Elf build him one. In the back seat, the young Boss lighted one of his infrequent Havana cigarillos and pondered whether or not to take a chance on Devereaux Page.

Bobby DeStefano loved the Côte Basque. Arriving fifteen minutes early, he was shown to his favourite table in the corner where he sat alone waiting for Mark. Before him was the verandah overlooking a charming Basque town with pastel-coloured houses on either side of a small canal in which gaily painted fishing smacks were anchored in the blue green water; in the distance, high atop a flagpole, the French tricolour seemed to be briskly snapping against the Delft blue sky. It was a giant mural, of course, covering the entire back wall; but when people were dining out on the verandah and you had a martini or two under your belt, you could look up suddenly and swear for an instant you were in another land where the air was clean and it was quiet enough to hear the sea gulls over the Bay of Biscay. The illusion was heightened by small leaded windows around the room through which you could see little houses and the cobblestone streets of a Basque village. This was New York dining at its best, in Bobby's opinion, with its splendid ambiance and superb cuisine of provincial France.

Bobby considered himself several cuts above his counterparts elsewhere in the Syndicate. For most of them, two and even three generations in this country were not quite enough to shake out the last vestiges of peasant crudeness inherited from their Calabrian or Sicilian forefathers. When dining out, their choice was invariably an Italian restaurant where the meal would start with torn hunks of white bread washed down with Chianti, followed by the pasta course and entrée, all swimming in oily sauce and laced with garlic. Two Italian restaurants in the city were excellent: the Villa Pensa on Grand Street in the heart of little Italy, and Gian Marino's across the street from Bloomingdale's department store. Otherwise, Bobby preferred the delicate seasonings and textures of French cuisine, complemented by the seemingly infinite variety of shades and bouquets of French wine. And of all the French restaurants in the city the Côte Basque was much the best. The food was marvellous, and there was none of the self-conscious, self-serving bullshit of Maxim's or Pavillon where the waiters fluttered and flitted around you throughout the meal. At Côte Basque customers were beautifully attended, but once served, they were left alone. What's more, in the five years he had patronized the restaurant, not once had he seen anyone he knew; by now he felt he could dine in relative obscurity and not have to wear one of those goddamn silly disguises.

Bobby had spent the week pouring over Mark's 300-page budget and game plan and had pretty well sorted out in his own mind the figures and the concept of how an election was won. But there were still questions about the mechanics and structure of the campaign organization, as well as about Mark Altschul himself. Naturally there had been detailed investigations of Mark and Devereaux Page, along with rather cursory checks into the past of the five others who would be managing the campaign. The investigations had turned up nothing except in the case of Jimmy Lee, the designated Chief of Research, whose Chinese father had entered the country illegally sometime in the late 1930s and had never applied for citizenship. Other than that, the records were clean, with no prior associations with the underworld, good credit ratings, and excellent recommendations from their previous employers.

Also, the more Bobby studied Devereaux Page, the more he liked him as a candidate. In his youth, Page was a hell of a guy – not only captain of the debating and riding teams at Princeton, but voted most likely to succeed by his class. While still in college he rode in the 1956 Olympics in Melbourne. A knee injury shortly after college cut short his riding career, but his reputation as a horseman plus his social connections brought him a fine stable of customers in his early years on Wall Street. Several of his former associates of that period were interviewed, and each of them said the young Dev Page had a remarkably quick mind and an instinctive ability to grasp the intricacies of the market. He was, in fact, well on his way to becoming an associate partner of the firm when he married Kay Mellon, whose net worth was around $30 million. After that, he just conked out, preferring the social whirl of the jet set to the pressure of business. True, he kept working, Kay having put up the money for him to become a general partner in Bannon, White & Co.; with Kay as his major account, he produced a quarter of a million a year. But he worked to keep up appearances rather than for any need or real interest. The combination of Kay and all that money had sapped him, and it was not until after he was offered the presidency of the Horse Show Association that his life began to have any purpose again.

Normally Devereaux Page would be somebody to sneer at. Hardly would his record seem to inspire an investment of $10 million or more in his candidacy for mayor, especially after an indiscretion in Berryville, Virginia, with a seventeen-year-old girl. However, lately there seemed to be flashes of the old Devereaux Page. It was most evident by the tenaciousness with which he had held on to the presidency of the Horse Show Association in spite of the divorce, when all the financial odds were against him. Further, he had served the Syndicate well, cleanly disposing of a lot of cash and securities of questionable origin without raising an eyebrow of suspicion, either in his own firm or with the law. In addition, he had a first-class mind, as evidenced by the tests he took in New Jersey; the handwriting analysis revealed no alcoholism or narcotic addiction, but on the contrary indicated he was a rather strong and stable person, a finding corroborated by the doctors who studied the results of the psychological tests; and finally, he seemed to be able to take punishment and learn from his mistakes. Through the week, Bobby had run the films and tapes of Page's performance during his weekend in New Jersey, from that first clenched-jaw fiasco on through to a final speech Sunday afternoon in which he was extremely convincing. Yes, Devereaux Page had the stuff. But did Mark Altschul? Bobby wanted some very straight answers this evening. If he got them, he would at this dinner table give Mark the go-ahead for Phase A of the campaign, with an initial war chest of $2 million.

Chapter 9

Mark arrived promptly at six and was shown to the table where Bobby was waiting. They shook hands solemnly, Mark sat down beside him on the black leather divan, and the table was pushed back in front of them. Mark ordered a Tanqueray martini on the rocks, and Bobby ordered Scotch. When the captain left to place the drink order, Mark scanned the dining room, pausing to gaze out over the little French town on the canal. 'Nice place,' he commented curtly.

'Been coming here for years,' Bobby replied.

Mark turned and confronted Bobby with his deep-sunk eyes. 'What have you decided?' he asked suddenly.

'I haven't decided anything yet. I read over your budget carefully, and there are a lot of things I want to clear up.' Mark's directness jarred Bobby's sense of tradition; normally business was never discussed until after dessert.

'I have some reservations about it too,' Mark admitted. 'Particularly about the candidate.'

Bobby laughed. 'You're worried about the candidate, and I have serious doubts about the campaign.'

'You mean you think Devereaux Page is all right?' Mark was really surprised.

'If you're going to pick a candidate out of the blue, I think Page is as good as any.'

'But what about Kay?' Mark asked. 'Won't she make trouble?'

'I had a long talk with her in person,' Bobby smiled smugly.

'With Kay? What's she like'?

'She's like forty and needs a swift kick in the ass.'

'You're sure she won't make trouble?' Mark persisted.

'One phone call from me, and she'll be on the next plane for Switzerland with the little girls.' There was no expression in Bobby's voice, 'Next problem.'

'The divorce. How do we keep that quiet?'

'It'll come out in the course of the campaign, all right. But shit, it didn't hurt Rockefeller.'

'I meant this particular divorce. If it ever got out he was caught necking with a teenager . . .'

'You want the whole story?' Bobby interrupted.

'There's more?'

Bobby broke into a wide grin and said in a very low tone, 'He was balling her in the stable, okay?'

'Balling? You mean screwing?'

'I mean screwing. Her three older brothers caught them, and Page was tarred, feathered, and ridden out of town on a rail.'

'Tarred and feathered!'

'Actually they didn't have any tar, so they used heavy motor oil.' Bobby chuckled mischievously.

'Jesus, if a thing like that got out . . .'

'Don't worry about it. She was a nymphomaniac who'd sucked or screwed half the boys in Clarke County by her fourteenth birthday and Page was drunk out of his mind.'

Mark put his head in his hands. 'I can't bear it,' he muttered. Just then the waiter arrived with the drinks on a tray. 'Are you all right, Monsieu'?' he asked.

Mark looked up. 'Just in a state of shock, that's all.'

'This should help,' he said, placing the martini before Mark who absently twirled the ice in his glass with his forefinger. The waiter finishing serving Bobby a short Scotch on the rocks with a small carafe of water. When he left, Mark said simply, 'We're dead,'

'No we're not. You see, the girl is married now, with a child, and nobody wants to bring this up.'

'But everybody down there must know what happened.'

'No, we talked to both brothers – the third brother was killed in Vietnam last year – and they said it happened late at night after a party. They were the only ones who knew about it, except for their sister, and, of course, Kay.'

'You're sure?'

'As sure as I can be of anything in this life.'

'Tarred and feathered,' Mark mused. 'Jesus.'

'It's an old Virginia custom. Back in 1933 a bunch of guys in

Warrenton tarred and feathered Igor Cassini for something he
said in his column. It never hurt him.'

'He wasn't running for public office.'

'Look, don't worry about it.'

'Do you think Page would do it again?'

'Do what again?'

'Get into trouble with a teenager.'

'He was driven to it. Since he split with Kay, he's matured. I
can't conceive of his doing anything like that again.'

'With his track record, it might be wise to keep him away from
that pretty daughter of yours.'

'Mia?' Bobby's mouth twitched. 'If he touched her, I'd kill
him.'

'Just a thought.'

'Look, Mark, let's talk about the campaign.'

Mark sucked in his breath. 'Okay, let's.'

'Can I believe the numbers in your budget?'

'Which numbers?'

'Average overhead of thirty thousand a week for twenty-six
weeks for a total of seven hundred and eighty thousand dollars.
Isn't that high?'

'It may be. It includes salaries for approximately sixty paid
workers, from top management on down to secretaries. It includes
rent for a main headquarters plus one hundred storefronts and
tele—'

'I know what it includes. I asked if it wasn't high?'

'It's a fair budget. Obviously we'll be spending considerably less
than that at the outset, but as we gear up and begin renting
storefronts around the city, it may come to more later on. I think
thirty thousand a week average is fair.'

'Why sixty salaried people? Why not volunteers? Aren't most
political campaigns run with volunteers?'

'Volunteers are the lifeblood of any campaign. But you've
got to have professionals running it. Sure, we'll try to get more
volunteers and cut down on other expenses. But the salaries
aren't high. For example, I'm taking a ten-thousand-dollar cut.'

'I meant to ask you about that.'

'I'm a bachelor without a lot of obligations. But the others,
they'll be taking a leave of absence from their jobs, and they have

to get the same salaries. Why should they take a loss to go into debt, especially for an unknown candidate? And remember, people in a campaign work a steady eighteen hours a day; volunteers come in when they can. You can't count on them.'

'How're you going to keep the big secret from these people?'

'What big secret?'

'Who we are. Who's really bankrolling this campaign. I mean aren't they going to wonder where all the money's coming from?'

'That depends a lot on you,' Mark stated flatly.

'What do you mean?'

'I mean if you're going to assign a bunch of your thugs to the campaign to hang around headquarters and generally treat people the way you treated Devereaux Page, for example, yes, they're going to be suspicious.'

'Just watch that talk,' Bobby growled menacingly.

'I mean it, Bobby. This is precisely the kind of thing I'm worried about too. You may be smart as hell, but you've had no experience with politics; there may be things going on in the campaign that won't make sense to you, and we'll all be too busy to explain it to you.'

'Well, goddammit, if I'm spending two million or maybe even eleven million, I want to know where the hell it's going.'

Mark stared moodily out across the restaurant. 'You know, I could have gone to Tony Scotto with the idea.'

Bobby gritted his teeth in silent rage. 'Scotto's a punk and an idiot,' he snorted.

'He understands politics, and he understands labour.'

'Yeah, and in 1969 he got into the *Congressional Record* by being fingered as one of Carlo's boys. Since then, he's been in the papers for all the wrong reasons. Being fingered like that made Scotto ineffective.'

'That's why I came to you.'

'Remember one thing about my group.' Bobby was anxious to prove the point. 'Not one of my people on the inside has ever been arrested or even fingerprinted. Neither have I. As far as the law is concerned, we're clean. All of them – P.J., Nick, Johnny, the Elf – they're all clean as a hound's tooth. If any of them should get photographed with the candidate, nobody would recognize them. And I intend to keep it that way. Because once you're found out, they'll hound you to death, just like what's happening to Scotto.'

'I feel secrecy is something we have to discuss.'

'Just don't ever compare me to Scotto again.'

'Okay, let's have another drink and forget it.' Mark signalled to the captain for another round. 'The point is, we can't let anybody know where the money is coming from.'

'You're fucking-a right we can't.'

'So in the budget there's provision for a finance chairman who'll do nothing but try to raise money legitimately. Using direct mail and other standard techniques, we can come on like Ralph Nader or Common Cause. The finance chairman will be the red herring; he'll make such a stink, nobody will realize we're spending fifty times what we take in.'

'Hopefully.'

'Hopefully.'

'I'll tell you something else, Mark. If I go along with this thing, it's going to be strictly a cash operation. Salaries, rent, phone bills, advertising, everything is cash. I don't want any traces of what we're doing.'

Mark sat back and looked at the ceiling. 'That's interesting,' he mused. 'Of course there'll be problems in handling large amounts of cash, but that's the way Huey Long operated in Louisiana. Everything was in cash.'

'What about filing?' Bobby was suddenly worried. 'Don't you have to file your campaign expenses at some point?'

'No problem. A political campaign is like an iceberg; the public only sees the tip. If we were running a candidate for federal office, we'd have to cope with the new Federal Election Campaign Act. But in a city election, it's easy. Besides, everybody lies about campaign expenditures. Nixon lied. Rockefeller lied. Lindsay lied. Even Gerald Ford of Michigan lied. In New York State, you're supposed to file your expenses, But there's no penalty for not filing. And once a candidate's in office they can't kick him out for having spent too much. Besides, since this will be a cash campaign, nobody'll know a thing. It's beautiful!'

'Hold on, Mark, nothing's definite yet.'

'What else are you worried about? We've got a candidate, money, and a campaign team.'

'What's he running on?'

'What do you mean?'

'What's his platform?'

'Ah, well, let me describe this to you.' Mark rubbed his hands together with obvious pleasure at the prospect of detailing the techniques of how to win an election. This was to be the most responsive and sensitive campaign in American political history.

'Where John F. Kennedy's 1960 run for the presidency might be called the first-generation campaign of the New Politics, this upcoming mayoralty will be the fifth generation in terms of sophistication.

'In this campaign, every election district captain will have not only a print out of the name and address of each voter, but a record of how the five hundred voters of that election district performed at the polls over the past four elections and the variance from the assembly district. In this way, each worker will know whether his district is liberal, conservative, or middle of the road.'

Bobby belched and pushed a lock of hair out of his eye.

'We can do it, Bobby,' Mark said earnestly. 'This is not going to be any half-assed effort where nothing is coordinated. We're all professionals, and we're going to go about this in a systematic way, using the newest techniques in market research and campaign communications. Give us the go-ahead, and we can win it.'

Mark's enthusiasm was infectious. City Hall was the prize. If it could be won, then you could have Albany next year, and two years later – the White House itself! Bobby was close to saying yes, at least to the two million dollars needed for Phase A. But there were still nagging doubts. He wished he were more a student of politics so he could articulate his visceral sense that something was still not in place. Everything Mark said seemed valid; the preparation of the budget appeared flawless. Yet the fact remained that here was just another candidate – an unknown, untested one at that – who was going to toss his hat in the ring with an appeal to the voters to listen to him on the issues; the other candidates were men whom the voters already knew and who would be more likely to hold their attention than an unknown. There should be some big, overriding new issue that could be created to give Page a real leg up. As Bobby's late friend Tony Anastasia once said, 'All I want is a fair advantage.' Well, dammit, something more than just Devereaux Page and a flashy campaign was needed before Bobby would commit for even two million, let alone for Phase B.

'Everything you say seems right,' Bobby said slowly. 'But I'm still not convinced.'

'Why?'

'This is just another guy going out and talking about the issues – the same issues every other guy will be talking about. It's not enough. There's something missing. And I won't spring for two million bucks until that missing piece is found.'

'But you've never been in politics before, Bobby.'

'That's correct.' He was getting irritated now, because Mark was playing on his inexperience; that was patronizing. Yet in his gut he knew there was an answer not very far away. 'Look at it this way,' Bobby suggested, 'if you could play God and solve all the problems of New York City, how would you do it?'

'It's basically a financial problem,' Mark answered instantly. 'The sources of income available to a city increase only about 6 per cent a year while the expenses increase about 17 per cent. The result is a fiscal gap. It happens year after year, and every year there is less and less money to pay for more and more expenses. This is true of all the cities, by the way, not just New York.'

'That's not a very interesting issue, is it?'

'That's why it's not mentioned in the budget; it's an abstract problem.'

'I repeat the question; if you could play God, what would you do?'

'I'd get more money out of the federal government. New York City sends twenty-three billion dollars a year to Washington and only gets back about one billion in the form of aid programmes. The same is true with Albany where we only get forty-three cents back on every dollar we send up there.'

'And how do you get more money out of the federal government back into the cities?'

'You get Congress to vote it.'

'And why hasn't Congress voted it?'

'Because Congress doesn't give a damn for the cities.'

'That's got to be crap! Isn't Congress based on population?'

'The House of Representatives, yes,' Mark looked a little

quizzical at Bobby's sudden excitement. 'In the Senate, there are two from each state.'

'Well, if all the cities have the same problems, why in hell don't all the congressmen from all the cities get together and swing some weight? I don't understand it. Christ, how many congressmen does New York City have?'

'Nineteen, but they've never agreed on anything.'

'They've never agreed on anything?' Bobby was incredulous.

'Hardly anything.'

'What the hell's the matter with them. ?'

'I think you'll find most congressmen in this country pretty mediocre people – ward heelers, hacks who've hung around so long that they're rewarded by a seat in Congress. Furthermore, since they have to run every two years, they have to spend most of their time feathering their own nests so they can get re-elected. They simply don't have the time or the ability to function in Washington the way they should. What's more, most of the New York City delegation is more interested in foreign affairs than working out the problems of the city. I mean Vietnam is a hell of a lot more interesting than welfare.'

'Well for Chrissakes, there's your big issue!'

Mark was puzzled. 'I don't understand.'

'I mean if we have a bunch of bums in Congress, we run a mayoral campaign where we expose them as such. It's simple!'

Mark scratched his head. 'But they're not running for mayor. They're not the opposition.'

'Look, if I read you right, the city is a shambles because we've got a bunch of hacks in Congress.'

'That's true of New York, and it's true of every big city in the country. But what can one guy running for mayor of New York do about it?'

'We smear those bastards from one end of the city to the other. We rub the voters' noses in it! Page can say, "Elect me mayor this year, and next year, together, we'll work to get a team in Congress that is really responsive to the needs of the city." Jesus, I'll bet every single issue is related to this, isn't it?'

'I guess . . .' Mark began ticking them off on his fingers: Narcotics . . . Education . . . Welfare . . . Housing . . . Transportation . . . He looked at the young Boss next to him. 'You know, you're right. If it's not Congress, it's the State Legislature in Albany.'

Bobby reached over and patted Mark's shoulder. 'You just talked yourself into two million dollars. Let's order dinner and have some champagne!'

Mark took a deep breath and sat back, sinking into the black leather of the divan. 'It'll be a one-issue campaign.'

'And what an issue.' Bobby laughed maliciously. 'The feds have given me enough trouble in my life. Now it's my turn!'

Chapter 10

Twenty-six rooms had been rented on the eighth floor of the Commodore Hotel with a promise by the hotel management that more space was available if needed. Mark had chosen the Commodore for its location in the heart of midtown Manhattan, right next to Grand Central Station and the huge hexagonal Pan Am Building that glittered skyward across Park Avenue, its millions of tons of steel and glass resting precariously on a plexus of subway, railroad, and pedestrian tunnels which crisscrossed the whole area like catacombs deep below.

The Commodore itself, completed in the 1920s, must have been a stunning headquarters for Jimmy Walker's 1925 mayoralty campaign. Today, however, it was a nondescript heap of dirty brown brick and once-white rococo marble trim, now grey with the grime of years. The lobby, three stories high and half the size of a football field, had the flavour of an ersatz medieval castle with its white marble floor and arcade of rounded Roman arches of white stucco; jutting out from the four walls overhead was a series of flag poles from which multicoloured flags and banners were hanging. High above was the glass ceiling of leaded panes lighted from behind. Upstairs, the great marbled hallways leading to the ballroom had all the charm of the Criminal Court Building; in the public rooms, the grit of ten thousand catered affairs was ground into the swirls of the green-and-barf-brown carpeting. In the upper floors where the guests stayed, the rooms had recently been redecorated with bright reds and blues, gay striped draperies, new furniture and paint jobs; but getting there meant an endless trudge down murky, narrow corridors, where the grey walls were peeling and you had to squint to see the faded gold script room numbers on the rounded Serv-a-Doors in the dim light of an occasional 20-watt bulb.

To be sure, the Organization could have afforded better, such

as the Waldorf, or the Biltmore on the other side of Grand
Central Station, where to this day the children of the rich can
meet under the fabled brass clock in the lobby, just as they did
in the era of Scott and Zelda Fitzgerald. But both Mark and
Bobby DeStefano agreed instantly on the Commodore. It was
centrally located, reachable by any number of subway lines and
bus routes, easily accessible to the hoards of office workers from
all parts of the city from whom they hoped to recruit volunteers.
In addition, there were adequate public rooms from small and
medium-sized gatherings, on up to the Grand Ballroom which
could hold 2200 for dinner. In close proximity to the Commodore were all the services essential to a campaign – quick-service
typographers and printers, film processing laboratories, dry
cleaning and laundry establishments, the huge stationery and
office supply emporium of Goldsmith Brothers, a fair assortment
of restaurants, and a small outdoor parking area situated on a
ramp overlooking Park Avenue for the fleet of campaign cars
that would take the candidate and his aides to the ends of the city
and back.

In short, the Commodore was somewhat less than a first-class
hotel, abounding with salesmen and airline pilots. It was a place
to find a decent hooker or take your secretary for a drink with no
chance you'd be recognized. Although this campaign might become the most costly in the history of New York, it was imperative to keep up the appearance that the candidate was continually
hard pressed for cash. For this reason, the Commodore was the
perfect headquarters.

The candidate's ex-wife and two daughters were en route to
Switzerland in a matter of a few days. Within three weeks, the
top management team for the campaign had arranged to take
leaves of absence from their respective jobs and were working
full time at the Commodore. Besides Mark Altschul, four others
would fill the top slots in the organization. Borough Coordinator
was Paul Berman, paunchy and balding at thirty-seven. A lawyer
by training, Berman had none of Mark's grim precision; rather
he would burst on the scene like a star shell, destroying any
semblance of order as he reached into every corner and pocket of
the campaign. Always wearing the same oatmeal jacket, grey
flannel slacks, and rumpled white shirt, unbuttoned at the collar

and billowing about the stomach, he would whirl through the various offices like a cyclone, barking orders, giving forth with the latest bawdy joke, or waving his arms like an orchestra conductor crying for 'Ideas! I need ideas! What can we do in Bay Ridge?' He loved needling the staff to use imagination, from the lowest receptionist to the managers, and if an idea was at all feasible, he'd try it, if for no other reason than to keep up the enthusiasm and make each person feel part of the effort. That was the key to Paul Berman: he couldn't possibly manage the intricacies of a street and storefront campaign, but he could manage the managers. He was one of those rare birds who didn't care about personal power; he would delegate authority to anybody in sight, with the result that all his people matched his 18-hour work days in order to live up to the responsibility he had entrusted to them. Where Mark was to be the campaign manager, Berman was to be the head coach, bouyant, bubbling, constantly exhorting the players to give, even after there was no more to give. Everywhere he appeared (and he appeared to be everywhere at once) he created a sense of urgency and enthusiasm. Some thought he was a genius; others felt he was just plain crazy. But whatever the prevailing opinion, Paul Berman, as resident extrovert, was very effective.

Perhaps the most low-key member of the top management quintet was Lou Klein, Director of Communications, whose quiet, almost professional manner was the direct opposite of Paul Berman's flamboyance. Tall, with a full head of black curly hair flecked with grey, Lou was always impeccably attired in a dark grey or blue suit and rep tie. He walked with a slight stoop and wore rimless glasses; both affectations made him appear older than his forty years. When not involved in politics, he was vice-president and creative director of an advertising agency whose specialty was direct response advertising – coupon ads in magazines or newspapers, catalogues, and junk mail. Lou Klein got into politics not because he had any great love of candidates or issues; his agency got the Republican National Committee account to raise money for the '68 election via direct mail, and was enormously successful. In 1969, Lou worked on John Lindsay's campaign where Mark found him to be not only knowledgeable about advertising but an expert on all kinds of communication, both print and broadcasting, from ancient times to the present. He was able to quote long passages from Cicero and Caesar on up to Hitler and McLuhan.

Then there was Jimmy Lee, the diminutive Chinese computer expert who was going to be the campaign's Chief of Research. Now in his late thirties, Lee had spent ten years with IBM, starting as a computer operator on the System 360 models, gaining 'hands on' experience, and gradually working his way up through programming into systems where he eventually became one of the senior systems designers assigned to new accounts. His primary expertise was market research, having supervised installations for General Motors, Colgate Palmolive, and the world's largest advertising agency, J. Walter Thompson. It was in 1967 that the State Legislature in Albany voted to allow New York City to collect a city income tax. Instead of simply adding one line to the state income tax form, which meant no collection costs to the city, Albany decreed the Lindsay Administration had to set up the mechanism to collect its own tax, which meant a system had to be designed and operative within 90 days. Jimmy Lee was assigned to the Finance Administration and, working round the clock for three months, the deadline was met. The following week, a grateful Mayor Lindsay invited Jimmy Lee to dinner at Gracie Mansion along with the brilliant, mercurial young Finance Administrator, Firoavante Perrotta. Jimmy had come a long way from the little railroad flat off Chatham Square, and he was easily persuaded by the mayor to leave IBM for a full-time job with the city. Later, Jimmy ran the entire computer operation for John Lindsay's mayoral campaign in 1969 in which Lindsay was re-elected, while Jimmy's boss, Perrotta, was defeated in the race for Controller.

Monday, April 30. By 9.30 AM, a full half-hour before the candidate's scheduled appearance, it was evident the room was going to be three-quarters empty. Parlours B and C of the Hotel Commodore, when opened up to make one big room, could comfortably accommodate two hundred at a press conference such as this; there were less than forty, and it did not look as though many more were coming.

Four news camera crews were setting up their tripods and paraphernalia midway down the room along the walls so they could record the action at the long green table with the speaker's lectern mounted on it. A fifth camera, Johnny DiSantis' Auricon with its 400-foot film magazine that looked like giant Mickey Mouse ears, was on its wooden tripod and ready to roll. Elsewhere, a few rumpled and disinterested reporters wandered about, pausing occasionally to blink at the electric blue walls with white fleur-de-lys designs all over them. A dozen or so were gathered at the far end of the room where a hotel waiter was dispensing coffee and Danish pastries, and a half dozen more were lounging list-lessly on the squat gold chairs neatly lined up row on row facing the speaker's table.

In the mirrored hallway outside, P. J. Costello stood by a table piled high with blue folders containing the press kits – a news release announcing Devereaux Page's candidacy, a copy of the announcement speech he would be delivering, a glossy photo-graph and a short biography. As a greeter, P.J. was marvellous, flashing his great smile and handing each new arrival a press kit, seeming totally unconcerned that of the three hundred folders he had stayed up most of the night preparing, only about thirty had actually been taken. Circulating among the newsmen were a few members of the fledgling campaign staff; most vociferous was the effervescent Paul Berman who scurried about shaking hands with those he knew, introducing himself to strangers. The others, Klein and Jimmy Lee, hovered quietly in the back-ground; these were the introverts, the thinkers, who came to observe but not to mix. None of the team had laid eyes on the candidate except for Steve Loomis a former advertising copy-writer who had written this first speech and spent an hour with him going over it to make certain there were no lines he was having difficulty with. It was Mark's and Bobby's idea to make this kick-off a real surprise for everybody by unveiling the candidate to the public, the news media, and the staff alike. After this point in time, Page wouldn't have a free minute to call his own for the next seven months; Mark planned to run his ass all over the City of New York, stopping only to let him eat, sleep, and learn a new speech.

At 10.00 sharp, Mark Altschul stepped behind the lectern and tapped the centre microphone with his finger nail, causing an amplified *clunk . . . clunk . . . clunk . . .* to reverberate around the room. From all ends of the room, reporters came to sit in the chairs down front, before the speaker's table. The motion picture camera men squinted into their viewing lenses for a final focus while the sound technicians checked the recording levels from Mark's voice.

Mark introduced himself as a lawyer, a former member of the Lindsay Administration, and a New Yorker who was totally disenchanted with the City. 'When you're fed up with a situation,' Mark said, 'you have three choices: you can grin and bear it; you can get out; or you can try to do something about it. Most of us grin and bear New York City. Others of us are leaving, fleeing to the suburbs or just plain getting out completely, only to be replaced by the poor and disadvantaged – a situation which is turning the city into a place for the very rich and the very poor, and a terrible place for everybody. Doing nothing or running away has never appealed to me. I spent five long years in city government trying to change things. We all know what happened. It might be said of the Lindsay Administration that never in the history of human government have so many owed so little to so few.'

A number of reporters burst out laughing; several actually applauded. It was uncharacteristic for Mark to get a laugh; he obviously enjoyed it.

'Shortly after Lindsay's re-election in 1969, I left city government along with dozens of others from the top commissioners on down; we were all totally disenchanted with what was happening. To those of us who departed, it seemed unconscionable to be on the public payroll while working for a man who was simply using the mayoralty as a springboard to national prominence.

'Several weeks ago I met a man who said that probably what the city needs is not a politician in Gracie Mansion, but an ordinary citizen, and that he'd love to have a whack at being mayor, because he couldn't do any worse than the current administration, and he might do a lot better. It was a fascinating proposition. After a long talk about this, I told him if he wanted to run, I'd manage the campaign.

'Ladies and gentlemen, the president of the National Horse Show Association, stockbroker with Harris-Hutton, and now

The Citizen Candidate for Mayor of New York, Devereaux Page.'

There was no applause. Only a murmur rippled over the small crowd as Page came through the double doors of the room and threaded his way to the speaker's table. He looked good, with his triangular face tanned from several hours under a sun lamp, medium sideburns and his sandy hair neatly barbered and parted back from his widow's peak. He was immaculate in a dark grey tailored suit, nipped in at the waist with subtle pinstripes and wide lapels. To the old-timers in the audience, he brought back vague recollections of Jimmy Walker. As Page neared the front of the room, the blinding sets of photographic lights snapped on, and the motion picture cameras recorded his entrance into politics. At the little wooden lectern, Mark Altschul, his head barely visible behind the cluster of microphones, waited to shake hands with the candidate, and then sat down at the table next to the lectern. Page was alone. This performance – the speech and the possible barrage of questions from the floor afterward – had been rehearsed for three gruelling days and nights in the basement room of Joe DeStefano's New Jersey estate, aided by the little Sony closed-circuit television system. Now, here was the real thing.

I think Mark Altschul pretty well summed up who I am and why I'm here. New York is the wealthiest city in the world. It has a higher population than 43 states and 66 members of the United Nations. It's name is synonymous with international power, and yet its government is powerless to deal with the problems of people who live here.

He was speaking in a flat monotone that made him sound somewhat tentative about the whole thing.

New York City provides 43 per cent of the state's tax revenue, but the state retains control of such details of city government as the power to decide what taxes the city may impose, how many hours a policeman may work, and even whether a dog licence can be raised from five to six dollars. The city provides jobs for 500,000 commuters, but the city government does not operate most of the bridges and tunnels they use to get here, nor its own transit system.

On the national level the situation is worse. New Yorkers send $23 billion in taxes to Washington and get back less than $1 billion in federal aid.

According to the President's Council of Economic Advisers, the federal government in the past 12 years has spent $680 billion for defence, $60 billion for agriculture, $42 billion for space exploration, *and only $15 billion on the cities.*

This is unacceptable.

Page looked over the small crowd and the dozens of empty chairs in the middle of the room. He blinked occasionally at the white hot lights. P.J. was there, and Bobby with a droopy false moustache – one of his ridiculous disguises – stood by the electric blue wall while Nick Gigante's hulk filled the doorway. Elsewhere, the other members of the campaign staff studied the candidate intently, while the reporters, quiet for the most part, scribbled notes or exchanged a whispered confidence. The candidate was speaking very softly into the microphone. There was no identifiable accent. His voice was resonant and medium pitched.

New York City's problem lies entirely with the State Legislature and State Senate in Albany, and with the Congress of the United States. Specifically the trouble is with the New York City representatives to those bodies.

New York City's congressmen are more concerned about national and international affairs than they are with their own districts. They make speeches about the Anti-Ballistic Missile and Civil Rights while their colleagues on Capitol Hill are scrounging around Washington trying to get money for the folks back home.

For years the New York Congressional delegation has not agreed on anything. In Queens, Benjamin Rosenthal and James Delaney aren't even on speaking terms. This is true of Shirley Chisholm and John Murphy of Brooklyn. Relations between our two United States Senators, Jacob Javits and James Buckley are, in the words of the *New York Times*, 'decidedly frigid.'

For the duration of this primary campaign one million New Yorkers won't have any representation whatsoever in Washington because their Congressmen – Herman Badillo and Mario Biaggi – are running for Mayor. They are using their offices as political stepping stones. So is Assemblyman Al Blumenthal . . .

On the Republican side, John Marchi is in the race, leaving his constituents with no representation in the State Senate in Albany . . .

We have to make our elected representatives do the job for us in Albany and Washington. We have to persuade them, cajole them, perhaps even embarrass them. And if they don't start performing, we'll vote the rascals out and replace them with men and women who can work together for the good of the cities . . .

Above all, we must have control of our own city government, and that can only come from Albany.

And we must have more of our tax money back, and that can only come from Washington.

Otherwise, we might just as well pull the plug now, and let New York City sink bubbling and steaming into the sea.

Page ended his prepared statement with a plea for volunteers to come down to the Commodore and help get the city away from the professional politicians and back into the hands of the people.

The questions came in rapid fire, and Page disposed of all of them relatively quickly. Any candidate who has done his home-work will emerge unscathed from a press conference. The lead questions are easily predictable; a vague generality can suffice for the tough questions, and a good-natured rebuff will take care of the impertinent ones. Most of the questions had been antici-pated and rehearsed over the past three days in New Jersey.

On the question of campaign finances, Page told them he was putting up some of his own money and hoped his candidacy would spark a real grass roots movement which would result in contributions from all over the city by disenchanted citizens. He made it clear that regardless of who won in the major party primaries, his was an independent candidacy, and he would be on the ballot in November.

When one reporter asked about Albert Shanker's recent threat to call a school strike, Page held up his hands to emphasize that he was not prepared to go into specific issues at this time; the campaign plan called for a full discussion of each issue before Election Day, and that once a week a new issue would be introduced and discussed in depth. 'Believe me,' he added with a wry grin, 'this campaign will be as much of an education for me as it will for the voters.'

When the subject of his divorce came up, he disposed of it as quickly as he could, saying that Governor Rockefeller had a far messier divorce, and was elected by a seven hundred thousand vote plurality in 1970. His own was simply a case of two people who couldn't get along, and he felt the voters were fairly sophisti-

cated and understanding about such things these days, especially
with one out of every three marriages ending in divorce. If there
were any criticisms of his performance thus far, it was that he let
them linger too long on his marital situation. Then came the
closing exchange:

Q. Don't you think that coming out against every single congressman
and legislator will hurt your chances?

A. I'm not against every single congressman and legislator. They're
probably all honourable and decent human beings. But they're not
working together. What we need is a *team* in Albany and a *team*
in Washington – not a bunch of individual players. This is a case of
where the whole chain is even weaker than its individual links.

What I propose to do in this campaign is look at the performance
of all our elected representatives. For instance, Ed Koch in the
Eighteenth District has apparently made real progress in getting the
New York City delegation to at least talk to one another. Unfortunately Koch blew it by running for Mayor.

Q. What do you mean he blew it?

A. I think he should have resigned from Congress or stayed out
of the mayoralty race.

Q. Does this mean you're calling for the resignation of all congressmen and legislators if they want to enter the mayoral race?

A. I think so. After all, they were elected to represent their constituents. Instead, they're taking their salaries and expense accounts and
running for some other office, leaving their districts flat. I call that
dishonest. Running for office is a full-time job. I've resigned as president of the Horse Show Association and quit my job on Wall Street.
My opponents should do the same at the very least.

At this point, Mark Altschul arose and came to the microphones. 'I'm sorry to cut in here, but we have another scheduled
appointment for the candidate. Mr Page will be back at the hotel
this afternoon and completely available to any of you who want
to pursue this.'

'Just one more question!' called a reporter from the second row.

'Okay, one more,' said Page. 'Shoot.'

Q. Robert Kennedy used to quote Emerson and Camus. John
Lindsay carried around St. Exupery's book, *A Sense of Life,* and
quoted from it often. I'd like to know what writer or thinker most
influenced you.

A. Kipling.

Q. *Kipling?*

A. That's right. Kipling. My father was reading Kipling to me before I was able to talk, and in the course of my boyhood I memorized a lot of his poetry. I guess Kipling isn't in much favour today, but he's due for a revival. I think he was one of the greatest poets of the English language.

Q. Do you feel with this campaign you're taking up the white man's burden?

A. I'm just going to try to keep my head while all about me are losing theirs.

Mark cut off any further discussion. 'Thank you all very much,' he said, and added, 'Incidentally, we have set aside Suite 616 upstairs as a kind of press lounge. Any accredited representative from the media is welcome to use the facilities. That's Suite 616. Thank you again.'

As they came off the podium, Paul Berman was there to greet them, and together he and Mark steered the candidate into the cluster of newsmen and technicians, shouting over the babble of voices, 'Meet the next Mayor of New York City!' and 'Shake hands with the Citizen Candidate, Devereaux Page!' It was a technique of introducing a candidate quickly to an assemblage of people whereby everyone got to shake his hand and have a close look; but the campaign aides would always manage to hustle him off to meet a new group before somebody collared him for a discussion of the issues, which was certain to happen if he were left alone. When the campaign was really rolling, and there was tremendous pressure to meet tight schedules, this was the only way to move a candidate in and out of an appearance and still make the next stop on the itinerary.

The hot photographic lights remained on as the motion picture cameras recorded Page's progress through the knots of newsmen, all of whom were trying to get at the candidate with microphones and questions. While Berman was introducing him, Mark was explaining they had another engagement for which he was already late. Thus they steered Page rather smartly to the hallway, and taking his elbows, led him to the elevator which Nick Gigante was holding in readiness. The door of the elevator closed and they were alone. Page was flushed with excitement. 'How'd it go? How'd it go?'

'It went all right,' Mark said. 'This is Paul Berman, our borough coordinator.'

Page shook hands with him perfunctorily, while saying to Mark 'Really? Did I do all right?'

Mark's face suddenly contorted into a scowl, and he pointed a finger in the candidate's face. 'Don't you ever treat anybody like that again.'

Page was confused. The elevator door opened and he was shoved rudely out into the eighth floor hallway. Paul Berman and Nick Gigante followed into the small lobby where they stood in a circle. 'What do you mean, Mark?'

'What you did in the elevator to Paul Berman. It was inexcusable.'

'What'd I do?'

'I introduced you to Paul, and you slighted him. That was fucking rude.' The candidate looked hurt. 'But he's in the campaign. I thought –'

'I don't give a shit whether he's Jesus Christ reincarnate or a hotel busboy. *He's a voter*. When you're running for office and you're introduced to somebody, you look that person straight in the eye and tell him how glad you are to meet him. Do you understand that?'

'Yes, but –'

'When you meet somebody, *nothing else in the world matters*.'

'Gee, I'm sorry.' He turned to Paul Berman. 'I didn't mean it.'

Paul's usually relaxed face was a serious mask. 'Just remember what Mark told you,' he warned. 'That kind of thing could cost you the election. If you don't believe me, go read about Charles Evans Hughes; he snubbed one guy once, and it cost him the presidency.'

'I'm sorry,' Page repeated dumbly. 'I'm sorry.'

'Don't be sorry. Just learn from your mistakes.'

Chapter 11

At 10.00 AM the following morning the candidate was taken to Armand's film studio where he sat through a showing of the entire announcement press conference of the day before, along with Mark Altschul, Lou Klein, Paul Berman, and speechwriter Steve Loomis. It was agreed the performance was generally good, with only a few criticisms. The biggest gaffe was his disarmingly candid remarks about his divorce. In the future, he was told, he should avoid the subject completely; if it came up at all, for Chrissakes to gloss over it. When one of his answers began with, 'Let me make one thing perfectly clear . . .' everyone in the viewing room groaned and hissed. Other Nixon phrases to be avoided were, 'With regard to . . .' and 'Make no mistake about it . . .'

When it came to the part where Page said he was most influenced by Kipling, Berman asked, 'How in Christ's name did you manage to pick Kipling?'

'He was a great poet.'

'He was a goddamned imperialist. He talked of Niggers and Wogs.'

'I don't think he ever mentioned Wogs,' Page replied.

'Okay, okay,' Mark snapped. 'But he talked about Niggers and thought of Indians as his inferiors. And this kind of stuff doesn't go in a modern campaign.'

'*A woman is only a woman, but a good cigar's a smoke,*' intoned Loomis. 'The Women's Lib crowd will love that.'

'I think you'd better find yourself another writer, Mr Page,' Klein suggested quietly.

Bobby DeStefano operated out of a plush suite in the Commodore two floors above the regular campaign headquarters. Even though he expected to be there no more than two days a week, he had stripped the five rooms bare of furniture, draperies, carpets, replacing them with furnishings of his own. The huge salon was turned into his office and bar; he brought in a lush black leather modern sofa fully nine feet in length with matching overstuffed chairs, and a giant semicircular desk with a high-backed swivel chair, also of black leather, and a round, rosewood conference table with matching chairs. And on the floor was one of those vibrant, iridescent yellow-and-blue Persian rugs brought in from New Jersey. The hotel drapes had been replaced with heavy blue damask, and there were four ultra-modern lighting fixtures, including a light over the desk on the end of a fifteen-foot chromium pole which arched clear across the room from a block of concrete next to the sofa. A console containing three television sets and a glass kidney-shaped coffee table completed the decor.

The outer door of the suite which opened directly into the hallway had been boarded up, and one small bedroom was converted into the anteroom; both the outer and inner doors of this room had been reinforced by bullet-proof steel, and a locking mechanism controlled from Bobby's desk had been installed. The anteroom was comfortably furnished with a hotel couch and chair; on the wall beneath the tiny TV camera with wide-angle lens was a button and speaker with the sign, Please Ring.

The bedroom was redone to Bobby's taste, with his own linens on a queen-size bed and Mediterranean bureaus and tables. Off the main room was a small kitchen unit stocked with an array of liquor and cordials, bar tools, and the DeStefano's family crystal, monogrammed with a Gothic S.

The third bedroom in the back was used as the vault. Here was a gun-metal grey Mosler safe with multinumbered combination and two desks. In the safe was the guts of the campaign – the supply of cash from which every invoice and every salary would be paid. Three men knew the combination – P. J. Costello, Nick Gigante, and Bobby himself. No one else was to be trusted. Although Bobby had great faith in Mark Altschul, he had known him for less than six months – not long enough to let him in on that little million-dollar secret.

'What do you think of him?' Mark asked Bobby at their first meeting in the young Mafioso's newly redecorated suite.

'Page? I think it's too early to tell.'

'He's wishy-washy.'

'He's got a lot to learn.'

Bobby spun in his chair so its high black back was facing Mark. 'I think we ought to marry him off.'

'What do you mean?'

'Don't you think a wedding in the middle of a campaign would be good publicity?' Bobby wheeled back around to face Mark. 'I mean a politician ought to have a wife, for Chrissakes. Look at the Kennedys. Look at Lindsay. They all had wives.'

'Koch is a bachelor.'

'Who?'

'Ed Koch, congressman from the Eighteenth. He's not married.'

Bobby stared out over Mark's head. 'Find Page a woman,' he ordered. 'Find him a Mary Lindsay type.'

'Am I a *shatchin* or a campaign manager?' Mark wanted to know.

'Just do as I say,' Bobby retorted. 'We're gonna need all the help we can get.'

Mark shrugged and made no reply, but as he drove back to his apartment he decided to put aside Bobby's suggestion of finding a wife for the candidate. This was one of the few times he had deliberately disregarded the Boss. A wife for Page was basically a good idea, and maybe there would be time later in the summer but for the moment there were far more important problems facing Mark Altschul and his campaign team.

As a result of the 1969 primaries, New York City found itself with six separate political 'groupings,' locked in a struggle to elect a mayor. The regular Democratic machine had supported the conservative controller, Mario Procaccino, who had eked out a victory over his four primary opponents with only 32.8 per cent of the vote; the regular Republican party and the Conservative party had backed State Senator John Marchi, who had whipped John Lindsay in the Republican primary; and the dissident Democrats, together with the liberal Republicans and the Liberal party, had rallied to the support of Mayor Lindsay for re-election. To this motley array had been added an additional group – the 20 per cent undecided vote.

As if all this weren't complicated enough, the total vote could

also be broken down ethnically: Jewish – 32 per cent; Irish – 15
per cent; Negro – 14 per cent; Italian – 12 per cent; German
Protestant – 10 per cent; Puerto Rican – 7 per cent; Scandinavian
and Oriental – 1 per cent each. It all added up to making it
impossible for a candidate to be elected by any one political or
ethnic group. Theoretically the Democratic party which claimed
65 per cent of the enrolled voters in New York City could do it.
But, as Mark was well aware, this year's Democratic primary,
to be fought throughout the spring with four contestants tearing
each other to shreds, was going to leave the party just as splintered
as in 1969. The fact was, Mark reflected, the Democratic party
in New York City hadn't agreed on anything since the end of
the boss system in the early 1960s. Things were in a state of confusion, and Mark could see no point in adding to it at this
juncture by going on a get-the-candidate-a-wife hunt. There was
enough – too much – to teach Page about the city, about campaigning, about people – about everything – to have his valuable
time cluttered up with a series of broads.

Page's first live appearance was before the Lexington Democratic Club on the Upper East Side of Manhattan, and it went
badly. In the car on the way up Mark handed Page a set of 3 by 5
cards with the names of the club president and district leaders,
along with a brief history of the organization. It was the largest
and most influential Democratic club in the city, Mark explained,
with about 3000 members and a network of election district
captains that could still turn out the vote if any of them could
agree on a candidate, which was unlikely. It was a so-called reform
club, meaning its members were liberal and were constitutionally
opposed to the regular Democratic organization and the old boss
system. Inside they found less than 100 people scattered throughout the huge barn of a meeting room whose shoddiness was
matched by the membership. The club president introduced
Devereaux Page.

As the candidate stepped forward, about half the audience
arose and marched to the back of the room where they stood
conversing with one another in loud voices. It was, undoubtedly,
a protest against Page's calling for the resignation of their own
Ed Koch from Congress. Later in the campaign if such a disturb-
ance occurred, Page hopefully would be able to lay aside his

prepared speech and handle the action directly. But the candidate was inexperienced. The sudden evacuation and subsequent din from the back of the room visibly jarred his composure. He went ahead with the prepared remarks which were to become 'The Speech' to the Democratic clubs the city over. It wasn't a particularly good speech, but it was all-purpose; to the regular Tammany clubs, he could hold up the spectre of a liberal nomination – Al Blumenthal's or Herman Badillo's; to reform clubs such as this, he would raise the threat of Beame. He said:

This year the Democratic party has a long primary campaign, after which there are four long months to the general election.

A primary fight is America's most original contribution to the art of democracy, and at any level it is that part of the art most hated by every professional who practices politics as a trade.

Theodore H. White wrote that a genuine primary is a fight within the family of the party – and, like any family fight, is apt to be more bitter and leave more enduring wounds than battle with the November enemy. Primaries suck up and waste large sums of money from contributors who might be better tapped for the November finals; the charges and counter charges of a primary civil war provide the enemy party with ammunition it can later use with blast effect against whichever primary contender emerges victorious; primary campaigns exhaust the candidate, use up his speech material, drain his vital energy, leave him limp before he clashes with the major enemy.

Page was not speaking up, and his words were lost to all but the few in the first two rows. To Mark who had worked with him in rehearsal, his inflections were all right, but he simply wasn't relating to the audience, and even those in the front rows were growing restless. He continued:

It was the poet Kipling who wrote:

> When Pack meets Pack in the Jungle
>   And neither will go from the trail,
> Lie down till the leaders have spoken
>   – it may be fair words shall prevail.
> When ye fight with the Wolf of the pack,
>   Ye must fight him alone and afar,
> Lest others take part in the quarrel,
>   And the Pack be diminished by war.

It was the first time the candidate had used Kipling; Mark wanted the passage struck, but Page had suggested it, and both speechwriter Steve Loomis and Lou Klein agreed the quotation was very relevant to the business of primary fights. However, for poetry to be effective in a speech, the audience has to be with the speaker all the way; Page had lost this crowd almost at the outset. As he began to talk about how Kipling's Law of the Jungle was not practical these days, there was a commotion in the back of the room. Congressman Edward I. Koch entered the hall and sauntered down the side aisle where he took an end chair in the empty fifth row. He was followed by the nattering band of button-wearing protesters who moments ago had marched out on Devereaux Page; now they too filtered into the seats in front, hoping for some verbal fireworks. The room was suddenly quiet as Page wound up his otherwise unheard remarks, saying simply he wasn't soliciting their support at this time, but rather asking only they watch his campaign, listen to what he had to say on the issues, and keep an open mind; then, perhaps, after the primary, if they could not bring themselves to support the Democratic nominee, they might well find his independent Citizens' party candidacy a reasonable alternative to four years of a Republican or a Conservative in City Hall. After thanking them politely, Page started to leave the podium. Suddenly Ed Koch jumped to his feet and shouted, 'Just a minute, Mr Page!'

The candidate stopped in his tracks. 'What is it?'

'I'd like to ask you a few questions, if you don't mind.' He was a tall man, with a huge, shiny bald forehead, big ears, and except for a large hooked nose, tiny features all squashed together at the lower end of his face.

'I don't mind a bit,' Page said. 'Who are you?'

'Who am I?' Koch seemed incredulous that he wasn't recognized. 'Why I'm Ed Koch, your congressman.' Page paled. 'I'm surprised you don't know me!' Koch exclaimed. He spoke in a high-pitched voice with sing-song intonation. 'You live in my district, don't you?'

'I – I guess so.'

'Well, what Congressional District are you in?'

'I – I'm not sure,' Page stuttered.

'Well, where do you live then? Do you know that?'

'East 57th Street. It's 333 East 57th Street.'

'That's my district. That's in the 18th Congressional District. Did you know that?'

'I know it now.'

Mark stood up and nervously held up his wrist watch. 'Mr Page,' he said loudly, 'I'm sorry to break into this, but we're due at the Felt Forum in five minutes.'

'I've just come from the Felt Forum,' Koch shouted. 'That thing's going on till midnight, and your candidate can appear any time.'

'Yes, but –'

Koch cut Mark off with a wave of his hand. 'Mr Page called for my resignation the other night, and I want to ask him some questions while I have the chance.' He turned to Page who looked like he might throw up at any moment. 'Do you know who your state senator is? Or your assemblyman?' Page admitted that he didn't. 'How long have you lived at that 57th Street address?'

'About a year and a half.'

'*A year and a half?* You know, Mr Page, to run this city you have to know about this city, and you don't even know who your congressman is!' There was a burst of applause from the audience. Mark was up again and over by Dev Page who seemed totally paralyzed by what was happening. 'You called for my resignation, didn't you?' Koch continued to bore in. 'Didn't you?' Page nodded; Mark was standing beside him looking pained. 'You said I should resign because it's dishonest to use my congressional office for the purpose of running for mayor. Isn't that what you said?'

'Running for mayor is a full-time job,' Page said hesitantly. 'I merely said I didn't think you could be an effective congressman and run for mayor at the same time.'

'What do you mean not effective? I seldom miss a roll call vote! I've introduced legislation in the Congress of the United States on mass transit, on withdrawal from Vietnam, on establishing a presidential commission on marijuana, on welfare, on the citizen's rights to the information about himself in government and credit company computers. I have a travelling office in the district plus a full-time staff, and I'm available to anybody who wants to talk to me from Friday morning right through the weekend. What do you mean, I'm ineffective? You've been living in this city for a year and a half and you don't even know who your congressman is. I say *you're ineffective!* I say your candidacy for mayor is a joke!'

There was an additional burst of applause that clattered through the big room. Mark turned to the audience and said, 'Mr Page has another engagement now. I'm sorry we can't continue this.' With that, he grabbed a dazed Devereaux Page by the elbows and hustled him out past the jeering membership and down the rickety stairs to the seclusion of the waiting black sedan.

As they pulled away from the kerb, Page sank back into the soft leather upholstery and covered his face with his hands. He felt as though a hand grenade has just gone off in his gut. Beside him Mark rode in silence. P.J. was up front with Jimmy the Dwarf who was invisible behind the high front seat. 'Jimmy wants to know where to,' P.J. said.

'The Felt Forum,' Mark replied.

'No more tonight,' Page pleaded. 'I can't make another speech.'

'This is just a drop-in, Mr Page. No speech.'

'Call me Dev,' the candidate said to Mark. 'It's short for devastated.'

'Don't worry about it, Ed Koch is a master speaker and debater.'

'I looked like a jerk in front of a club of 3000 members.' Page's voice broke. 'Nothing like that has ever happened to me in my life.'

'It was bad luck Koch was there, that's all.'

Page was trembling. 'I don't think I could take that again.'

'Happens all the time in politics,' Mark reassured him. 'Think of what Nixon went through all those years.'

'I'm not Nixon.'

Mark looked at the candidate. 'You know what Norman Mailer called that club when he was running for mayor?' Page shook his head. His hands were still covering his face. 'Mailer called them a pack of plastic cunts.'

P.J.'s sudden laugh was infectious, and Dev Page himself began to chuckle in a kind of helpless relief.

'Mailer got up and insulted them to their faces,' Mark added. 'At least you didn't do that.'

'But you said it's the most important club in New York.'

'It's a paper club.'

'A paper club?'

'They have 3000 members on paper, of which 95 per cent have nothing to do with politics; they just joined so they could take advantage of the charter fares to Europe and group rates for ski weekends in the winter. What you faced tonight was about half the active membership. They're a bunch of bickering assholes with no power, no patronage, and very few election district captains. Don't worry about it.'

Page felt a little better, but not much. The hand grenade in his gut was now a string of Chinese firecrackers. 'Could we stop for a drink?'

Mark nodded, and they pulled up next to Kenny's Steak Pub on Lexington Avenue. Leaving Jimmy the Dwarf with the car, P.J., Mark, and the candidate went inside and stood at the dark, noisy bar. Page ordered a double Wild Turkey on the rocks; the others ordered Scotch. When the drinks came, Page took a slug of his favourite medicine and asked Mark if Koch was an effective legislator.

'What do you mean by effective legislator?' Mark retorted.

'I don't know. I guess I mean is he good at his job?'

'Most people think a congressman is doing a great job if he introduces a lot of legislation. That's bullshit. An effective legislator is one who gets legislation *passed*. Introducing a bill doesn't mean a thing; it's a grandstand play, so a politician can come back and crow about how he introduced this bill and that bill which didn't get passed, but boy, does he care about this problem and that problem. It's all bullshit. By any criterion, Koch is terrible. But they all are – Rangel, Badillo, Chisholm, Bingham, Rooney – the whole crew. Christ, they don't even vote the same on most bills. They make a lot of racket, but they don't get a fucking thing done. The same is true in Albany.'

'Koch seems to get re-elected all the time,' P.J. remarked.

'That's because he spends so much time massaging the people of his district. The voters see him on street corners, read about him in the papers, see him on television, and think he's doing a good job. People simply don't know the difference between getting your picture in the *Daily News* and getting bills passed.'

'Who are the effective congressmen?'

'Guys you never heard of. They're the quiet men who round up the votes – Hebert of Louisiana, Bolling of Kansas, Andrews of North Dakota – Staggers, Mills, Patman. Because of them, the the farmers of this country have got $60 billion in the past 10 years while the cities have got less than $15 billion, and yet 70 per cent of the population live in the cities.'

'Why can't we say this?' Page wanted to know.

'Say what?'

'Why can't we educate the voters as to what an effective legislator is? Can't I incorporate this into my speeches?'

Mark downed the rest of his drink and left a $10 bill on the bar.

'Why not?' he said. 'I'll talk to Loomis and Klein.'

Both Mark and Paul Berman subscribed to the Bobby Kennedy theory of politics that there was no such thing as rhythm in a campaign, nor was there any point in trying to 'peak' just before Election Day. The candidate was in it to win, and you kept him running flat out from the day he declared right on up to the election itself. You took care not to schedule too many speeches close together so the voice could rest, and you forbade the use of cigarettes by the candidate or any of his aides who were travelling with him; a politician's voice is all he has, and it must be protected. And, of course, you let him take time off to eat and sleep. But beyond these elementary precautions, you ran him ragged. His hours are excruciatingly long. When he wants to get drunk, he must do it quickly – and in private – with time to sober up for his next appointment. There can be five testimonial dinners in one evening, yet not a morsel of food will pass his lips. Meals when eaten are bolted; and friendships made and cemented in minutes. It is generally conceded most politicians are lousy lovers, with little time for the niceties of foreplay. Although they probably have a sexual urge less often than normal men, it can come with overpowering intensity; if a woman is handy, it's a skirt-up-pants-down piece of ass in the nearest empty office or coat closet without one scintilla of charm or love in the process. If a woman is not readily available, a good politician will service himself in a hot shower and proceed with his schedule; a poor one, like one state governor, will chuck everything – even the presidency of the United States – for a lay. Page was fortunate to have found Mia DeStefano who instinctively understood this and made few demands on the candidate whenever she would slip into town for a visit to his apartment which occurred two or three times a week.

On the campaign trail, Page found everything was compressed in time. He had to shave and dress quickly; meetings and discussions were very intense and necessarily short, because there was the schedule to maintain. There was never really time to study the 3 × 5 cards describing the next meeting; rather much had to be committed to memory in a hurry, used and then forgotten. Remembering names was easy; putting them together with faces was difficult. And so it was in the weeks that followed that Devereaux Page changed from an ordinary mortal to one of that frantic, driven breed, the politician. At first he suffered terribly from headaches and sluggishness under the rigours of campaigning; Bobby and Mark thought for sure they were stuck with a lemon. But after a half-day session with a Park Avenue internist, at which every conceivable kind of test was run on the candidate, it was finally determined he was suffering from the simplist of ailments; the pressure, long erratic hours, and rich meals were causing constipation. Several mild laxatives were tried, but each caused difficulties: one would hit him in the campaign car as they were dashing from place to place; another caused him to give off odoriforous manifestations of his malady. Finally it was found that prune juice, taken at 4.00 AM would produce the desired effect two hours later when the candidate had to get up anyway. And so, still another pressure was added. Not trusting an exhausted, sometimes drunk candidate to set his clock radio for so ungodly an hour, Mark hired a wake-up service to phone on the dot of four; when Page answered, he was greeted with a cheery female voice saying, 'Time for your prune juice!'

Chapter 12

'You want I should fuck a bottle?' Nick Gigante asked in disbelief as he regarded the glass object on the low table by the emperor-size bed.

'No, Nick, we do it like always,' Rosemary said, 'only at the last minute you pull out and come in the bottle.'

'Then I take it to the doctor.'

'What does he do with it?'

'I don't know. He said to bring it to him, that's all.'

The single wrap-around eyebrow that crossed Nick's forehead wrinkled. It was three in the afternoon. He had just flown in by helicopter from two straight days of campaigning in the city. All that was on his mind was to screw Rosemary, take her for a steak dinner, and then come home to get some sleep; he was assigned to pick up Page at 6.20 the next morning for a subway stop, and according to the schedule, the following 36 hours were to be more hectic than ever. 'I ain't gonna fuck no fuckin' bottle,' he said at length.

Rosemary, who was sitting on the end of the bed, burst into uncontrollable sobs, causing her big breasts to jiggle under the see-through nightie. 'I want children, Nick!' she wailed. 'It wasn't so bad when you were here all the time, but now you're gone, and I got nothing.'

'Don't cry, Rosemary,' Nick pleaded. 'I can't stand to see you cry.' He went over and sat next to her and she buried her tormented face in his lap. He was nude. His killer fingers probed through the shiny black hair, gently massaging her skull. The tears were flowing freely now, trickling on to his genitals which began to stir. Suddenly his massive instrument sprang alive like the top of a tenpin; Nick was embarrassed that Rosemary's woe should turn him on, but everything about that broad had had the same effect on him for the past sixteen years – her walk, her laugh, the way her big tits hung straight down when she bent over, even her tears. 'Okay, okay,' he acquiesced, 'I'll fuck the bottle. Just please don't cry any more.'

'Oh, Nick!' Rosemary sobbed. 'Oh, Nick, thank you!' Raising her head slightly, she went down on him, and a moment later was impaled astride him, the little nightie around her waist. 'Don't come yet, Nick!' she cried, twisting rodeo-style to snatch the bottle which she held in one hand over him. 'Tell me when you're gonna come! Tell me!' Nick gasped, and Rosemary leapt dripping from the saddle like a trick rider. In a trice she had the mouth of the bottle jammed against the massive freckled corona Nick was too big for the opening! She held it hard against him and he cried out in pain, 'For chrissake, you're gonna break the fuckin' bottle!' With that he cracked her across the face, sending Rosemary and the bottle flying off the bed just as his load shot all over the crucifix on the wall behind him. 'Ya dumb cunt!' he screamed. 'Ya dumb cunt! What the fuck are ya doing?'

Now it was Nick who was sobbing, covering his face with his hands. 'I'm sorry, I'm sorry. I didn't meant to hit you, Rosemary. My God, forgive me; I didn't mean to hit you!' Slowly he sat up and regarded his wife on the rug beside the bed; she was trembling like a wounded animal. He went over and tried to comfort her. 'I'm sorry,' he repeated again and again. 'I'm sorry. I thought you were going to break the bottle on me, and it woulda cut up my cock.'

Finally she looked at him, her lip beginning to swell from the blow, her face red from crying. 'I wouldn't hurt you, Nick,' she stammered. 'I just want your child.' The big man gathered her clumsily in his arms where they clung to each other for a moment 'Maybe we can get some of it off the wall,' Nick said at length 'Or I'll do it in the bottle again if I have to.'

Any political campaign is made up of two separate efforts: the candidate's appearances on the campaign trail – the Kennedys called it the 'road show'; and the scramble at headquarters to reach the voters through the media, by telephone, with doorbell ringers, and via the US mails. From a management point of view, Page was the dream candidate who did what he was told to the best of his ability. However, within a week, Mark Altschul realized his mayoral hopeful was something less than dynamite as a public speaker. Perhaps in Page's brash student days would be found an incipient Billy Graham quality which could set his listeners afire and win for himself the captaincy of the Princeton debating team. But during the arid years with Kay, his oratorical skills fell into total disuse. Although he made a great many speeches after his appointment to the presidency of the National Horse Show Association, his audiences were captive and his remarks always brief. Furthermore, of all sporting subcultures, one of the biggest collection of drinkers was the horsey set; when Dev Page addressed them, both he and his audience were generally pissed to the eyeballs, so it mattered little what he said or how he said it.

On a personal basis, the candidate was great. Talking to a small roomful of ladies at cocktails or at a *kaffeeklatsch*, he could draw in the entire crowd and create a nice rapport – so long as the room was small and there were no more than thirty present. He was also excellent at dealing with people on a one-to-one basis, where he could ease through a throng, pressing the flesh with genial urbanity. Television, too, was a fine medium for Page, because he treated the camera as though it were another human being. But in big halls and in front of large audiences, he simply didn't have it. There was a wooden quality to his delivery; his speeches sounded as though they were being read; above all, he could not relate to his listeners. After a particularly dismal appearance at a candidate's night in Brooklyn where the big high school auditorium seemed to overpower him, Mark and Lou Klein decided to concentrate more on television.

Klein, Altschul and Loomis designed a show which combined the folkiness of a late-night talk show with the formal aspects of Cronkite or Chancellor on the early evening news. Half the programme would be given over to a documentary presentation of an issue; the remaining time would be devoted to the candidate answering questions phoned in by the viewers. The title of the programme was to be non-political: 'The Citizen's Spotlight.'

The first programme was to concern the economic plight of the city, with Page's narrative being a rerun of his regular speech, but with one wrinkle: over his shoulder on the rear-projection screen was a montage of motion picture footage showing every-

thing wrong with New York . . . slums . . . traffic . . . a purse
snatching . . . cockroaches crawling across a child's face . . . filthy
streets . . . He said in part:

So I ask you to judge your legislators – your own congressmen, your
own state senator, your assemblyman, and your city councilman as
well. I ask you to judge them not for their smile, or their handshake,
or their statements of foreign policy or civil rights. Instead, judge
them by their actions, by what they are doing to stem the tide of
hard-earned dollars flowing out of your family's pockets and into the
Pentagon . . . into farm subsidies . . . into rockets to the moon . . .
and into the billion-dollar Albany Mall . . . all of which seem to have
higher priorities than our children in overcrowded schools . . . narcotics addicts creating terror in our neighbourhoods. . . our houses and
apartments crumbling away . . . our streets filthy and full of potholes,
our mass transportation with its dirty, dilapidated, dangerous equipment . . .

The talk was delivered in conversational tones, but it packed a
wallop. Page was not attacking any particular legislator, but
rather asking innocently if all four of the viewer's own representatives – congressman, assemblyman, state senator, and city
councilman – were doing the best possible job. Since 80 per cent
of all professional politicians were inveterate hacks, the answer,
of course, was that at least three of the four should be replaced.

The moment Page's narration was finished, there was a blast of
sound from the ringing telephones which had been turned on, and
the cameras showed the rows of volunteers where an announcer
was seen picking up messages from the operators. The studio
announcer turned and invited the viewers to phone in their
questions and said the candidate would answer as many as there
was time for on the air; all would be answered with a personal
letter from the candidate. Then the announcer sauntered across
the studio with a handful of questions and sat down opposite
Page. Naturally all the questions had been pre-selected, and Page
had rehearsed the answers. All that remained was for the operators
to assign the real name of a viewer who had phoned in with
roughly that question, and ask it. The whole thing went very
smoothly.

At the programme's end, the viewers were invited to keep calling
in their questions (or complaints), because everyone would get

an answer by mail, so long as they gave their full name and address.

As they were leaving the studio, Page turned to Mark and asked, 'Did we mean that about every person who calls getting a personal answer from me?'

'Of course we meant it. The letters will go out Tuesday morning.'

'But how?' Page was incredulous. 'I won't have time.'

'By computer, you dummy,' Mark snarled impatiently. 'Now quit asking questions and study these cards for the next stop.'

After two solid weeks on the campaign trail, Devereaux Page was exhausted and running on pure adrenalin. He had been to every borough, making as many as ten and fifteen stops a day, eating on the run, seldom getting to bed before midnight, only to be roused at 4.00 AM by the answering service for prune juice, and at 6.00 by Mark or P.J. and given a half hour to be ready before being picked up for the first stop. Between stops were long car journeys to the distant ends of the sprawling metropolis, during which he was not allowed to rest; instead, he was having his head crammed with facts, figures, statistics, names, and numbers, and then being peppered with questions to make sure he remembered them.

Now that he had quit the brokerage house, he had no income whatsoever, and finances were suddenly a nightmare. When he asked Mark how he would pay his bills, he was told to give them all to the campaign and they would be paid. 'But I don't have any money of my own,' he had protested. 'What are you going to spend it on?' was the retort. 'I don't know. Toothpaste or a hamburger.' Mark repeated, 'Give me the bills and we'll pay them.'

So, not only was Page bone weary, with every waking minute of his days and nights spoken for, but totally dependent on Mark and Bobby DeStefano for even his tiniest needs. Nor would they tell him how the campaign was going beyond showing him an occasional news story. To Page it was a continual wild whirl through crowds on the streets, short speeches in funny little apartments to babbling women in hair curlers, his literature and handouts grudgingly accepted by sullen commuters, dinner parties at which he was faint with hunger, but too busy shaking hands to have so much as a single morsel of food. Every day in the late morning there was scheduled a 'television event' – a walking tour in a strange neighbourhood or a tour through a home for the aged or an orphanage. Anything that was visually interesting was fodder for the television news broadcasts; and by scheduling it in the late morning, there was plenty of time for the footage to be processed and sent to the television studios for use on the evening news.

From the daily and nightly pounding around the city in the campaign car, Page began to realize how huge a place the city was, how varied its make-up, how chock-a-block full of people pushing, rubbing, pressing body against strange body. At community meetings in the outlying boroughs he saw terror in the eyes of the participants who shouted angrily about their fear of going out at night because of purse snatchings, muggings, and assaults. He heard firsthand the outrage at higher real estate taxes, the poor sanitation service, and narcotics openly sold in the schools. Heretofore only vaguely aware of this side of New York, he was suddenly eyeball-to-eyeball with the despair, the raw fear, the anger, the frustrations. One night it took an hour to get to Far Rockaway to address a Kiwanis meeting. During the twenty-mile run back to Manhattan, Page said, 'You mean the mayor of New York is also the mayor of Far Rockaway?'

'That's right,' Mark replied in the darkness of the car.

'It's madness.'

'What's madness?'

'That a guy sitting in New York City should be responsible for the people of Far Rockaway. It's idiocy!'

'We've known that for a long time.'

'So why doesn't somebody do something?'

'Like what?'

'Like Lindsay, for instance. Why didn't he appoint a deputy mayor for Far Rockaway and one for Brooklyn and another for the Bronx. He could have had them be like executive vice-presidents.'

'The structure is there, Dev,' Mark said. 'There's a borough president for each of the five boroughs; but as you know from your recent handy-dandy course in New York City government, the borough presidents are just figureheads, with only the power to recommend legislation.'

'Do they have to be just figureheads? Why didn't Lindsay make more use of the borough presidents. Or why didn't Mayor Wagner before him?'

'Because in the era of civil service, it's very difficult for a politician to seize enough power to govern effectively. Giving over some of your power to the borough presidents gives you less power to work with.'

Page thought a moment. 'What makes you think the same won't hold true for me?'

'Because you're backed by the most efficient Organization in the world. When they turn over power to somebody, they know how to retain tight control. Just like they have complete control over you and me. We're the only Organization that can change New York. Remember that.'

Page shuddered. They were hurtling across the upper roadway of the Queensborough Bridge. Before them, lay the hundred million lights of Manhattan winking and shining like an immense crown jewel.

Mark said, 'There's only one politician in America who understands how to exercise power, how to parcel it out and yet maintain complete control over his fiefdom and over the people who work in it.'

'Do you mean Nelson Rockefeller?'

Mark sneered.

'Who then?'

'Richard J. Daley of Chicago.'

Chapter 13

Monday, May 28. At 6.45 AM, Devereaux Page emerged from the self-service elevator of his apartment building and crossed the lobby to the main door where P. J. Costello was engaged in his usual early morning discussion with Willie, the doorman, on Joe Gelardi's choice in the feature race at Aqueduct in the *News*. P.J. looked up as Page approached. 'Got a little surprise for you today, Mr Page.'

'You mean you guys finally had a winner yesterday?'

'Nothing like that,' he replied with his toothpaste smile. 'But come on outside.'

Page stepped into the bright sunshine of the sidewalk on 57th Street. It was strangely deserted at that early hour. Parked by the hydrant was a sparkling white Chrysler sedan emblazoned with huge bright red lettering:

DEVEREAUX PAGE FOR MAYOR
The Citizen Candidate

Jimmy the Dwarf and Mark were leaning against the car with broad smiles as Page approached. 'How do you like it?' P.J. asked.

'It's gorgeous,' Page said. 'What's the occasion?'

'The Boss got tired of never having a car, so he ordered this.'

Inside, the car was completely customized with brown leather upholstery throughout, like Bobby's own car, and it bristled with electronic gear. By the rear window was a Bell telephone unit of black plastic with five channel buttons; a companion unit was placed on the floor next to the driver. In addition, Page learned, the campaign had leased from Hertz a dozen more sedans which had been equipped with Lafayette Telsat 23-channel two-way radios mounted under the dashboards, so all the vehicles in the fleet could communicate with each other and with headquarters at the Commodore without having to rely on the New York Telephone Company's mobile operators whose lines were frequently tied up. Next to the telephone in the back was a tensor high-intensity lamp for reading.

As well as the regular AM/FM radio, Page's car had a tiny television set mounted between the two front seats so the candidate could watch developing news as he travelled through the city. 'Just don't get hooked on any soap operas,' Mark cracked as he got in next to Page.

It was an incredible machine; it seemed to enfold the passenger like a marvellously soft, air-conditioned womb, filled with the fresh odour of a new car and heightened by the perfume of expensive leather. P.J. and Jimmy the Dwarf got in front and moments later the car leaped from its parking place and was rolling silently through the waking city.

'How do you like it?' Mark asked.

'It's a beauty car.'

'Enjoy it while you can. We've got a bitch of a week.'

'Tougher than last week?'

'In terms of what you're going to see, this is the worst week of the campaign.'

'What subway stop are we hitting today?'

'Today's Memorial Day. There's no subway stop'

'What the hell'd you get me up so early for then?'

'You'll see, Dev. You'll see soon enough.'

It was more of a foetus than a human baby, a tiny twitching rat-like thing, loose-fleshed with skin the colour of a bad burn and glistening with sweat. Barely six inches long and weighing less than three pounds, the bony form lay in a glass incubator, its puny brittle body racked with spasms. A feeding tube had been inserted into one nostril, while other wires were taped to the skin to record temperature and breathing. Suddenly the little body was in convulsions, the spindly legs and arms thrashing desperately. The air was shattered by a high-pitched scream which caused the four men peering in on it to draw back, wincing in discomfort.

This was a heroin baby, barely twelve hours old, born two

months prematurely to a Puerto Rican addict, and was in the first stages of withdrawal. The scene was a municipal hospital, a decaying wreck of a building in Central Harlem.

'Is it capable of feeling pain?' Dev Page asked softly.

Dr Bob Buralli, a man with wild eyes whom Page had met two weeks before at a rehabilitation centre on 116th Street, turned to the candidate. 'Mr Page, if you were to take all the physical pain you ever had in your life, put it together in one lump, and multiplied that by fifty, it would just about equal what that little creature is feeling right now.'

'When will he come out of it?'

'Heroin detoxification will last for the next ten to twenty days,' murmured Dr Philip Brown, a tall, sad-eyed black man who was the associate attending paediatrician at the hospital. 'Just the same as for adults.'

Page turned from the incubator; the child's pitiful squeals were crackling into his brain. He looked down at the dirty marble floor. 'Is there nothing you can do?'

'Prescribe chlorpromazine or phenobarbital to ease the pain a little bit,' Dr Brown said. 'And then wait it out.'

'What are the after effects?' the candidate wanted to know. 'I mean is there brain damage or anything like that?'

'We don't know, and probably never will know,' Dr Brown said. The bones in his jaw were bulging with tension. 'When that kid gets out of here, he'll go right back into the ghetto, and we'll lose him.'

'Does this happen to every baby born of an addict?'

'About two-thirds go through some stage or other of withdrawal.'

'And how many total are born here?'

'One out of every twenty-five in this hospital,' said Dr Brown. The baby stopped shrieking for a moment and they turned to look. The tiny humanoid creature yawned, gagged slightly, and started to scream again, and clawed at its face and chest. The four men stood in silence.

'God! This is awful,' Page muttered.

'By 1975, we figure there'll be one million heroin babies born every year.'

Mark, his hands jammed into his pockets, shifted his weight

from one foot to the other. 'I'm sorry about this, Dev,' he said, 'but if you're going to become an expert on narcotics, you've got to see it to understand it.'

The four men left the puking, mewing, writhing baby and proceeded down the narrow labyrinthine corridors that were teeming with humanity – in wheel chairs, on wheeled beds awaiting surgery, or just out of surgery, bobbling about on yellow wood crutches and aluminium walking devices or sitting on folding chairs staring blankly off into space. The corridors were dark and hot, lighted only by occasional naked bulbs high overhead; the smell of urine seemed to be everywhere. Most of the crowds in the hallways were black, although there were some Puerto Ricans. All were in untidy bed clothes – nightgowns or pyjamas – except for the few nurses who looked harried, and the visitors. The young were intermixed with the old, the pregnant in with the diseased. Corridor on corridor, floor on floor. Where most hospital rooms might hold two and four beds, these had six or eight jammed in together, tiny hot rooms ready to explode with patients and visitors and sickroom gear. The only amenity was segregating the men from the women wherever possible. They walked down the stairs (the elevators weren't working), and in the dingy lobby of the hospital, they left Dr Brown to return to his hopeless task and joined P.J. and Jimmy the Dwarf at the new car; the vehicle was a gleaming anachronism amid the slum. Page was shaken by what he had seen; to Mark and Dr Bob, it was old stuff – just a question of how much worse things had become since the last visit. The candidate stood by the car rubbing his head; the Harlem air seemed clean and fresh after the inside of that filthy jungle. For a moment he was afraid he would retch. Finally he got in the back seat of the car next to Dr Bob. Mark followed him in and closed the door. 'Something's got to be done about that,' Page said as they started downtown through the garbage-strewn streets of Harlem.

'Done about what?'

'That hospital,' Page said. 'I mean, what the hell is happening to this city?'

They rode in silence, the only sound being the whoosh of the car's air conditioner. 'I feel dirty all over,' the candidate added. 'And that's not the way you should feel coming out of a hospital.'

'This week and next, Dev, we're going to concentrate on the problem of narcotics,' Mark said. 'I told you this morning, this will be the worst week of the campaign, and I think you now see why.'

'Much more of this, and I'll throw in the towel.'

'What if everybody in this town threw in the towel?' Dr Bob said suddenly. 'What if I said the hell with it, and left my clinic on 116th Street for a nice cushy post at the Mayo or N.Y.U. What if Judianne Densen-Gerber –'

'Who?'

'Dr Densen-Gerber. She started Odyssey House for the help and rehabilitation of addicts. What if she threw up her hands and said it's no use? What if all the men and women working sixteen hours a day, like Phil Brown there at the hospital and the thousands more, all gave up? You know what would happen? This town would be worse than India.'

'I never knew it before,' Page replied slowly, 'but I think this town *is* worse than India. No, not the part I live in or in the areas I used to work in or shop in – Wall Street, Fifth Avenue – but up here, where the people don't have a chance.'

He gestured to a block of blackened brownstones with broken windows and garbage heaped on the sidewalk where a dozen little black children were playing. 'Maybe physically the poverty in India is worse,' the candidate added. 'Maybe the rats are bigger, the people hungrier, the shelter more run down, and the filth waist deep instead of ankle deep. But goddammit, we're the richest country in the world, sending millions of dollars in foreign aid out of here, and yet we treat our own people like this. It makes me sick. If India was as rich as we are, they wouldn't let this kind of thing happen. No, this is worse than India, if not physically, then certainly from a moral point of view.'

'Spoken like a true candidate,' Mark said with a smile.

'After what I've seen,' Page said, 'I wish now I had been more of an activist in college so I would have learned it all much earlier. But it wasn't fashionable then. We never thought about it.'

The car turned onto 116th Street and pulled up in front of the two adjoining buildings that made up Dr Bob's shabby clinic. 'You know, Mark,' Page said, 'for the first time since we started, I think I could do a better job as mayor than is being done now.

When you consider what I had as a child – the start in life I got – and then think of that poor tiny baby we saw today, and all those desperate people in the hospital, it just destroys you.'

Dr Bob grasped Page's shoulder. 'Mr Page, whatever you do, don't give up.' Getting out of the car he added, 'Too many people are counting on you.'

'Thanks, Dr Bob.'

Dr Bob closed the car door and went inside the clinic.

'It's the Mafia's fault, isn't it?' Page said when they were alone in the car. 'The DeStefanos and all of them are responsible for this.'

'Not the DeStefanos,' Mark replied quickly. 'They've never been into drugs, and have tried to persuade the others to get out of it. It's too dangerous and destructive for Bobby.'

'But it's profitable, isn't it? That little prick would do anything for a profit.'

'Wrong,' said Mark. 'Bobby is a bit of a philosopher. And he's a businessman. So long as society is healthy, Bobby will make money, whether it's gambling or moneylending or in legitimate business. Anything that destroys the fabric of society, like narcotics, Bobby wants no part of.'

'Are you sure?'

'I've looked into him pretty carefully. That's one reason I approached his family in the first place with this scheme, and not the Gambinos or the Lucheses.'

'I hope you're right,' Page said grimly. 'Because if I find out Bobby DeStefano is even remotely connected to what happened to that little baby, I'll kill him.'

'Where to, Mark?' P.J. wanted to know.

'Let's get some breakfast.'

'You mean you could eat something after what we just saw?'

'You'll get used to it, Dev.'

Devereaux Page did not get used to it. During the following week there were more tours of city hospitals, each more crowded and filthy than the last. There were street appearances in Harlem where hostile bands of blacks pelted the candidate with obscenities and occasionally bits of garbage. Then there were the Brooklyn slums of Bedford-Stuyvesant and Brownsville, looking like bombed-out cities of World War II, with trash in the streets and rats. The inhabitants seemed neither hostile nor friendly; rather they were just there, vacantly standing in knots by the corner streetlights or leaning in doorways, swaying stupidly, their eyelids drooping with the vacuous, moronic look that blankets the faces of all addicts. As the candidate approached them to introduce himself and ask what they needed if he were elected mayor, they merely looked up fuzzily and said quietly, 'Motherfuckin' honkey' or 'Shee-it.' Several times Page was propositioned, once by a raggedy little black girl who couldn't have been more than nine. Startled, he said, 'Do you know what you just asked me?'

'I need a fix, man,' she looked at him with dazed eyes. 'Lemme suck y' off fo' two dollers. How's that?'

Perhaps the worst neighbourhood of all was Hunts Point in the South-east Bronx, just north of Manhattan Island on the East River. There, the two main industries were narcotics and welfare. Amid the abandoned buildings where police, sanitation, and fire services were meagre at best, clusters of addicts lived roach-like in debris-strewn cellars or rooms. 'Who owns all these deserted buildings?' Page wanted to know.

They were city property now, Mark explained. They were once privately owned, but the city's rent laws were so screwed up that taxes on the buildings became higher than the amount of rent the landlord was allowed to collect; the landlords simply walked away and left them.

Page was taken into one of these buildings by Mark and Nick Gigante who knew the neighbourhood. After climbing the dark and dangerous stairs with no railing they came to a second-floor room where four children, ranging from an infant up to maybe five, all filthy and stark naked, were living on mattresses amid an odour that made the visitors gag – it smelled as though a thousand diapers filled with shit and soaked in piss had been lying around for months. With them on this trip was Johnny DiSantis and his Bolex; his photographic lights suddenly flashed on, bathing the room in near daylight.

'Where's the mother?' Page asked.

'A junkie,' Nick replied sombrely. 'She's out trying to turn a trick so she can feed her habit.'

'But the kids –' Page looked over the room in disbelief.

'Kids don't matter none when you got the habit,' Nick muttered.

'Can't we leave some money or something?'

'The mother would find it and use it for a fix,' Mark said.

They went back to the stairway where they proceeded to go up a couple of floors, picking their way through piles of wine bottles, beer cans, garbage, and dog shit. On another floor they came across a bare room with an addict, naked to the waist, sitting cross-legged on a mattress. Page judged him to be in his late twenties and white, although it was difficult to tell in the darkness of the room. He was surrounded by his worldly goods – a blanket, a shirt, and a pair of shoes – and seemed to be in a kind of trance; he didn't even move when Johnny DiSantis's photographic strobes went on and the camera began to roll.

Out on the streets and sidewalks, where pedestrians had to literally wade through raw garbage, they came to the Bronx Casino on 149th Street where pushers were hawking heroin out in the open to all passers-by. A little black boy followed the candidate's party. 'Hey, baby, you wanna deuce?' the boy shouted, trotting alongside them. 'You want a tres? You wanna eye dropper? You wanna piece of ass? My momma'll fuck you and suck you real good – she's a virgin . . .'

Page walked on, trying to pretend not to hear. Until this past week, no one had ever spoken to him like that in his life; here for the first time he was hearing the normal patois of ghetto. Some of it Mark had to translate for him: a deuce, for example, was a $2 bag of heroin; a tres, a $3 bag. In this Hunts Point section of the Bronx, Mark explained, the residents were living in a state of seige; they had a one-in-twenty chance of dying a natural death. It was here in the Twenty-fifth Precinct that there was the highest per capita crime rate in the city – more than 11,000 crimes reported last year. Addicts were everywhere, either living here, or travelling here to make a contact and buy their stuff, and, of course, stealing here. What few policemen were assigned to the area were all on the pad, either being paid off to look the other way, or wheeling and dealing in heroin themselves, making thousands of dollars a week over and above their salaries.

Once again Page got into the new car feeling dirty all over, frustrated, and powerless.

'You have to see it first hand to understand it,' Mark said.

Johnny DiSantis, so tall his head nearly brushed the ceiling of the car, stared moodily ahead. In the front seat, Nick Gigante called the Commodore on the two-way radio to say they were heading back.

'But it all seems to be tied in together,' the candidate mused aloud. 'There's narcotics, housing, crime, hospitals falling apart, welfare, law enforcement, poverty – it's everything rolled into one.' He looked over at the campaign manager next to him. 'What do you do?'

'The first thing is to keep it all separate in your mind. Any discussion of narcotics naturally leads into the situation of the ghettos; that can immediately take you off on a tangent of welfare or housing or health services.' Mark shook his head. 'They're all wired together, it's true. But if we keep them separate – at least for the campaign – then we'll be able to maintain our schedule of one issue at a time. The trouble with most candidates and most politicians is they lump everything together and it confuses the campaign, and it confuses the voter.'

'But take Hunts Point.'

'You take Hunts Point,' Mark quipped. 'Please.'

The tension in the car broke for a moment. 'Hunts Point has everything wrong with it – narcotics, housing, crime, sanitation. It's ghastly.'

'So?'

'There must be something that could be done,' Page insisted. 'There must be one single thing which could alleviate the situation. Like a big bunch of federal money just ploughed in there to clean it up, rebuild the neighbourhood, help the addicts. Am I crazy, or isn't this true?'

'Right on, baby,' Mark said. 'Now how do you get federal money?'

'Congress has to vote it.'

'Right again. And if you were the congressman representing the East Bronx, wouldn't you be scurrying around Washington trying to scrounge up every possible dollar for your district? Wouldn't you be working night and day trying to get money to make the place better?'

'Well sure.'

'Guess who their congressman is.'

'I have no idea.'

'Herman Badillo.'

'But he's running for mayor!' Page exclaimed.

Mark looked at the candidate. 'That's sort of the point of this campaign.'

Chapter 14

Dev Page spent the entire week on the run. During all of his tours, he was followed by the ubiquitous Johnny DiSantis, who filmed every grim scene, and Tony the Elf Mauro with his ever-present Nagra tape recorder. Tony the Elf also took stills of the various scenes, and turned his recordings over to the film laboratory to be used for the sound on film. And when Page was not actually touring or making 'The Speech', he was being fed enormous funds of back-up material put together by the campaign research staff, handed to him piecemeal by Mark during every free moment – in the campaign car, over lunch and dinner, and for bedside reading. By the end of the week, the candidate was glassy-eyed with fatigue, his head spinning and whirling with numbers, with images of slums, dilapidated hospitals, naked children, starving addicts, abandoned buildings.

The real problem was that no one could agree on the narcotics problem. Some experts, like Dr Judianne Densen-Gerber, the hefty, knowledgeable director of the Odyssey House Centre, insisted that marijuana should be legalized, but that anyone found with heroin in his bloodstream should be summarily charged with a crime and forced into a rehabilitation programme under constant supervision; if that didn't work, he should be put away for three to five years. Governor Rockefeller was for jailing everybody. Yet how could any government – federal, state, or local – cope with detaining perhaps 400,000 addicts? Others, such as Dr Bob, maintained heroin addiction was a sickness, not a crime. Dr Bob's answer: methadone and intensive psychotherapy. Methadone was a drug, also addictive, which blocked the craving for heroin and permitted the addict to lead a reasonably normal life. Then there was the Ford Foundation study which suggested the British system whereby the addict could receive maintenance doses of real heroin; the addict simply registered

with the narcotic control board, who in turn would send a prescription around to the addict's local pharmacy, permitting him
to pick up one or two doses a day. While obviously not the final
answer, at least it might cut down on the horrendous crime rate –
some $6 billion in thefts in New York City alone each year. And
legalized heroin would short-circuit the underworld.

But at the mention of heroin maintenance Dr Bob would
pound the table in rage and shout the British system had done
nothing but make heroin addiction more rampant. As for the
legalization of marijuana, he again would shake his head.
'Marijuana is the first step. Our youngsters try grass first and like
it, and then go on the hard stuff!'

It was a confusing divisive issue, and both Page and the
campaign staff were under tremendous pressure to come up
with a newsmaking television show which was scheduled for a
full hour of prime early evening time scheduled for airing in just
ten days. That Friday night, Mark, Lou Klein, Dr Bob, and
Page spent a fruitless dinner at Pen and Pencil trying to thrash
the thing through. They all came to respect Dr Bob for his
commitment and knowledge, but he was inflexible in his position.
In his opinion, methadone was the only solution. Yet methadone
presupposed the addict wanted to undergo treatment. The fact
was that many addicts liked being on heroin. This had been
driven home the previous afternoon as they stood talking to a
junkie amidst the ruins of Brownsville, a black who was unusually
literate for the ghetto. 'I'm twenty-five years old now,' he said
to them, 'and if I put together all the sex I've had in my whole
life, and all the Christmas mornings, and birthday parties, and
multiplied the feeling by a thousand, that's how good it feels
when you mainline.'

'What's mainline?' Page wanted to know.

'You stick a needle directly into the vein,' Dr Bob explained,
'and you get a tremendous rush of feeling.' The addict then rolled
up his sleeve to reveal a festering plexus of scars and holes running
the length of his inner arm from wrist to elbow.

'Wouldn't you like to get off this stuff once and for all?' Page
asked him.

The addict's dull eyes met Page's. Then with a tired gesture toward the garbage in the streets and the filth of the deserted

buildings, his lips went into a kind of grin. 'Look around you, man,' he said, his voice calm. 'If I go off junk, this is what I can look forward to.'

As the dinner broke up, Page was drained of energy, tired of the subject, and physically aching for bed. Once during dinner he had actually dozed off and when nudged awake by Mark, excused himself to go splash cold water in his face in the men's room. It was midnight now. They were driving along Madison toward 57th Street. 'Maybe there's no solution,' Page said. 'I've never in my life seen a situation where there was so much hopelessness, both in the ghettos where it's happening and in the minds of the so-called experts. Even if the government voted five billion dollars to wipe out the problem of heroin, nobody could agree on how to spend it.' He tilted his head against the soft leather of the high back seat. 'Maybe we should drop the whole thing and go on to the problem of housing or welfare.'

'And come back to narcotics later?'

'I don't know,' the candidate muttered. 'God, I'm tired.'

'Look, Dev, you can't cop out on this.'

'What do you mean?' Page's eyes were closed. 'You guys own me. Come up with a position on narcotics, and I'll be your parrot.'

'Nobody ever asked you to be a parrot,' Mark snapped. 'If we come up with a position on narcotics, it's got to be a position you can live with.'

'I'll live with anything you tell me to live with,' the candidate replied drowzily.

The white car swung a U-turn on 57th Street and pulled up in front of Page's building. As he got out of the car and stumbled sleepily toward the lobby, Mark called out the window of the the car, 'Sleep on it, Dev. We've got to come up with something damn soon!'

Mark heard the phone ringing as he stepped out of the elevator. Ringing, and ringing, and ringing, it knifed through the silence of the wide hallway. He hurried past the line of doors toward his apartment with the ringing getting louder. What terrible news was he about to hear? Was his mother all right? Had something finally happened to his uncle with the respiratory condition? He flung open the door and threw himself at the ringing phone with dread in his heart. On the other end was a wide-awake, slightly hysterical Devereaux Page. 'I've been robbed!'

'You what?'

'I got upstairs and found my apartment's been robbed! They got the television and the stereo and my jewellery! The whole place is turned upside down!'

'How about the suits?'

'What?'

'Look in the closet to see if they got your suits.' There was a thump and a scramble on the other end of the phone. Moments later Page was back. 'Yeah, they got my suits, my overcoats, and my suitcases too.'

'Junkies,' Mark said.

'Junkies? How do you know?'

'They take anything that's portable and can be easily sold on the street. TV, stereo, clothes, that kind of thing.'

'I'll kill the sons of bitches!'

'They're sick human beings,' Mark said. 'They're not responsible for their actions.'

'They're a bunch of goddamned criminals!' Page shouted back into the receiver. 'Now what the hell do I do?'

Mark thought fast. 'Don't do anything, understand? Just call the police and tell them what happened. I'll be over in about twenty minutes.'

'Jesus!' the candidate cried. 'I just noticed they slashed my Picasso lithograph!'

'Calm down, Dev, and don't move anything,' Mark counselled. 'Just call the police and I'll be right over.' He hung up and looked at his watch; it was 12.20 AM. The late city editions had been put to bed, so the story would have to break in the afternoon papers. Mark called the city desk of the *New York Post*, and after identifying himself, explained that the citizen candidate for mayor, who was in the middle of preparing a one-hour television special on narcotics, had himself just been robbed by an addict. 'That's funny!' hooted the editor, and promised to send over the radio car. Next, Mark alerted *Newsday* and the *Long Island Press*, both afternoon papers with heavy readership in Queens as well as Long Island. Finally the *Times* and *News* were called, along with Johnny DiSantis who fortunately was staying overnight at the

Commodore, as was Tony the Elf. Mark ordered Johnny to get his Bolex up to the candidate's apartment pronto, because they had the makings of a dandy news story. 'Get hold of Berman, too,' Mark added. 'And Tony the Elf with his still camera.'

Not trusting Page to have a decent liquor supply, he grabbed two bottles of Scotch from the shelf and left hurriedly to find a taxi. It was imperative to get there fast, because this would be the candidate's first real impromptu encounter with the news media, and from the way he had sounded, Page was not at his coolest and most reasonable.

The candidate's apartment was a minor disaster area. The thieves – at least two were involved to have removed so much stuff – had jimmied the lock out of the cylinder and then replaced it so it wouldn't be noticed by anyone passing down the dim hallway. Inside, all the furniture was turned turtle in the desperate search for anything of value. Every bureau drawer had been systematically pulled out and spilled onto the floor so the contents could be pawed through. The little desk had been ransacked and there were cancelled cheques, bills, letters, strewn about the room like confetti. The portable typewriter was gone. Two policemen were on the scene.

'Why the suitcases?' Dev Page wanted to know. 'They were old and battered.'

One of the two patrolmen looked at him sympathetically. 'To carry out the loot, Mr Page.'

The little hall closet had also been sacked for most of his winter wardrobe, including his favourite maroon velvet lounging jacket from Hong Kong. 'This town is a goddamned jungle!' he raged as Mark walked in the door. 'If I lived in Keene, New Hampshire, I could go to bed knowing I was safe and the air I was breathing was pure, and the streets were clean, and there was practically no crime!'

'And when you woke up in the morning,' Mark said with a grin, 'you'd be in Keene, New Hampshire.'

'That's not a bad alternative!'

'Relax, Dev,' Mark soothed. 'The press will be here any moment, so you have to give the appearance of being calm and in complete control.'

'The press?' Page looked quizzical. 'You called the press?'

'This is a hell of a story,' Mark said matter-of-factly. 'Have a slug of Scotch.' Mark pulled a bottle of Dewars from the paper bag he had brought.

Page paused . 'I'd rather have Wild Turkey.' He went to his little liquor cabinet in the wall unit. It was empty except for a few drops of Surrey gin and a half-filled bottle of vermouth. 'I don't believe it! They even got my booze!'

'When he got there, the cupboard was bare,' cried Paul Berman who suddenly appeared in the doorway. He let out a low whistle. 'What a messy housekeeper.'

'Screw you, Berman!' The candidate was angry.

Johnny DiSantis walked in with Tony the Elf and in minutes the floodlights were on so they could photograph the carnage. A reporter and photographer from the *Post* arrived, followed by a team from the *Long Island Press*, and shortly thereafter, the *News*, causing the tiny apartment to be aswarm with people, all with tumblers of Scotch, gingerly stepping over and around piles of debris, or sitting in a row on the box spring of the daybed or on the mattress on the floor. Page himself was perched on the overturned easy chair, glumly surveying the scene. As the reporters asked questions, it was evident the candidate's mood kept shifting from fist-pounding fury to real depression. The approximate tally was $3500, including the Sony colour television set, the portable Olivetti electric typewriter, and the seven suits, a tuxedo, several sports jackets, and the lounging jacket from Hong Kong. Three topcoats were also missing. The biggest single loss was the Scott Model 477 AM/FM stereo receiver and the Garrard Zero 100 turntable whose combination cost had been over $600. Kay had given it to him two Christmases ago. It was small consolation the AR-5 speakers were just too big, and still remained, the connecting wires frayed from where they were yanked from the terminals. Instead of the speakers, the burglars had opted for the digital clock radio; and the one good piece of art, a signed and numbered Picasso lithograph, was slashed beyond recognition.

How did the candidate feel? 'In a word, damn discouraged. And angry,' Page added. 'You can spend a week learning about narcotics and the root causes of the problem. Yet it's all a bunch of theory until something like this actually happens to you.

Then suddenly you really care.' What solution did he propose to the narcotics problem? Mark Altschul fielded the question, saying that this was something the entire campaign was focusing on at the present time. 'Nobody can agree on anything,' Page added cheerlessly. 'No one inside the campaign, not the experts we've talked to, not the law enforcement people, the doctors, the psychiatrists, not the social workers – not even the addicts themselves.'

Would what happened here tonight have any bearing on the candidate's position? 'You're goddamned right it will!' Page asserted.

Within a half hour, the reporters had their stories and departed. The two patrolmen stayed for a short Scotch. Then they too went on their way, pausing to leave their names and phone number at the 17th Precinct station house; he was to contact them if he found anything else to be missing. 'Cheer up, Mr Page,' one of them said on leaving, 'anything that's not insured is tax deductible.'

Page muttered gloomily, 'Nothing is tax deductible if you don't have any income.'

The robbery made national news in the first real publicity break of the campaign. Johnny DiSantis had carried his footage down to the processing lab while speechwriter Steve Loomis journeyed to the Commodore and knocked out a 30-second narration. They met at Armand's studio at 3.30 AM with the raw film, edited it, and sent it back to the lab for final printing, while Loomis returned to the Commodore office to retype his script and xerox it. Seven copies of the film and narration went out, one to each television station in town. The 'Today Show' used it nationally, as the usually sombre Frank Blair ended his morning newscast on an up note – the sad tale of a New York citizen candidate who was stolen blind by narcotics addicts while he and the staff were out researching a position paper on that very subject. Cronkite and Chancellor used it on the early evening news, and Johnny Carson mentioned it in his opening monologue.

The *New York Post* ran a front-page picture of Page in his ransacked living room, and a story on page 5. Most of the evening news broadcasts used it either that day or the following day, and there was a page 7 story and picture in the *News* and a small item in the *Times*. Loomis also wrote a news story which went out over the AP and UPI wires along with one of Tony the Elf's photographs.

But the real impact of the robbery on the campaign occurred the morning after, when Devereaux Page stormed into headquarters at the Commodore and put forth a perfectly logical programme to deal with narcotics. When he awoke after a restless night amid the wreckage of his private world to find his underwear and socks still all over the floor – nothing to wear but yesterday's suit because all his others had been stolen or were at the cleaner – no cuff links because they were gone along with his jewellery box – shoes under the bed where they had been flung by the thief rooting through the closet – he had worked himself into another fury.

Then the whole thing suddenly came clear in his head. That morning he cancelled two appearances (a *kaffeeklatsch* and a walking tour of the Park Slope section of Brooklyn) to call a meeting of Klein, Loomis, Mark, and Berman where the candidate laid out the Devereaux Page narcotics control plan, a step-by-step compilation of the best of everybody's thinking on the subject – from the British, to Dr Bob, to Dr Densen-Gerber, with a smattering of Bronx District Attorney Burton Roberts and one-time mayoral candidate Mario Procaccino. There was none of the affable good humour on his part; he was tight-lipped as Mark, and deadly calm. It was perhaps the first time in his life he'd ever taken complete charge of a situation with no help from anyone, and Mark Altschul was ecstatic. Here was a leader of men. Now if only Dev Page could translate that kind of leadership into live appearances before big audiences and before intimate groups and on television, spice it with a little humour, and still carry that impact, they would have a viable candidate. When Page finished with the outline, he asked if there were any questions. None were forthcoming, so he got up and walked out of the room, with Mark trotting behind. 'We've missed the Brooklyn stops, Dev,' the campaign manager said in the hallway. 'What do you want to do with the time?'

'How do you feel about campaigning a naked candidate?'

'What do you mean?'

'I haven't got any clothes, for Chrissakes!'

'We'll replace everything that was stolen; Bobby's already agreed to that.'

'Okay,' the candidate snapped. 'If anybody wants me, I'll be at Saks Fifth Avenue.'

Rosemary Gigante was scared. In the sixteen years of blissful marriage to Nick, she had never before been the bearer of ill tidings. Nick was not a complex man. He liked his sex, his sleep, his food, and presumably he enjoyed his work, although he never mentioned it at home; Rosemary was still not sure exactly what he did. But on those occasions when Nick's temper flared, such as the previous week when she was trying to get a jissom sample, it was truly frightening. Now as she studied the massive, muscular sleeping form next to her in the early morning light, she wondered how he would take the news that he was sterile.

Should she even tell him? Wasn't this the ultimate insult to a man – particularly to Nick Gigante to whom masculinity was everything? The doctor assured her this was a common occurrence and in no way had anything to do with virility or ability to satisfy a woman. Many women were taking the alternative of getting pregnant by artificial means. You didn't have to go to bed with another man, which would be unthinkable. The doctor explained it could be accomplished right in the office with a squirt thing which wouldn't hurt a bit; in fact, the newest idea was to have the husband actually squeeze the stuff into the wife so the couple would feel they did everything themselves, even though it was somebody else's juice. And the chances were very good the baby would have the same characteristics of the parents – same skin and hair colour – so no one would know it was not really all their child.

But should she tell him? Or should she find a doctor who would perform the task and not say anything to Nick at all? No, that was out. Rosemary was a terrible liar; she couldn't possibly walk around for nine months with somebody else's child and keep it a secret. And if Nick ever found out, he'd kill her. If she wanted a child – and she did, desperately – Nick would have to be told, and they would make the decision together.

Rosemary looked at the clock. It was 6.30. She got out of

bed and went into the kitchen to make coffee. She had slept fitfully, tossing and worrying about how to tell him, and what he would do when he found out. Last night it was pretty straight in her mind how to tell him, but now she was confused again and began to weep.

Finally at breakfast she told him they couldn't have children together. 'The doctor said I can probably get pregnant, but you can't – you don't make enough . . .' Rosemary couldn't go on. She started to cry. Nick was very calm. He took her in her arms and held her sobbing next to him. 'It doesn't mean you're not a man or anything like that. It's just that your body doesn't make enough – enough – little sperm things.'

Nick soothed her and asked some questions which she answered as best she could. Then he got up and went to the window where he looked out over the beach and the ocean beyond. 'Do you believe the doctor?'

'He's Mr DeStefano's doctor,' Rosemary said. 'He should be pretty good.'

'And there's no hope.'

'The count is just too low.'

Nick said nothing.

'Do you love me, Nick?'

'I love you.'

'Are you sorry I told you?'

'I don't know.'

'I'm sorry,' she said. 'After sixteen years of nothing happening, I just had to know. We can adopt, or we can do it artificially.'

Nick returned to the table where he took a final gulp of coffee and then went into the bedroom to finish dressing. When he came out, there was a distant, hurt look in his eyes Rosemary had never seen before.

'When am I going to see you again?'

'Day after tomorrow, probably,' he said. There was the sound of a car horn; Jimmy the Dwarf was outside waiting.

'Nick, I love you.'

'Yeah,' he replied. 'I love you too.' He went out of the house and drove off with Jimmy the Dwarf.

Chapter 15

Both mornings of the weekend, New Yorkers who turned to their copies of the *Times* and *News* were jolted by a full-page advertisement with the headline:

> **IF YOU LIVE IN NEW YORK CITY**
> **YOU WILL BE ROBBED AT LEAST**
> **ONCE IN THE NEXT THREE YEARS!**

There was a large photograph of Dev Page sitting amid the rubble of his once tidy apartment, chin in hands, looking dejected. Beneath was the caption: *This Candidate for Mayor Was Robbed Last Week. Are You Next?*

The ad, which also ran in the weekend editions of the *Post*, *Newsday*, and the *Long Island Press*, was cooked up by Klein and Loomis to promote the one-hour television special Sunday evening on the subject of narcotics. It was generally agreed this scare ad was in less than good taste, but more than effective.

By 6.30 PM the candidate was thoroughly primed and ready for the broadcast. Attired in a grey pin-striped suit with blue shirt and a collar clip under his striped tie, Devereaux Page arrived at the NBC studios on the sixth floor of the RCA building where he was greeted with a crossfire of blinding strobes and flashbulbs. The press was there in force, having been invited to watch the programme in the gallery overlooking the studio audience.

Page paused by the elevators to pose for pictures, shake a few hands, and – for the first time in the campaign – sign some autographs, which delighted him. The press was barred from the dressing room. 'You never want a photographer around when the candidate is being made up for television!' Paul Berman cried when Page asked why there were no reporters around.

At 6.45, P. J. Costello went around to every person who had worked on the show, from the Bell Telephone men to the cameramen and technicians, right on down to the NBC page boys, and handed each of them an envelope with his name typed on it. Inside was a note of thanks (computer generated, but who was to know?), signed by the candidate, and a brand new $50 bill. Thus, when Devereaux Page made his entrance down the stairs through the audience who was giving him a standing ovation, the cameras panned around the studio, and the viewer saw electricians, stage hands, assistant directors, all cheering and joining in the applause. The show was off to a good start.

Page took his seat in the pedestal chair, and the big colour cameras wheeled in as his narration began unrolling on the Teleprompter machine over the lenses of the camera. His talk opened by addressing the eighteen New York City congressmen and their colleagues in the suburbs, saying that narcotics was entirely a federal responsibility, and until now, the federal government had failed miserably in dealing with it. This programme was an attempt by one citizen, with the aid of a fine research staff, to focus on the issue. The viewers were invited to phone in their questions, and there was a cut to a shot of the volunteers talking on the phones and writing down questions. Even if the question wasn't answered on the air, everyone would receive a reply by mail. The telephone number to call was flashed on the screen, and throughout the programme, viewers were reminded of it.

Page started with the premise that all drugs were illegal unless obtained with a doctor's prescription. Some drugs – marijuana, heroin, cocaine, absinthe, for example – were banned completely by federal law. Yet one out of every nine Americans had tried marijuana, and one in twenty was a regular user. There were approximately 60 billion amphetamine pills produced every year, enough for about 50 tablets for every man, woman, and child in the country; at least two-thirds of that production was diverted into illicit sales, via fake prescriptions, fake doctors, and manufacturers who simply wanted to unload their pills. In terms of heroin, another completely illegal drug, there was an estimated 500,000 addicts in the country, half of which were in New York City.

The heroin habit costs each addict from fifteen to one hundred fifty dollars a day, with the average being thirty-five dollars. There was no way a black or Puerto Rican with little education and no skills could *legitimately* earn the necessary $35 a day to support his need. Once on heroin, the addict has two choices: he steals, or he himself becomes a pusher, converting others to the drug and supplying them. A girl can turn to prostitution.

If you have some stolen merchandise [Page said], you can sell it on the street for about fifteen per cent of the retail value. Thus to earn his needed thirty-five dollars every day, the addict has to steal two hundred dollars or more worth of television sets, suits, radios, or small appliances. That two hundred dollars a day means more than sixty thousand dollars a year stolen by each addict. If there are one hundred thousand addicts whose business is stealing, that's *six billion dollars a year being stolen by addicts right here in New York City!*

On the rear-projection screen was footage of the Devereaux Page robbery, with the police talking to the candidate amid the topsy-turvy mess that was his apartment. 'No one is safe in this city from the narcotics addict,' Page said. 'Not even a candidate for mayor, as most of you read in the paper last week.' [Disarming grin.] 'Fully 25 per cent of all crime in New York City is drug-related; half of all muggings, hold-ups, and armed robberies are committed by addicts.'

On to the screen was projected a purse snatching, then a mugging and finally the looting of a store. 'We are not safe in our homes; we are not safe on the streets; we are not safe in our places of business. Clearly something has to be done.'

Page divided drugs into three categories: soft, medium-hard, and hard. Marijuana, the soft drug, he said should be legalized. There were thirty million Americans who had tried it, and ten million regular users. Legalizing marijuana meant it must be manufactured under strict government standards and, like liquors sold only to adults through specially licensed outlets; and no advertising. Finally, marijuana should be taxed to a fare-thee-well, the revenue being used exclusively to fund drug-related programmes.

In the case of the medium-hard drugs, such as amphetamines, barbiturates, and hallucinogens, strict federal controls should be imposed on the manufacturers, these drugs to be sold only on a doctor's prescription.

Finally, with heroin, Page proposed a three-part programme. First, methadone, the substitute drug, should be available to any addict who desired to kick the habit. In every assembly district of the city there should be a drug centre offering methadone treatment, medical advice, and psychiatric counselling if it is wanted. But for methadone to be effective, the addict has to want to kick the heroin habit, and in Dr Judianne Densen-Gerber's words, 'Junkies seldom volunteer for anything.'

The second part of the Page heroin programme was the adoption of the British system – free heroin to any addict who wanted it. To obtain his free heroin, the addict would merely have to report to his local drug centre once every two weeks, whereupon a prescription would be sent to his pharmacy; there he could pick up the necessary paraphernalia, such as sterilized syringes and doses of heroin, on a daily basis, or oftener if necessary. No compulsory psychotherapy, no probing questions, or demeaning physical examinations. He would get his heroin in any form he wanted it, and as strong as he wanted. In addition to the free heroin, the addicts would be issued government food stamps, so they would not have to worry about getting money for food.

The third aspect of the Devereaux Page drug plan, first proposed by Bronx District Attorney Burton Roberts and taken up by mayoral hopeful Mario Procaccino in the 1969 campaign, was the most controversial: any person caught committing a crime would be given a urinalysis, and if the tests showed the presence of heroin, that person would be automatically locked away for from three to five years for complete detoxification and rehabilitation.

As Robert Claiborne wrote in a recent article in the *Village Voice*, 'The fact is the heroin addict is not a black man or a white man any more. The junkie is a predatory animal.'

A junkie will steal from his mother, knife his brother, put his wife on the street; he'll kill your children or bash your grandmother's head against the sidewalk if that's what it takes to feed his habit. He is an animal.

I'm sure [Page said] there are a lot of liberals and organizations like the American Civil Liberties Union who will say automatic jailing is unconstitutional and outside the law.

But laws were made for men. And the narcotics addict has to be considered a non-person. Legal heroin and free food stamps will make it possible for him to exist without turning to a life of crime, without bothering the rest of us.

Our only concern is that the addict receives enough heroin for himself and no one else, and that he is off the streets. Under this plan, he has no reason to commit a crime to support his habit or get food. But the fact remains that a crime committed by a heroin addict is still a crime, and that criminal should be taken out of society and instantly put away

If any liberal disputes this, I hope his apartment gets broken into and his television set and his suits are stolen and his pictures slashed. And I hope his children do not get beaten and knifed in the process, because I wouldn't wish that on anyone . . .

But in dealing with the heroin addict . . . the non-person . . . the predatory animal . . . the words of Dr Densen-Gerber are the ones we should listen to when she said, 'The firm hand is the loving hand.'

Then Page made one final announcement:

There are right now in the city numerous programmes to keep you from getting into drugs, and more to pick you up and help rehabilitate you once you're looking to get off drugs. But there's nothing yet established devoted to getting you – and your children – through the inevitable years that fall between education and rehabilitation.

What do you do, for instance, if you come home and find your teen-age daughter in deep shock from an overdose of heroin?

Recently the *Village Voice* pointed out what is most urgently needed is an overdose 'hotline' – a place where you can call and say, 'My kid just took an OD,' and be told more than the routine 'Take him to a hospital.'

Therefore, this campaign is setting aside funds for such a programme, and it will continue after I'm elected mayor. Basically it will serve as an information centre. It doesn't take long to tell someone what to do in case of a heroin overdose. With this hotline, maybe we can save a few lives.

Page gave the number to call, and told the viewers there would be volunteers on duty twenty-four hours a day beginning that moment.

With the end of that announcement, there was a blast of sound as the phones were turned on and began to ring. On screen, the

viewer saw tables of volunteers busily writing down questions.
In addition to the approximately forty volunteers taking calls in
the studio, there were 75 operators across town handling the
overflow, plus a distributor system with which the tape recorded
voice of the candidate would answer, saying, 'Hello, this is
Devereaux Page. I want to thank you for calling. Would you mind
holding for a moment until one of our operators is free? Thank
you.'

At the close of the broadcast, the studio audience rose from
their seats as instructed and streamed on to the set to engulf the
candidate, while an off-stage announcer repeated the numbers to
call – for a question about narcotics which would be answered
by mail, or the new OD Hotline which was to be in service round
the clock to handle emergency calls. What the viewer saw on
screen was bedlam, a smiling candidate mobbed and jostled by the
cheering crowd. Even though this was all prearranged, it seemed
a genuine outpouring of affection and enthusiasm which Page
had never before experienced. In the dressing room, he asked
Mark and Lou Klein how it went. 'It was great,' Mark exulted.
'At last count we got over five hundred calls, and they're still
coming in like gangbusters!'

'When're you going to be ready to do another show?' Klein
wanted to know.

'Just as soon as your guys can write it,' Page replied happily.

Thirty minutes after the broadcast, an exhilarated Devereaux
Page pushed his way through the milling throng to the elevators.
Once in the street, Paul Berman, Loomis, Mark, and the candidate
piled into the white car for a procession up to Harlem for the
opening of a sixth storefront headquarters at 130th Street and
Lenox Avenue. With them were two of the secretaries from the
Commodore, Bev Fujiwara and Berman's assistant, Judy, sitting
on laps in the back seat. Two other cars full of staff followed
behind. Page was buoyant. It was the first time since the start
that he felt he was getting the hang of this campaigning business
and that people were beginning to respond. 'I think it went over,'
he said shaking his head in wonderment. 'I think I could get
elected.'

All the way to Harlem spirits remained high as they cracked jokes and gleefully guffawed at the idea of Page actually moving into Gracie Mansion.

Their ecstasy was short lived. Outside the new Page headquarters was an angry crowd of perhaps 200 blacks being whipped into a fury by black militant Jesse Jones, an ex-basketball player who stood fully seven feet tall with burning eyes, a satanic black beard, and a six-inch-high Afro haircut. In a flowing *dashiki* he stood towering over the crowd, shouting into a very powerful electric bullhorn that carried his booming, resonant voice hundreds of yards, and attracted a growing crush of onlookers in addition to his band of followers. 'Here comes the honkey now!' he shouted, the words reverberating up and down the garbage-strewn avenue. 'Git out of that car, muthafucker, and tell us what you gonna do for the black man!'

P. J. Costello, who was advancing this stop, came around to the window of the lead car and said to Mark. 'Holy mackerel! I tried to call you on the car telephone.'

'It wasn't turned on,' Mark said. 'What's happening?'

'Terrible scene,' P.J. said. 'They've been here for a half hour with this guy shouting at them.'

'What's their problem?'

'They're pissed off at the free heroin idea, I think.'

Mark looked out the car window at the wall of black humanity. 'I'd split,' P.J. suggested. 'Come back some other time.'

'Nobody ever won an election by running away from a crowd,' Mark retorted. 'Come on, Dev, let's see what we can do.'

'Here comes the imperialist pig!' Jones roared into the bullhorn. 'He gonna tells us how to solve all our problems with free heroin. Mr Page gonna give all the soul brothers free horse so we can go off somewhere and shoot up and not bother the honkey no more!'

There were whistles and cat calls from the mob, along with cries of 'Yeah, man!' and 'Right on, brother!'

'You know what honkey's gonna do next? I'll tell you what honkey's gonna do next. Honkey's gonna bus us all out of the city so we don't give him no more trouble! Just like Buckley wanted in 1965!'

'Yeah, brother!' came the shouts. 'Right on!'

Jones whirled and faced Dev Page who was standing nearby with Berman and Mark. 'How many black people you got working on your campaign, Mr Page? How many black people you got down at your fancy offices at the Commodore Hotel?'

'Tell him seven,' Mark whispered.

'We have seven,' Page called over to him.

'That's *bullshit*! Ain't no black people down there! Now you get out of here!'

'Why should we?'

'Because the white man should civilize his own!'

With that a large rock went sailing out of the crowd and through the big display window of Page Headquarters causing sheets of jagged plate glass to go cascading on to the sidewalk next to the terrorized campaign staff. There was a shout as a gang of about fifty blacks surged forward into the building and began ripping the place apart, smashing furniture, overturning tables, stripping posters and bunting from the walls. Soon squad cars were converging on the scene with sirens whooping and flashing red and blue lights, followed by riot police in blue helmets thrashing through the crowd with billy clubs dispersing the angry mob. Page and the others cowered next to the building wall while the shouting blacks hurled more rocks and battled with police. When the incident was finally under control, Jesse Jones was nowhere to be found, and about 15 blacks – mostly boys in their teens – had been lined up with their hands pressed against the wall of the adjoining building.

Mark stepped forward to introduce himself and tell the police captain in charge that nobody wanted to press charges. The captain looked at Mark. 'Mr. Altschul,' he said slowly, 'there's been a lot of damage here . . .'

'I don't think any purpose will be served by taking all these kids in to be booked.' The campaign manager looked around at the cordon of police behind which was a sullen assemblage of onlookers – blacks and Puerto Ricans. 'Why don't you just let these kids go before the TV and newspapers get here and this thing is blown up all out of proportion.'

The captain looked quizzical. 'What do you say, Mr Page?'

'Let's just try to forget the whole thing.' Dev was shaking.

The captain conferred with another officer and two black sergeants, and then told all the boys lined up to scram. 'Just clear everybody out of here, if you can,' Mark told the captain. 'We'll take care of the damages.'

The police sheathed their billy clubs and began to walk slowly through the knots of ghetto residents, asking them to leave quickly and go home. Soon the street was virtually deserted, so if the media boys arrived there would be nothing to photograph but a bashed-in headquarters. Mark ordered Paul Berman and P.J. Costello to remain behind to talk to them in case they should show up. Also a policeman would remain on duty so there would be no looting.

'What do we tell the press?' Berman wanted to know.

'Tell them they missed a helluva party.'

Devereaux Page was scared. Never before had he witnessed an angry mob cut loose in an orgy of mindless destruction. He was confused, too. His narcotics plan, he believed, was a reasoned and necessary approach to a complex problem that was plaguing the city; yet, within an hour, he had been the object of savagery and violence unlike any he had ever seen, and by the very people he was trying to help. Perhaps they were beyond help. As far as he could see, the blacks wrecked everything nice the white man had given them. He remembered driving through Brownsville in Brooklyn and seeing the Van Dyke project, marvellous fourteen-storey slabs rising out of the surrounding ghetto like towers of hope in the distance. Here was low-income housing, Mark had told him, and Page was excited at the idea that some progress was being made to eliminate the dreadful living conditions of the poor. From close by, however, these new buildings were themselves slums of the worst order, with garbage and litter strewn over the grounds, graffiti on the walls, and, according to Mark, vandalism, roaches, filth, and an exorbitant crime rate. This was a carbon copy of the $36 million Pruitt-Ingoe project in St. Louis, thirty-three ultra-modern, high-rise apartment houses designed for low-income families by architect Minorou Yamasaki (who also designed New York's giant World Trade Centre). In fifteen years, Pruitt-Ingoe had been literally destroyed by the poor; they stood abandoned and windowless, looming against the skyline like a contemporary ghost town, havens only for junkies and muggers, until finally blown to bits by demolition teams in 1972.

Page spoke aloud in the subdued, crowded car.

> Take up the White Man's burden –
>   Send forth the best ye breed –
> Go bind your sons to exile
>   To serve your captives' need;
> To wait in heavy harness
>   On fluttered folk and wild –
> Your new-caught, sullen peoples,
>   Half devil and half child.

His quotation from Kipling was greeted with silence. The gaiety and optimism of the ride uptown had been smashed along with the plate glass window and the new headquarters that a volunteer staff had worked so hard to get ready for the grand opening. 'Anybody in politics today is taking up the White Man's Burden,' Page said sadly. 'No goddamned liberal is going to tell me different. Kipling was as relevant today as he was in his own day.'

'I hate to admit it, but you're right,' Berman agreed.

At 70th Street Mark said, 'No more stops tonight, Dev. Do you want to go out for dinner?'

'No,' the candidate replied softly. 'No, you all go on without me. I think I'll go home and try to catch up on some sleep.'

They left him off in front of his building. He knew the apartment was still a shambles from the robbery, with only the basics put away and the bed made. But it was better than that dreary room at the Commodore. Page wasn't looking forward to getting home. In fact, he wasn't looking forward to much of anything any more.

Mia DeStefano stood in the steamy shower, letting the hot needle spray stream down the gentle arcs and incurves of her tanned body. She was back home, having spent four hours in New York putting Dev Page's little apartment in order, relaxing only for an hour to watch 'The Citizen's Spotlight' programme on the tiny seven-inch portable she had brought with her from New Jersey. Dev had done well; she was immensely proud of him. The outpouring of affection by the studio audience at the conclusion seemed real enough, and for the first time since she'd known him, there was an infectious radiance to his smile that came across even on the mini black-and-white screen. Perhaps this was at last the end of the long, tortuous road to finding himself as a person and as a candidate.

Stepping back from the hot deluge overhead, Mia palmed a big blue cake of Estée Lauder soap and began passing it slowly over her wet shoulders and breasts, luxuriating in the gentle fragrance and the sound of the water. Would Dev be pleased with what she had done to the apartment? At least it was outwardly picked up and vacuumed, instead of the dreadful pigpen that had been left by the intruders ten days ago. If he had come home right after the broadcast, they would have slept together as they had eight times before in as many weeks. But apparently the press of campaign business must have kept him at the Commodore, and she couldn't stay on to wait for him without raising suspicions in New Jersey. But at least she had made his world a little more bearable. Often she would sign out of the DeStefano compound ostensibly to do some shopping in the city, and instead slip into the apartment to just sit by herself for a few hours, surrounded by his things, and then leave without a trace.

She soaped up the rest of her lean torso, letting her strong hands travel the length of her legs, up between her thighs to the ample black pubic bush where she worked up a full white lather. Dev loved to do that for her when they showered together after one bout of love-making and before another. Would little Paulie Coppola appreciate her body as Dev did, with the nipples the size of pink bottle stoppers and firm buttocks and belly? She winced in disgust at the thought of her fat husband-to-be, a common punk in comparison to Dev Page who had style and charm. Why were so many of the Syndicate offspring so revoltingly obese – Philly Dioguardi, the grossly flabby nephew of the debonnaire and elegant Johnny Dio, Tony Colombo, Caesar Vitale, and her own Paulie Coppola, chinless with fat, whose rotundity was but slightly disguised by the $350 double-breasted suits.

She put Paulie out of her mind. There was to be some kind of grand jury indictment against him which she hoped would delay the wedding; it was an event she dreaded but knew she must go through with someday or her father would kill her. Besides, there was a new and terrible element in her life for which she could be killed – a situation that both thrilled her and sent shockwaves of panic through her. She was pregnant with Dev Page's child.

Chapter 16

Bobby DeStefano loved to run. Often he would arise at 6.00 AM to don a sweat suit and run barefoot along the beach on the hard sand nearest the water. Running allowed him to push his body to the limit. When he became thoroughly winded, he would press on, until his aching flesh case would seem to leave him and he was only aware of moving and the crash of the ocean and the cold water splashing over his feet. Few people understood what it was to run, to break through the barrier of the body to where you could seem to operate without it and be at one with God. Heroin might be something like that, but not nearly as good for you. When he stayed at the Commodore, which he generally did on Monday and Thursday each week, a car would take him to Central Park at dawn, dropping him at 50th Street and meeting him at 96th Street and Fifth Avenue to get him back to the hotel for a shower and breakfast before his 8.00 meeting with Mark to discuss the progress of the campaign.

Nobody ever accused Bobby DeStefano of being a fool. Perhaps in his youth, as a stringy, tousled-haired kid growing up in the shadow of his older brother Joe, he was patronized by both adults and his peers. They had good reason then to look down on the gangly runt kid brother. But West Point and a stint of combat in Korea had changed all that. By the time that fulminate of mercury bomb blew Joe DeStefano, Jr, through the top of his Cadillac convertible, Bobby was ready to step into his brother's shoes, and never once since had he faltered or relinquished the reins. Although a West Point graduate, Bobby realized there was much to learn, so a month after he took over, he enrolled in night courses at Rutgers, studying accounting, management, finance, and business communications. He even took a semester of Cobol programming just to find out more about computers. No one in the Family had any idea Bobby had been going to night school once a week for the past five years, let alone that he was an A student. Nor did his professors have an inkling that the serious, silent young man in the back row, known to them as Bob Stevens, was one of the most powerful men in New Jersey.

When Bobby undertook a new venture, he tackled it with gusto and thoroughness. Politics was no different. Just as soon as the money had been committed for Phase A of the campaign, Bobby began reading everything he could get his hands on about modern politics and history. Most of it came from the research department's extensive files and library downstairs which were brought surreptitiously to Bobby's suite at the Commodore late at night and returned by the following morning. After eight weeks, Bobby began to understand what the hell was happening.

The campaign was now seven weeks old, and Bobby had found some serious flaws.

Mark arrived exactly on time for his early morning conference with Bobby DeStefano in his private suite at the Commodore. The young Boss had just finished his room-service breakfast of poached eggs on whole wheat toast and was engrossed in the *Wall Street Journal*. As usual, an extra orange juice and coffee had been ordered for Mark.

Ordinarily there were some pleasantries before the serious discussion, but this morning Bobby was all business. 'We need more volunteers,' he snapped without looking up from his paper. 'How's your computer letter system working?'

'Perfectly. We have the capacity to get out a hundred thousand letters a day.'

'I want a little programme written whereby each new person who signs up with the campaign gives us twenty-five names of people they think would volunteer, and we'll send out letters from the candidate.'

'Okay.' Mark pulled out a scrap of paper and began making notes with his gold Cross pen.

'We need more storefront headquarters and we need more volunteers. I'm really worried.'

'All I can say is wait till after Labour Day. That's when people start getting interested in politics.'

'By Labour Day we have to decide whether we're going ahead

with Phase B. By Labour Day we should have at least 1500 people out in the streets getting signatures on the nominating petitions. We can't wait until Labour Day. I want an all-out effort to get volunteers *now*.'

'We've got ten new headquarters opening up next week and seven more the following week. That should bring in some.'

'I want parties going every night and ads running in the papers inviting people to come in for the openings. We'll have booze and food, and the candidate will be there.' The flat of Bobby's hand was smacking the breakfast table causing the dishes to rattle. 'Go for the singles crowd. There're thousands of horny little boys and girls all over this town who are dying to meet each other, what better place than a campaign? Give them free what they're paying for at Maxwell's Plum and Mr Laff's.'

Mark shrugged. 'Whatever you say, Bobby.'

'Get the *kaffeeklatsch* programme going. Christ, we'll pay six bucks a guest if people entertain their friends so they can meet the candidate and join the campaign. That's great. A gal can give a luncheon or cocktail party or anything. We need volunteers.'

'Okay,' said Mark. 'I'll get right on it.'

'You found a wife for the candidate?'

'Uh – no.'

'You introducing him to a lot of girls at least?'

'We – uh – haven't had time.'

'Goddamnit! I told you a month ago I want that guy married off. A candidate needs a wife. Christ, the biggest publicity break you got was that robbery. The voters don't give a shit about the issues really.'

'Oh, yes they do,' Mark contradicted.

'Okay, I take it back. Issues are important. But the voters also love the personal stuff. And the candidate getting married in the middle of the campaign would make them cream in their drawers. Why the hell haven't you been introducing him to women like I told you to?'

'I just felt a series of broads would take his mind off the campaign and learning about the issues.'

'Don't ever disobey me again.' His voice was icy quiet. 'Do you understand that, Mark? When I tell you to do something, you do it.'

'Do you have anybody in mind?'

'I don't know. Somebody not too good looking. A Mary Lindsay type. With kids, maybe. Yeah, a divorcee with kids.'

'A divorcee would hurt him. The voters don't like divorce. And he's divorced himself.'

'A widow then. Bobby clapped his hands. 'That's it! Find Page a Vietnam widow with some kids! That'll make a helluva story!'

Mark shrugged. 'I'll try.'

'I'll get my people working on it too,' Bobby enthused 'What a helluva story!'

Mark poured himself another cup of coffee. 'How do you think things are going generally?'

'Except for the volunteer problem, okay,' Bobby replied. He seemed somewhat more relaxed, now that he'd got what was bothering him off his chest. 'You're pretty close to your progress schedule in the budget.'

'The narcotics show got good coverage. Voter attitude and awareness profiles were up as a result. Everybody feels it was a success in spite of what happened in Harlem.'

'Oh, fuck the niggers,' Bobby snarled impatiently.

'I'd like to, but they make up 25 per cent of the population and 14 per cent of the voters.'

Bobby returned to scanning his *Wall Street Journal*. 'Page is good on television. He understands it and wins your confidence when you watch him. When's the next show?'

'One week. Subject is housing.'

'How're Page's live appearances?'

Mark's jaw tightened. 'Not good.'

'What the hell do you mean?'

'He's excellent on television.' Mark's words were measured. 'He's great in a small group or in a one-to-one situation. But he can't handle big crowds.'

'Jesus! What're you doing about it?'

'We've stopped scheduling him before large groups. We've cut out the Democratic clubs. Instead we're concentrating on small gatherings and television.'

'He'll never learn that way. You gotta keep pushing him out in front of big live audiences. He'll catch on.'

'We tried it. He kept getting worse and worse. No confidence. Being attacked in Harlem didn't help. Now he's just plain frightened of big crowds.'

Bobby's fingers drummed rhythmically on the breakfast table. He started to say something but checked himself. Then he said, 'Look, Mark, you can't win an election with just television and handshakes. The guy has to be able to make a speech. He's gotta be able to get up there and give everybody in the place a hard-on.'

'I don't know what to do,' Mark admitted. 'It's going well except for that.'

Bobby thought a moment. 'I'll tell you what. We'll get Jack Leokum in.'

'Who is Jack Leokum?'.

'He works as consultant to big corporations. He'll teach Page how to hold an audience by the balls and not let go till they're screaming.'

'Has he ever worked in politics?'

'I don't know.' Bobby stood up impatiently; it was the signal for Mark to leave. 'Look, Mark you're doing a good job. You just worry about bringing in more volunteers and getting more people out on the streets, okay? I'll get hold of Leokum and we'll teach that idiot how to make a speech.' Mark nodded and started for the door. 'And another thing,' Bobby added.

'What's that?'

'Find Page a wife.'

It was Gene Fowler who wrote that New York City speaks and lives in the present tense. It daily enthrones new gods, who seem to spring from nowhere and, more often than not, as swiftly return to their source. These temporarily exalted deities hasten their own heart-breaks, at the polls or other places of judgment. They learn too late that a honeymoon with notoriety is not a marriage to fame.

By July first, Mark Altschul was a troubled young man. Everything possible was being done to make his candidate an instant deity, yet Page was not attracting enough workers to run a viable campaign. Plans for opening some forty-five neighbourhood headquarters had to be held up indefinitely because there simply weren't enough bodies to man them, let alone canvassers to ring doorbells or run a phone operation.

There was, of course, money in Phase B of the budget for a fully paid campaign staff. But professional political operatives were a cynical, coarse lot and could have an adverse effect in terms of morale. What a successful campaign needed was a flock of eager, dewy-eyed volunteers to fan out through the electorate and ask for the vote. Mark knew the idea of a grass-roots movement was very much a possibility in modern politics, especially with the proper manipulation of the media, the polls, and the computer.

Unfortunately history was not on the side of the Devereaux Page candidacy. Perhaps if the former president of the National Horse Show Association had been a real spellbinder on the stump a Mussolini or a Huey Long, a Jimmy Walker or a Franklin D. Roosevelt whose patriotic oratory could make the wings of the eagle flutter – then the necessary voltage would have surged through the terminals and drawn the rank and filings into the campaign. But the candidate was crowd-shy. He was believable on television, but so was every candidate these days whose constituency was larger than a congressional district; you had to be good on TV.

In New York City, only two men had ever been elected mayor without the support of a major party: Vincent Impelitteri in 1949, and John V. Lindsay twenty years later. In both cases, however, they were up for re-election. As City Council president, Impelitteri had become acting mayor when William O'Dwyer resigned. Lindsay had been previously elected on the Republican ticket. So although these had been independent races, both candidates had the considerable leverage of being the incumbents. This election was going to be tough.

Over the Fourth of July Weekend, Devereaux Page took to the beaches of Brooklyn and Coney Island where the crowds had the raucous, cheery, wise, hard middle-class New York smarts, take the measure of everything and still give a politician a cheer because he's there. Page was photographed in bathing trunks cavorting in the ocean, doing a creditable swan dive from a high board, shaking countless hands among the sunbathers and swimmers of every age, sex, shape, and size. It was during this weekend that Page was first told of Bobby DeStefano's scheme to spice things

up by introducing the candidate to a string of eligible women.
'What exactly does Bobby have in mind?' Page wanted to know.

'Matrimony.'

'Matrimony! Christ, I've just got divorced!'

'In terms of publicity, it's a hell of an idea.'

'What do you mean?'

'Look at the coverage we got from the robbery.'

Page grimaced. 'You mean that little son of a bitch thinks he
can tell me to get married just for the publicity? I won't do it.'

'Dev, he owns you,' Mark said. 'Like it or not, you're going to
get married before Election Day.'

'Down to Ghenna or up to the Throne/ He travels fastest who
travels alone . . . Tell Bobby that.'

'Is that Kipling?'

'Of course it's Kipling. I don't have time for a wife at this
point; she'd only be a hindrance. Besides, I happen to be rather
seriously involved with somebody.'

'That's great! We'll get her involved in the campaign and save
us all a lot of trouble.'

'Somehow I don't think Bobby would quite approve.'

'Who is she?'

'I can't tell you.'

'What's the matter? Is she black or something?'

'I can't tell you anything.'

Mark shrugged. 'Whatever you say.'

The first of the young women was Gayle Shack, in her mid
thirties, with a reedy, willowy body and an aristocratic nose that
arched out over a pouty lower lip. A Vietnam widow with three
children (the campaign was paying for baby sitters), Gayle gamely
made the rounds, watching with bemusement as Page was photographed wolfing frankfurters, knishes, pizzas and pop with evident gusto. By nightfall, she was too flaked out to go on to dinner
or the theatre which had been arranged. The same was true of
Claire Burnett, a faded, porous-faced blonde of forty whose alcoholic husband had demolished himself on the Taconic Parkway
two years previously; Claire, too, succumbed to the strain of
campaigning and begged off from further involvement. Tina Peter-
son, a dark-haired and brittle socialite of thirty-one who had never
married, lasted two days before dropping out. It was evident

Page had been right: there simply wasn't time for women. The candidate, while perfectly gracious, was totally preoccupied with the business at hand. There were the inevitable 3 × 5 cards with names to memorize before each appearance, and during breaks, he was being prepped for 'The Citizen's Spotlight' show dealing with the next major issue, housing and urban renewal. This meant fatiguing treks, mostly on foot, through what appeared to be bomb-blasted neighbourhoods such as Brownsville and East New York, where the candidate was photographed by Johnny DiSantis in front of block after block of abandoned buildings, interviewing landlords and tenants. It was a tedious, tiring procession of days and nights. Several more supposedly eligible young ladies were dragged along one at a time. They were stolid, plain-Jane types for the most part; although perfectly presentable, all seemed emotionally bruised by widowhood and perpetually worried about their children at home with the baby sitter. A political campaign is a superb environment for a courtship, but definitely not for the candidate. He's too busy and full of himself to relate to anybody new, unless it's a voter or a prospective contributor.

When Mark reported to Bobby their efforts to interest the candidate in a prospective bride were totally unsuccessful, the young Boss stormed. 'What the fuck's the matter with him? Doesn't he like women?'

'He's too busy to be turned on by a woman.'

'That's bullshit!' Bobby retorted 'All guys get horny and have to get laid occasionally. Don't the girls know they're supposed to screw?'

'They've been briefed.'

'Then what's the matter?'

'At the end of the day, I guess everybody's just too tired. I don't know.' Mark took a deep breath. 'Anyway, the idea just isn't working.'

Bobby wheeled and pointed a finger at Mark. 'You know what Capone used to say? "If a guy don't fall for a broad, he's through." Capone used to test his bodyguards out with real sexy women, and if they didn't respond, he'd fire them. I think there's something to that.'

'Well, we can't fire Page; he's the only candidate we've got.'

'Well, goddammit, I want him married.'

'He says he's involved with somebody now.'

'Who is she?'

'He won't say.'

'Well, find out, for Chrissakes!' Bobby waved Mark out of the room. 'I want that guy married!'

Later in the car Page asked where the latest entry in the matrimonial sweepstakes was.

'She had cramps,' Mark retorted.

The candidate was feeling relaxed and rather expansive. 'You know, I wouldn't mind being married again, but all the girls so far have been really ordinary.'

'That's not true. They're all perfectly nice.'

'Ordinary,' Page repeated.

'What the hell do you have in mind? After all, this marriage is for your political career, not your sex life.'

'There have been some attractive politicians' wives. Look at Jackie Onassis; I wouldn't mind something like that.'

'Jackie Onassis was no help to John Jennedy during his lifetime. In fact, many people felt she was too fancy. They couldn't identify with her.'

'Well Joan Kennedy, then. Or Justice Douglas's wife.'

'We've discussed this at length.'

'Who discussed what at length?'

'Bobby DeStefano and I. A wife that's too glamorous tends to detract from the candidate.'

'So I've got to marry an Eleanor Roosevelt?'

'We had Mary Lindsay in mind.'

'Mary Lindsay is not my cup of tea.'

'That's too damn bad; she has a lot of class.'

Page sighed and stared out the window of the car.

'Mary Lindsay is the best political wife on the circuit,' the campaign manager maintained. 'She's admittedly less snappy than a Jackie Onassis, but polls have shown that women voters don't feel threatened by Mary Lindsay. Anybody as attractive as John Lindsay who can be faithful to someone as – as –'

'Go on,' Page prodded with a smile.

Mark inhaled deeply. 'Anybody as attractive as John Lindsay who can remain faithful to someone as plain as Mary can't be all bad. That's the way women feel. In other words, Mary Lindsay is a plus.'

'I think we can do a hell of a lot better than Mary Lindsay. That's what I think.'

'Okay, Dev,' Mark snapped. 'Name another politician's wife who is an asset and who doesn't turn you off.'

The candidate turned to Mark. 'I was at a party at Gracie Mansion once, and she was wearing a shirtwaist dress. A shirtwaist dress in Gracie Mansion. Jesus, Mark!'

'Name a political wife you might consider,' Mark repeated.

'Ethel Kennedy.' There was silence in the car. 'Find me an Ethel Kennedy, and maybe I'll go along with the gag.'

'Let me check it out with Bobby, and we'll see what we can do.'

Paul Berman sat alone in the empty control room. The programme on housing had gone well. Once again Page's performance in front of the television cameras was smooth and convincing. Through the glass Berman watched absently as the studio stage hands were striking 'The Citizen's Spotlight' set and replacing it with a daytime quiz show scheduled for the following morning. The usually ebullient Berman was in a sombre mood. The campaign was in deep trouble. The idea of resigning in order to work for someone who had a chance of winning was very much on his mind. He hated losing elections. Besides, after Election Day, he wanted a job with the city. Otherwise, he'd be out on his ass with two ex-wives and three children to support.

As borough coordinator, it was his responsibility to bring the candidate and his message to the people, and in turn, recruit workers for the campaign organization. Of everyone in the Page operations, only Berman, with his years of experience in politics, understood how critical the situation was in terms of not enough volunteers. In order to get Devereaux Page on the November ballot, it was necessary to collect at least 10,000 valid signatures on nominating petitions during the six-week period from August 28 to October 8. But because of the narrow definitions of what was a valid signature and the complexity of the petition form, Page really needed more like forty to fifty thousand signatures in order to head off a possible challenge by the other candidates. A successful court challenge meant your candidate was kicked off the ballot. And to get that many signatures, a candidate needed better than 1500 workers spread out all over the city; at present there were about 400 volunteers, most of them in the borough of Manhattan; it was barely a cadre to teach the petitioners and canvassers their jobs.

For days now, Berman had been living in real fear. At the present rate, there was no way to get enough volunteer workers in time for the petition drive, even though it was still almost two months off.

Berman let his eyes scan the rows of silent grey television screens around the darkened control room. If only Page were a member of some organization that could get behind him to provide the necessary bodies to man the headquarters, ring doorbells, hand out literature, ask for signatures, and generally drum up voter interest. It was true that with so many candidates vying for city-wide offices, plus all the councilmanic contests, the number of available political workers had been reduced to just about zero. Even if there was a tremendous influx of workers after Labour Day, there would be left only five weeks to train them and get the bulk of the signatures; that was mathematically impossible. The whole thing was a nightmare.

Pushing himself out of his seat, Berman shuffled from the control room into the deserted hallway outside the studio and headed slowly for the elevator. He hated losing causes, and this Page was a loser. The television show on housing might suck in a few volunteers eager to own a building, but at the same time he had no doubt alienated one of the larger power blocs in the city – the landlords. That was what New York politics was all about – getting the party workers out to talk to the voters while the candidate concentrated on enough power blocs and interest groups to gain the needed plurality.

Of course, party machinery in the old sense no longer existed, having gone the way of the boss system. The current Democratic nominee was unacceptable to at least half the party. Few of the disaffected would go so far as to switch parties; rather they would simply not work this time around, and hope for a change in four years. No, a lack of volunteers was not unique to the Page campaign; everybody was faced with it.

The red light overhead blinked on to signal the coming of a

down elevator. At the same time a little red light blinked on in Berman's brain. Why think in terms of the past? Why assume the only workers in town were to be found among party regulars? In 1968 the old thinking changed when Allard Lowenstein and Eugene McCarthy put together a children's crusade that changed the course of modern history. Never mind the fact that McCarthy was a dud as a candidate, or that Bobby Kennedy, in joining the race late in the game, had diluted the effect by more than half; there had been deep antiwar sentiment in the country, and the call for workers had been answered by legions of fresh-faced youngsters streaming to New Hampshire and states west to volunteer for the cause.

Who were the disenchanted of New York City? The teachers . . . the civil service . . . the police . . . the transit people . . . the Jews . . . the blacks . . . there were all kinds of blocs to whom Page, as the citizen candidate, could make a direct appeal. Couldn't he write a powerful campaign platform which promised the teachers everything they ever asked for in terms of money, benefits, and extra protection from the little bastards? Suddenly the most important issue to the citizen candidate is the education of our children, and he becomes the candidate of the teachers. The teachers, in effect, are his political party, going out in their spare time to comb the neighbourhoods for votes and money. Or the police or firemen. It was fantastic! Nobody in New York politics had ever tried this! By God, Devereaux Page could be mayor after all!

Berman burst out onto 50th Street and started walking toward the Commodore. By the time he had reached the Rockefeller Centre skating rink he was running, his heart pounding with excitement. At Fifth Avneue, he saw an empty cab and hailed it. Ten minutes later Paul Berman had let himself into the research office with a master key; there he was to spend the entire night poring over the records and files. By Monday morning he had the outline of what could become the most incredible campaign in the history of New York City politics.

Chapter 17

Bobby DeStefano was in a black mood. The campaign was not going well. In spite of all the newspaper and television advertising, the flow of volunteers was at a trickle. Furthermore, little Paulie Coppola, who was slated to become his son-in-law, had just been indicted in Buffalo; it was a federal charge of conspiring to melt down $300,000 in United States silver coins into more valuable ingots. Mia's October wedding would have to be put off until after the trial. Bobby had never thought highly of fat little Paulie; he was a drunk and incredibly vain. But he was the only male Coppola left. Subconsciously Bobby was fanatically possessive about Mia; the idea of some slim handsome young greaser ramming his hard cock into her while she writhed and screamed in pleasure stabbed him in the deep heart's core.

Arranged marriages were a thing of the past, Mia had argued over and over again. Bobby dismissed her protests out of hand. His own union with the grandniece of Guiseppe Masseria had been reasonably satisfactory, and the same should be true for Mia. With one out of every two marriages failing, the young were obviously unfit to choose their life partners. And the need for peace with the Coppolas far outweighed Mia's personal desires. This was especially true if his candidate should win the New York mayoralty and Bobby decided to go after the governorship in Albany next year; then he would have the Arm – the ruling Family in the state's second largest city along with all the clout they undoubtedly wielded in the Erie County political machinery.

When Bobby called Mia with the news of the indictment, he was already irritated at Paulie's stupidity; his daughter's reaction – hoots of laughter and squeals of delight – really pissed him off. He banged down the receiver and tilted back in his leather chair. The phone rang. It was Mark who wanted to see him right away.

Here would be more disastrous news about the campaign, no doubt; just what Bobby needed to add to his present woes.

The campaign manager arrived five minutes later. After a brief preamble about the difficulties they were still facing in terms of recruitment, Mark began to outline Paul Berman's plan to put on a huge dinner at the Commodore for the New York City Sanitation Department. Bobby leaned forward across the desk. As he listened, a smile gradually formed on his lips that had widened into a broad grin by the time Mark had finished. It was a great idea, he agreed. 'But why garbage men? Why not the police or firemen?'

'The city charter won't let them. Besides, the Sanitation Department covers every single election district in the city at least twice a week. They know the neighbourhoods; they know the people. Furthermore, their union is organized along assembly district lines, so we – '

'Anybody who'd spend his life hauling shit had to be a dumb shit himself.'

'That's just the point. These guys are the plodders, just like the old Tammany politicians. There's no glamour in garbage; just a lot of hard work and a lot of abuse if you're late with a pick-up. That's why if we got them on our side and gave them a chance to get hold of some real power in this town, they'd do anything for us. And there's nothing in the city charter that says they can't work in politics.'

Bobby tugged at his forelock and brushed it back. 'I really can't get it up for the garbage men,' he said. He swivelled around to face the wall, leaving Mark to confront the high leather back of the judge's chair. 'When's the dinner going to be?' came the young Boss's voice.

'In five weeks. August eleventh, if you agree to it. There are no bookings on the ballroom floor of the hotel that night, so if we draw a thousand we can handle it.'

'What if you get more?'

'We'll use both ballrooms plus other rooms if necessary, and tie them all together with closed-circuit television.'

'How about invitations?'

'Computer services has the home address file of every member of the Sanitation Department. Personal letters signed by the candidate are going out late this week. We're also enclosing cards and stamped envelopes for easy reply.'

Bobby spun around to face Mark again. 'What's this dinner going to cost?'

'Thirty dollars a head. That includes cocktails, hors d'oeuvres, two bottles and set-ups on every table, and a complete dinner. If we get a thousand people, that's thirty thousand dollars.'

Bobby's face was impassive. 'That's a lot of bread to spend on a candidate who can't make a speech.'

'What do you mean?'

'Between now and August eleventh, Page is going to have a week in Acapulco with Jack Leokum and learn how to become an orator.'

'Jesus, Bobby, the candidate can't spare a week from campaigning.'

'Fuck you, Mark. I'm not spending thirty big ones to have that guy bomb out, understand?' Mark's jaw tightened. Bobby added, 'I'll call Leokum and set it up. The sooner the better, too.'

Mark sighed.

'And this idea of yours better work,' Bobby snarled, 'or there's going to be blood all over the walls of that campaign office downstairs.'

Jack Leokum sprawled in the cockpit of the *Pan Am*, his 51 foot Columbia sloop anchored in Acapulco harbour. He was reading *Mein Kampf*. Overhead, a specially built awning that traversed the boom and attached to the stays kept the fierce Mexican sun off him. Still, it was 87 degrees in the shade that August morning in southern Mexico. Only a fool would be away from an air conditioner in weather like this. And, in many ways, Jack Leokum was a fool. For one thing, three ex-wives had nicked him for an average of $15,000 a year, so that his alimony bill was a cool forty-five grand before he put a forkful of steak between his big teeth or turned a winch motor aboard the *Pan Am* which rolled gently under him in the wake of some water skiiers who had whizzed by to port.

By any standard, Jack Leokum was a conspicuously homely little man. At forty-eight he was reasonably trim, with only a small paunch bulging out over his Pucci bathing trunks of red and yellow swirls, But German measles as a child had left his vision so impaired that he had to wear horn-rimmed glasses with quarter-inch thick lenses; when you looked him in the eye, it was literally through concentric circles of glass to pupils the size of pin heads. Five divorces and a wild, peripatetic life in the upper echelons of big business had turned his ample thatch of hair snow white. His drinking had caused tiny capillaries to surface, so now his puffy cheeks looked as though they were tatooed with road maps; and beneath his fleshy lips was a round ball of a chin disconcertingly off centre, the result of an automobile smash-up in his teens when he was too poor for decent plastic surgery.

Once at a New York cocktail party he met Chester Gould, and a year later, to his delight he found himself a ringer for the newest Dick Tracy villain. During the four months it took Tracy to track down Pin-Eyes and run him off a cliff in Big Sur, Jack was constantly being stopped on the street by passers by who wanted his autograph. Once in Indianapolis a woman got hysterical and tried to have him arrested.

He had met Devereaux Page only briefly in New York when he stopped by Bobby's office to firm up the deal and take a check for the first month's fee. The candidate with his triangular face had struck him as a perfectly ordinary fellow with intense eyes and a weak mouth. Since that meeting, Leokum had poured over a xerox copy of the massive master dossier, and spent hours in one of the projection rooms in his house studying Johnny DiSantis's films of Page in action and tapes of the television appearances. Page had great presence in small crowds and before the television camera, but he was a flop before an audience of more than twenty or so. Instead of reaching out to enfold a big crowd with his words, he seemed to punch his speeches at them in a kind of hesitant monotone. Leokum's task was to make Page into an orator by August 11, the date he was scheduled to appear before the Sanitation Department at a dinner at the Commodore Hotel. If possible, Leokum was to imbue the candidate with some instant charisma as well.

He closed *Mein Kampf* and added it to the pile of books on the cockpit seat: T. Harry Williams's biography of Huey Long;

Nixon Agonistes by Garry Wills, and Francis Russell's *The Shadow of Blooming Grove*. Politics was a new bag for Jack Leokum.

As an expert in corporate communications, Leokum had been on his own for nine years teaching businessmen how to be effective speakers and writers. Often an executive with a brilliant head for figures would be elevated to a vice-presidency, only to turn out to be a fumbler in front of an audience, and sometimes to screw up the syntax of his letters and memos so roundly that the meaning would be totally lost. At this point Leokum would be called in for high-level lessons in elocution and business English. The week-long session was held in Leokum's fabulous Acapulco house, half of which was a great audiovisual centre. Usually it was confined to speaking and writing, but one client, as crude as he was brilliant, had to have a course in table manners and good grooming thrown in.

For his efforts, Leokum was well paid. Five steady clients retained him at $50,000 a year each. This was augmented by a series of special jobs, such as the Devereaux Page project; however, these were invariably from the business community, funnelled in by such industrial consultants as McKinsey and Company or Arthur D. Little, who in turn, demanded 50 per cent of his fee as their commission. His overhead was fairly high. He had two assistants, both graduates of the Harvard Business School, three secretaries, six servants, and a full-time engineer for the maintenance of his electronics equipment worth hundreds of thousands of dollars. Even so, he managed to clear $400,000 a year before alimony and before taxes, which weren't very high in Mexico.

The Devereaux Page assignment posed a real challenge. Leokum had never before taught anybody how to be a spellbinder on the speaker's platform. It was more important for a businessman to be poised and able to exude confidence about the future than to be an orator. In industry there are no blacks and whites; only shades of grey. The corporate world wanted the Ed Muskie or George McGovern type; the voters liked a Franklin Roosevelt, or Huey Long, or even a Richard Nixon. One thing was damn sure; as things stood now, Devereaux Page wouldn't stand muster in either politics or business. Jack Leokum meant to change that.

When Dev Page stepped off the plane in Acapulco, he was ready for a solid week of sleep. For two and a half months there had been up to 15 appearances a day, seven days a week, starting at dawn, seldom finishing up before midnight. Any spare time was given over to Mark Altschul's mind-bending instruction in New York City history and government, learning the issues, and shoring up the sagging spirits of the staff. With all the hoopla of the campaign, Page had managed to keep going. But when Mark and Nick put him on the aircraft for the flight south, the turmoil and confusion seemed behind him, and he slept the whole trip. Now, standing on the apron beside the huge silver jet in the heat of the Mexican sun, he could think of only one thing: more sleep.

Jack Leokum had other ideas. 'You're here so that I can transform you into a speaker for mass meetings,' he told Page over rum and tonics beside the kidney-shaped swimming pool high above the blue green Pacific. 'All great, world-shaking events have been brought about, not by written matter, but by the spoken word. Always remember that.'

'My television appearances have gone pretty well.'

'That's not enough. You take two candidates who are pretty much equal on all counts; the guy who wins is the one who can sway a large crowd.' Leokum noisily gulped the remains of his drink and called the houseboy for a refill. 'The crowds have to see a guy in the midst of a tangible, physical fight for office. They've got to see him in the flesh, eyeball to eyeball. Television is good only up to a point. You don't respond to a piece of glass in your living room the way you do live, with the real candidate standing up there in front of you with the crowds pushing and shouting. Before this week is over, Mr Page, we're going to teach you how to handle a crowd, like Hitler or Huey Long or Mussolini.'

'I really don't think I'm quite the demagogue type.'

'Not a demagogue, Mr Page. Let's use Eric Hoffer's phrase – a "mass leader".'

'A mass leader?'

'A man who articulates and justifies the resentment dammed up in the souls of the frustrated, and kindles the vision of a breath-taking future.'

'Me? Do that?' Page shrugged. 'I don't know . . . I don't know.'

'Tonight we're going to listen to the voices of the great orators of modern history and look at them on film. Tomorrow we learn breath control exercises which I want you to perform every day of your life from here on out. We're going to study diction and pronunciation and crowd psychology. We'll get into phrasing and body movements. The day after tomorrow two people from your campaign office are coming down to put together a speech for the Sanitation Department dinner.'

'Who's coming?'

'I don't know their names.'

'Loomis? Mark Altschul? Paul Berman? Lou Klein?'

'Loomis is one. Maybe Klein is the other.'

Page sat back. 'So this week is pretty well planned out.'

Leokum smiled. 'My clients get their money's worth.'

'Are you going to start me with a mouthful of gravel like Diogenes?'

'If necessary, I'll do anything.'

Later, after a fine steak and salad, they went to work in one of the small curtained projection rooms. 'There are many great orators in recent history,' Leokum said, 'and I've picked six of them. All have one thing in common: they were successful in getting elected, or, in the cases of Hitler and Mussolini, in reaching positions of power mostly because of their ability as public speakers.'

'Hitler, Mussolini, and who else?' Page asked.

'Roosevelt, Huey Long, John Kennedy, and Warren G. Harding.'

'Warren G. Harding! You're joking!'

'How do you think he got elected President of the United States?'

'I never thought about it. His good looks, I guess.'

'Harding was one of the greatest orators of this century. Listen to this.' Leokum pressed an intercom button and asked the unseen engineer to roll Harding. The lights in the room dimmed, and curtains parted to reveal a movie screen. 'This was before talking pictures,' Leokum explained, 'but you're going to see footage of Harding at Arlington Cemetery for the dedication of the Tomb of the Unknown Soldier, and hear his address which he recorded later. I want you to try to put them together in your mind.' On the screen there was grainy, blotchy brownish footage of a vast assemblage of dignitaries in the columned amphitheatre of Arlington with the President's arrival, shots of Harding with the coffin, and photographs of the huge crowds gathered on the grassy slopes beyond. Suddenly the little room was filled with the virile, silver tones of Warren G. Harding; when it was over, Page had goosebumps.

For the next two hours they watched footage and heard the voices of mass leaders of the twentieth century. There was Adolph Hitler with his demonic fury which whipped the crowds into a frenzy of wild patriotism, and Mussolini rolling out the t's and r's with the staccato of a machine gun, while the adoring populace continually interrupted him with shouts and applause. Page watched in fascination at the freewheeling, folksy technique of Huey Long, head, hair, arms, shoulders – everything seemed to be moving constantly in different directions. Then followed the stark contrast of Roosevelt and John F. Kennedy, with their sparse, almost wooden gestures and the ringing precision of their words.

'Now watch Kennedy at the 1960 Alfred E. Smith Dinner at the Waldorf,' Leokum said. 'It was an informal occasion and he played it strictly for laughs.' On the screen was shown the incredibly handsome young nominee, elegantly attired in white tie and tails. Virtually every line of his speech was punctuated with guffaws and applause.

When the film ended, Leokum said, 'In the 1960 elections, you watched a duel between the two greatest orators in the country. The greater of the two won it. You know why? John Kennedy like every great politician in history, was an actor. He was able to adapt to any crowd he addressed, whether it was a television camera, a small luncheon, a large banquet, or a huge mass rally. Furthermore, every man you've seen here so far – Harding,

Roosevelt, Huey Long, Hitler, and Mussolini – had the very same ability.'

'But all these men were able to develop their technique over many years,' Page protested.

'Mr Page, in the course of this week, you're going to work harder than you've ever worked in your life. To aid you, you'll have some of the most fantastic electronic gear ever put together for the sole purpose of teaching communications. Using rear-projection screens, I can recreate audiences of any size, sex, make-up, from giant rallies to small banquets. I can produce laughter, applause, hisses and boos even, and I'll use them. You will be photographed on film and on closed-circuit television for instant replay so you can watch yourself in action, much as Kennedy could do instinctively. You will learn to project your voice to the very last row so that not one member of an audience of one hundred thousand will miss a single word of what you are saying. And through it all you'll be concentrating on the style, technique, mannerism, and delivery of one man – the most compelling speaker in America today.'

'Who in the world are you talking about?'

'Billy Graham.'

'Billy Graham?' The candidate winced and muttered, 'Jesus H. Christ.'

Chapter 18

Invitations had been sent to 17,000 active and retired sanitation workers all over the city of New York. Close to four thousand acceptances were received – far more than the poor old Commodore could handle. So the dinner was switched to the grand ballroom of the Waldorf Astoria which would feed 2500. In addition, they contracted for the Starlight Roof, the Gold Room, and the Jade Room, all of which would be connected to the proceedings in the Grand Ballroom by closed-circuit television. The cost to the campaign went from thirty to forty dollars a head; in one wild splash of spending, the Page campaign coffers would be poorer by a whopping $160,000. Mark and Bobby decided that if they could get 50 per cent of the attendees – or 2000 sanitation workers – to sign up as volunteers, they could mount a successful petition drive and change voter awareness and attitudes enough to get the necessary vote to squeak by. Any less than the targeted number of volunteers, and the whole thing would be called off.

Thursday, August 11. At 6.00 PM, some 4200 city sanitation workers began arriving at the Waldorf. For the most part, they were white males between the ages of 19 and 42; while the Police Department was primarily an Irish organization, sanitation workers were principally Italian, with a sprinkling of other ethnic groups, including perhaps 4 per cent Negro. The press was not invited.

As the guests disgorged from the outsized ballroom elevators, they were greeted by the smooth sound of the full Ben Cutler orchestra, thirty musicians playing a medley of Neapolitan songs. It was primarily a string sound, with an undercurrent of woodwinds, vaguely reminiscent of the old country, even to those who had never been there. If there was one thing the Syndicate knew how to do, it was put on an Italian party. Liquor was flowing like

Niagara, with waiters passing drinks even through the crowds waiting briefly at the registration tables to pick up name tags. Each man was given a packet of play money, and on entering the main reception room outside the ballroom, he found himself at a carnival; there, virtually reproduced, was the St Anthony street fair that came every June to Little Italy on Sullivan Street, with dozens of booths set up where he could bet on dice, throw darts at balloons, play wheels of fortune, and have a go at a score of other games of chance and skill. Interspersed among the games were food booths, offering clams on the half shell, corn on the cob, Italian cheeses and salami, pieces of roast chicken, stuffed clams, spare ribs, beer and soda pop. Everything could be paid for with the play money. Prizes were awarded for the various games of skill and chance. Overhead were banners and streamers proclaiming the Devereaux Page candidacy. And in the middle of the whole carnival was the band with its infectious Neapolitan melodies. Hotel waiters wandered down the 'streets' of the fair dispensing drinks, and bars were set up all around the room. In short, it was a gas.

The ballroom itself, an immense hall, half again the size of the Commodore's, with murals on the walls and gold trim everywhere, was fully five storeys high. A huge banner across the closed curtains of the stage proclaimed DEVEREAUX PAGE – THE CITIZEN CANDIDATE. On the main floor of the ballroom were 170 round tables for ten, while additional tables were set up in the two tiers of arcades overlooking the festivities, and in the Starlight Ballroom and the Jade Room. Every place setting included a packet of campaign materials, a souvenir ashtray and Zippo lighter embossed with Page's signature, a blue velvet box containing a sterling silver medallion specially created by the Danbury Mint to commemorate the event, and a set of matching ceramic cuff links and tie pin of green, white, and red – the Italian national colours. On every table stood a quart of Seagram 7, Johnny Walker Red, and Tanqueray gin, a bucket of ice and set-ups. In addition, there were four bottles of chianti with their wicker casings, several loaves of Italian bread, mounds of sweet butter, and two big platters of antipasto on which were artistically arranged salami, provolone cheese, celery, red peppers, hot little green pepperincini, giant black and green olives, eggplant salad, sardines, anchovies, and ham. After the cold antipasto had been demolished, hot plates appeared with a spectacular offering which included capicole and stuffed clams. This was followed by the main course of veal scallopini, eggplant parmigiana, and spaghetti with marinara sauce. No sooner would a man's plate be empty than the waiter was at his elbow urging him on to new heights of gluttony with a serving fresh from the ovens. After a salad course, the whole gastronomic orgy was topped with cannoli from Farrara's pastry shop on Grand Street. Through dinner, the music from the Ben Cutler band floated over the room, and from the noise pitch of the voices, it was evident everyone was having a hell of a good time.

After dinner, espresso coffee, cognac and liqueurs were served, and as the speechmaking was about to commence, 4200 satiated guests pushed themselves away from the tables, hooked their thumbs into now tight belts, and puffed contentedly on their ten-inch Havanah cigars. As the lights dimmed, a spotlight illuminated an American flag set up in front of the curtains of the stage. In the darkened room over the loud speaker boomed an announcement: 'Gentlemen, our national anthem.' Four thousand men were on their feet and the room fell silent as the strains of 'The Star-Spangled Banner' soared out over the room in a splendid rendition crowned with solo violins picking out the 'rocket's red glare' passage, and the full orchestra coming in for the finale. Amid the cheers that ensued, the announcer said, 'Gentlemen, Devereaux Page!'

The candidate approached the stage with apprehension. Following his return from Acapulco, he had made a total of 39 speeches all over the city – on street corners, in parks and playgrounds, at subway stops, and at beaches and boardwalks. After each appearance, Jack Leokum would be waiting in the campaign car to begin his critique, suggesting different timing, changes in wording, more fluid gestures. In the past couple of days, Page had begun to feel comfortable in front of live audiences. It was apparent, as some of his listeners began to come forward to sign up, that his urgent appeal for volunteers had finally started working. There was a new air of confidence about his appearances, and his delivery was becoming crisp and vibrant.

But this dinner was the largest and most influential group he had thus far addressed. Before him was an ocean of faces, virtually all of them indifferent to his candidacy. They were here only for a free dinner with the boys; the politics was an afterthought. The patter of applause that greeted Page was far from enthusiastic. The pivotal moment was at hand. If he could evangelize the New York Sanitation Department successfully so they would come out and work for his campaign, there was a real chance of getting elected. But if he blew this one, the group headed by young Bobby DeStefano indicated the money would dry up, and the race would be called off. And after three months of campaigning, Devereaux Page wanted very much to be mayor.

He began by saying he was running for mayor because the professional politicians had destroyed the city, and as a citizen candidate he was offering the voters a real alternative for the first time in years. To help him learn about the issues, he had one of the finest research organizations in the country. Each week they came up with a research report on a new issue which he had to study and learn. 'Gentlemen, I show you the volume I received last week devoted to the Sanitation Department.'

From beneath the lectern he pulled a black spring binder, fully two inches thick, and held it up for all to see. Here, suddenly, was Billy Graham with a Bible, and every eye in the room focused on the black book. Page leaned way into the microphone and said in a very low tone while still holding the book in the air, 'You know something?' He paused, and there was absolute silence in the vast hall. 'You men have been screwed!' This was followed by hoots of laughter. The candidate had the book in one hand and opened it. Then shaking his head in apparent confusion, he told them he was astounded to learn that there had been ten Commissioners of Sanitation in the past seven years. Lindsay's first Sanitation Commissioner, Page reminded them, had been Joseph F. Periconi, who resigned when his first deputy, Vincent A. Starace, was sentenced to a year in prison for conspiring to accept payoffs for promotions within the department.

The mayor's second Sanitation Commissioner, Samuel J. Kearing, Jr, was dismissed for insubordination. The third commissioner, James L. Marcus, was sentenced to 15 months in prison on bribery-conspiracy charges. And the fourth, Griswold Moeler, was fired for incompetence. Then came a string of acting commissioners – Maurice Feldman, James Marron (who died between his appointment and his swearing in), an insurance lawyer named Fioravante Perrotta, and a former state assemblyman from Manhattan, Jerome Kretchmer, who quit to run for mayor and had used the department as his political base for three years. Page reminded them that Mrs Kretchmer was quoted in the *Times* as saying how fantastic it would be for her, a little girl from Brooklyn, to be living in Gracie Mansion with the mayor. Page looked out over his audience. 'I'm sure Mrs Kretchmer is a nice lady, and I'd be quite willing to try a one-night stand with her. But before she moves into Gracie Mansion with me, I'd like to get to know her a little better.' There was a rumble of ribald laughter from the crowd.

Page then brought his black book right up to his nose and feigned puzzlement. 'This brings us to the current commissioner – Herbert – Eyelash?' [*Laughter*] 'I'm sorry, it's not Eyelash – it's Elish. Herbert Elish. A distinguished name in sanitation!' [*Laughter*] 'What can you say about Herbert Elish . . . except I'm sorry?' [*Laughter and applause*]

Suddenly Page slammed the book shut and erupted into the microphones, his voice picking up force and clarity as the words zinged out to the farthest reaches of the huge ballroom.

Every man on this list was a political appointee. Every man on this list got the job because he helped Lindsay get elected – *not* because he knew anything about sanitation. *I say that's wrong!* [*Beginning applause; Page gestures for quiet*]

I say that's a *crime*! It's a crime against you loyal men of the department and a crime against the people of New York City! [*Applause*]. The fact is there has only been one qualified man to hold the job of commissioner of sanitation in the past twenty-five years – a man who began on the streets of New York and worked his way up through the department. He was a man who knew sanitation and who knew city government and knew how to make the Sanitation Department perform its tasks and hold its head up high. I wish he could be here tonight. Of course, I'm talking about the one – the only – the great – Paul R. Screvane!

At the mention of Screvane's name, the room exploded with cheers and huzzahs. What Page said was perfectly true; Screvane had been the most effective and best-loved sanitation commissioner in recent years, and the only one who had actually risen from the ranks. When the ovation died down, Page declared the city of New York was too big, too spread out for just one commissioner of sanitation. It was imperative to have five deputy commissioners – one for each borough – who would have line responsibility for that borough. The candidate was using broad, sweeping gestures with his arms now, sometimes clenching a fist, often throwing out both arms like a symphony conductor. He continued, the pitch of anger in his voice rising with each sentence.

And I'll promise you men something right here and now. My commissioners of sanitation are not going to be a bunch of insurance lawyers, or assemblymen, or political hangers-on, or clubhouse hacks. My sanitation commissioners are going to be men from the ranks like *you* – or *you* – or *you* [*Jabs with his forefinger toward different parts of the room and to the balconies*] or *you* – or *you!* [*Applause*]

And do you know why? Because professional politicians don't know shit from shinola! And that's one one thing you do have to know when you're commissioner of sanitation . . . [*Wild cheers and applause*] . . . in this great city of ours!

Suddenly 4200 men were on their feet howling and stamping and beating their hands together until numb with pain. The candidate gestured for silence, but it was a half-hearted effort. For the first time in the campaign a crowd had really reacted positively, and he was loving it. Strange juices seemed to be surging within him, and he felt light-headed. He stood there impassively as the waves of noise reverberated around the room. Some of the men were clapping each other on the back; others held their glasses high in a toast. Here, at last, was a candidate who wasn't afraid to call the shots as he saw them!

Gradually the room calmed down as the men reclaimed their seats, relighted their cigars, and poured another cognac. Steve Loomis, Lou Klein, and Jack Leokum had composed and orchestrated this speech with the precision of a Bach Brandenburg Concerto. Now would come the *andante* movement, a relatively slow portion in which Page would sound very much like Billy Graham, with every word enunciated with clear, dramatic force that carried to the back of the second tier overlooking the vast assemblage below. Page let the tone of moral outrage show through by means of a slight tremor in his voice. Like Kipling's technique of dealing with a pony, Page had hit them over the nose at the outset, and they would be taking a deep interest in his movements ever afterwards. But he would not be leaving them with empty rhetoric; the citizen candidate had a plan.

As soon as he was elected, Page said, it was his intention to press the Albany legislature for a bill that would split the Department of Sanitation away from the Environmental Protection Administration and turn it into a private corporation in which each member of the department was a shareholder. The reasons for doing this were obvious. Under the present system, where the Sanitation Department was part of city government, there were layer on layer of little bureaucrats every step of the ladder. There was one bureaucrat sitting in an office shuffling paper for each man out on the street collecting refuse. It was an exact match, Page said. There were 10,500 sanitation men, and a total of 21,000 in the Environmental Protection Administration. What does this mean to the city of New York? It means that it costs $60 a ton for the department to collect and dispose of refuse ,while private carting companies can do the same job in this city for $26 a ton – less than half – and make a healthy profit!

The fact is that when John Lindsay created the ten superagencies in order – he said – to streamline city government, he created a monster. In the Environmental Protection Administration alone we've seen half the people sitting on their asses shuffling paper, while the other half are out on the streets working their asses off! And that half is you! And I say you're being screwed! [*Applause*] And the people of New York City are being screwed! [*Applause*]

Page went on to describe the San Franciso sanitation system, a private corporation in which each man has 32 shares of stock. With their annual dividend, the average sanitation man in San Francisco makes $17,000 a year; here he makes about $14,000 a year. Thus, in New York City, where the cost of living is 20 per cent higher, the workers make 20 per cent less. 'That is called a screwing!' Page reiterated.

Furthermore, each worker in San Francisco is guaranteed nine hour's wages, including a paid lunch hour, for working an eight-hour daily route. But the men go home when the work is done, and virtually every truck in town careens through its paces at breakneck speed; yet it's one of the cleanest cities in America.

What's more, Page added, the president of the San Francisco corporation, Leonard Stefanelli, makes just what the men make – $6.40 an hour – while in New York City, the commissioner makes $37,500 plus benefits that include a limousine and three full-time chauffeurs on call.

What's the real advantage to the City of New York? Where the taxpayer here pays $60 a ton, in San Francisco they pay $30 a ton. In Boston, where the setup is slightly different, a private carting corporation does the job for less than $20 a ton – or one-third the cost here.

Could such a scheme become a reality? Page assured the men it could. There was precedent for such a private corporation. The old Department of Hospitals was legislated out of existence by Albany, and replaced by the Health and Hospitals Corporation.

I know many of you men now live outside the city where you work – in Nassau and Suffolk Counties on Long Island, in Rockland or over in New Jersey. But by being members of the department you have a deep personal commitment to the city of New York and its people. In the past eight years, we have all watched this great city of ours go down hill. It hasn't been a gradual slide; it's been like a roller coaster, going faster and faster. Lindsay's answer has been to hire more people to try to stop it. But we all know our laws of physics: the more people who jump on a roller coaster, the faster it goes and the harder it is to stop. As I see it, there is only one organization that can stop the roller coaster, and that is you men of the Department of Sanitation.

Page then unfolded the master plan. It was the Department of Sanitation alone that went into every nook and cranny of the city, covered every election district at least once or twice a week. These men knew the city like a book – its people, its problems, its neighbourhoods, its attitudes. During the coming election, Page was going to open a campaign headquarters in every single assembly district of the city. It was his intention to keep those offices open after the election and turn them into little city halls – neighbourhood centres where residents could come to find a representative of the mayor to talk to about the individual problems concerning them. Each of the little city halls would be staffed by mini-mayors who would be the city's direct representative in that district. This system of mini-mayors would not be limited to assembly districts, which after all, were artificial boundaries drawn up by the Albany legislature, but would also embrace neighbourhoods and communities. The job of mini-mayor would be to act in effect as district leader, mediator, friend, father confessor to the people of the district. Through these neighbourhood offices, the people of the city of New York for the first time in decades would have a direct line of communication to City Hall. Under Page, city government would become responsive to the needs of the people.

The job of mini-mayor would not be a full-time job. But it would be a paying job. Page estimated that there could be two mini-mayors responsible for each of the city's 4500 election districts, or 9000 mini-mayors, plus an additional thousand workers to staff the 200 headquarters a– total of 10,000 men working two to three evenings a week. The pay for the mini-mayor would be a flat $50 a week, or $2,500 a year, which would mean an annual expenditure of $25 million, plus a headquarters budget of a thousand a month, or $12,000 a year for each of 200 headquarters costing a total of about $2½ million more. In other words, the entire project would cost less than $30 million a year.

Where will the money come from? There were several possibilities. Page estimated that turning the Sanitation Department into a private corporation would save New York City taxpayers $100 million a year. Furthermore, there was corruption and waste in every single department of government. Right now the city was paying out $2½ billion in welfare benefits, and it has been estimated that 30 per cent of all recipients are ineligible; in other words, the city is being cheated out of $700 million right there. Or perhaps the new Sanitation Corporation could begin charging the residents for trash removal. All over the country there were cities and communities – including San Francisco – that charge for garbage collection – say, a nominal 40¢ per can per month. That money could go directly into the new corporation which in turn would underwrite the costs of these little city halls and the salaries of the mini-mayors. There were all sorts of possibilities.

This then, is the deal [Page told them]. If I'm elected mayor, my highest priority will be to make the Sanitation Department a separate corporation in which each of you receive shares of stock and a base salary of $17,000 . . .

In addition, any man who wants to volunteer his services as a mini-mayor, working two or three evenings a week, we'll pay you an extra $2500 a year, bringing your pay up to $19,500.

You benefit, the city benefits. Instead of 37 representatives in the City Council, we'll have 10,000 mini-mayors, or one mini-mayor for less than 2000 citizens. You and I together can save the city of New York!

Page surveyed the thousands of upturned faces in the room. A heavy silence filled the hall, not unlike the air before a summer thunder storm. Like a bullfighter in a great *faena*, Page was in total control of the action and the crowd. Suddenly the candidate raised his arms and shouted: '*Are you with me? Will you help me save New York City!*'

There was a scattering of applause at first as the audience was letting the whole awesome concept sink in. Gradually more and more men began clapping and the noise swelled into an ovation that grew in intensity until the huge ballroom was rent with the thunder of acclaim; 4200 men rose again to their feet to begin shouting, cheering, and then jumping up and down, clasping their hands overhead like prizefighters. It lasted fully five minutes, culminating with the entire audience in all four ballrooms taking up the chant: 'We . . . want . . . Page! . . . We . . . Want . . . Page! . . . We . . . Want . . . Page!' over and over again. The candidate remained at the podium, a part smile on his lips, nodding his head as the walls shook with the cannonade of kudos. Finally he looked down at the opened book and gestured for quiet. Getting their attention again was not easy. Once the ovation began to die down, everyone wanted to talk about the Page plan; where before there was a wild salvo of acclamation, now a babel of voices filled the room. Page pleaded for quiet, saying he had just a few more minutes to talk, and then they could discuss the proposition and ask any questions. The hubbub was slow in subsiding, but at last there was enough quiet for him to continue.

The criticism will be twofold, Page warned. Lindsay and the City Council will say that another layer of personnel is being added to further complicate the city government, further separating the mayor from his constituency. The other criticism is that the plan will take money away from other essential city services.

But the real fear is that a group of decent, honourable, hard-working men will get into city government and begin to take it away from the bureaucrats and professional politicians who've been screwing us for the last hundred years – and that's exactly what's going to happen! [*Applause*]

Page told them he couldn't do the job alone. The first order of business was to get elected, and he needed help. It was imperative to have several thousand campaign workers taking to the streets beginning in two weeks to get signatures on the nominating petitions. There were some 50 campaign headquarters all arranged for, but with no one to man them; volunteers were needed desperately to open them and keep them open. Following the petition drive, there would be a canvassing operation in which every single voter had to be contacted in every area of the city and told about the citizen candidate and his master plan to save New York . . .

As Page was speaking, the curtains slowly parted behind him, revealing hundreds of red, white, and blue streamers of bunting, and a huge white banner stretching across the back wall proclaiming SANITATION POWER. There, at long tables set in semicircular rows were about two hundred campaign workers waiting to sign up volunteers. The candidate closed his big book and looked out over the vast throng. Then with outstretched arms he cried:

Right now I'm asking you men of the Sanitation Department to make a decision for New York. I want you to get up out of your seats and come forward down the aisles to me here – hundreds of you, I would hope – come on down front and you will be greeted by my campaign staff, and you can join the team that's going to save New York City . . .

In minutes the aisles were clogged as hundreds and hundreds arose, almost as one, and started for the stage. In each of the four ballrooms there was chaos, with men pushing and shoving in the scramble to be the first to volunteer. The Ben Cutler Orchestra began blaring out fast-paced renditions of 'Happy Days Are Here Again,' 'There's a Tavern in the Town,' and 'For He's a Jolly

Good Fellow.' Up by the lectern, the candidate was engulfed by well-wishers who wanted to shake his hand or exchange a few words. Lines began to form at the volunteer tables on stage, backing up to the doorways clear across the giant ballroom; it was the last great traffic jam of humanity. Virtually every member of the audience was volunteering enthusiastically.

Page was exuberant. Still clutching his black book, he left the podium. In the kitchen he was greeted by an ecstatic Jack Leokum who grabbed him in a bear hug and danced him into the pantry. 'You did it! You did it!' Leokum cried. 'I knew you could do it!' Campaign Manager Mark Altschul appeared radiant with excitement. 'We've finally got a candidate and a campaign,' Mark shouted as he and Leokum pumped each other's hands and danced around the candidate. More members of the campaign staff charged into the kitchen to congratulate him – Loomis and Klein, P.J., Johnny DiSantis and Paul Berman. Even Nick Gigante's usually sullen face was wreathed in smiles.

Page, his heart pounding and beads of perspiration glistening on his forehead, stood in near disbelief. 'I can do it,' he repeated over and over again. 'By God, I'm going to be the next mayor of New York City!'

Chapter 19

Within a week, there was a whole new look to the Devereaux Page candidacy. Suddenly Paul Berman had the manpower to open some fifty neighbourhood headquarters all over the city.

Instantly the campaign began to take hold. It was Paul Berman's peculiar genius that he could not only whip up enthusiasm in a lagging effort with too few volunteers, but that he could juggle an army of workers, making each one feel terribly important, even though he might be kept waiting for several hours with nothing to do. Berman might well have been a social director on a cruise ship, for he always seemed delighted to see anybody and could generate excitement no matter how late the hour or how tired he was. He bubbled, he steamed, he exulted, he was constantly in motion, working 18 or 20 hours a day, falling near dead on the leather couch in his office for a few hours sleep, only to be up and at 'em at six or seven in the morning. Berman, too, was a public relations artist and con man without peer.

Using a kind of pyramid technique, Berman's team managed to process these 10,000 volunteers within a week, getting them assigned to local headquarters, giving them cash budgets to rent furniture, desks, work tables, sending out loads of campaign material, bunting, photographs of the candidates, and getting signs painted for over their doors.

As for the candidate, he suddenly found himself racing around the city, opening headquarters, often at the rate of five and six a day. And as the storefronts became organized and the positions of the candidate known, invitations to speak increased, so that from pre-dawn to almost midnight a caravan of cars containing the candidate and a retinue of campaign workers chased around to the farthest corners of the five boroughs in a dizzying whirl of appearances at synagogues, meeting halls, private homes, high school auditoriums, street corner rallies – anywhere people might gather.

Any doubts Bobby DeStefano had as to the efficacy of garbage men as political operatives quickly vanished; they were superb. Many weren't very bright, he thought, nor were their wives and children who turned out in droves to work for Page, but by God, they were dedicated. And they were organized. It turned out that John DeLury, head of the Sanitation Union, had under wraps the best political machine left in town, one that had never before been tapped. Although there were only a total of 10,000 sanitation men – all city employees – the union had a current file on every member, every former member, every retired member, every deceased member's widow, arranged by assembly district and election district. In addition, it had a sanitation man for every street or group of streets in the city, and they got there at least once or twice a week. Where the regular political organizations might have 20–40 per cent coverage in an assembly district, the Sanitation Department had 100 per cent coverage. Furthermore, if a political candidate wanted the names of thirty to fifty potentially friendly local residents, the names were there in the union files.

Most of the city chauffeurs who drive high officials around were on the payroll of the Sanitation Department; these men, too, volunteered to drive the candidate and the campaign cars around the city, delivering campaign material, transporting equipment from rally to rally, and dropping off advance men and picking them up at various stops. The importance of this might never occur to a candidate until he turned up late for a date in the wilds of Brooklyn or Queens with a driver who didn't know the way. But for want of a knowledgeable chauffeur, many an appearance was lost, and for want of that appearance, the district was lost.

One other facet of the Sanitation Union made it an extraordinary political operation – it was overwhelmingly Italian. And Italians are very family and clan-oriented. Thus, when a volunteer was processed, he was given a stack of IBM cards and asked to fill them in with the names and addresses of friends and relatives in the city. He was to use his private telephone book or Christmas card list – anything with the names of people. These cards were then given to Jimmy Lee to have programmed through the computer. A series of letters were generated, printed on parchment paper and signed by the auto pen which reproduced

Devereaux Page's signature in water-soluble ink. Tens of thousands of letters a week began pouring forth from campaign
headquarters that began, 'My Dear Mrs Vitterini, I am writing
you at the suggestion of your cousin, Harry Santini . . .' and
went on to say why he was running. Along with the letters went
questionnaires asking for the recipient's advice and for his
feelings as to what were the most important issues. These answers, too, were programmed into the computer, and more
letters were generated at each step of the campaign. The system,
called the Doughnut Letter Operation, used different form letters
with holes in the middle to allow specific paragraphs to be
inserted by computer on issues in which the person indicated
interest or fear. These began, 'I, too, share your concern about
the problem of crime in the streets . . .'

All of this was costing huge sums of money, and Bobby decided
on several tactics designed to whitewash the question of finances.

First, a fund-raising chairman was found, a Wall Street lawyer
who, like the mayoral candidate, was into the Organization rather
deeply, and who was also well connected. It was the job of this
lawyer, a fortyish WASP named Gerald Tippy, with a florrid
face and a love of sailing, to head up what was essentially a dummy
finance committee. It didn't m atter whether he succeeded or not;
it was just imperative that the effort be made.

As a result, Tippy, who was not a very good lawyer, but quite
personable, found kimself with an enormous expense account
that enabled him to take all kinds of people to dinner at the best
restaurants, give huge fund-raising parties, and generally tear
around town visiting with potential fat-cat contributors. It
was the dream job for a dumb, well-connected WASP; it would
have been rough if he had had to produce, but he didn't, and he
was perfect at giving the illusion of success.

In addition to Tippy's committee, Lou Klein's staff put together a series of advertisements for the newspapers reiterating
some of the candidate's positions. The ads proclaimed this was
the only man who could save New York from the professional
politicians, and he needed help. This media campaign ran in the
daily and weekly papers as well as the local magazines – New
York, the New Yorker, Cue and the New York Times Magazine.
Bobby DeStefano arranged to have thousands of coupons clipped

and mailed in with real names but with dummy contributions from all over the city amounting to tens of thousands of dollars a week – all of which came out of his pocket.

There was, of course, a lot more interest on the part of the press and television now that some 50 headquarters had opened around the city and the neighbourhoods were swarming with Page campaigners. Devereaux Page began having frequent contact with the media. But Mark and Bobby had little to worry about. By now, Page was maturing as a candidate. If a question was too technical, he said frankly that he didn't know the answer, because he was just a citizen candidate and was trying his best to learn the issues as fast as he could. But he promised to damn well find out and let the reporter know his answer to a question once he had studied the issue thoroughly. And there was always a campaign aide at Page's elbow to note the question and the name and affiliation of the reporter who generally had his answer, usually in writing, in no more than 48 hours.

For the most part, the media treated the candiate well. The press suite at the Commodore was open twenty hours a day, staffed with pretty campaign workers and perpetually stocked with plenty of food and liquor. Lou Klein held press briefings twice daily at which he would give out the candidate's schedule for the following day along with a press release containing the transcript of a speech or a position paper on a new issue. There were also glossy photographs with captions describing the day's doings. Each morning's 'television event' was photographed, showing the candidate touring a prison or a hospital, or taking part in some ceremony or parade, or speaking out on a new issue. The footage was processed and sent to each of the city's seven television stations along with a narrator's script – always in plenty of time to make the evening news, which it frequently did.

In addition, the radio stations were supplied with daily tapes of the campaign doings, and a special answering service was installed whereby the newspaper or radio station could call, and the daily tape would be played automatically for them. One of Lou Klein's cardinal principles was making good use of instant news. For example, three days after the sanitation speech, two policemen were shot and killed in the Bronx. Page, who was

touring Brooklyn at the time was reached on the car telephone
and told what had happened. He and Mark quickly composed a
statement expressing horror and shock, which Page read over a
pay phone to headquarters at the Commodore where it was
recorded and immediately put on the daily telephone tape.
Campaign workers then phoned all the radio stations in town
and told them to call in to hear what Devereaux Page had to say
about the shooting, As a result, the citizen candidate was on the
air with a statement within twenty minutes of the shooting, well
before any other politicians or city officials could be reached for
comment.

The *Times* ran a tongue-in-cheek editorial twitting the so-called
'citizen candidate for choosing as his guiding literary light a
hard-core imperialist such as Rudyard Kipling.' Colonialism,
the *Times* said, was not only out of fashion, but since our Vietnam
involvement, positively repugnant to the majority of the people
Page was trying to reach. Page promptly composed and issued a
reply.

Rudyard Kipling has always been my favourite poet. Had it been
Shakespeare, I'm sure the *Times* would have remarked on a politician
looking for the Jewish vote and at the same time quoting the creator
of the character Shylock.

Kipling was a colonialist, it's true. But because of British colonialism, and the many thousands of loyal, decent public servants who spent
their lives in the colonies, a country like India is not now part of
Communist China.

Kipling was a product of his time. Some of his views may not
be fashionable; but he was a great writer, and I have drawn inspiration
from his words all my life. Trying to dismiss Kipling as a colonialist
is the same as trying to dismiss Bach as a composer because he didn't
have a twelve-tone scale.

It was the *Voice* reporter Jack Newfield who once wrote that a
political campaign is a dehumanizing rite. Its only purpose is
power, and tends to bring out the worst in men. Repetition,
exhaustion, anxiety, and pressure must be endured cheerfully.
Instincts have to be disguised. Sleep and privacy are elusive.
Each day brings some new temptation to compromise a little.
Yet, the personal campaign is not to be despised, despite its
carnival air and the mindless character of the slogans and political

speeches. President Johnson's press secretary, George Reedy, called it an educational device. The people learn something from it. It gives the voters an opportunity to observe a man under conditions where he would be unguarded in his reactions and his comments. And a man cannot play a role for week after week of gruelling travel. Sooner or later he must reveal his true character.

In the case of Devereaux Page, politics seemed to forge within him a steely resilience to the onslaughts of fatigue, hysteria, and histrionics that are so much the part of any political foray. The pressures were especially severe on the road show, where the candidate was eyeball-to-eyeball with thousands of people daily, many of them confused and openly cynical to the blandishments of any who would promise a change for the better. Although the car and most city buildings were air conditioned, the August sun was merciless, beating down on the candidate and giving his face and hands the quality of rawhide. Yet, the grinding round of rallies, walking tours, *kaffeeklatsches*, and speeches to large and small audiences, followed by the inevitable mingling with the electorate – pressing the flesh, as LBJ called it – seemed to give Page a new physical vigour that enabled him to go back for more, day after exhausting day. Even his digestive problem cleared up, with the result that the answering service no longer had to awaken him in the early hours of the morning with the prune juice call.

It has also been said that the more one uses the human brain, the better it gets. As the campaign wore on, Page found himself able to absorb information quicker, sorting out that which was important and filing it away in his memory drum to be called up when needed. Like Mark Altschul, his mind began to function like a small computer.

Jack Leokum often travelled with the candidate, giving critiques of each appearance, helping Page to read the faces in the crowd, to know whether he was registering or not, and to change his speech accordingly. He found that a politician had to speak in several idioms. In some cases he had to address the masses only with figures of speech that were part of their experience. Yet at the same time, the masses wanted their leader to be different from them, to be in some ways of a higher order, and to talk sometimes in a language they but dimly understood. This was the oratorical tightrope a politician had to walk. And Page was getting good at it.

As the campaign wore on, his attacks on the Establishment grew sharper. He emulated the technique of old Senator Theodore Bilbo of Mississippi; every town where Bilbo spoke, he would begin by denouncing in violent language the wealthiest citizen or citizens, causing his listeners to perk up and say, 'Did you hear what Bilbo said about So-and-So?' Page's targets were the do-nothing congressmen and legislators against whom he railed and snarled, accusing them of letting the city come apart while they feathered their political nests. 'By the most brutal view,' he cried, 'New York City is today a legislative pail of dismembered organs strewn from Washington to Albany. And the real fault is not the present administration. It's your own congressman, The Honourable Charles Rangel!' (Or Rooney or Delaney or Chisholm, depending on what district he was in.) Then he would cite their absymal legislative records, pointing out the number of bills they introduced that were defeated, which he called a colossal waste of time. In the home districts of the other politicians who were candidates, Page was particularly rough, calling for their resignations from Congress or the state legislature before they continued on with their campaign. The recipients of these barrages often replied in such shrill, violent language that the people believed there might be some justification for the attacks. The result was a lot of publicity for Page, and the growing image of a idealistic young reformer. Along with individuals, Page began blasting away at the New York Telephone Company, Consolidated Edison for its pollution and power failures, and the Port of New York Authority, his speech writers realizing the truth of the old Huey Long dictum that corporations were the finest political enemies in the world, and that if you wanted to attract attention and support, you denounced the biggest and the closest at hand.

It was apparent to all those around him that Devereaux Page was no longer role-playing. The daily pounding through the sprawling, filthy city, and the sense of hopelessness he felt everywhere he went was having a very real effect on him. Often the juxtaposition of appearances would stagger him, such as the time he went from a tour of the Brooklyn House of Detention to a posh fund-raising affair in Manhattan. At the Brooklyn jail, where the prisoners were confined for twenty-one hours a day, four men to a tiny, dark six-by-eight-foot cell, the cell block was without air conditioning, and steaming with the stench of humanity, sweat and urine. Lying semi-nude in a stupor on the concrete floor in front of one cell in the corridor was a boy no more than sixteen years old, his hands manacled to the steel bars of the cell door. The warden hastily assured Page, 'That's a police case, not our concern.' He explained the boy had been brought in off the street by police a few minutes earlier and was being secured until he could be processed. Page looked down at the boy, wasted and thin, and then turned to the warden and exploded: 'You fucking little bureaucrat! How dare you tell me that's not your concern!' The warden, a mild, medium man with rimless glasses, blanched. The candidate, shaking with rage, pointed a finger at the warden and said in a quivering voice, 'Buster, you get a key for those handcuffs and loosen this boy and get him to a doctor. And I'll tell you another thing. I've got a fair chance of being elected mayor of this town, and the first thing I'm going to do when I take office January first is come down here and fire you personally, you little weasling son of a bitch!'

Back in the campaign car, Page sat in the corner of the back seat by the window, completely unapproachable, tears glistening in his eyes, and a new, curiously ravaged look on his face. 'I don't want to be mayor of this evil, evil city,' he muttered.

Ironically, the next stop was a Gerald Tippy fund-raising party for the beautiful people at the Regency Hotel on Park Avenue, where Page was expected to be his old charming social self. There were about a hundred people gathered, and when he came through the doors, a trio played 'East Side, West Side,' and there was the usual pattering applause. At the front of the room a single microphone on a chromium stand was set up. After being introduced by Tippy, Page stepped up to the microphone and let his eyes travel around the room with its bright red drapes of lush velvet, its red-and-gold damask walls. Before him was arrayed an elegant, well-dressed crowd, a few of them friends from his Horse Show and college days, and all the kind of people he grew up with and saw socially all the time prior to this race for mayor. He said simply:

I've just come from the Brooklyn House of Detention. What I saw there was not pretty. It was just one of the many unpretty things I've seen travelling around this city.

There are some who have implied that my candidacy is not serious, and that I'm just out to make a name for myself. My answer to them is: anyone who runs for office in this city, with the shape this city is in, and takes it as a joke, is committing a mortal sin.

[Voice breaking] We've got to get this city out of the hands of the professional politicians – and – and the bureaucrats. *We've got to.* And with your help, we will. Thank you all for coming.

As Page left the microphone to go into the crowd for some hand-shaking, many noticed there were tears in his eyes, and one man who had known him slightly through the years, described him as having the brooding stare of a man who had 'just looked on the face of the devil himself.'

For any candidate, politics is a colossal paradox, taking him sometimes in a matter of minutes from the glorious to the grotesque, the tragic to the comic, mixing hilarity and despair in a giant shaker and spilling out a potion guaranteed to singe the heart of anyone who drinks of it. Yet, taken too seriously, the election will be lost just as surely as if the whole thing were played for laughs. And so Page, with a politican's instinct, managed to develop a rather sharp sense of humour, sometimes self-deprecating, more often savage. When asked by a reporter how many people were working on his campaign, the candidate answered, 'About half.'

He was asked if he thought his Democratic opponent could win. 'There's a remote possibility he could beat me,' Page replied, 'But only if they keep him locked up in a broom closet.'

And one day the *New York Times* called him at home to say that he was quoted as saying he wasn't in this race to win, but rather to illuminate the issues. Was it true?

'Illuminating the issues is a lot of bullshit,' Page retorted. 'If you're going to get into this thing, you do it to win.'

'Could you rephrase that answer?' the *Times* man asked.

'Why do you want me to rephrase it?'

'Because the *Times* can't print "bullshit".'

'The *Times* prints it every day.'

Chapter 20

According to the New York State election law as amended in 1970 and 1971, in order for the name of an independent candidate for citywide office to appear on the ballot, his supporters had a six-week period in which to gather 10,000 signatures on nominating petitions; these had to be filed with the Board of Elections four weeks prior to election day. But it couldn't be just any 10,000 signatures. To be valid, a signature had to be that of a registered voter, and one who had not previously signed a nominating petition of another candidate for the same office. With a half dozen other candidates having run for mayor in the various primaries, each of whom had got a minimum of 10,000 valid signatures to enter the primary in the first place, it was obvious that a huge number of people had signed nominating petitions already; if those same signatures were to appear on a Page petition, they would be detected and thrown out in any challenge by other candidates. They only way to avoid a challenge in court was to get many times the required number of names, probably around 40,000, and hope that 25 per cent of them would be valid.

Even with the distinct advantage of having the Sanitation Union in his hip pocket, with some 10,000 workers fighting for him out of 50 neighbourhood headquarters, and another 18 storefronts scheduled to open within two weeks, the Page candidacy was somewhat stalled. True, his appearances were getting better each day, with his attacks on the present administration, the do-nothing legislators, and the other candidates; his speeches were sharper and more effective. But the fact was he simply wasn't drawing the big crowds. Ideally, what was needed to catapult Page into the consciousness of the electorate was some kind of news break, preferably of a personal nature. The robbery back in June had had that effect. Bobby and Mark seriously discussed the possibility of marrying Page off, figuring that the sound of wedding bells would drown out some of the oratory, hysteria, and headlines. 'Could you imagine the crowd he'd draw appearing with his new bride two days after the wedding?' Bobby chortled. 'They'd all come to stare and wonder if she was any good in bed!'

But there wasn't time for a marriage at this point. With the petition drive starting in eight days, it was imperative that the candidate visit every single storefront headquarters for a kickoff rally. The schedule was rough – five stops a night during the week and ten stops on the weekends.

This was such a hectic period that virtually nobody caught the fact that Nick Gigante was undergoing what was tantamount to a nervous breakdown. P.J., who roomed with him at the Commodore when they stayed over in the city had an inkling of what was happening to the big man. But to the rest of the staff, Nick, huge in stature, always rather sullen and uncommunicative at best, had only become more so. He carried out orders in his usual mute, deliberate way, lugging boxes of materials around, going on errands, even serving as advance man for some stops that didn't require any public relations expertise or thought. Outwardly, it was the same old Nick, reliable, plodding, hard as steel, and lightning fast. Inside, he was apparently going like a pneumatic jackhammer. Everything would have been all right but for two concurrent events: finding out he was sterile, and the long separations from Rosemary – as much as three and four days at a time – resulting from the horrendous pace of the campaign. While he loved Rosemary, his sterility made him feel inadequate whenever he was with her. He couldn't get it up for Rosemary any more, which only heightened the tension at home and caused Nick to prolong his stays in the city, even when he didn't have the duty.

He was perpetually aroused, almost to the point of male nymphomania and priapism. After his last stop in the evening, he would begin drinking heavily, and then go over to one of several massage parlours, or pick up a whore on 42nd Street; about the only satisfaction he got was watching the eyes of these girls, black and white, bug out when they first caught sight of his monstrous equipment. The act itself, performed in the squalor of a dingy hotel room or a massage parlour cubicle, was quick and meaningless. Nick, who had been used to sex three and four times a night with Rosemary, was in perfect physical shape; he simply needed more satisfaction than one little streetwalker could give him. So he prowled the streets of the city, sometimes picking up as many as two or three girls a night, which cost him up to $100 and more. And still he wasn't satisfied.

Nick pretty much left the girls in the campaign alone. While the sight of dozens of leggy little creatures in miniskirts and no bras running around the Commodore left him throbbing with desire, he made it a point to try to find release with the girls of the streets and massage parlours. In fact, the only one at headquarters he had touched had been Lou Klein's big Hungarian secretary, Louise, and she had actually seduced him. It was Louise, whose German husband had been away on an extended business trip, who had propositioned Nick and sent him off on this binge of liquor and sex. For about a week, Louise had completely re-placed Rosemary as a wild and constant sexual partner, alter-nately submitting to and subduing Nick anywhere they were alone – up in the room he shared with P.J., fully dressed on toilets or lying in empty bathtubs in hotel bathrooms, several times at Louise's apartment, and more often than not on the couches of empty campaign offices in the wee hours of the morn-ing when headquarters was deserted.

Then one day, Klaus, Louise's engineer husband, returned from Germany, and for Nick the well dried up. Louise decided her marriage was more important than being serviced by a big Italian goon, so she broke the affair off, resisting any further advances, and treating Nick with the cool professionalism she reserved for any other campaign worker.

At first Nick was stunned by her attitude and tried to reason with her. Later, he in turn rejected her, never going near Klein's office if he could avoid it, not even speaking to her in the halls or out at a neighbourhood headquarters if she happened to be along on the evening's activities. But he brooded about her constantly, as well as fantasizing over the way her haunches and belly would shimmy when she was astride him, the effluence streaming from her grand canal; he seldom saw her breasts, because their encounters were usually quick, wildly passionate, and not in a place where they could take the time to get completely undressed.

It has since been suggested that Nick's marriage to Rosemary might have been saved by a marriage counsellor had one got into the picture at the point when Nick found he was sterile and before his first bout with Louise – saved, that is, if the counsellor could relate to two confused people whose IQ's together might add up to sixty. More likely, a priest might have put Nick straight, because the Catholic Church – or at least the memory of the way it was – was still a force in his life, even though he quit going to mass on Sunday when they started using English. But by this point, Nick's case was almost hopeless. The rupture with Rosemary, although not final, was certainly severe.

Nick's womanizing and drinking became more pronounced, as did his lust to have big Louise again, as much out of spite as anything else. So late one Sunday night in the deserted offices of the Commodore, Nick, after hours of solitary drinking downstairs in the bar, stumbled into Klein's office where Louise was typing a speech for Page in the giant IBM Orator typeface for delivery the following night. He slammed the door shut and locked it, subdued the terrified girl with a crack across the mouth, threw her on the floor, and stripped her naked; he thereupon unzipped his pants and angrily rammed his giant limb into her. It was skin against skin and excruciatingly painful. Louise, frozen with fear, lay there trembling; Nick drunk and rock hard, was unable to reach a climax, which only increased his rage. Any whimper from the big nude girl beneath him brought a cruel iron hand across the face. He pumped away on her until she was bleeding and raw; still he couldn't come. Mercifully Louise blacked out in pain, and after a few more minutes. Nick withdrew his bruised and bloody shaft, still erect, and in mighty frustration, smacked it with the back of his hand, sending shock waves of pain shooting into every extremity of his body. He let out a roar, cleared both desks with a sweep of his arm, sending the contents, – books, papers, computer printouts, desk lamps – cascading onto the mute nude figure on the floor. Then picking up the IBM Selectric she had been working on, he hurled it across the room where it smashed into one of Klein's five television sets causing a shower of jagged glass slivers to land on the rug not far from where Louise lay. His fury finally expended and once again calm, he fastened his pants and lurched upstairs to his room where, fully clothed, he passed out cold on the bed. P.J., sound asleep in the other bed, heard nothing.

It was Paul Berman who discovered Louise about a half hour later. A hopeless insomniac, with a constant and morbid fear of death that kept him from getting to sleep because he was scared he wouldn't wake up again, Berman often roamed the streets of New York until five or six in the morning, finally getting home to drop from sheer exhaustion into a deep sleep. During a campaign he would come down to headquarters to grind out massive a-mounts of work in the quiet time when nobody was around. And it was on this night, as he headed for his office, that he heard moans issuing from Klein's room, and, on investigating, found Louise nude on the floor amidst the papers and debris. She was semi-conscious and suffering terribly. He covered her with a bedspread and brought her around with a cool compress. She sat up and began to sob uncontrollably, stammering out that she had been raped by Nick Gigante and was in terrible pain. Berman called his own doctor who rushed down by cab and took charge, giving Louise a sedative and examining her, while Berman went into the next office to call Mark.

An hour later, in Bobby DeStefano's suite upstairs, a tight-lipped furious Mark confronted the young Boss with the news that one of his henchmen had raped an innocent campaign aide. The fact of the rape was bad enough, Mark told him, but if the word got out to the rest of the campaign staff, there would be a lot of questions as to just who Nick Gigante was and what he was doing there. This in turn could well blow the cover on who was really underwriting this campaign for the citizen candidate, and the whole effort would go up in smoke.

'Who knows about this?' Bobby asked.

Mark ticked off the names of those involved so far: Berman, the doctor, Louise, Bobby and Mark.

'And the rapist,' Bobby added.

'And the rapist.'

'Are you sure it's Nick?' Bobby looked puzzled. 'Christ, it can't be Nick! That's the straightest guy I ever had working for me.'

'All I know is what Louise told Berman when she was rather incoherent.'

Bobby was wearing green silk pyjamas with white piping and a monogram on the breast pocket; he padded across the room to his big semicircular desk where he picked up the phone and dialled P.J.'s room. 'Where's Nick?' Bobby demanded.

'He's asleep on the next bed.'

'Get your ass up here right away,' Bobby snapped. 'Don't bother to shave or anything.'

Minutes later P.J. arrived. Even with a monumental hangover and unshaven, the Irishman looked as alert and fresh as if he'd just come back from a month's vacation. With a certain amount of reluctance, P.J. confirmed the fact that Nick and Rosemary were undergoing marital difficulties and that Nick had been drinking very heavily in the past few weeks.

'Why the fuck didn't you tell me?' Bobby snarled. 'I can't have guys working for me who aren't happy at home.'

'What happened?' P.J. wanted to know.

Mark recounted the events of the preceding few hours, and P.J. told what he knew about Louise and Nick – how she had seduced him one night and then a week later had broken it off when her husband returned.

'So it wasn't entirely Nick's fault.' Bobby ruled. 'The lousy cunt was a goddamn cock teaser.' He looked at Mark and P.J. 'I mean you don't turn a guy on and then turn him off the next week without asking for trouble. Especially a guy like Nick.'

'I still don't want him working on the campaign,' Mark stated. 'He's dangerous, and it could happen again.'

It was decided that word of what happened would go no further. Louise was to be taken to the hospital, and then she was to look for employment elsewhere. She would be warned that if she said anything to anybody or made trouble for the campaign, her husband would be told the whole ugly story.

'What about Berman?' Bobby wanted to know. 'Can he be trusted to keep his mouth shut?'

'I'll tell him it was an unfortunate lovers' fight and that both people involved had been discharged from the campaign, and not to say anything about it. I've known Berman for close to ten years. He's not a gossip or a troublemaker. His whole aim is to get his candidate elected.'

Bobby asked, 'What about the doctor?'

'If no charges are brought, he doesn't have to report it,' Mark said. 'We'll call it a lovers' quarrel.'

'You take care of the doctor, Mark.'

Mark nodded.

'And Berman. You handle Berman, too.'

There was a momentary silence.

'That leaves Nick,' P.J. said quietly.

Bobby winced. 'I ought to cut off that big cock of his and make him swallow it,' he muttered, 'but I'm just going to fire him.'

'From the campaign or from the Family?' P.J. asked.

Mark stood up to go. 'This sounds like an internal matter among you guys.'

Bobby waved him back to his seat. 'You're part of the Organization, Mark, whether you like it or not.' Mark sat down again. 'I hate to fire the bastard,' Bobby muttered, 'but I have to do it. He lost control. There are two things you can't do in this business: you can't get too greedy, and you can't go haywire.' Bobby looked at P.J. 'Have Johnny DiSantis and Tony the Elf here at nine sharp this morning. In fact, get two or three of our boys from Jersey – Tommy and Vic and maybe Meatball. Get them here on the chopper by nine. Then I'll call Nick in and can him. But I want a lot of guys around me when I do it. Otherwise, he might go crazy and kill us all. The son of a bitch is big enough to do it.'

P.J. nodded and rose to go. 'What kind of shape is Klein's office in?' Bobby wanted to know.

'A wreck,' said Mark.

'You and P.J. clean it up so it looks like nothing happened. Then we'll tell Klein his girl called in sick – permanently.'

The secret was kept. Nick, while not happy about the judgment against him, seemed to understand, and took the news quietly; he was not only banished from the DeStefano Family, but from any employment east of the Mississippi.

Lou Klein took Louise's departure with somewhat less than equanimity; she had been a damn good secretary, and he wanted to know what the hell had happened. But she was quickly replaced, and in a very few days, Louise, Nick, and the whole unpleasant incident were forgotten in the hustle of the campaign.

Two weeks into the petition drive, the Page organization had already collected some 30,000 signatures; a quick check showed that about one in four was valid. If the enthusiasm and numbers held, this would mean they would file close to 100,000 signatures, of which 25,000 would be valid, many more than was necessary to guarantee the candidate a place on the November ballot. Page himself was bone weary. Someone estimated he had walked 20 miles a day in his quest for signatures and keeping his army of workers in good spirits. He looked tired and acted tired. The smile that was usually genuine became automatic and forced. He needed rest, and yet was almost too tired to sleep nights which only compounded his fatigue. Finally he told Mark he didn't think he could go on without a day off; this was reluctantly agreed to. So after a short dinner with Mark and P.J. at Moriarty's, Page was driven back to his little apartment where he took two sleeping pills, hoping to pass out undisturbed for the night and most of the following day. At four in the morning he was slowly awakened from his drugged sleep by the persistent ringing of the telephone. Shaking loose the cobwebs in his aching brain, he grappled for the receiver and put it to his ear.

'Mr Page?' came a crisp male voice.

'What is it?' he mumbled.

'This is the Associated Press city desk.'

'What the hell do you want at this hour?'

'We're asking if you could confirm for us the death of your wife, Katherine Mellon Page, in an automobile accident in Switzerland yesterday.'

Chapter 21

Kay's body had been found in the twisted wreckage of a Mercedes-Benz 280B sedan at the foot of the St. Gothard Pass where the road to Airolo snakes back and forth up the 6000 foot mountain in a series of extraordinary hairpin turns. The Swiss police estimated she had gone off the road at about the 4000 foot level and had careened and bumped down the mountain side, smashing on to some sections of the road below and then hurtling on, gathering such momentum that many trees along the path were torn up by the roots. The car didn't burn, probably because a promontory of rock had ripped the gas tank out on the way down, leaving it two thousand feet up the mountain. Nevertheless, both the automobile and the woman's body were demolished. It took professional welders four hours to extricate Kay's body from the car. By great good luck, the two girls were not with their mother, but were staying with friends at the nearby summer resort town of Faido.

The following morning, it was decided the candidate would fly immediately to Switzerland to bring home the two children and Kay's body for burial in this country. Page himself was distraught, both from the shock of Kay's frightful death, and for his two daughters, Gelsey and Johnna, whom he had seen all too seldom in the year and a half since his separation from Kay. The accumulated guilt began to eat at him until he felt himself a hollow, aching shell.

Mark had come over right away, as had P.J.; finally at six in the morning after dozens of desperate phone calls, the choked voice of Gelsey had come over the transatlantic wire, crying, 'Oh, Daddy, Daddy, it's awful! You've got to come! Please come!' His voice breaking with emotion, he promised to be on the next plane to Switzerland. The travel arrangements were made. He would take the evening Swissair flight to Geneva. Fortunately his passport was still valid, although he hadn't been abroad for three years. At 6.00 PM, with a suitcase packed by Mark and P.J., Page descended to the waiting campaign car with Jimmy the Dwarf at the wheel. Waiting for him on the sidewalk was a horde of reporters, TV cameramen, photographers, and a knot of curious onlookers who had heard the news and had come like locusts to swarm around the tragedy-stricken candidate, hoping to get a picture, a quote, or just a glimpse. The moment Page appeared outside the building, his way to the car was blocked by a wall of newsmen jostling and pushing. Everybody seemed to be shouting at once. High-intensity photographic lights went on as motion picture cameras began recording his departure for the airport. Flashbulbs popped and cameras clicked. Half a dozen microphones were shoved in Page's face as the radio and tele-vision boys shouted their questions. 'Where are you going, Mr Page?' 'How do you feel?' 'Are you still a candidate?' 'What's this going to do to the campaign?' 'When are you coming back?' 'Are you bringing the body back with you?'

Page could only mutter over and over, 'Jesus, can't you leave me alone at a time like this?' and 'I don't know anything, I really don't.'

In the Swissair departure lounge at Kennedy Airport, things were no better. Many of the newsmen and camera crews had followed the campaign car out to the airport while others were already there waiting. Had Page not been so excruciatingly tired from the strain and grogged from the two Seconal capsules he had taken the night before, he might have been capable of dealing with the press. But his fatigue plus the emotion of the situation had left him zombie-like, to the point where he almost had to be led around like a small boy. His reaction to Kay's death was disbelief. 'I can't believe it,' he said several times. 'Kay was an excellent driver, I can't understand what happened.'

Given the magnitude of the tragedy, to begin immediately to assess the effect of Kay's death on the Page candidacy might appear unforgivably tasteless. Nevertheless, neither a campaign manager nor the public can ignore the fact of front-page banner headlines in the *New York Post* – the city's only afternoon paper. The story of the beleaguered candidate, coupled with photo-graphs of his departure, was bound to sell papers and, in turn, would engender a great deal of voter awareness and sympathy. Most heart-rending about the *Post* coverage was the close-up on page 7 the following day where the lens man had caught the grief-stricken Page looking as though he were about to burst into tears.

Further, the timing was perfect for the television evening news. Every channel carried footage of the story. There was a debate at headquarters as to whether Johnny DiSantis should photograph the candidate's departure and send prints of the story over the broadcasters, but this was quashed. Berman argued for it, but Mark and Lou Klein vetoed the idea as being in less than good taste. It turned out not to have been necessary; the stations used their own footage.

The following morning, the *Times* put the story on page 1; the *News* put it on page 3 along with the other major political news and had additional pictures in the centre spread. In terms of publicity, it could not have been better if the whole thing had been planned.

For Devereaux Page, the scene in Switzerland was grim. Gelsey and Johnna were relieved to see their father; yet after four months of separation, preceded by over a year of minimal contact, Page and his daughters were virtual strangers to one another. In addition, it was immediately evident that Kay had been less than complimentary whenever the subject of their father or the divorce came up, an attitude shared and amplified by her friends, the Talbots, an American couple summering in Switzerland with whom they were staying when the tragedy occurred. As a result, the Talbots were hostile; Gelsey and Johnna were confused and frightened, bursting into storms of weeping that lasted from a few minutes to an hour. To complicate matters, Swiss authorities were reluctant to release the body until there had been a complete investigation. A hasty transatlantic call to Mark was followed by a peremptory cable from Bobby DeStefano to a banker in Zurich; this secured the release of Kay's body within eight hours. But before Page could take actual possession, it was necessary for him to view the remains.

When the coroner pulled back the white sheet, Page regarded the carnage before him. Kay's head had been split open like a grapefruit with brains smeared about like dough. Her jaw and

teeth were crumpled up into the cranium, forcing the eyes out of
the sockets, and there was a coating of dried blood and matted
patches of scalp and hair everywhere. To compound the horror,
she had been squashed like a tomato by the 4000 foot fall, and in
order to free the body from the wreckage, welders had literally to
leave her decapitated and quartered like a chicken, with jagged
white bone fragments sticking out of the flesh. At the sight of it,
Page promptly threw up on the tiled floor of the morgue.

There had been a lot to be said against Kay during her lifetime;
she was spoiled, domineering and mean. But he wouldn't wish
that end to any life, especially the misguided girl he'd married and
spent fourteen years of his life with for better or worse. It was a
grisly spectacle in the morgue drawer, one that was to haunt his
consciousness for weeks, becoming yet another element to compound the guilt of Devereaux Page.

'Did you see Mommy?' little Johnna asked him. He nodded.
'How does she look, Daddy?' Gelsey, in tears, wanted to know.

'She's – she's sleeping peacefully,' Page lied, and suddenly
hugged his two children to him so they wouldn't see his tears.

They flew back to New York on the Swissair 747 evening flight
that left Geneva at 6.00 PM. Fortunately the huge aircraft was not
crowded, so they had a small section with four seats across curtained off to themselves. The girls were frightened about what was
going to happen to them. Would they be able to keep the house
in Brookville? Would Daddy come out and live in the house
with them? Very early in the flight, Page realized that the girls
were somewhat suspicious of him; at the same time, they had no
one else to turn to. Whether Kay had consciously poisoned their
minds, or whether all the bitterness of the divorce had seeped
through involuntarily, Page didn't know. But it was soon evident
he had to do a selling job on himself. And this time, there was no
Steve Loomis with the words or Jack Leokum with the technique.
There was no faking the sincerity or bombing out with this audience.

He began by telling them that his life had changed radically
since they last saw him. In fact, things were so different he probably
wasn't the same man they knew. Gelsey furrowed her brow, and
Johnna, red-eyed from crying, looked at him through her horn-
rimmed glasses. As they knew, he said, he had been in politics for

the past four months and was running for mayor of New York City. He was famous now. When he walked down the street, strangers recognized him and stopped to shake his hand. His pictures were all over New York and he was on television a lot. Reporters were always following him around asking for quotes, and he spent all his time giving speeches and meeting people.

'Do you want to be mayor of New York?' Gelsey asked.

Page didn't answer directly. He said a group of people had asked him to run. As he started campaigning and travelling around the city, for the first time in his life he saw how other people lived. He saw slums and hunger; there were children who didn't have proper clothing or good schools. The city was dirty, and there was so much crime, people were scared to go outside their houses. And as he went around the city, he began to see all the things that could be done to make it a better place, and he had come to believe that maybe he could change things.

'Can we come live with you when you're the mayor, Daddy?' Johnna wanted to know. She was crying again.

'You are going to come live with me right now,' he reassured her 'The three of us will be together from now on.'

Later, after dinner, the stewardess removed the armrests from between the seats so the girls could stretch out and sleep. Page sat across the aisle keeping a silent vigil. He wanted to be near them in case they woke up and wanted something.

Across from him, Johnna tossed and moaned slightly. Page arose to put the blanket back up around her shoulders. Nine-year-old Johnna was a little thing, chubby with buck teeth and very nearsighted. Gelsey, at thirteen, had slimmed way down to where she had a boyish figure with narrow hips and beginning breasts. Both girls wore their brown hair straight and long, below the shoulders. Of the two, little Johnna was the more outgoing, with a kind of bubbly personality; Gelsey was quiet, almost distant sometimes.

He thought of the accident again. How could it have happened? Kay was a superb driver, one who took almost sexual pleasure in the smooth operation of an automobile, much as the women in Ian Fleming's novels; unlike James Bond's women, however, driving was about the only sexual pleasure Kay ever got. But Kay knew that road; she and Dev had driven it on their honeymoon, and again ten years later. Maybe a tyre blew. Or she could have fallen asleep at the wheel. Or something. Page closed his eyes and slept fitfully, only to waken an hour later in a cold sweat. In the recent brawling scramble for votes and the sudden, almost surreal trip to Switzerland, he had forgotten completely about Mia DeStefano. Jesus, how would he explain that one to the girls, let alone to Bobby or the electorate? He loved Mia, but as of now there was no place in his life for a woman. Yet, could he simply cut Mia off? He shook his head. More and more his life was beginning to look like a daytime soap opera.

Although there was no announcement of Devereaux Page's return to New York, the press had smelled out his arrival. Fifty newsmen and camera crews were milling around on the sidewalk in front of the International Arrivals building at Kennedy Airport. Mark Altschul and P.J. were waiting just outside the door of the customs room. With them were two old friends of Kay's from Brookville, Peggy and Stu French, who once had also been close to the candidate. Stu, a rotund, black-haired man with pudgy red cheeks was treasurer of the National Horse Show; Peggy French, tall and deeply tanned, with a regal nose and hatchet face, was co-chairman of the Cerebral Palsy Ball. Both were in their forties, and both spoke with their jaws and teeth tightly clenched. When Page left for Switzerland, Mark had telephoned around and found the Frenches who volunteered to handle the funeral arrangements. They now saw Page for the first time in months as he came out of customs, and like everyone else who had known him before the campaign, were shocked at the changes politics had wrought – the deep-etched lines in his face and the sunken eyes that bespoke his perpetual fatigue. When Page saw them, tears began to well in his eyes. He embraced Peggy, then Stu, and said simply, 'Thank you for coming. You don't know what this means to me.'

'Are you all right, Dev?'

Page nodded. 'And thank God the girls are all right.'

The Frenches greeted Gelsey and Johnna with hugs while Page shook hands with Mark and P.J. 'How was it?' Mark wanted to know; he seemed quite agitated and upset.

'Grim. Really grim.'

'The press is outside and want a statement.'

'Won't those guys ever quit?' Page looked at Mark and saw a flicker of uncertainty in those cold black eyes.

'They want to know if you're still a candidate.'

'What do I tell them?' Page searched the faces of the six people around him, and instantly everyone knew this was not the old Dev Page, but a public man, a politician who looked at you directly with one eye while the other seemed to be focused on some distant scene yet to be played – in this case, a statement to the press.

'Do you want to be mayor of New York, Daddy?' Gelsey again asked.

'It's something I think I have to do,' he said.

'Don't do it, Dev,' Peggy French said. 'Don't do it for the sake of the girls.'

'If it's important to you Daddy,' Gelsey said firmly, 'then do it.'

He looked at Johnna, small and round, her hair in pigtails now. Johnna blinked back through her thick glasses. 'What do you say, Johnna?'

'All we want is to come live with you, Daddy.'

Page dropped to his knees and hugged the girls to him. 'It's going to be very rough on all us us,' Page said. 'Especially you girls.'

'Maybe it'll help keep our minds off what happened to Mommy,' said Gelsey fighting back her tears.

Page nodded and arose slowly. 'I'll be back,' he promised, and went out to face the press.

During the two days immediately preceding the funeral, which was to be on Saturday, Page stayed in one of the guest rooms of the big house he and Kay had shared for thirteen years. It was frankly eerie. In the morning he woke up to find Jennie, the children's governess ever since Gelsey was an infant, bringing him breakfast in bed just as she always had on Saturday and Sunday mornings. A hefty Norwegian woman, Jennie spent all her spare time in front of a colour television set knitting incredible cable-stitch sweaters of Indian cashmere which she would give as presents to members of the family. Even after Page was divorced, he received one every Christmas.

At a brief meeting at the house with the trustees – Manhattan lawyer Ray Khan who had handled Kay's divorce and a rather stiff young vice-president of the Fiduciary Trust – it was decided that the big house in Brookville would be kept going, servants and all, so that the girls would feel the security of a familiar home. Curiously, of all the former friends and relatives Page saw during that week, Kahn, whom he personally detested, was the only one who encouraged him to go on with the campaign 'Kay was very protective of the girls,' he told the candidate. 'It might be good for them to see a little bit of the other side of life. It never hurt the Kennedy children.'

It was further agreed that Page was to receive $5000 a month from the $20 million trust fund. Out of that he had to maintain an apartment in town and pay for food and clothes for the girls. Jennie would continue to live with them full time, but her salary plus extraordinary expenses such as the girls' tuition and doctor bills would be paid directly out of the trust funds. Mark had already rented a four-bedroom apartment in Page's building and was about ready to hire a decorator; but the candidate reminded him they might all be moving to a big white house on the East River in January. So the new apartment was furnished simply but well. In two weeks, the girls would start at Brearly, one of the finest, most exclusive girls' schools in the city.

For Page, those two days in the old house were a nightmare. While the press hung around outside the grounds, Page found himself imprisoned in his past. A steady stream of former friends trooped through to pay their respects. To a person, they implored him not to continue with the campaign 'for the sake of the girls, Dev. You owe them something, you know.' Others, with a gesture to Kay's house, asked how he could expect Gelsey and Johnna to give up all this for a dingy apartment in New York City; to which he replied that Gracie Mansion wasn't really that dingy.

Not only was he resentful of all the gratuitous advice, but acutely aware that this whole crowd was unchanged in the two years he had stopped seeing them; on the other hand he, Page, was developing into an entirely new human being. Bluntly put, he had outgrown them. They prattled on about the club and the horse show, while his concerns were with the big issues – narcotics, crime and the poor. In the words of the great American novelist, Page found you can't go home again.

Kay's funeral at St. John's of Lattingtown Episcopal Church in Locust Valley was well attended by all the social types who had already come to the house to pay their respects. In addition, there were Kay's few relatives from Pittsburgh and a contingent of friends from New York City. The press was also there in force, ghoulishly recording the whole scene and asking anyone who happened by for a quote. Even Gabe Pressman, the best known local television reporter in the New York area, came out to narrate the proceedings for WNEW-TV news. With his black plastered-down hair and jowly face, Pressman always seemed to Page to typify television news at its worst. When he tried to interview Gelsey as she was leaving the church, it prompted Page to say to him, 'You'd stick that microphone under the nose of Jesus Christ on the cross, wouldn't you, Gabe? You'd ask him which hurt more, the nails in his hand or his feet.'

Page returned to the campaign trail on Monday. Gelsey and Johnna turned out to be game little campaigners, trotting along behind the candidate as he swept through crowds of well-wishers and autograph seekers. The 'television event' staged for the benefit of the early evening news programmes was a tour of the Coney Island Aquarium where Johnna was photographed shrieking with delight at the giant white beluga whales. Later Gelsey stood on a wooden platform while the trained porpoises leaped high out of the water and took food from her hand. To the viewing audience, it was a father on an outing with his daughters with everyone having a lot of fun. After visiting the sixteen new headquarters in an exhausting whirl of speeches and handshaking, they headed home to the new apartment on 57th Street. Page flipped on the tiny television set in the campaign car, and they all saw themselves on ABC news. Johnna was so excited she wet her pants. When they got back to the apartment, Jennie was there with a good hot supper all prepared for the girls, and Page spent an hour alone with them, as he was determined to do every night of the campaign thereafter.

Naturally there was criticism, especially from the other candidates' campaign offices, that Page was exploiting his children for political gain. But whenever the question came up, he said simply that he had made a commitment to the eight million people of New York and that his daughters understood this. And although they would never forget their mother, Page explained, these outings did take everybody's mind off the terrible tragedy, as well as being a terrific educational experience. In fact, as the candidate, he was spending a lot more time with his children than if he had a nine-to-five job. Furthermore, both girls would be starting school the next week, so they would be on a very regular schedule during the week. Any campaigning they did would be confined to weekends only. What Page didn't say was that if he dropped out of the campaign, he would probably be on the bottom of Eastchester Bay wearing a pair of cement shoes.

Bobby and Mark were persuaded to allow Page a full hour with the girls – from six to seven every night – a set time in his busy schedule that was inviolate, no matter how urgently he was needed elsewhere. For the first time in the campaign, he was guaranteed a short period to relax, have a drink, and recharge his batteries by forgetting about politics and completely devoting himself to the girls and their day in school. By having that break in the day, Page found he could drive himself even harder on the stump, and in no time was even more effective a performer than before. This was an hour they all came to treasure, and at the end of it, when the buzzer from downstairs signalled the car was waiting, Page reluctantly kissed the girls good night and returned to the grind of trying to get elected.

Chapter 22

It took Page a day or two to get back into the routine of the campaign. Jack Leokum returned to travelling with the candidate in order to critique his speeches, and in no time they were back up to the old standard. After Page's trip to Switzerland with all the attendant press coverage, the size of the crowds who turned out to hear and see him just about quadrupled. Everywhere the Page motorcade went, he was greeted by a large and sympathetic audience. Whether the people came to hear what he had to say or just to stare at him mattered little. The important fact was he was drawing crowds. What's more, his concentration was better, his timing more precise, and there was a little more ring in his voice. He was not only drawing crowds, he was beginning to touch them with his rhetoric.

It wasn't in Mark's game plan to bother with the minorities: the blacks made up only about 14 per cent of the vote; the Puerto Rican segment was even smaller – 7 per cent. This was not a constituency Page's advisors cared about. The Jews, the Irish, and the Italians were far more important. Although there were Page headquarters in the ghetto areas, these were only to head off a confrontation with the new breed of self-styled black revolutionaries who had sprung up in the mid-sixties and elbowed aside the moderates such as Martin Luther King and Whitney Young. The fact was, people were tired of Negroes and their rights; no one knew what they wanted any more.

Page himself had no feeling for blacks or Puerto Ricans. During the two weeks devoted to narcotics, the campaign through the ghettos was the first time Page had ever moved through the houses of the poor and examined the way they lived. To be sure, he had always had a natural sympathy for such people; that was not something one acquired suddenly on the road to Damascus. But he didn't relate to them. And after that early incident up in

Harlem where Jesse Jones led a contingent of militants who had totally demolished his new headquarters, he had been completely turned off.

It was to everyone's astonishment then that Devereaux Page became the hero of the ghettos. It happened during that first week after his return from Switzerland; the campaign entourage of three cars was returning to Manhattan from the last stop of the night. They were driving through the Bedford-Stuyvesant section of Brooklyn, a slum much poorer than Harlem, the place where people land when they fall out of Harlem. Some 500,000 people – about the same population as Kansas City or Cincinnati – were jammed into 500 square blocks. Humanity was so thick you could stir it with a stick. Suddenly in the middle of a trash-strewn block they came upon a building on fire. The fire engines and police were just arriving, sirens screaming, bells and whistles blaring. Blacks were pouring out of the adjoining buildings, and the scene was one of total confusion, bordering on bedlam. The car had stopped, and Page, acting on an irresistible impulse to help somehow, leaped out without warning before anybody could restrain him, pushing through the crowds toward the burning building. Mark and P. J. got out of the car to follow him, as did the campaign aides in the other two cars. It was an incredibly hot night, and the stench of garbage and sweat was soon overpowered by the smell of smoke from the fire. Pushing and shoving their way through the throngs of black spectators blocking the street, past police and firemen who were trying to get people out of the way so the hoses and ladders could be brought through, Mark and P. J. finally arrived in front of the burning building. The orange flames from the top-floor windows licked out at the black sky with an ugly crackling sound, casting an eerie light that danced on a sea of black faces beaded with sweat and wide-eyed with fear. Adding to the whole grotesque scene was the rhythmic high-intensity light show of the emergency vehicles – the vicious red of the fire engines and the blue and green lights of the police vans. As Mark and P. J. broke through to the cleared area directly in front of the burning brownstone, they came upon a startling tableau – a painfully thin black woman perhaps in her thirties, in a torn and dirty nightgown kneeling on the drenched sidewalk, surrounded by a half dozen black children, all of them shrieking and crying for help. In their midst was Devereaux Page, squatting with one arm around the woman, the other around as many of the children as he could gather to him. He was trying desperately to comfort them, saying, 'Please, please, the firemen are going to put out the fire. Everything will be all right. Please don't cry.'

It was obvious from the size of the conflagration that everything was not going to be all right. The top two floors were alive with flames; timbers and burning curtains were cascading into the streets nearby. An unholy scream came from inside the tenement next door, and a tiny black face appeared in one of the first-floor windows – a child trapped within. Without a moment's hesitation, Page sprinted up the steps of the rude brownstone, and darted inside, appearing moments later with a tiny screaming boy in his arms. The child's only garment was a pair of white underpants which vividly contrasted with the tar black body and Page's dark suit. The candidate stood for a moment at the top of the stairs, swaying slightly as though dazed, and then slowly descended to the sidewalk where he rejoined the hysterical family group; still holding the child in his arms, he tried again to calm them down. As Mark came up to them, Page looked up at him and shouted, 'These people are completely burned out. Get money! We've got to help!'

Mark looked at the candidate, not comprehending his words. 'Are you all right, Dev?'

'Of course I'm all right!' he snapped. 'How much money do you have on you?' The heat and noise from the fire were overpowering. Mark fumbled in his pocket and found a few ten-dollar bills and some singles. 'Don't you understand?' Page cried. 'These people are completely burned out! Ruined! They need help! Go back to the cars and get as much money as you can. We'll pay everybody back.'

Mark turned dumbly and pushed his way back through the press of spectators, returning five minutes later to find Page and the burned-out family gone from the front of the buildings. Racing around the fringes of the crowd, he found them seated on the steps of a building across the street, Page in the centre with his arm around the crying woman and a group of black children hanging around his shoulders. Between Jimmy the Dwarf, P. J., and Johnny DiSantis, Mark had collected close to $600 cash. He started to give the fistful of bills to Page who waved it away, saying, 'Give it to this lady. Give it to this lady!' Mark pushed the money at her, and she was so startled that it fell into her lap and fluttered over the stoop where she was sitting. 'Pick it up!' Page ordered the children. 'Pick it up and give it to your mother!'

A quarter-hour later Page was still sitting with the family. Across the street, their house was being flooded by great streams of water from a half-dozen hoses; smoke and steam were hissing out of the dancing orange flames into the black sky. The woman was silently rocking back and forth, the candidate's arm still around her shoulder, mutely watching the devastation on the other side of the street. By now some friends of the woman had come up and were adding their words of comfort to the children. Several recognized the candidate and cried, 'God bless you, Mr Page.' At length Page stood up. Huddled around him on the stoop were poor blacks – women and children – clutching one another, while the candidate, his hand still on the cheek of the woman beside him, shook his head in sorrow. 'You'll take care of her, won't you?' he pleaded to another woman nearby. 'Please take care of them and give them a place to stay.' Slowly he descended the steps to the sidewalk. A little black girl, not a member of the family, was standing on the bottom stop. Her hair was done in spit curls and she peered up at him through thick glasses. Their eyes met, and Page suddenly knelt down and hugged her. 'My little girl has glasses just like yours,' he said. Then he arose and with Mark at his elbow, was led back to the waiting campaign car a block away. As he pushed through the teeming crowds of curious onlookers, they reached out to touch him. Some knelt as he passed by; others burst forth and hugged him. 'Take care of that poor woman,' Page kept telling them. 'Take care of the children. They need help.' As the candidate walked towards the car, the crowds parted to let him pass. Jimmy the Dwarf was waiting with the rear door opened, and before getting into the car, Page turned to shake some hands and reach out to touch the grateful throng. Then he was inside the car, tears streaking his smoke-blackened face, repeating over and over again, 'Those poor, poor people. I've got to do *something*'.

It was old-fashioned luck that Johnny DiSantis had been in the second car and had just finished loading his Bolex with a new roll of colour film. Arriving on the scene, he opened the lens to the widest f stop and began filming just as the candidate emerged from the doorway with the black child in his arms, and he kept the camera rolling as Page descended the stairs to the street and knelt with the frightened family. The film was processed and delivered to the television news departments at 4.00 AM; it made the 'Today' programme, and all the evening news broadcasts. The next day, when interviewed by the press, Page said modestly, 'I wasn't a hero. I did what anybody would do in the circumstances. I only wanted to help out. I'm glad I was able to get to that child in time.'

Overnight, Page had become the saviour for the people of the ghetto – the poor, the culturally deprived, the black and the tan.

To a wildly cheering throng in Co-Op City in the Bronx the following evening, Page announced his Citizens Emergency Relief Fund, which later became known as CERF. Any needy family who was turned out of their home by an act of God – fire, explosion, flood – was eligible for an instant cash payment out of the campaign funds to help them buy food and clothing and find lodging. A directive, he said, had gone out to each of his 67 storefront headquarters to be on the alert for any personal tragedies such as the one he came upon the preceding evening and to notify his headquarters at the Commodore. A car with cash would be dispatched immediately at any hour of the night or day. The Citizens Emergency Relief Fund was to be given the highest priority and would be available in response to the request of any of his district campaign managers, no questions asked. Furthermore, if elected, he would see that a certain portion of the city budget was set aside for this operation. It was his intention to try to counteract the random evil of the city with a programme for random good. Speaking to a crowd of several thousand gathered outside the massive high-rise complex of middle-income housing, Page pulled a Richard Nixon trick out of his hat by putting words in the mouths of his political opponents (who in actuality had nothing but praise for the citizen candidate's actions):

There are those who will say that what happened last evening and the Citizens Emergency Relief Fund we're setting up today were done for purely political motives.

This is true.

The purpose of politics, as I see it, is not to seize power, but rather to create a government dedicated to truth, to justice, and to the value of a single human life.

In just about every speech I have made in this campaign, I have criticized our congressmen and state legislators for their do-nothingism. As a result, I have been accused of being a one-issue candidate.

I stand before you now and agree with that charge: I am a one-issue candidate.

Now let us call that one issue by its rightful name. That issue is Humanity. [*Cheers*].

That night when Page returned home, he found among the telephone messages Jennie had taken that Mia DeStefano had called. It was past midnight when he dialed her private number in New Jersey. At the sound of his voice, Mia began to sob hysterically on the other end of the line. 'Dev, what's to become of us?' she cried.

'What do you mean, sweetheart?'

'So much has happened since – since we were together.'

'I know. I've got the girls now, so we're going to have to cool it for a while.'

'Dev, I'm pregnant!' she said desperately. 'I'm going to have your child. You've got to help me.'

The candidate was suddenly weak in the knees; his head felt as though a tuning fork had been struck in his brain. 'Jesus, Mia, are you sure.'

'Am I sure?' she whimpered. 'Oh yes, yes!'

Page was silent. The obvious solution at this point was an abortion. His life had changed so radically over the past two weeks, with Kay's death and the girls coming to live with him, that he simply didn't have time to cope with Mia. Yet she had been there when he needed her; he couldn't abandon her to the abortionist's table. At some point he would have to face up to his love for her and to Bobby DeStefano's wrath. 'Look, it's only seven weeks to the election,' he said. 'Can you fake it till then? Once I'm the mayor, I can get away with marrying you.'

'You don't understand. It's almost four months. I'm swelling. The baby is showing. Help me, Dev!' She was crying into the phone. 'You've got to help me.' She hung up.

How would Bobby DeStefano react to the news that he was

going to become a grandfather? Page shuddered and poured himself a Wild Turkey. How would the electorate take the news that the new hero of the cities, the inconsolate widower, the bachelor father, was really a cocksman, a dirty old violator of young girls? Page winced. Yet out in New Jersey, and very much alone, was Mia, whom he loved and to whom he felt he owed a great deal. But what to do about it? He shrugged and after pouring another Wild Turkey, vowed to think it through at some point. Mia could wait until after the election. Meanwhile, there were calls to make – to newsmen, columnists, workers, contributors, who expected to hear from him no matter how late the hour. As the daily schedule became more crammed with events, and as more people rallied to his side, Page began conducting more and more business over the phone from his apartment at all hours. His time alone with Gelsey and Johnna was being cut into. The schedules became tighter. The pressures were mounting.

Page seldom needed coaching any more on how to make a speech. Leokum, preoccupied with corporate clients, came along only occasionally – once or twice a week – in the campaign car. For the most part, Mark had only to hand Page the 3×5 cards minutes before each appearance, and the candidate would know how to handle it, remembering the names of the key people, the main concerns of the audience, and exactly what to say. He and Mark conversed like two computers as Page concentrated on absorbing vast quantities of information, sorting it, and feeding it back on call.

Page had come a long way from his aloof, distant demeanour in the early days of his quest for the mayoralty. Now he rather enjoyed the physical contact with crowds. He learned how to enter a room like a big man, with a serene sense of his own importance, shoulders back, chest out, winning smile flashing. Before each appearance, he would wait until the introduction was over, and then walk slowly through the assembled throng to the podium, letting the applause sweep over him while the people in his path reached out to shake hands and touch him. Every speech was preceded by a massive case of stage fright. His hands trembled uncontrollably whenever he was being introduced, but once the applause for him began, it seemed to fill him with confidence, and his speeches went off without a hitch. The polls, both those of his own organization and outsiders, showed him running well behind the party regulars who were his opponents; but he was gaining all the time. When Kay was killed, with all the ensuing coverage, voter awareness jumped ten points, and there was an attitude shift in his favour of four points; following the fire in Bedford-Stuyvesant, the polls went up another five points, with a startling sixteen-point rise in the ghettos.

As he gained experience and confidence on the campaign trail, life at home became more tense. Gelsey and Johnna, enrolled at Brearly, saw their father all too seldom. Jennie, the family retainer, older and fatter than when she was engaged almost fourteen years before, had neither the energy nor the patience to discipline the girls. Both became unruly and disobedient. Johnna threw at least one tantrum a day; Gelsey all too often spent hours alone in her room sulking. Page tried desperately to establish some home life for himself and the girls during the one-hour break he got at night, but he was really too preoccupied with campaigning to be an effective father. In addition, there were nightly calls from Mia, each more hysterical than the last, wanting him to make a decision for either marriage or abortion.

Then one night Page returned home late to find Mia at the apartment waiting for him. There were tears and kisses and then she hiked up her skirt to show him how she had begun to swell. Page, bewildered and tired from the day's campaigning, wished to hell she would go away so he could get some sleep; but she stayed, insisting he make a decision one way or the other. More than once she called him an abject coward for not going to face Bobby with the fact that they wanted to get married.

'Don't you love me, Dev?' She looked at him earnestly.

'I guess I do,' he replied glumly. 'Honestly, I'm so tired, Mia, I don't know anything any more.'

Mia began to cry, and Page, pressured into it by a monumental sense of guilt coupled with revulsion at the idea of abortion of his child, finally agreed to see Bobby. Besides, Mia was so hysterical that he feared Gelsey and Johnna would wake up which would mean a lot of explaining; in his state of total exhaustion, that was one scene he did not care to play at the moment.

Mia finally left, and the citizen candidate slept fitfully.

When Page awoke the following morning, marriage to Mia didn't seem like a bad solution. She could move into the apartment and help cope with the two girls who desperately needed more attention than he had time to give or Jennie was capable of. The marriage could take place in a quiet ceremony, and after the election, the secret could be let out. He called Mark to say he wanted to have a meeting with Bobby DeStefano at the Commodore, and it was arranged.

Bringing bad news to Bobby DeStefano with that terrible temper of his was a dicey proposition at best; only a fool would ask to marry his pregnant daughter and expect to come away without deep and lasting scars.

Chapter 23

Page and Bobby had not seen each other face-to-face in over a month, although they'd spoken a number of times on the phone. During that period, a great deal had happened to change Devereaux Page. As a candidate, he had finally learned how to move audiences of any size. Whether he was talking to one person or a thousand or ten thousand, he had power over people. There was an overwhelming presence about the man; as with any celebrity, wherever he went, people's eyes riveted onto him. And his confidence was infectious. Minor snafus like a lost advance man or being hopelessly late for an appearance could cause Mark to grind his teeth in rage, thus setting everyone in the campaign car on edge. It would be Page who would toss off a quick remark that would calm things down. In short, it was a different Page who went to ask for Mia's hand in marriage. Here, indeed, was a leader who might well be the next mayor of New York City.

It was not Bobby DeStefano's custom to rise for anybody, but when the candidate was ushered into the big sitting room with the deep carpet and the modern leather furniture, Bobby rose up out of his big leather chair and came around the curved desk to greet Page. Johnny DiSantis and P.J. also snapped to attention when the candidate came in.

Page and Bobby greeted each other warmly, firmly clasping hands and arms. 'You're doing a great job, Dev, just great,' Bobby told him. 'Every day the polls look better and better.'

'You've put together a great campaign organization,' the candidate replied with a smile. He was at ease with Bobby. Instead of feeling owned by the Mob, as he had so many times before, Page felt completely equal if not a bit superior to Bobby. One was the candidate, the other the guiding genius. They were a team. Bobby gestured for Page to sit on the long black leather sofa that faced his curved desk while he slid into the big matching easy chair across from him. They were separated by the large coffee table with kidney-shaped glass top and polished ebony base. P. J. and Johnny DiSantis were standing at parade rest on either side of the room. Page got to the point immediately. 'Bobby, I want to get married.'

'You what?' DeStefano sat forward, pushing a wavy lock of brown hair away from his forehead. He stared at the candidate intently, his bony face with the big Adam's apple and bent nose an expressionless mask.

'I want to get married,' Page repeated. 'I have my daughters living with me, and frankly they need supervision which I can't give them. They're like wild Indians. So it makes sense for me to have a stepmother for them.' The candidate was positive in his approach, as though he were arguing for legalized heroin or a federal takeover of welfare.

Bobby suddenly relaxed and smiled. 'That's great,' he said. 'I've been after Mark to find you a wife for months. Jesus, we've come up with some of the most eligible broads in New York, but you wouldn't have any of it.'

'Well, I've met somebody, and we want to get married.'

'That's great! Let's have a drink on that!' Bobby was suddenly on his feet. 'P.J., make Mr Page and me a drink to celebrate. What are you drinking, Dev?'

'No drink before an appearance,' Page replied. 'It dulls the perception, and takes the edge off.'

Bobby wheeled around to face Mark who was sitting in a small chair by the door. 'Jesus, Mark, the polls will go up another five points. Think of the coverage!' The campaign manager stared blankly back. 'Who is she, Mark?' Bobby wanted to know. 'What do you think of her?'

Mark shrugged. 'This whole thing is news to me.'

'Who is she, Dev?'

The candidate smiled confidently. 'Mia.'

'Mia –?'

'Your daughter Mia. We want to get married.'

'*What!*' Bobby suddenly stiffened. His eyes flashed. 'What the hell do you mean by that?' His reedy nasal voice took on a steel edge.

'Mia and I have been seeing each other on and off for the past four months. We're very much in love, and we want to get married.

'Mia's marrying Paulie Coppola!' he snapped.'What the hell do you mean, you've been seeing each other for the past four months!' The room was suddenly charged with Bobby's anger. P.J. edged forward slightly; Mark slumped in his chair, putting his head in his hands. 'Well?' Bobby shouted.

'Look, Bobby, Mia and I are in love,' Page said confidently. 'It's barbaric to think you can arrange your daughter's marriage in this day and age – especially to a fat little turd like Paulie. Anyway, we need each other, and we want to get married.'

In an instant, Bobby was at the candidate's throat, yanking him upright by his necktie and spinning him backwards over the glass coffee table and onto the floor where Bobby leaped onto Page's chest. Grabbing him by the ears, he began pounding the candidate's head into the thick carpet. 'You son of a bitch!' he was shouting. 'You fuckin' little son of a bitch! Just who the fuck do you think you are!'

P.J. dove at them from across the room, pulling Bobby off the fallen candidate. 'Take it easy, Lieutenant!' P. J. soothed. 'Cool it. Nothing's going to be solved this way.'

Bobby continued to shout obscenities. 'You goddamn little WASP asshole! I wouldn't let you marry my daughter if she were three months pregnant and you were the father!'

'It's more like four,' Page said weakly from the floor.

'*What*?'

'Mia is four months pregnant. We *have* to get married.'

Bobby was suddenly hysterical, screaming and cursing and thrashing at P.J. Johnny DiSantis rushed over to help keep Bobby down until the fit passed; if P.J. and Johnny hadn't been there, Dev Page would have been a dead man. Instead, he was very much alive and quite controlled. Page got to his feet and stared down at the young Boss who was being pinned by his two bodyguards. 'I've been through these histrionics with you before, Bobby, and frankly, I'm too tired for violence.'

'You little fuck!' Bobby snarled. 'I'll kill you!'

'Kill me if you like,' the candidate replied calmly. 'But it won't solve Mia's problem, and it certainly won't help elect me mayor of

New York, which you've already spent five million dollars trying to do.'

The candidate returned to his place on the big leather sofa and began rubbing his head where it had been punched into the carpet. On the floor before him Bobby DeStefano was shaking all over, his mop of brown hair in tousled disarray; little gurgling sounds came from his throat. At length he sucked his breath and said, 'Okay, guys, I'm all right now. I won't kill him.'

Gradually P. J. and Johnny DiSantis released the arms and legs and backed slowly away, leaving Bobby sitting in the middle of the room on the great blue-and-gold Persian carpet. 'You certainly know how to hurt a guy pretty good, Dev.'

'The point is, I'm a different Dev Page than the one you dragged out to New Jersey last April. I was like jelly then. You owned me. But I don't feel you own me any more.'

'Oh, you don't?' Bobby's voice dripped with sarcasm. 'Do tell me more, *Mister Page*.'

'There's not much more to tell. I've become a person. A positive personality. I think I could probably become mayor now without you and your Organization.'

Bobby got up off the floor slowly and stood in the centre of the room with his hands on his hips regarding the candidate. There was the faintest trace of a smile on his lips. 'Tell me, Dev, when did you first feel you could get along without us?'

'Oh, I don't know, really. I started getting my confidence a couple of months ago, and it's been building ever since.'

'Was it the robbery three months ago? Mark told me that the next day you called a meeting and outlined a comprehensive plan for narcotics. Apparently that was the first time you really began to act like a candidate.'

Page nodded. 'I'd say that was true.'

'Do you remember how you felt when you came home to find your apartment robbed?' the young Boss asked.

'I was suddenly mad as hell. I figured if they could get into a luxury building on Fifty-seventh Street, then nobody in the city was safe. And if I was going to be mayor, I had to do something it.'

'When you say "they," Dev, what do you mean?'

'What?'

'You said *they* got into a luxury building. Who is the *they* talking about?'

'The burglars. The narcotics addicts who got in and took all my stuff. They took everything that could be quickly sold off on the street – television, stereo, clothes, jewellery. The police were sure they were narcotics addicts.'

Bobby was smiling broadly. He gestured toward a door across the room. 'Take a look in that closet, Dev.'

'Don't do it, Bobby,' Mark said.

'Shut the fuck up.' He turned to the candidate. 'Go on, open that closet.'

'What's in it?' Page wanted to know.

'Just do as I say.'

'Bobby, for Chrissakes – ' Mark stammered.

The candidate crossed the room and pulled open the closet door. There, stacked on the floor, was every item that had been taken from the apartment three months before – the Sony colour TV, Scott stereo, jewellery box, even the liquor; all his clothes were hanging neatly from hangers on the cross bar. At first Page didn't comprehend what he saw. Finally he muttered, 'This is all my stuff. Where'd you find it.'

'*We* broke into your apartment and took it, Dev. Nick and Johnny and P.J. did the job. They paid off doorman and the janitor and simply carted the stuff out the service entrance.'

'You mean it wasn't junkies?'

'It wasn't junkies.'

Page shook his head in bewilderment. '*You* robbed me?'

'We robbed you. That's all your stuff right there.'

Page knelt down on the floor of the closet and examined the television set and ran his fingers over the turntable of the Garrard Zero 100 changer. Still confused, he separated the suits hanging from the cross bar, fingering the material and looking at the labels in disbelief. Even his maroon velvet smoking jacket with the black satin piping on the lapels was there. 'You mean you guys robbed me and then made me and the press and the police and everybody think it was junkies?'

'That's right, Dev. The polls jumped five points.'

'But that's – *that's dishonest!*'

The room suddenly rocked with the laughter from the on-lookers. The candidate was not amused. He slowly shut the closet door and turned to Bobby who was perched on the edge of his big round desk, weak with laughter. 'I tell you,' Page repeated, 'that was dishonest.'

All at once Bobby was deadly serious. He pointed a finger at the candidate. 'Now listen to me, you little son of a bitch. There's nothing that's happened in this campaign that we aren't directly responsible for. Do you think for a minute you could have learned to make a speech without Jack Leokum? *Do you?*'

'Well – no.'

'Or pulled the big crowds without Paul Berman? Or produced the campaign material without Lou Klein or the research without Jimmy Lee? Do you? *Do you?*'

Page drew himself up. 'Now just a minute –'

'You were nothing when we found you,' Bobby snarled. 'Everything that has happened in this campaign was directly caused by us, understand? Without us, you would still be nothing! Zero! A cipher!'

'I suppose you caused that fire in the tenement in Bedford-Stuyvesant just so I could go rescue that black kid.' There was the same smug expression on Page's face that Bobby remembered from his appearance before the cameras that first weekend in New Jersey.

'No, Dev, we didn't set that fire,' Bobby said slowly. 'But in the last couple of weeks we did learn one interesting fact.'

'What's that?'

'Your wife was one hell of a driver.'

'What do you mean?' Page was puzzled.

'Bobby! Jesus!' Mark shouted. 'Don't do it!'

Bobby dismissed Mark's explosion with a wave of his hand. 'I mean your dear dead Kay almost got away from us.'

'I don't understand –' The candidate was standing in the middle of the room shaking his head.

It was Bobby now, his arms folded across his chest, who wore the smug, cat-that-ate-the-canary smile. Directly beside Bobby's head was the shiny hemispheric desk lamp on the end of the fifteen-foot chromium pole that arched high across the room from a concrete block base. Bobby cupped the lamp in his right hand and savagely shoved it on a trajectory away from him; it caught Dev Page on the temple, sending him staggering into the far wall which he hit with a thump. His knees buckled and he slid to the floor. 'You . . . killed . . . Kay?' he asked, stunned. 'Oh Jesus. Oh, Jesus Christ . . . Oh, no . . . no . . . no . . .'

'We chased her ass all over that fuckin' mountain, and if she'd been driving anything but a big Mercedes, she'd have made it.' Bobby's lips were in a contemptuous sneer now. 'She wasn't exactly murdered, Dev. She missed a turn and went over the cliff by herself. But we'd have got her one way or the other. There was a contract out on her.'

'But the girls – they might have been killed too.'

'The contract said it was to look like an accident, and the girls were not to be harmed.'

'But why? Why would you do a thing like that?'

'You dumb little fuck! *It made news!*'

'But that's – '

'We wanted to get you married, but you turned down every broad we got for you. We had to do something.'

'But you don't go – killing people. Oh, my God!'

'The polls jumped five points in your favour. It was beautiful!'

There was a silence in the room, finally broken by a strangled sob from the candidate, then another and another, each one seemingly wrenched from his diaphragm and threatening to rend him to pieces. 'My God! My God!' The memory of Kay's broken and battered body was fresh again in his mind. 'I can't go on with this campaign knowing a thing like that,' he sobbed. 'I can't go on.'

'You shouldn't have told him, Bobby,' Mark said quietly.

Page looked up. His face was contorted with anguish. 'You knew about this too, Mark? You knew all along?' The campaign manager's face remained impassive except for the furious blinking of his eyelids. 'Jesus, Mark! I mean this is – *murder*. We could all go to jail!'

'Nobody's going to jail, Dev.'

'I can't – I can't go along with this,' Page said.

'What are you going to do about it, Mr Page?' It was P.J. who asked the question.

'Jesus, I don't know.' He put his head in his hands and began to sob again. 'I just can't believe it.'

'We own you, Dev,' Bobby said quietly. 'We own you body and soul, and don't you ever forget it.'

'You shouldn't have told him, Bobby,' Mark repeated. 'He's going to be no good as a candidate after this.'

'Nobody fucks around with my daughter and gets away with it!' Bobby shouted, and picking up a ceramic ashtray from the desk, he hurled it across the room where it narrowly missed the candidate and crashed into the wall, shattering, with the pieces burying themselves in the deep pile of the carpet. 'Nobody fucks around with Mia!' he screamed, his voice a full octave higher, making him sound like a wounded bird. 'Nobody! Not the mayor of New York! Not the President of the United States! Not God Almighty! Now get this sniveling fuck off the floor and out to his next stop before I kill him!'

Page remained on the floor unmoving.

'Up! Up! Goddammit!' Bobby shrieked. P.J. and Johnny DiSantis rushed over and pulled the stupefied candidate to his feet. 'Get him out of here!' Bobby ordered. 'Now!'

As they were dragging him across the room to the door, Page moaned, 'I can't go on . . . '

'The only reason you're alive is because I got such a big investment in you!' Bobby cried.

'It's a lie,' Page whimpered. 'I'm living a lie.'

'Wait a minute, guys!' Bobby shouted. They stopped and wheeled the stricken candidate around to face the young Mafioso. Bobby's cheeks were florid, and there were flecks of foam on his lips. 'Let's not talk about living a lie, Mr Page. For the past year you've been making a damn good income investing stolen cash and securities.'

'But – but if what you say about Kay is true, that's *murder*.'

'It's only a question of degree, isn't it? *Isn't it?*'

'But – murder –'

'When the stakes are this high, anything goes.'

'We're all in Rome, Dev,' Mark said quietly, 'and like it or not, we're all wearing togas.'

Page was silent, propped up by P. J. and Johnny DiSantis like an effigy of himself.

Bobby pointed a finger at the drooping figure by the door. 'You're going on with this campaign, and you're going on with it tonight as if nothing happened, understand?' There was no response. 'You'll do it, you little prick!' Bobby ranted on. 'You know why? Because I've learned a thing or two about politics this last couple of weeks. And one thing I've learned is the media and the press love personal tragedy. They revel in it like pigs in shit! And I'm telling you right now, if you show me one trace of giving up, I'll toss one of those brats of yours off the Brooklyn Bridge, and the polls will go up ten points!'

Page's whole body seemed to collapse; he would have slumped to the floor if he hadn't been supported on either side by the two bodyguards.

'Now get his ass out to the next appointment, or they'll find Gelsey's body floating around in the East River like a dead fish!'

P.J. and Johnny dragged the limp candidate backwards out the door which closed behind them. The special precision-lock mechanism clicked shut.

'You were rough on him,' Mark said, breaking the silence. Mark could not look Bobby in the eye.

'*Me* rough on *him*? Bobby jammed his hands in his pockets and strode angrily to the window. 'That weasling little fuck knocked up my daughter! I should have killed him on the spot.'

'What do you want me to do?' Mark asked in a monotone.

'Give him Librium and get his ass back on the campaign trail. What's the next stop?'

'A rally in Harlem.'

'Get him up there. The quicker he gets back into the campaign, the quicker his mind will be occupied with other things.'

'I still think you shouldn't have told him,' Mark said, getting up to go. 'It may wreck him.'

'He has to remember who's the boss. There are three rules which I've always operated by. One of them is never let a guy get too big for his fuckin' britches. That was happening to Page.'

'What are the other two rules?'

'Absolute loyalty up and down the ranks; and I never go after somebody else's territory.'

'That's bullshit. You're going after New York City, and that's the property of the five Families.'

'Mark, if Page gets elected, we'll have the police working for us, right? And we'll own the jails, won't we?'

Mark nodded.

'The first thing you're going to see is the biggest crackdown on organized crime in the history of this country. I'm going to round up every one of those gumbahs and greasers and moustache Petes and chuck them all in jail, and their lawyers are going right along with them. And the public will love it. Then the city won't belong to five Families. It will belong to one Family – *mine!*'

'Wait a minute, Bobby. When we made our agreement, you promised to help clean up this town, and there'd be no funny business.'

'Cleaning up this town means chucking Carlo and Tony and Joe Yacovelli in jail with all their henchmen.'

'You just implied you were going to take over the rackets.'

'Mark, how big is the city budget?'

'In round numbers, ten billion dollars.'

'How much of that is waste?'

'What do you mean?'

'On a city-wide basis, how much of that ten billion is pissed away in graft, corruption, fraud, inefficiency, double payments for the same lousy service? How much? Ten per cent? Twenty per cent? Give me a guess.'

'Thirty per cent, I'd say.'

'That's three billion dollars a year.'

'I'd say that's about right.'

'With that kind of money to play with, we don't need the rackets. We'll abolish the rackets. Believe me, there's a very nice profit to be made just by running this fuckin' city legitimately. The same is true for the country. Jesus, just turn me loose on the Pentagon and give me 10 per cent of what I save!'

Mark shrugged. 'I hope you're not shitting me.'

'Just get Page back on the campaign trail. Let him go on Librium for a while and then gradually reduce the dosages, and he'll be all right.'

At the door Mark turned. 'I hope you're levelling with me, Bobby. I couldn't live with myself otherwise.'

'Your job is to get him elected. And I meant what I said about tossing Gelsey into the East River. Make sure he knows that.'

Mark shuddered and left. Bobby, alone now, went to his big curved desk where he unlocked the top drawer and took out a black book to look up the number of his friend, the abortionist.

Chapter 24

The candidate was given six green-and-yellow Librium capsules and taken down the service elevator of the hotel. Jimmy the Dwarf was told to go twice around Central Park on the way to Harlem so the drug would have a chance to take effect. They rode in silence, the candidate staring mutely ahead, Mark and Johnny DiSantis on either side watching him intently. At last the candidate sighed aloud.

'How do you feel?' Mark wanted to know.

'I don't know.'

Mark ordered Jimmy the Dwarf to head for the Harlem rally and told P.J. in the front seat to turn on the car telephone; the advance man would be calling about the size and mood of the crowd. The mobile operator was paging them. It was Paul Berman and Lou Klein from the Commodore with news of another national tragedy: Jesse Jones, the black militant leader, had been shot by a sniper in Savannah.

'Jesus, is he dead?' Mark asked.

'Seriously wounded,' came Berman's voice crackling over the loudspeaker. 'They don't know whether he'll live. He's been taken to the hospital.'

'Who's Jesse Jones?' Page asked.

'Do you remember the black guy in Harlem who got the crowd all worked up, and they started heaving bricks through our headquarters? That's Jesse Jones.'

'Oh, Christ!' Page muttered. 'Another killing.'

'Does the crowd in Harlem know yet?' Mark asked Berman over the phone.

'It just happened minutes ago, so they probably don't.'

Mark looked out the window. They were stopped at 115th Street for a light. Ten blocks to go. 'You better get the hell up there quick,' Berman urged over the mobile phone. 'There's a chance Page can keep Harlem from going up in smoke.'

'You heard the man, Jimmy,' Mark shouted at the driver, and the white car leaped forward through the night. Mark turned to the candidate next to him. 'Now listen to me, Dev.' Page seemed in a daze. 'For Chrissakes, Dev, listen to me! This is perhaps the most important speech you'll ever have to give!'

The car raced and bucked through the streets while Mark instructed the candidate on how to handle the situation.

'Jesse Jones has been shot. We don't know if he's dead or not. But it could have a worse effect on the ghettos than the Martin Luther King assassination. Do you understand? Do you?' Page nodded. 'You have to tell them about it, Dev.'

'What do I say?'

'You give them BOMFOG. Can you remember that? BOMFOG.'

'What's BOMFOG?'

'The all-purpose speech. BOMFOG stands for the Brotherhood of Man under the Fatherhood of God. BOMFOG.'

Page repeated the acronym twice. 'Oh, God,' he muttered, 'why is the world like this?'

There was no time for an answer. The car careened around the corner of 125th Street and came to a screeching stop behind a wooden speaker's platform. The street had been cordoned off with sawhorses, and there were several thousand people gathered to hear the candidate. The night was stifling, with the overwhelming humidity that causes prickly sweat to trickle down the neck within minutes of emerging from an air-conditioned car or building. Page was hustled up the steps of the platform. A rock band was playing gospel music at a deafening level over the loudspeakers. Mark told the pianist to cease playing; an important announcement was about to be made. Then Mark went to the microphone. The music stopped. 'Ladies and gentlemen, your attention please. I want to introduce Devereaux Page.'

There was applause which began to swell and roll like a vast ocean of sound. It was an outpouring of affection for the man who had rescued a black boy barely a week ago, and had given hope to the poor with CERF – the Citizens Emergency Relief Fund. The raised wooden platform under Page's feet vibrated with cheers and applause, causing a warmth to surge through him, giving him renewed strength and purpose. 'Remember,' Mark shouted in his ear, 'Jesse Jones has been shot in Savannah. Give them BOMFOG, a prayer, and tell them to go home!'

Page nodded and stepped up to the microphone. The Librium had taken effect; his insides were calm, and it was as though he were in a dream. His gesture for quiet seemed almost like a papal blessing, causing the crowd to increase the pitch of their ovation. It was obvious they hadn't yet heard the news of the Jones shooting.

When there was quiet, Page looked out over the vast assemblage of blacks in the sweltering night air where the heat of the day was still rising from the garbage-lined pavement beneath. There were many men with tee shirts or naked to the waist, and women in halter tops and shorts. He could see sweat on the faces down front. And despair in their eyes which he knew he was about to add to. He started by asking everybody to kneel in prayer. 'Just get down on your knees right where you are. Get down before Almighty God.'

A murmur rippled through the crowd, but these people obeyed; they knew it was not a good idea to offend their Maker. Then Page drew the microphone to him; the cool steel of the stand felt good against his sweating palms. He spoke softly and slowly; the sound system magnified his words many times, echoing down the street in a kind of weird caricature of how he really sounded. In the distance there were police sirens and car horns.

We live in terrible times [he said]. Even though this is a free and democratic country, it seems we are powerless to determine our own destinies.

We all know the roll call of national tragedy by heart . . . John Kennedy . . . Martin Luther King . . . Robert Kennedy . . . and others. Now it is my sad duty to bring you news of yet another tragedy. Jesse Jones has been shot by a sniper in Georgia.

The entire street suddenly erupted in shouts of anger and disbelief. Many rose from where they were kneeling to shake their fists in frustration and shout 'No! No!' Page exhorted them to remain calm and finish hearing what he had to say. Where before the crowd was quiet, now there was an eerie recitative of moans, interrupted by occasional cries of anguish. Some on the fringe of the crowd broke away to run for their radios and television sets. Most remained kneeling. Page told them that he didn't know Jones' condition, but that he had been taken to a hospital in Savannah. Then he said:

Brothers and sisters, the Bible tells us there is a time to love and a time to hate, a time to win and a time to lose. It is natural that all of us should feel this is a time of loss and a time to hate.

But nothing in this life was ever accomplished by hate . . .

Right now I ask you not to hate, because hate triggers unreason and violence; and violence only undoes all the things Jesse Jones has tried to do in his life.

Instead, think with love about Jesse Jones and what he gave to this country and to his people, and be grateful to God Almighty that against all probable odds, Jesse Jones was conceived and born, and walked this earth, and was able to do the things he did in the time he had to do them.

And let us pray.

Page's voice faltered. He glanced down front and saw a black woman with a massive Afro hair-do, on her knees cradling an infant in her arms. She wasn't listening to him, but was dissolved in tears, her face buried in the baby's tiny form. A little black girl standing next to her was trying to give her comfort.

And let us pray for the recovery of Jesse Jones, and for the recovery of this sick, wounded country. And let us pray that someday all of us – black and white – rich and poor – men and women – Christian, Jewish, Atheist – can walk together, hand in hand, in the common Brotherhood of Man, under the Fatherhood of God. . . .

May I ask you all to remain on your knees in silent prayer for Jesse Jones and for his family. And then rise up quietly, calmly, and go back to your homes. . . .

And put your hands on your radio or television, and listen for the news and pray. And just as the news comes to you from Savannah, Georgia, where Jesse Jones is fighting for his life, so will your prayer carry up to God Almighty and down to Savannah, Georgia. We ask it in the name of the Father and the Son and the Holy Spirit. Amen.

Page turned from the microphone to find Johnny DiSantis panning the subdued crowd with his Bolex. Page tapped him on the shoulder. 'No more pictures, Johnny, okay?' Then the candidate moved to the front of the wooden platform and jumped down onto the street. There he began moving like a healer through the kneeling assemblage of blacks, gently touching their hair, stroking their cheeks, occasionally hugging a young child. From the platform loud speakers came the sound of a single deep contralto singing:

> We shall overcome
> We shall overcome
> We shall overcome some day.
> Deep in my heart
> I do believe
> We shall overcome some day!

It was one of those great gospel voices with that underlying tragic tremolo embodying four hundred years of despair. The clean, clear voice soared out and over the filthy, hot, close-packed street. Others took up the words, until by the end of the second chorus, virtually everyone was singing. Soon the entire throng was standing, hands joined, singing 'We Shall Overcome'; the candidate was surrounded by black people, most of them singing through their tears. He moved slowly, through the distraught, weeping crowd. There were no words of comfort in him now; he could only touch, and they in turn touched back, saying, 'God bless you, Mr Page,' and 'We love you.' Gradually the people did as he bade them and went quietly to their homes.

Back in the campaign car, Mark was elated. 'Boy, I've never seen BOMFOG work like that,' he crowed. 'Dev Page, you were fantastic!'

'Fuck off,' Page retorted quietly.

'Come off it, Dev. Jesse Jones was a bastard.'

'Those poor, wretched people,' the candidate muttered to himself. 'Oh, Christ!' He reached forward to turn on the tiny black-and-white Sony portable that faced them in the back seat, and watched the special report on the Jones shooting. The silver light filled the back seat of the car. The black leader had been shot in the neck and shoulder, and had died in a Savannah hospital. Page snapped off the set and all was dark again as they rode downtown. At length the candidate asked what the name of the song was they all sang at the end.

'Everybody knows that song, "We Shall Overcome".'

'It's – it's beautiful. Do people sing it a lot?'

'All the time. It's the great black freedom song.'

'Can you teach me the words?'

Mark nodded and shrugged in disbelief.

The Librium was at work on Page. With the motion of the car he felt a kind of euphoria, as though he were floating along through the city on a cloud. He spoke slowly, his lips barely moving; the words came out slurred, as though he were drunk. 'If somebody else but me had been up there on that platform when the news of the Jones shooting came, there could have been trouble.'

'You bet your ass there could have been trouble. There could have been a riot that swept Harlem like a tornado.'

There was a silence in the car. On the way downtown, they passed several police cars and fire engines, sirens screaming, their high-intensity roof lights spinning, speeding through the night toward Harlem.

'Even though you guys own me, it was better for the city that I was up there, and not some angry black whipping up a crowd.'

'That's for damn sure,' P.J. agreed from the front seat.

'What are you saying, Dev?' Mark asked.

'I hate you bastards. I hate you for what you did to Kay. And I hate you for the way you beat me up and the way you threaten to hurt my little girls –'

'Dev, we only –'

'Let me finish. I hate you bastards. But at the same time, because of you, *I am somebody*. Even with you evil people behind me, I was a force for good tonight, wasn't I?'

'Absolutely.'

'I hate you bastards. But I couldn't do it alone.'

'We're the only Organization that can change things, Dev. Never forget that. We've never been given any power; we've seized it. And naked power is the only thing that's going to make this city work again.'

'You won't make me a liar, will you?' Page looked over at Mark.

'What do you mean?'

'If I'm elected, you guys won't get in and screw the city worse.'

'There's no way it could be screwed worse.'

'You know what I mean.'

Mark stared absently out the window. They were passing the

Plaza Hotel, massive and spotlighted, a nineteenth century relic, incongruously surrounded by stark, soaring edifices of steel and glass. 'There's a good living to be made in running the city legitimately, Dev. We'll run it well. Efficiency is the first priority. Then, wherever possible, humanity.'

'I hope so,' the candidate sighed. 'Otherwise, I'd probably kill myself.'

'And leave Gelsey and Johnna to be the wards of Ray M. Kahn and the Fiduciary Trust?'

'Jesus, I don't know any more.'

They turned on to 57th Street. 'Hey!' Mark said suddenly. 'Where'd you get that idea for the people to put their hands on the radio and pray?'

'When you're running for office, you remember a lot of things – things that happened to you, and things that you learned. It's sort of as though my mind were – I don't know – bubbling and boiling like a great stew, and all kinds of memories come to the surface.

'We used to get a Negro station from Ohio when I was in college, and the preacher would tell everybody who was listening to put their hands on the radio and pray for sinners. Listeners sent in the names of people who were sinners, and all over the Midwest, people would put their hands on the radio and pray for them. We sent in the names of the president and the dean of Princeton, and by God, one night if they didn't say a prayer for those sinners in New Jersey, Harold Dodds and Bill Lippincott.'

The car pulled up in front of Page's building, and the campaign manager went upstairs with the candidate. The apartment was quiet; Jennie and the girls were in bed. In the bathroom, Mark found a bottle of Seconal. He returned to the living room with a glass and two red capsules. 'Take these, Dev. They'll help you get a good night's sleep.'

The candidate obeyed, popping the pills on to his tongue and downing them with the glass of water. He stood holding the empty glass in the middle of the room; he swayed slightly. It was obvious he was very groggy. 'I hated Kay,' Page said slowly. 'She was mean to me all the years we were married. There were lots of times I wished she was dead.'

Mark said nothing.

'Bobby shouldn't have told me what happened to her. That'll make a hell of a difference in the way I think.' He paused. 'Or maybe he should have told me. It'll keep me honest. Or dishonest. We're all dishonest, aren't we? We all wear togas, like you said.'

'The end will justify the means.'

'What about Mia?'

'Forget Mia. That's finished.'

Page kicked off his shoes and bent over to pull off his socks. 'Make me one promise, Mark.'

'What's that, Dev?'

'For God's sake, don't give me time to think about what's happening to me!' The candidate turned and stumbled into his bedroom.

When Mark Altschul first went to Bobby DeStefano with the proposal that the Syndicate was the only Organization that could run New York City, he hadn't figured on being a party to murder, which Kay's death most certainly was. Although he had not ordered it, nor was he even aware of it until after the fact, by continuing on as campaign manager, Mark was, in effect, an accomplice to a heinous crime. As a result, he awoke each morning with a distant ache in his gut. A Librium quelled it, and the pace and furor of each campaign day managed to make him forget the fact momentarily. Yet there were nights when he woke himself up screaming, and even with the air conditioning in his apartment on full, he would sweat profusely as he paced restlessly up and down, cursing the sleep that would not come. Almost nightly after he learned Kay's death had been by contract, he pondered the possibility of going to the *New York Times*, or to the United States Attorney with the whole story. But he would undoubtedly be disbarred and perhaps jailed for conspiracy. Worse, there would be an open contract on him, so there was nowhere in the world where he would be safe.

In essence, Mark Altschul was hoist by his own petard. As he had put it to the candidate, 'We're all in Rome, and we're all wearing togas.' For the campaign manager – a lawyer who knew perhaps better than anyone the difference between right and wrong – the toga had now become a kind of hair shirt.

Devereaux Page, too, woke up daily with a pain in his gut. He was trapped but good. But the presence of Gelsey and Johnna forced him to do as he was told to the best of his ability each day.

During the week, Gelsey and Johnna had been living in the apartment and attending the Brearly School for girls. On the weekend, they generally motored out with Jennie in Kay's limousine to the big house in Brookville where they could spend Saturday on horseback, returning Saturday evening to make campaign appearances with their father on Sunday. Page had three of Kay's horses brought into New York by van and stabled on West 89th Street. Every day when the weather was decent, he and the girls arose at first light and slipped away for a ride in Central Park. This was the private time for Page, and he relished it. The city was still silent, and the only sound was the hoofbeats on the dirt trails. The air was clear and cool; often there was dew on the grass. And as they rode, they could talk father-and-daughter things without the ever-present retinue of campaign aides and volunteers.

On the stump, Page ran to greet the crowds, savouring the adulation and exchange of electricity. Once he was before an audience, his timing was flawless. He had learned to read the faces of those down front while addressing his remarks to the listeners in the very back. No matter what his topic, he had in his repertoire a couple of dozen socko lines guaranteed to bring cheers and applause; these were dropped into each speech with the precision of a great matador working with a Miura bull that was charging straight and true. He gestured more, until in the final month of the campaign when he was making a speech, some part of him was always in motion. He waved his hands, hunched his shoulders, rocked on his heels as he cried out about the professional politicians, the waste, the graft and corruption, the need for decency and humanity in government.

Only on television did he revert to the old, quiet, charming Page who politely came on to the home screen to discuss some new issue in a professional bedside manner that radiated cool confidence and engendered total trust. But out on the stump, he seemed to toy with his audience as though it were a wounded animal. He could whip up the anger of a throng at will, and when they responded with their plaudits and chants of 'We . . . want . . .

Page!... We... want... Page!...' it seemed to send an electrical
charge through him; his words became magnets, drawing himself
and the people closer until at the end of his peroration, he would
plunge into the crowd, much the way Robert Kennedy had,
seeming to relish the pummelling, the jostling, the bumping of
people stripping away his cufflinks and necktie and mussing
his hair. This body contact was almost sexual in its intensity,
as though he were making up for the years of cool and aloof
women – first his mother and then his wife – by being grabbed
and shoved in a kind of huge, sweaty orgy of flesh against flesh.

From the low-key, hesitant approach of the early campaign,
he had become a charged personality. He began to move quicker,
until no one who described him ever said that he walked; the
usual expression was that 'Dev came running up.' As the pace
of the campaign quickened, the candidate became unable to
relax, even while eating and drinking. Often late at night in a
restaurant at the end of a gruelling day with Mark and several
aides, Page would suddenly empty his pockets of dozens of scraps
of paper on which were written notations of names and phone
numbers. Then, completely ignoring his food and his companions,
he would order a phone brought to the table so he could begin
calling people – columnists and commentators, local campaign
managers all over the city to whom he wanted to say thank you,
or ask about a problem, or just touch base. Suddenly ravenous
after not eating for hours, he would gobble up his own dinner, and
then pluck bits of food from other people's plates, still talking
furiously as he wolfed it down. Once, a headwaiter asked him
which dinner he wanted, to which he replied, 'The nearest.'

When Leokum was along, these late-night sessions were wild,
as the candidate and his coach nattered away at each other in a kind
of bizarre shorthand as they dreamed up new bits of business
for the candidate to try. One night at the Brasserie, Leokum
suddenly stood up to demonstrate a gesture and clunked his head
against a huge tray full of chocolate pastries that a waiter was
carrying, sending the entire gooey mess crashing down on to the
heads and laps of the people at the next table, almost precipitating
a fist fight. Mercifully, they were from Ohio, or there would have
been four votes lost.

Politics was truly in Page's blood now. It occurred to Mark that the white-hot fervour with which the candidate was running for mayor was really his way of running away from the ghastly truth of his Mob involvement and the reality of Kay's murder. More than once the campaign manager found himself remembering the candidate's final plea before lurching off to bed: 'For God's sake, don't give me time to think about what's happening to me!'

Chapter 25

Tuesday, October 9. At ten in the morning, a procession of eight campaign vehicles pulled up in front of the Board of Elections building at 80 Varick Street in the heart of the vast and useless lower Broadway section of the city that separates the financial district from Greenwich Village. On hand to meet the caravan was a crush of newsmen and camera teams, reporters, sound technicians, and the usual motley assemblage of onlookers that builds up when the media boys descend. As the first car slid up to curbside, there was a surge to see who was inside. When Johnny DiSantis and Tony the Elf Mauro leaped out, there were shouts of 'That's not them!' and 'The next car! Try the next car!' Johnny DiSantis, Bolex in hand, joined the throng of newsmen which moved amoeba-like toward the second automobile, from which stepped P. J. Costello, Mark Altschul, and Devereaux Page. From the other six cars came three dozen campaign aides, many of them girls in miniskirts, bearing big books of nominating petitions all neatly bound in long, green pressboard bindings. This was the final day for filing, and Page's organization, working like beavers, had gathered an astounding 100,000 signatures in the past six weeks. The candidate grabbed a couple of books, which were some 300 pages thick and a foot and a half long, and pushed his way through the shouting mob of newsmen, followed by his campaign aides all carrying more big books of petitions. Inside, the procession took the elevator to the third floor and marched noisily down the linoleum-covered hallway into a big room with fluorescent lighting and green walls. With a startled group of city employees looking on, the candidate and campaign aides proceeded to dump book after book of nominating petitions on to the counter until there was a wall the length of the counter and high as a man's head. Page then signed the proper forms declaring his wish to be on the November ballot and left the building. There was no question now about his name appearing on the ballot; a quick check by lawyers for the opposing candidates revealed that approximately 20 per cent of the 100,000 names were valid signatures of registered voters who had not signed other nominating petitions in this election. Thus Page had 20,000 signatures – about double the required number to assure a place on the ballot.

Now that Page was officially a candidate, press coverage increased dramatically. Those papers and broadcasters who had previously given only sporadic attention to his campaign now assigned full-time reporters to follow the day-to-day progress of his effort. Additional cars were provided for the newsmen, so that wherever the candidate appeared, his arrival was presaged by a caravan of vehicles snaking through the twisting hot streets of the city with all the attendant brouhaha the media adds.

It was now three weeks before election. The campaign was humming along like a well-oiled machine. Personalized computer letters were going out to the voters at the rate of 300,000 a week. The candidate was stumping the city, making fifteen to twenty appearances a day. There was constant exposure on television and radio, some of it pick-up material from the 'Citizen's Spotlight' programmes which were being aired once a week, each being a new issue – transportation, crime, welfare, municipal government, hospitals and health. Also appearing fairly constantly on the home screen was footage taken by Johnny DiSantis and patched into commercials showing Page out in the streets talking to voters, touring the city, or happily plunging into a wildly enthusiastic throng of well-wishers – always with the candidate's voice reassuring the viewers that he was the one man who really cared. Each week as the campaign focused on some new area of city government, the message was always the same: the only way to save the city from more scandals and irresponsibility was to get the government away from the professional politicians and back into the hands of the people.

A New Yorker couldn't turn around without seeing Page's name somewhere – on billboards, in newspaper advertisements, and on big signs inside every bus and subway car as well.

Skywriters proclaimed THE CITIZEN CANDIDATE every weekend high overhead the beaches of Brighton and Coney

Island. And on street corners in every neighbourhood of the city from the North Bronx to South Brooklyn, from Staten Island to the Nassau County Border, card tables and kiosks were set up to dispense literature and buttons, and to collect the nickles and dimes which helped keep the local headquarters in beer and sandwiches. Nightly and on weekends, Page's devoted army of volunteers trudged through the city knocking on doors and talking to the voters face to face.

To supplement the canvassing, a vast telephone operation was set up in a midtown office building under the direction of ComCam, Inc. (Communications for Campaigns, Inc.) For the citizen candidate's ticket, there were two hundred professional operators calling registered voters from ten in the morning to nine at night. The conversation to a registered Democrat would go something like this:

Voter: Hello.
Operator: Is this Mrs John Smith?
Voter: Yes, it is.
Operator: This is Joan Cunniffe. I'm calling from the headquarters of Brooklyn Democrats for Page, the citizen candidate. How are you, Mrs Smith?
Voter: I'm fine, thank you.
Operator: Would you hold on for a moment while I put on Devereaux Page, the citizen candidate for mayor? You'll be hearing his voice in just a moment.

There would be a click, and a recording of Page's voice would come on the line, first apologizing for it being a recording and then saying he wanted to get the voter's opinion on some matter or other. Usually he mentioned a problem that was of intense local interest, such as the proposed low-income housing project to the residents of the Forest Hills area, or Brooklyn waterfront renewal which was of concern to the residents of the Red Hook section. Page would outline the problem and then proposed three or four solutions. At the end of his short talk, he would ask the person on the other end of the phone to dial either 1, 2, 3, or 4, depending on which position was most attractive. The voter would dial; Page would thank him for his time, and after reminding him to be sure and vote on Election Day, would hang up. Two days later, a personal computerized letter would be in the voter's mailbox. The letterhead would proclaim Brooklyn Democrats for Page, and the letter would thank the voter for helping out with the survey, tell him the results of the survey, and devote a short paragraph to the voter's own opinion of it, which he had indicated by dialing 1, 2, 3, or 4.

These same telephone operators would call registered Republicans in the Bronx saying they were calling on behalf of Bronx Republicans for Page. If the person called had a Jewish name, the operator identified herself as Muriel Bernstein or Paula Schwartz; to an Italian she would be Pat Gaglione or Liz Patrarcha. Like the direct mail effort, this telephone operation was secret, and the press had no way of tracing how much was being spent or how extensive it was. Mark and his team, using the computer to its outer limits, knew how to reach the voters on a personal basis, maintaining a meaningful dialogue between the individuals – even the ones huddled behind locked doors and afraid to go out at night – and the candidate who was promising law and order, cleaner streets, and a new day for New Yorkers. Truly this was the New-New Politics. The voter would see the candidate on television, an appearance all the more meaningful because on the coffee table was a personalized letter from the guy discussing the viewer's problems and *his* neighbourhood. And the real beauty of the New-New Politics was that a rich candidate could be spending millions and appear to be spending only one-tenth the amount.

In American politics, it is virtually impossible to lose if you have an attractive, articulate candidate with a good organization that is intelligently outspending the opposition five-to-one; the exception is if one of the opponents is the incumbent or is so well known in the district that he couldn't lose to anybody. Both the Louis Harris and the *Daily News* straw pools showed Page running neck-and-neck with his opponents with two weeks left in the campaign. Each of the three major candidates had about 25 per cent of the expected vote with another 20 per cent undecided. And Page was still gaining. He had come from absolute zero voter awareness in June to about 25 per cent, with a nine point gain in the past month, during which time his opponents' positions remained relatively static. Thus, by Election Day, Page should get in with about 33 per cent of the vote as against

29 per cent each for the opposition. Page and the entire campaign organization were giddy with anticipation. Bobby DeStefano was reported on the verge of perpetual orgasm, puffing expansively on big Havana cigars and occasionally leaping from his seat to click his heels in mid air with delight. It would be close, to be sure. But if they could just keep gaining the percentage points, then Page would win.

They would win, that is, unless something catastrophic happened. And on Friday, October 26, just 11 days before the voters were to go to the polls, the *New York Times*, with all the attendant hoopla that accompanies a gorgeous political scoop, startled not only New Yorkers, but the entire nation with banner headlines that read:

PAGE CAMPAIGN FOUND
TO HAVE MAFIA TIES

$10 Million in Campaign Funds
Funnelled from Organized Crime

New Jersey Mafioso
Direction Campaign

What followed was an old-fashioned political hatchet job, an eleventh-hour exposé designed to totally discredit the candidate, and timed so close to the election that there was no way to refute it. The main story was written by the *Times* Mafia expert, Nicholas Gage, and it accurately outlined how Mark Altschul first went to see Bobby DeStefano in February with the idea of running a candidate for mayor, detailing all the events with incredible accuracy all the way up to the conversion of the Sanitation Department. Included were the attempts to get Page married off, the false robbery which everyone – press, television, and the candidate himself – had believed to be real, and the fact that all expenditures were being effected in cash, so the money was very difficult to trace.

In the breakover, two full pages were devoted to the story, as it recounted the campaign's huge, hidden direct mail effort, and the involvement of ConCam Inc., where hundreds of paid operators were calling voters all over the city, claiming to be from various volunteer organizations working for Page. There were biographies of the campaign staff: Mark Altschul, Jimmy Lee, Lou Klein, and Paul Berman. And the daily 'Man in the News' column was a piece on Roberto DeStefano titled: 'The New Breed: Businessman Mafioso.'

At first glance it appeared that Nicholas Gage had done an incredible investigative job, practically rivalling Lucien Truscott of the *Voice* for thoroughness, no doubt heading a staff of operatives who secretly gathered information for weeks while no one on the campaign team suspected anything. On closer reading, however, it was like the Pentagon Papers' story; the *Times* had somehow come into possession of Mark Altschul's budget and game plan. Even the profiles of the top men in the campaign organization were lifted verbatim from Mark's rather drab, legal-sounding prose. There was, of course, a great deal of material not contained in the massive budget. This must have been supplied by someone on the inside – perhaps a disaffected campaign worker who had found out about the underworld involvement, got his hands on the budget, and decided to blow the whistle. It could also have been someone in Bobby's own Organization, but that was highly unlikely; these people were too deeply imbued with the old Sicilian law of *Omerta* – silence under pain of death.

About the only original piece of research the *Times* came up with was a story on Jack Leokum, his fabulous executive retreat in Acapulco, and his role in turning the candidate into an orator. There was an historical piece about the Mafia involvement in New York politics through the years which included lurid tales of gangster Frank Costello's support of past Democratic administrations, the various scandals of the Lindsay administration, a brief paragraph devoted to Tammany Boss Carmine De Sapio who was recently released after serving time in federal prison for extortion, and a short history of corruption in New York City which reached its zenith under boss William Marcy Tweed, who with his henchmen, managed to loot the city of more than $100 million in the mid-nineteenth century, when a dollar was really a dollar.

Finally, the lead editorial, running a full column, demanded not only his withdrawal from the race, but a full investigation that would bring all the facts out into the open, so that such a 'gross conspiracy would never again be added to the already stained and sorry history of New York City politics.' By any standards, coming when it did so soon before the election, the *New York Times* exposé would be called the most scurrilous kind of yellow journalism in the tradition of James Gordon Bennett and William Randolph Hearst, and hardly worthy of the world's greatest newspaper. Except for one small fact: every word of it was absolutely true.

By nine that morning, the campaign of the citizen candidate was a shambles. The bandwagon had turned into a hearse.

Chapter 26

Devereaux Page's apartment building was under siege by the press. The hallway outside his door was aswarm with dozens of reporters. Camera crews waited for him to make an appearance, their cameras set up on tripods, lights and sound equipment in place. In the lobby below, an additional crowd was milling about, also hoping to catch a glimpse of the candidate. The media had put virtually every spare reporter on digging up more facts on this story. As a result, the situation was much the same at the apartments of the operating heads of the campaign – Klein, Jimmy Lee, Mark Altschul, Berman, and even their secretaries. Those whose functions were too minor to be worthy of a full interview by a reporter were called on the phone by the city desks. In fact, the attempts by the press to call people meant that the members of the campaign team were unable to communicate with one another because their phones were all busy. The only ones not affected were Jack Leokum, who was staying anonymously at the Waldorf, and Bobby DeStefano in New Jersey who who had several unlisted telephones. Outside the DeStefano compound, however, was a cluster of newsmen; they were kept at bay across the street by the presence of some hefty body guards and two large guard dogs.

At the Commodore, all the campaign offices were locked; there was not even a receptionist in the hall. All sixty-seven storefront headquarters remained locked and empty. When the story broke, everyone connected with the campaign was terrified; the murders of Tommy Eboli and Joey Gallo were too fresh in everyone's mind, with the result that volunteers and paid staff alike remained indoors with the phones off the hooks. By two in the afternoon, the press and television boys were wild with frustration. All they could get were interviews with the other candidates and the city officials who were howling for the blood of the entire Page organization.

At 3.00 PM Manhattan District Attorney Frank Hogan called
a press conference to announce there would be a full-scale
investigation; subpoenas were being issued to all principals to
appear before a county grand jury specially empanelled to hear
testimony. At 4.30, the United States Attorney announced that
the federal government was entering the case, and subpoenas were
being issued for those involved to appear before a federal grand
jury as well; normally it would be a city matter, but since a New
Jersey Mafia Family was directing the campaign, interstate
commerce was involved. Over in Trenton, the capitol of New
Jersey, United States Attorney Herbert Stern announced he was
going to hold his own investigation.

Finally, late in the afternoon, Lou Klein and Paul Berman
released a statement in which they denied all knowledge of Mafia
involvement and offered full cooperation with all investigative
efforts. Jimmy Lee broke silence to pledge his full cooperation,
and at the same time vociferously denied any knowledge that he
had been the pawn of Organized Crime.

Page himself remained at home, doors locked, blinds drawn,
following developments on radio and television. Finally at five
in the afternoon, an envelope was slipped under his door. In it
was a scrap of yellow paper with a telephone number scribbled
on it; the area code was 609 which meant New Jersey. He
dialled, and Bobby DeStefano came on the line. At the first
sound of Bobby's reedy, nasal voice, Page froze with fear; but
curiously the young Boss sounded warm and quite relaxed.
'How are you bearing up?' he asked the candidate.

'All right, I guess,' Page replied. 'It's like a zoo outside my
door.'

'I want you to keep cool, Dev. We're going to get you elected
yet.'

'Are you crazy?'

Bobby laughed. 'Look, Dev, there'll be someone to pick you up
at eight sharp. You, Mark and Leokum are coming out here so we
can regroup and figure out what to do.'

'What do I tell the press? They're all over the place.'

'Tell them you have every intention of staying in the race, and
that you expect to get elected.'

'Bobby, you're crazy. It's all over, for Chrissakes!'

'Not according to my sources.'

'What sources?'

'Never mind that now. Just remember, we're going to pull this election out, and you're going to be mayor of New York.'

'But the *Times* –'

'Fuck the *New York Times* and all those other sanctimonious shits trying to screw us! We'll fix 'em! You watch!' Suddenly over the phone came a demonic laugh that assaulted Page's ear and sent chills through him.

'You mean I'm still a candidate?'

'You're goddamn right! I'll see you out here about nine-thirty this evening.'

'What about the girls?'

'Gelsey and Johnna?' There was a pause. 'I'll have a car take them out to Brookville for the weekend. Okay?'

'Will they be safe there? I don't want the press around.'

'Some of my guys'll go along to watch out for them. Don't worry.'

'Bobby, what the hell do you have in mind?'

'I'll tell you when I see you.'

'Who broke the story?'

'I'll tell you that when I see you. Just remember one thing.'

'What's that?'

'Until you learn how to hate, you'll never get anywhere in this world. And if there's one thing I love, it's a good fight!'

'Well, you've got one on your hands this time.'

'Yeah, and we're gonna win it.'

'I think you're nuts.'

'*Iligitimi non carborundum*,' Bobby said jovially.

'What's that?'

'Don't let the bastards grind you down.' There was a click, and the line went dead.

The superintendent of Page's building called the police to ask that the mob of reporters in the hallway outside the candidate's door be moved downstairs to the sidewalk; other tenants were complaining. The result was relative calm on the candidate's floor. But at 8.00 PM when he went down to the lobby and out on to the sidewalk, an angry, teeming throng of newshounds who had been kept waiting all day with no one to interview, pounced on him. The moment the candidate appeared, there were shouts of 'There he is!' and 'Get him!' Fully a dozen pencil microphones were shoved under Page's face and the questions flew at him all at once. No one could possibly outshout the reporters – least of all, the subject of the interview. Finally Page was walled in by a solid phalanx of reporters, and there was a moment of relative quiet. Did he have any comment on the *New York Times* story? Not at this time. When he was going to make an announcement?'

'What kind of announcement?'

'When you're quitting the race.'

'I have no intention of quitting the race.'

'You're still a candidate?' There was incredulity in the reporter's voice.

'Of course, I'm still a candidate. This is a free country. The *New York Times* might try to act as prosecutor, jury and judge, but that doesn't mean I'm guilty of anything.'

'But what about the *Times* exposé?'

'It was a gloating, distorting piece that is irresponsible to the extreme, prompted by malice and full of lies and half-truths.'

'Who are your backers?'

'Standing behind me are ten thousand New Yorkers who are actively working for my election. They managed to get one hundred thousand signatures on the nominating petitions. And that's just the tip of the iceberg. The fact is most New Yorkers are totally fed up with the professional politicians and what they're doing to the city.'

'Do you think the Mafia will do better?'

Page looked at the reporter coldly. 'Anything's better than what we've got,' he snapped. 'I have nothing more to say at this time.' He pushed aside the microphones and thrust himself into the crush of reporters and technicians, elbowing them aside. Their reaction was a cruel bumping and jostling, kneeing him in the side, hitting him in the face with their microphones, and shouting questions. He pushed through by forcing bodies out of the way, his teeth clenched in grim determination to reach the waiting car. The press was hostile now. They had been lied to, and the camaraderie and good fellowship that had prevailed throughout the campaign had turned to viciousness; questions were shouted and snarled, microphones were jabbed in his face in a deliberate attempt to hurt him as well as get a comment. It took five minutes to reach the car by the curb. 'Where are you going now?' they shouted. There was no response from the candidate. He got into the car – Bobby DeStefano's black Chrysler with the luxuriant glove-soft upholstery. Three big men he'd never seen before got in with him, and they sped off, leaving reporters and camera teams shaking their fists and their microphones and cursing his evasiveness.

The helicopter ride from the West Side Heliport to Bobby's front lawn was uneventful. Leokum and Mark were already in the craft; when Page got aboard, the door was slammed, and they whirred off into the night, bouncing low over the Hudson River.

No one could remember seeing Bobby DeStefano in so expansive a mood. He greeted Leokum, Mark, and the candidate warmly as they alighted from the helicopter and led them immediately to the comfortable panelled study in his white clapboard house at the far end of the compound. It was a cool night, the breeze from the ocean smelled of salt, and it felt good. P.J. and Johnny DiSantis were taking drink orders. Bobby went right to the point. Sitting behind his big desk with an overhead spotlight playing on an opened book, he surveyed the tattered remains of his once-powerful campaign organization. There was silence in the room. Bobby looked up and brushed the brown forelock out of his eye. 'Gentlemen,' he said quietly, his reedy, nasal voice slightly hoarse, 'when this thing broke, my first impulse was to throw in the towel and take what came.'

'There aren't many options open to us,' Mark muttered.

'Not so, according to the *I Ching*.'

'The *what*?' Mark demanded.

'The *I Ching*,' Jack Leokum threw in matter-of-factly. 'The Chinese Book of Changes.'

'You use the *I Ching*, Jack?' Bobby wanted to know.

'Not personally. But I have clients who do.'

'What the hell are you talking about?' Page interjected.

'It's an old book of Chinese wisdom going back a thousand years before Christ.'

'Oh, for Chrissake,' the candidate snorted. 'Our lives are in ruins, and you're trying to solve it with some kind of mumbo-jumbo.'

'It has never been wrong for me,' Bobby said firmly. 'Now listen. After I read the *Times* this morning, I almost panicked. But then I cast the *I Ching*. It took me most of the day to figure out what to do. But I think we've got it. Are you ready?'

There was another silence broken only by the sound of the ice rattling in Page's highball; his hand was shaking uncontrollably. Finally he set the glass down on the coffee table before him.

'I threw the coins and came up with the Forty-sixth Hexagram – "Kuai, The Break-Through". Just listen to this.' Bobby paused and began to read:

The Judgment.
Break-through. One must resolutely make the matter known at the court of the king.
It must be announced truthfully. Danger.
It is necessary to notify one's own city.
It does not further to resort to arms.
It furthers one to undertake something.

'What the hell are you talking about?' Page asked.

Bobby repeated the key lines. 'It must be announced truthfully. . . . It is necessary to notify one's own city.' He stood up, and pointing a finger at Dev Page, he shouted, 'You're going to make a Checkers speech!'

'I'm what?'

The young Boss was smiling broadly. 'You're going to go on television and turn this whole damn thing around. Nixon did it in fifty-two; Teddy Kennedy did it after Chappaquiddick. You're going to do it now. That's what the *I Ching* is saying, goddamn it!' Bobby looked down at the book and read the lines again: 'It must be announced truthfully . . . It is necessary to notify one's own city.'

'A Checkers speech?' Leokum looked puzzled. 'What the hell can we say?'

'That, gentlemen, is precisely what you're here for. I've reserved one hour of air time on the three major New York City stations for ten o'clock Sunday night. All the weekenders will be home, and the whole city will be watching. I trust in the next forty-eight hours you'll come up with something pretty good. Otherwise –' Bobby paused and looked around the room. 'Just come up with something and win this fucking election.'

Mia DeStefano awoke to the sound of a horse whinnying. She sat up and looked at the digital clock on the bureau across from her. It was 6.30 AM, first light. Since the abortion, Mia had been confined to the compound and had spent just about every waking hour working with the horses, perfecting the dressage, cantering along the beach, currying, brushing, and loving them. It was a kind of retreat to her girlhood; she wanted to think of nothing beyond the big animals in the stable. Now she wondered if she had actually heard a horse or whether she had been dreaming. The neighing came again. She heard it distinctly through the open window. It sounded like Molly Pitcher, the brown mare. What was she doing out? Pushing aside the covers, she went to the window of her cottage next to Bobby's house and looked out at the great expanse of green lawn that stretched the length of two football fields to her grandfather's massive stucco mansion with the pink tiled roof. Four men stood in a group outside Bobby's white house next door. They were huddled down under their light jackets with their hands jammed into their pockets, their breath smoking in the crisp morning air. To one side of the lawn was a much larger man, completely nude, bound hand and foot, gagged with a white towel, and tied to a small birch tree. Shivering with cold, he threw his head from side to side as though trying to work the gag loose. Mia's curious gaze noted the contrast between the stark white of the birch bark and pasty quality of the man's body, punctuated in the centre by the big comma of pubic hair from which protruded genitals so large she could distinguish them fifty yards away. In the middle of the lawn was Shakespeare, her big grey gelding, stamping and pawing the turf. The horse was bridled and, oddly, fitted with a western saddle which it wasn't used to. Shakespeare was being led by a small man whom she made out to be Tony the Elf Mauro; of all her father's henchmen, the former jockey was the only one she ever allowed to saddle up or help curry the animals. Others had come riding with her – P.J. and occasionally Johnny DiSantis –

but Tony the Elf was the only one who had the experience and feel for horseflesh.

Mia reached for her little Nikon 6-power binoculars and put them to her eyes. The big man bound to the birch tree was twitching in obvious discomfort. Well he might, tied hand and foot and stark naked on a morning where you could see your breath. Focusing her attention on his genitals, she gasped; the man's limb hung down to mid-thigh. Who was he? The gag covered most of the lower part of his face, but suddenly his identity came to her. With that flat, bald head and single eyebrow going across, it had to be Nick Gigante, the mammouth goon with the oily, pitted face whom she detested. What in the world was going on?

Moments later her father appeared carrying a rifle which he jauntily tossed over to one of the four men, who, with the aid of the glasses, she made out to be P.J. The former Green Beret caught the rifle and performed a perfect Queen Anne salute, twirling the weapon back and forth, kicking it with his heel to send it spinning the other way, finally ending up at present arms. The other men, including her father, responded with laughter and applause. Then she heard Bobby shout, 'Okay, let's get this show on the road.' Johnny DiSantis loped across the lawn to the stucco wall where he opened the wrought-iron gate leading to the beach and the ocean. Tony the Elf led the big grey horse around in a tight circle until it was facing the opened gate, and away from where the men were standing; he repeatedly patted Shakespeare on the neck to reassure him. On the other side of the lawn, Bobby gave a curt nod to the fourth henchmen, whom Mia did not recognize, and he went over to the prisoner; producing a long stiletto which snapped open, he cut away the big white gag from the bound man's mouth. Suddenly Nick started screaming in a voice that boomed across the compound and sent chills into the deep heart's core. '*Oh My God! Stop! No! No! For God's Sake Stop Him!*'

He had a strange speech impediment; he was pronouncing the S's as though his tongue were tied. The words were coming out 'For God hakes, hop him.' It was a weird, almost surreal scene in the dawn light, with the big grey horse towering over the small man in the centre of the lawn, P.J. holding a rifle, Nick screaming from the birch tree to which he was bound, naked. The stranger with the big stiletto waited. Bobby nodded to Tony the Elf who reached up and slipped off Shakespeare's bridle and removed the bit from its mouth. He patted the horse and walked quickly away, leaving the animal alone in the middle of the lawn with only a western saddle on his back. She heard Bobby shout, 'Okay, P.J., shoot the son of a bitch!' P.J. raised his rifle and aimed – not at the prisoner, but at the horse. When Mia saw where P.J. was aiming, she let out a scream of her own. But it was too late. P.J. pulled the trigger. There was no report; just a tiny pop. It wasn't a rifle at all, but a child's BB gun. The tiny projectile hit the big horse in the flank, causing it to rear high on the hind legs and give forth a mighty whinny. When his front legs came down on to the turf, the big grey animal bolted across the lawn toward the opened gate to the beach and freedom. Invisible to Mia's eyes, even with the Nikon binoculars, was the strand of piano wire leading from the pommel of Shakespeare's saddle across the lawn to the back of Nick's tongue where it was tied with a slip knot; a second strand was similarly secured around his gentials. The doomed man let out one final blood-curdling howl of agony which became gurgling choke as his tongue was yanked out by the roots and bright red blood began spurting from his mouth. An instant later, his entire pelvic region was wrenched outward on his gentials were yanked off, bringing out with the force long coils of seminal tubes, urethra, and even part of his bladder along with the cascade of blood shooting out between his legs that turned the grass red. Bobby nodded coldly, and the man with the stiletto cut the bonds to Nick's hands and feet. He doubled over, choking, gasping, cluthing his throat with one hand and the gaping blood hole in his crotch with the other. His entire body was wracked with great spasms as he began swallowing blood and then inhaling it into his lungs. Bleeding profusely, he fell head first on to the lawn where he lay twitching, coughing, croaking for three or four minutes until mercifully blacking out, while the red stuff of life continued to spill out on to the grass. There was one more twitch; then stillness.

Mia began to tremble. She tried to scream in horror, but no

sound came forth. She doubled over and staggered into the bathroom, where suddenly crying and weak, she sat on the edge of the bathtub and vomited.

By Sunday morning, the fact of Mafia involvement in the New York City mayoralty race had become headline news all over the country. Officials from every corner of the land were outraged at so flagrant an attempt by Organized Crime to take over a municipal government. Mayor Lindsay called it 'a blatant, shocking incursion on the fundamental rights of the people.' while City Council President Sanford Garelik, himself a former chief inspector of the police force, mumbled that nobody was safe from anything any more. The United States attorneys of New York and New Jersey, as well as New York District Attorney Frank Hogan, had prepared subpoenas to be issued Monday morning. Even the President of the United States got into the act, guaranteeing the people of New York the full resources of the federal government and Justice Department to get to the bottom of 'what appears to be the biggest lie ever perpetrated in the history of American politics.'

Angriest of all were John DeLury and his Sanitation Union. They had been the real dupes. And now the fiery little labour boss denounced the Page candidacy with vituperation he usually reserved only for the mayor and city council during contract bargaining talks.

In editorials, every paper from the *New York Times* to the Statten Island *Advance* demanded Dev Page's withdrawal from the race, and cried out for a full investigation to insure nothing like this would ever happen again. The *Times* editorial page on Sunday morning even had some fun at Page's expense:

Since the citizen candidate has such a penchant for quoting poetry, he is probably saying to himself right now these words of Rudyard Kipling in preparation for his television appearance tonight:

> I could not dig: I dared not rob:
> Therefore I lied to please the mob.
> Now all my lies are proved untrue -
> And I must face the men I slew.
> What tale shall serve me here among
> Mine angry and defrauded young?

Chapter 27

By 7.00 PM Sunday evening, normally a quiet time in midtown Manhattan, the area around the RCA building was clogged with vehicles and humanity. The police had set up grey sawhorses along the sidewalks, barricading the hundreds of curious spectators who had shown up hoping to catch a glimpse of the embattled candidate on his way to the television studio. Inside the lobby beneath the NBC studios, an extra contingent of page boys had come in to take care of the expected crowds.

Anyone showing press credentials was whisked up to the 8th floor, usually deserted at this hour, where in the hallway, at great buffet tables, delicatessen sandwiches were being dispensed, while at either end of the hall were bars where reporters could get a free drink. One thing about the Page campaign everyone agreed on: win or lose, they were damn nice to the press.

Studio 8H, with its grim grey walls and concrete floor, was originally designed for Arturo Toscannini and the NBC Symphony Orchestra. This evening it was set up with hundreds of folding chairs and a giant screen at one end where the press could watch Devereaux Page's performance which was to be live from a studio elsewhere in the building.

The sixth floor, from which the actual broadcast would emanate, was sealed off, with Pinkerton men at the stairwells and corridors leading from the RCA Building; a desk at the elevators was manned by NBC pages who turned away everybody who was not on the approved list. Behind the bright red doors of studio 6B, under a blinding barrage of scoop lights, the candidate had been rehearsing since mid-afternoon.

Page was sweating profusely under the hot lights. It was not a speech he had to learn; the entire text would be unrolling in front of him on the Teleprompter machines which were mounted just over the lens of each camera. The words were typed on a huge typewriter on to big rolls of yellow paper and controlled by a professional who moved the speech along in consort with the performer's timing. But there were changes. All day, it seemed, new changes kept coming from either Mark or Leokum or Bobby DeStefano or the candidate himself; this meant a correction on the master script and a patch on the four Teleprompter rolls. All of this took time. In addition, there was to be a very complex arrangement of graphics – newspaper headlines which were to be shown on the rear-projection screen over the candidate's right shoulder. On the set, too, near Page's chair, were two additional chairs where Gelsey and Johnna would be seated; the layout was much the same as for a late-night talk show.

At 8.00 PM, the final run-through was finished, and Page relaxed in one of the dressing rooms. Dinner was sent up for the candidate – charcoal steaks from Charley O's downstairs. Page declined a drink, as he always did before an important speaking engagement. And so they waited. At one point while picking at his steak, Page turned to Bobby DeStefano. 'Say, Bobby, who the hell got us into this anyway?'

'What do you mean?'

'Who gave the story to the *Times*?'

Boby smiled slightly. 'It didn't take long to figure that out.'

'Who was it?'

'Nick Gigante.'

'Nick? Why would he do a thing like that?'

'He got into some trouble, and we fired him. He was bitter about it, so he went to the *New York Times* and told them everything.'

The candidate pushed aside his plate. 'What're you going to do about him?'

'We've done it.'

'I hope you weren't too rough on him.'

'We make the punishment fit the crime''

'What do you mean?'

'When a member of the Organization sins, we generally see to it he can't be a repeater. That's where we differ from the law, and why we're so much more efficient. For instance, if one of our guys is careless with a gun, we cut off his trigger fingers, get me? If he's caught eavesdropping, we remove his ears.'

'What'd you do to Nick?'

'I assume you were still in bed at dawn this morning.'

'You guys gave me two big red ones last night. I was out for the count.'

'It's probably just as well.' Bobby smiled enigmatically, and the subject was dropped.

A bare hour before air time, both NBC and CBS decided the Devereaux Page appearance had national implications and delayed their regular programming to put this special broadcast on the network coast to coast. Three floors below where the candidate waited, John Chancellor, who, much to his annoyance, had been called away from dinner at '21', was now being made up just outside the third-floor newsroom. Up the street, in the gargantuan black granite and glass tombstone-like edifice designed by Eero Saarinen that housed the Columbia Broadcasting System studios, Walter Cronkite deliberately removed his eyeglasses and laid aside his pipe. Across the table was Eric Severeid who, as usual, looked as though he were sitting on a thumbtack.

At 9.55 PM, Devereaux Page took his place on the darkened set and was immediately surrounded by cameras and technicians. He was obviously tense; it had been a gruelling two days, both emotionally and physically. The stage manager, a natty little man in a pink button-down shirt and black tie, fastened a microphone around the candidate's neck. 'Now say something, Mr Page, so we can adjust the audio.'

'If you can keep your head when all about you are losing theirs . . .'

The floodlights were being held off until the last possible moment; the intense heat they generated caused performers to perspire. Over to one side, Jack Leokum turned to P.J. 'Make sure you've got that handkerchief soaked in witch hazel. He can't do that sincerity bit if he's sweating.'

Finally at 9.59:30, all the lights in the place blazed on, causing the studio to become bright as day. Gelsey and Johnna were led over to the two chairs reserved for them. All was in readiness. Behind the candidate was a blonde panelled wall and a window overlooking the Manhattan skyline. Page was wearing a black pinstripe suit with wide lapels and nipped in at the waist. It was perfectly tailored and would contrast well with the light wood backdrop, making his image stand out on the home screen, whether colour or black-and-white.

With ten seconds to go before air time, Page suddenly spun around in his white pedestal chair and threw a big wink at his two daughters. Gelsey, looking quite grown up in a blue silk dress, smiled wanly at him. Johnna, in a red jumper, white socks and patent leather Mary Janes, stared back myopically through her thick glasses. Out of the rafters came a voice booming over the studio loudspeaker system, 'We're ready to go. Quiet on the set, please.' The candidate returned to his original position facing the two cameras, and, with the city and the entire nation tuned in, he waited to be introduced by an unseen announcer in another studio. Mounted just over the camera lenses were the Tele-prompter devices, with the words, 'My Fellow New Yorkers, Good Evening,' typed in huge letters. As Page began to speak, the words would roll by. A moment later, the red light on one of the big colour cameras went on, and the stage manager, standing just to one side, pointed a finger at the seated candidate. He was on the air for the biggest speech of his life.

My fellow New Yorkers, good evening. I come before you tonight as a candidate for mayor, and as a man whose honesty and integrity have been questioned.

As he spoke, all the tension suddenly went out of him. He felt in complete control of himself and his material. He was calm and confident, rising above all the abuse to which he had been subjected, meeting a giant crisis head on.

I'm sure you have all read the charge, and you have heard and seen it on television, that I, Devereaux Page, am the candidate of the Mafia, and that Organization has put up ten million dollars for my campaign.

Let me say first off, that despite what the Italian-American Civil Rights League and others say, there is a Mafia. It is a loose Confeder-ation of about five thousand men across the country. Its main business – 95 per cent of it in fact – is gambling and money-lending. By all estimates, these two areas of endeavour, gambling and money-lending, amount to about a hundred billion dollars a year business.

In other words, these five thousand men are doing the equivalent of the gross national product of Italy. This Confederation, then, is the most efficient organization the world has ever known.

So, it is true there is a Mafia.

Now as to the charge that this Organization has put up ten million dollars for my candidacy in an attempt to help elect me mayor of New York, this is also absolutely true.

There was a collective gasp in front of every television set in America. Viewers from Maine to California sat forward in wide-eyed fascination as one of the great political dramas of the century was unfolding. Three floors below, John Chancellor watching the monitor built into his news desk, removed his glasses and began to wipe them compulsively with a handkerchief. Up the street in the CBS studios, Walter Cronkite shook his head in disbelief, while across from him sat Eric Severeid, his long face the usual solemn mask. At 1600 Pennsylvania Avenue, the President turned to one of his top aides and snapped, 'Get the Attorney General on the phone and make sure he's watching.' All over the city of New York, activity had come to a standstill, as the voters to whom this broadcast meant the most clustered about television sets in homes and in bars, agog at the revelations that were coming forth.

On screen, Devereaux Page coolly continued with a brief history of the Mafia, outlining how the Organization began serving the needs of society in the 1920s, by supplying liquor to a thirsty nation. The Volstead Act was a bad law, Page said, rammed through Congress and the state legislatures by a bunch of do-gooders and Puritans. Instead of doing away with alcoholic beverages completely, it accomplished the reverse. People who never touched the stuff began using it; the per capita consumption of liquor actually jumped 10 per cent.

When Prohibition was repealed, this supply organization was effectively put out of business. So the Organization found new needs in society: specifically, gambling and money lending. Now, forty years after the repeal of Prohibition, the law was coming around to admit that maybe wagering a dollar on a horse, or a number, or an athlete wasn't immoral after all. Page smiled his little half smile.

Isn't it amazing how old-fashioned morality goes out the window when you're broke? If there's a chance a state senator isn't going to get his salary because there's no money in the treasury, he might be persuaded to shift his stand on the legalization of gambling.

Ten years ago a lottery was unthinkable. Now we have a state lottery.

Five years ago, betting on a horse away from the track was illegal and immoral. Now Off-Track Betting flourishes.

Two years from now, I predict there will be open gambling in New York State. Casinos will be offering all the standard games – dice, roulette, blackjack, slot machines, even betting on sports events.

I don't think the government will ever get into money-lending, not that there's anything immoral about borrowing money at high interest when you need it. Anyone who has ever been in the service knows the expression, 'Five will get you ten'. All that means is, 'Let me have five dollars now, and I'll pay you back ten on payday.' That's what money-lending is, or as the law prefers to call it, 'Slylocking'. Actually it's a perfectly reasonable proposition if all parties to the deal understand the terms and agree to them. However, the government wouldn't dare get into that business. It's obvious that a borrower wouldn't have quite the same respect for New York State as he does for one of our enforcers.

But with the state getting into gambling, a large segment of our business will be cut off. So, as was the case when Prohibition was repealed, we have to look for new areas of endeavour.

It was interesting that Page was using 'we', 'us', and 'ours', as though he were not only speaking in behalf of the Confederation, but was actually part of it, which he wasn't. He eased himself out of his chair and ambled rather casually back to the window through which was seen the Manhattan skyline. Reaching up, he pulled down a white shade which was to become a screen for the graphics that followed. He turned to the camera and smiled.

So with the government focusing so much attention on our activities, we decided to take a good hard look at government. It's amazing what we found.

The lights dimmed in the studio, and the camera dollied in for a close-up of the white screen behind the candidate. During this portion of the programme, the graphics filled the home screen while Page did voice-over narration. He told the viewers he was going to present the issues in alphabetical order, and on the screen they would be seeing actual newspaper headlines in the type style of either the *News*, the *Times*, the *Post*, the *Village Voice*, or title pages of magazine articles from *New York*, *Newsweek*, *Time*, and others. These were to be the actual headlines; there was no faking it. No trickery. As he proceeded from issue to issue, from A to Z, the viewer could judge for himself who was really fit to run New York City – the professional politicians, or the citizen candidate, together with the most efficient Organization in the world.

VIDEO	AUDIO
1. 'NEW YORK ABCs *An Alphabet of Horrors*'	*D.P.* There was no way to separate the issues in any logical sequence. To the man who's been beaten and mugged in Central Park, Crime in the Streets is the most important issue. To the parents in Brooklyn who have just discovered their teenage daughter is on heroin, it's Narcotics they're interested in. So we decided to do it alphabetically. I call this, The New York ABC's the Alphabet of Horrors.
2. 'A – AGED.'	A is for the Aged, our senior citizens, who are forced into old-age homes where there is gross overcrowding, filthy, dirty linens, the stench of urine, and poor health care.
3. MONTAGE OF PHOTO-GRAPHS – STILL AND MOTION–OF CROWDED OLD-AGE HOME: OLD PEOPLE SITTING IN THE PARK SURROUNDED BY GARBAGE CANS OVER-FLOWING; OLD WOMAN SITTING ON DOORSTEP WITH TORN, FILTHY CLOTHES; OLD MAN ALONE, WEEPING.	In any other country in the world ... France ... Germany ... the Orient ... Italy ... the old are treated with respect and love. Here, they're thrown aside, to live out the rest of their years – the so-called 'golden years' – in hope-lessness and filth.

VIDEO	AUDIO
4. 'B – BUILDING AND CONSTRUCTION.'	B is for building and construction.
5. 'STUDY FINDS $25 MILLION YEARLY IN BRIBES IS PAID BY CITY'S CONSTRUCTION INDUSTRY.'	Here is an industry so riddled with graft, in a city that desperately needs new housing, it is no longer profitable to build. Look at these headlines.
6. 'FIVE CITY BUILDING INSPECTORS ARE SEIZED AS GRAFTERS.'	To be a building inspector for the city of New York means you can increase your salary by double . . . triple . . . five and ten times.
7. 'BRIBES REPORTED ADDING 5% A YEAR TO BUILDING COSTS.'	All you do is threaten a builder with violations . . . hold up his licenses . . . lose his applications.
8. 'GOODMAN CHARGES CITY AGENCIES DO VIRTUALLY NOTHING TO ALLEVIATE CORRUPTION IN CONSTRUCTION INDUSTRY.'	The law calls this kind of practice extortion. The city agencies wink and look the other way. The result is builders now look for other cities in which to invest their capital.
9. 'CONSTRUCTION THEFTS COST CITY $50-MILLION A YEAR.'	This city is desperate for new housing, and instead of encouraging new construction, these extortionists in city government are strangling it.
10. 'C – CRIME.	C is also for Crime in the streets. This is one issue that's on everyone's mind these days.
11. 'THE CHANGING CITY: CRIME REPORTS RISE DESPITE MORE MODERNIZED POLICE.'	Former city Comptroller Mario Procaccino used to say there was once a time when people were afraid to go out of their homes at night. Now they're afraid to go out in the daytime.

VIDEO	AUDIO
12. 'EAST SIDE VIOLENT CRIME SEEN UP 145%.'	In the past twelve months, there have been:
	1,048 murders ...
	2,607 rapes ...
13. 'NEW YORK CRIME TWICE THE NATION'S AVERAGE.'	69,520 robberies.
	42,317 felonious assaults.
14. 'NY MURDERS LEAP 30%.'	273,582 burglaries.
	251,140 larcenies of fifty dollars or more.
15. '57 SLAYINGS HERE IN WEEK SET RECORD THE POLICE LINK TO HEAT.'	92,470 car thefts.
16. 'PROMINENT LAW PRO-FESSOR SLAIN NEAR COLUMBIA UNIVERSITY CAMPUS.'	All this in just the past twelve months. Incidentally, these were only the *reported* crimes. Police estimate perhaps as high as thirty-five per cent again go unreported.
17. 'ANOTHER COMMUTER KNIFED IN HARLEM.'	Under the Lindsay Administration, Crime has reached an all-time high.
18. 'TASS CORRESPONDENT BEATEN AND ROBBED IN CENTRAL PARK.'	Procaccino was right: it is no longer safe to go outside your home in the daytime.
19. 'C – CONGRESS.'	C is also for Congress.
20. 'REPRESENTATIVE CHISHOLM JOINS DE-MOCRATIC PRESIDEN-TIAL RACE.'	Our congressional delegation has been the target of much criticism in this campaign.
21. 'BADILLO THROWS HAT IN MAYORALTY RING.'	The fact is our New York delegation is doing a terrible job. Instead of working to get needed legislation for the cities, many of them were busy running for other offices.

VIDEO	AUDIO
	The result is the city is starving for funds, while farm programmes . . . space programmes . . . military programmes . . . are reaping the benefits of congressmen who are responsible to the needs of their constituencies.
22. 'KOCH DECLARES FOR MAYOR.'	
	New York City sends twenty-three billion dollars a year to Washington and gets back one billion in federal programmes.
23. 'BIAGGI TOOK 5TH 16 TIMES IN QUIZ.'	
	This is entirely the fault of our New York City congressional delegation. For all the good they're doing New York City, you can take every one of our congressmen – Koch, Abzug, Badillo, Biaggi, Chisholm, Rooney, Carey, Murphy, Rangel, all eighteen of them – and shovel the whole bunch into the ocean.
24. 'N.Y. CONGRESSIONAL DELEGATION SELDOM AGREES ON ANYTHING.'	
25. 'JAVITS-BUCKLEY RELATIONS DESCRIBED AS "VERY COOL".'	The same could be said for our senators.
26. 'C – CITY COUNCIL.'	C is also for the City Council.
	There are thirty-seven men and women in the city council. They make a salary of twenty-five thousand dollars a year; those who are chairmen of committees pull down from two to nine thousand extra in 'lulus' – lump sum payments *in lieu of* expenses.
27. 'THE CITY COUNCIL: IT'LL NEVER DIE FROM OVER WORK.'	What are the duties of the City Council? The city charter requires them to attend two meetings a month.
	Many do not even do that.
	Thirty out of the thirty-seven councilmen serve on a part-time basis, holding down full-time jobs.

VIDEO

AUDIO

I say anybody who takes twenty-five thousand a year out of public funds, with this city in the desperate shape it's in, and does so on a part-time basis, is nothing more than a common thief.

And thirty out of a possible thirty-seven is a lot of thievery.

28. 'D – DISTRICT ATTOR-NEYS.'

D is for our District Attorneys.

29. 'DA FRANK HOGAN: SOFT IN HIS OLD AGE.'

These are supposed to be the guardians of the law.

30. 'PROSECUTOR SAID TO FACE CHARGE IN BRIB-ERY STUDY.'

Yet their offices are just as riddled with do-nothingism as every other branch of government.

31. '9 IN DA MACKELL'S OFFICE CITED IN FED-ERAL TAX EVASION IN-QUIRY.'

And they are corrupt.

32. 'QUEENS DA MACKELL AND 2 AIDES INDICTED IN SWINDLE COVER-UP.'

The office of the Queens DA is a rat's nest of corruption.

33. 'HOGAN SAYS HE BACKED MACKELL IN-QUIRY.'

Here's where one DA investigates another . . .

34. 'ALL 5 CITY DA'S IN HIGH DUDGEON OVER LOW RATING BY KNAPP TEAM.'

Here's the first time in modern history where all five New York District Attorneys agreed on anything.

35. 'GOVERNOR SUPERSED-ING FIVE DISTRICT ATTORNEYS HERE. AP-POINTING A SPECIAL PROSECUTOR ON COR-RUPTION.'

They were doing such a terrible job and their offices were so corrupt, Governor Rockefeller had to appoint a special investi-gator – to investigate the in-vestigators!

36. 'E – EDUCATION.'

E is for Education.

37. 'STUDY URGES A Z-TO-A SHAKEUP OF SCHOOLS.'

One of the most inefficient and bureaucratic agencies in the city is the Board of Education. It wastes millions of dollars a year on archaic practices.

VIDEO	AUDIO
38. 'FISCAL METHODS OF SCHOOL BOARD FOUND "CHAOTIC".'	There are forty thousand more students in the public high schools than they are equipped to handle.
39. 'CITY SCHOOLS FOUND "SHAMEFULLY OVER-CROWDED".'	And there is constant danger. Last year there were over two thousand assaults on our teachers.
40. 'CRIME AND VIOLENCE RISE IN CITY SCHOOLS.'	Marauding gangs of teenage hoodlums are running wild. There is no school in the city in which life and property are safe.
41. '9 STABBED IN FIGHT OUTSIDE LOWER EAST SIDE SCHOOL.'	
42. 'BURGLARIES IN SCHOOLS REACH "EPI-DEMIC PROPORTIONS" IN SOME DISTRICTS OF CITY.'	No wonder eighty-five per cent of New York's elementary children have a reading ability below the national norm.
43. 'NYC CHILDREN LAG BEHIND NATION IN READING – THREE AND FOUR YEARS THE NORM IN MANY DISTRICTS.'	Given the situation of our city schools, our children would get a better education if they stayed home and watched television all day long. What's more, they'd be a lot safer.
44. 'F – FINANCES.'	F is for finances.
45. 'METROPOLITAN AREA LOSES 91,000 JOBS EVERY YEAR.'	In the hands of the professional politicians, the city has gone steadily down hill until it is bankrupt . . . bankrupt of money . . . and bankrupt of ideas.
46. 'MANY GARMENT MAKERS LEAVING THE CITY.'	Instead of growing, the city's job market is shrinking as businesses are fleeing by the hundreds to escape the dirt . . . the taxes . . . the crime . . . the poor schools.

VIDEO	AUDIO
47. 'REP. KOCH FINDS 27 MAJOR COMPANIES IN MIDTOWN AREA ARE WEIGHING MOVE FROM CITY.'	Of the ten billion dollar budget, fully thirty per cent – or three billion dollars – is wasted in duplication of services . . . illegal payments . . . embezzlement and fraud.
	What little money there is available to New York City is being criminally mismanaged.
48. '$65 MILLION US SLUM AID SNARLED IN CITY RED TAPE.'	For example, the pension funds and sinking funds – some eight billion dollars which generates income so the city can pay its pensions and loans – these funds have been growing at the rate of less than three per cent a year.
49. 'CITY PENSION COSTS SNOWBALLING.'	Comptroller Abe Beame – the supposed financial wizard – would have done far better putting this money in a savings bank.
50. 'HARD-PRESSED CITY OWES $119 MILLION TO RAINY DAY FUND.'	The result of this mismanagement means that you, the taxpayer, have to make up the difference. Fully seven per cent of the city's operating budget – or seven hundred million dollars a year – goes into paying pensions. This will triple in five years and, together with welfare, quite literally bankrupt the city.
51. 'G – GHETTOS.'	G is for the ghettos and slums.
	In our ghettos, rats nibble on our children's toes at night, and crime stalks you in the street.
52. 'INSIDE THE BLACK COLONY: OVERDOSE OF DESPERATION.'	Harlem is so densely packed with people, that if all America were to live that way, the whole country could be crammed into three boroughs of New York City.

VIDEO	AUDIO
53. 'HARLEM CRIME TOLL IS PUT AT $2.7-BILLION.'	In Harlem's 25th Precinct alone last year there were reported ...
	1105 robberies and muggings ...
54. 'FEAR IS STEADY COMPANION OF MANY HARLEM RESIDENTS.'	1841 burglaries ...
	382 assaults ...
	717 auto thefts.
55. 'BED-STUY UNEMPLOYMENT AMONG NATION'S HIGHEST.'	In the ghetto, unemployment runs as high as thirty per cent; able-bodied men and women simply cannot get jobs. In desperation, they turn to narcotics and crime.
56. 'THE BROWNSVILLE JUNGLE: CABBIES CALL IT VIETNAM.'	In the ghetto, the streets are dirtier, the prices are higher, the schools are worse, and there is hunger and malnutrition.
	Yes, believe it or not, in the richest city in the world in the greatest country on earth, there is hunger.
57. 'STUDY FINDS 40% OF NYC'S GHETTO CHILDREN UNDERNOURISHED; MANY CHILDREN OF ADDICTS ON "NEAR STARVATION" DIETS.'	Thanks to the professional politicians – in Washington, in Albany, and in City Hall – *Little children are going hungry in New York City.*
58. 'H – HEALTH & HOSPITALS.'	H is for Health and Hospitals.
	The United States has the worst health care system of the world's ten leading nations – including Russia and Communist China.

VIDEO	AUDIO
59. 'CITY HEALTH LEVEL FOUND FAR FROM SATISFACTORY.'	And New York City has the worst health and hospital system of any major city in the United States.
	Every year, 25,000 people die in New York City because of inferior medical care.
60. 'OUR SICK HOSPITALS: SOARING COSTS THROW SYSTEM INTO THE RED.	Our children do not get innoculations, so preventable diseases like whooping cough and measles still persist.
	People are dying of curable diseases like tuberculosis, because positive tests for the illness are not followed up with treatment.
61. 'HEALTH VIOLATIONS FOUND IN ALL THE CITY HOSPITALS.'	In Riverdale, the infant mortality rate is 11.7 deaths for every 1000 live births. In Harlem it's 39 deaths. On a city-wide basis, it's 24.2 deaths – higher than any other major city.
62. 'CITY IS CONSIDERING SALE OR CLOSING OF 5 HOSPITALS.'	There is malnutrition, resulting in actual cases of scurvy among the old, and rickets and physical underdevelopment among the young.
63. 'COUNCIL WATCHDOGS PLAY DEAD ON MEDICAID CUTS.'	That's right. Rickets and scurvy right here in New York City – two diseases for which cures were found in the Nineteenth Century. And those cures were simply a proper diet.
64. 'CUTS IN MEDICAID PUT INTO EFFECT.'	In 1970, the old Department of Hospitals was replaced by a new agency – the New York City Health and Hospitals Corporation.

VIDEO	AUDIO
	In the first year of operations, the Corporation boosted salaries from $1.8 million to $4 million, with most of it going to administrative personnel.
65. 'HEALTH AND HOSPITALS CORP. THE FAT "TECHNOCRAT" AND UNION CONFUSION.'	The number of executives earning more than $20,000 a year jumped from 75 to 169 in that first year.
	Dr Joseph English, the Corporation Administrator, made a salary of $65,000 – more money than the mayor.
66. 'HARLEM DOCTORS AND NURSES PROTEST "APPALLING MEDICAL CARE" AT HOSPITAL.'	That first year, the Corporation spent $1.5 million to re-model its executive offices, while the pap smear clinic at Coney Island Hospital was phased out for lack of $5,000.
67. '2 BRONX HOSPITALS SLASHING SERVICE OVER CITY BUDGET.'	It was Dr Seymour M. Glick, Chief of Medicine at Coney Island Hospital who said, 'You come to this hospital, and we're telling you somebody's going to take care of you. The fact is you're going to lie in a damp bed, develop an ulcer, blood poisoning, and perhaps ultimately die, because of inadequate nursing care.
68. 'HEALTH SERVICE HERE IS ACCUSED OF FRAUD.'	Not only are our hospitals an archaic disgrace – unsanitary and inhuman – there is corruption everywhere.
69. 'GRAND JURY FINDS A $1-BILLION LOSS IN MEDICAID HERE.'	Doctors and nursing homes have bilked the city out of $1 billion in overpayments from Medicaid – with the complete knowledge of many city officials.

VIDEO	AUDIO
70. 'BADILLO ASKS CITY INQUIRY ON BRONX HOSPITAL FUNDS.'	Medical groups engage in ping-ponging – referring patients from one another and back again. Patients lend their cards to friends who get services.
71. 'NURSING HOMES THAT WERE SHUT GOT CITY'S $475-G.'	City records are so bad, that the city could not defend itself against a lawsuit by a dentist for $358,000; that dentist had already made $1,312,752 from the city in 1968 and 1969.
	All I can say is, if you're going to get sick, don't do it in New York City. The odds are you'll get sicker and die.
72. 'H – HOUSING.'	H is also for Housing.
73. 'MANY RANK CITY WITH WORST SLUM-LORDS.'	Two million New Yorkers live in decaying, substandard housing.
74. 'HOMEOWNERS SAY CITY ABUSED THEM.'	We need one million new units right now. Yet the Housing Administration is so bogged down with red tape and bureaucracy, that it has not made full use of funds available to it under federal and state programmes.
75. 'TUMBLEDOWN BUILD-INGS SEND BRONX TAX RATABLES TUMBLING.'	In 1969, the Housing Authority lost $13 million.
76. 'CITY REPORT CITES LOSS OF HOUSING.'	In 1970, the Housing Authority lost $18 million.
77. 'FEDERAL HOUSING ABANDONMENT BLIGHTS INNER CITIES.'	In 1971, the Housing Authority lost $22 million. Last year it lost $26 million.

VIDEO	AUDIO

VIDEO

78. 'RAZING FOR OFFICES EVICTING THOUSANDS – STATE SENATOR ASSAILS "FOOLISH' TREND.'

79. 'HOUSING SUPPLY IN CITY ERODING AMID CONSTRUCTION STAND-STILL.'

80. 'J – JUSTICE.'

81. 'JUSTICE IS SLOW AND UNSURE IN NATION'S BUSY COURTS.'

82. 'FELONY TRIAL BACK-LOG HELD PERIL TO WAR ON CRIME.'

83. 'POLICE STUDY SHOWS 15.7% SEIZED IN PURSE-SNATCHINGS ARE JAILED.'

84. 'J – JAILS.'

85. 'POOR MEDICAL CARE BLAMED IN MANY PRIS-ON DEATHS.'

86. 'OVERCROWDING OF TOMBS WORSE THAN AT 1970 RIOT.'

87. 'J – JUDGES.'

88. 'JUSTICE SCHWEITZER BEING INVESTIGATED.'

AUDIO

What's more, of the money it gets, fully *one-third is used for tearing down old housing – housing that could be rehabilitated and rebuilt.*

Structurally sound buildings are being demolished at the rate of ten thousand a year, because the Housing Authority is impotent and inept.

This in a city desperate for new housing.

J is for Justice.

Our courts are so clogged with a backlog of cases that many criminals go free.

A recent *New York Times* story revealed that only 15.7% of purse-snatchers go to jail. This means 84.3% go free. This percentage holds up for other crimes.

The grim statistic is that roughly 80% of all crimes are committed by repeaters.

J is also for jails.

Even when criminals are put in jail, the conditions are so bad – so crowded, so crude, so under-staffed and under-funded, that when they get out, chances are *eight in ten they will repeat.*

J is also for the Judges.

And like everything else in this city, the judiciary is riddled with graft and corruption.

VIDEO	AUDIO
89. 'DILORENZO RELIEVED OF CIVIL COURT DUTY.'	Here you see the judges who were stupid enough to be caught. How many more are involved in shady deals ... bribes ... plea bargain payoffs ... favors ...
90. 'BROOKLYN JUDGE AC-CUSED OF BEAME CAM-PAIGN FRAUD.'	The reason the judiciary is in such bad shape is simple: judges, like everybody else in public life, are hacks – lawyers who never made it big ... clubhouse hangers-on who managed to scare up the money to buy a judgeship ... or cash in a favour.
91. 'SUPREME COURT JUS-TICE THALER CON-VICTED IN SECURITIES CASE.'	
92. 'BROOKLYN'S JUDGE RINALDI: THE PUSHERS AND MAFIA GO FREE.'	And make no mistake about it, every judgeship is bought – either with cash or political favors.
93. 'OUSTED CITY AIDE DUE TO BE JUDGE.'	In New York, a federal judgeship sells for $80,000.
94. 'JUDGE ON TRIAL IN BROOKLYN IS CHARGED WITH BUY-ING HIS POST.'	State judgeships go for about $50,000 – the equivalent of one year's salary – half of which goes to the party that nominated him, the other half to the judge's own county Democratic or Republican committee.
95. 'STATE JUSTICE PFINGST CONVICTED OF FRAUD IN DAIRY BANKRUPTCIES.'	Who judges the judges?
	Nobody judges the judges. And we all suffer.
96. 'L – LINDSAY.'	L is for Lindsay.
97. '90,000 ADDED TO CITY'S PAYROLL SINCE LIND-SAY'S FIRST TERM.'	To many across the country, John Lindsay is a reformer ... a great humanitarian mayor ... and the voice of urban America.

VIDEO	AUDIO
98. 'HOW OUR CITY HALL PAYS OFF IN JOBS.'	They say, 'Look what John Lindsay has done for the poor.' By executive order he added 90,000 employees to the city payrolls and sent many of them out into the ghettos and slums signing up the poor for welfare payments.
99. 'CITY 2ND ONLY TO US GOVERNMENT IN NUMBER OF EMPLOYEES ON PAYROLL.'	Today the city's welfare budget is $2½ billion. One out of every six people in New York is on the dole roll.
100. 'STUDY REVEALS WELFARE FRAUD COULD BE AS HIGH AS 30%.'	On closer inspection, about thirty per cent of those on relief are taking money from the city illegally. Three out of every ten welfare recipients are ineligible.
101. 'STATE AUDIT FINDS CITY JOB POLICIES WASTE MILLIONS.'	In other words, welfare clients are *stealing* $700 million a year from the city. And with the full knowledge of City Hall.
102. 'ROCKEFELLER LEADS ATTACK ON MAYOR: CALLS HIM "INEPT!"'	Why would John Lindsay sign up welfare clients like this? Why would his administration sanction $700 million being stolen from the city?
103. 'WITH LINDSAY IN THE GHETTO: "A WALK ON THE WILD SIDE".'	The answer is simple. In return for putting someone on welfare, he asked for a vote in return.
104. 'CITY PAID $200 MILLION SINCE 1969 IN FEES TO PRIVATE CONSULTING FIRMS.'	When the Democrats wouldn't vote for him, and when the Republicans wouldn't vote for him, he turned around and put one-sixth of the city on welfare and got that vote.

VIDEO	AUDIO

105. 'INSPECTORS CITED ON FUND SOLICITING FOR LINDSAY.'

No wonder John Lindsay could walk through the ghetto on the night Martin Luther King was shot and be completely safe: everybody in the place was on his payroll!

106. 'DUMMY COMMITTEES IN D.C. FUNNELLED CASH INTO LINDSAY CAMPAIGN.'

This makes John Lindsay *not* a reformer . . . *not* a humanitarian . . . but an old fashioned political boss in the tradition of the greatest days of Tammany Hall.

107. 'ON A CITY PAYROLL WHILE IN JAIL.'

Instead of building a machine down at the docks where the boats came in, Boss Lindsay found his votes in the ghettos.

108. 'CITY SCALE FOR THOUSANDS 1½ TIMES PRIVATE PAY.'

And since the poor can't come up with campaign funds, where did Boss Lindsay turn for money? He gave out hundreds of millions of dollars in contracts to private consulting firms, and then held up those firms for huge campaign contributions.

109. 'FORMER CITY AIDE GUILTY OF BRIBERY.'

110. 'US LOOKING INTO REPORT TYING CITY PURCHASING AIDE TO PAY-OFF.'

In the words of the old Tammany Hall boss, George Washington Plunkitt, 'He seen his opportunities and he took 'em.'

111. 'TAX COMMISSIONER LEVY FOUND GUILTY IN TICKET FIXING FRAUD.'

Meanwhile the city fell apart. We now have more employees than the whole state of California. Many of the city's employees earn more money from the city – one and a half times more – than they could get doing the same job for the state . . . or for the federal government . . . *or even in private industry.*

112. '5 HOUSING AIDES HELD ON EXTORTION.'

And while Boss Lindsay was building his political base in the ghettos, his cronies were bleeding

VIDEO	AUDIO
113. 'HIGH CITY OFFICIAL HELD IN ETHICS INQUIRY: COMPANY HE CONTROLS SOLD BURGLAR ALARMS TO BOARD OF EDUCATION.'	the tax-payers white, until every layer of his administration became rotten with corruption . . . rotten with graft . . . rotten with greed not seen in this town since the days of Jimmy Walker and the Seabury Investigation.
114. 'RANKIN TO GIVE UP HIS LAW PRACTICE.'	The amounts Boss Lindsay's people have stolen from this city makes Boss Tweed look like the March of Dimes Poster Child.
115. 'MARCUS, EX-LINDSAY AIDE, HELD WITH CORALLO, A MAFIA LEADER, IN KICKBACKS ON CITY CONTRACTS.'	The Corporation Council, J. Lee Rankin, who received a salary of $41,000 a year, for years maintained a private law practice on the side.
116. 'ALBANO REBUKED ON TIE TO MARCUS.'	Boss Lindsay's top commissioner, James Marcus, was jailed for extortion and receiving kickbacks on a city contract.
117. 'RUGGIERO IS FOUND GUILTY ON THREE PERJURY COUNTS.'	Vince Albano, Republican County boss and Lindsay's original sponsor, deeply involved in scandal.
118. 'GARELIK TOOK GIFTS AS CHIEF INSPECTOR.'	Joe Ruggiero, former chairman of the New York Republican Law Committee, deeply involved in a scandal.
119. 'DA PROBING TOP LINDSAY AIDE KRIEGEL: SAYS HE KEPT SILENT AFTER COMPLAINTS OF LAGGING INVESTIGATION.'	His City Council President a crooked cop. Jay Kriegel, Boss Lindsay's Legislative Aide, deep in scandal.

VIDEO	AUDIO
120. 'YOUTH SERVICES AGENCY HEAD QUITS AFTER BEING ACCUSED OF MISAPPROPRIATING $325,000.'	Youth Services Commissioner Ted Gross, deep in scandal.
121. 'CITY'S FIRST DRUG CO-ORDINATOR IS AC-CUSED OF MEDICAID FRAUD.'	And so ad infinitum.
122. 'LINDSAY DECLARES FOR PRESIDENT.'	And when Lindsay realized he couldn't get re-elected, he entered the presidential primaries. After ruining the city of New York, he felt running the country would be a challenge. The damage Boss Lindsay and his henchmen have done to the city will take a quarter of a century to undo.
123. 'M – MUNICIPAL LOAN SCANDAL.'	M. is for the Municipal Loan Scandal.
124. 'MUNICIPAL LOAN PRO-GRAMME: THE BIG-GEST SCANDAL IN THIRTY YEARS.'	The city lent out over $100 million to building owners and landlords to rehabilitate old buildings at special low interest.
125. 'MILLIONS IN HOUSING FUNDS REPORTEDLY MISUSED HERE.' 126. 'A GET-RICH-QUICK SCHEME FINANCED BY THE CITY.'	At 433 East 119th Street, where the city had paid the contractor $333-115, inspectors later esti-mated the construction work was worth a little more than $200,000. This means the landlord of that building cheated the city out of more than $130,000. To date he has not been prosecuted, and he still has the money.

VIDEO	AUDIO
127. 'CITY GAVE LOANS ON NONEXISTENT MORT-GAGES.'	The Municipal Loan Programme stipulated that all workmen were to be paid at prevailing rates – in other words, union scale. There were some 3000 ghetto workmen employed under the loan pro-gramme.
	By one estimate the average prevailing rate for the jobs these workers performed was $8.50 an hour.
128. 'NINE NAMED IN IN-DICTMENTS IN MUNI-CIPAL LOAN SCANDAL.'	Yet the average actual pay was only $1.50. In other words, $7 per man hour – or $21,000 per hour – went directly into the pockets of greedy contractors and Boss Lindsay's corrupt officials.
129. 'DUN & BRADSTREET AMONG 50 NAMED IN HOUSING FRAUD.'	One of New York's most res-pected financial corporations was waist deep in this scandal which has so-far bilked the taxpayers out of more than $100 millions.
130. 'N – NARCOTICS.'	N is for Narcotics.
131. 'OBITUARY OF A HER-OIN USER WHO DIED AT 12.'	Heroin touches the lives of every-one in the city – either with their children getting involved, or their houses and apartments being robbed.
132. 'HUNTS POINT: RULED BY ADDICTS.'	The fact is that 50% of the city's crime is directly caused by nar-cotics. Addicts steal $6 billion a year in the city of New York alone.
133. 'THE 13TH DISTRICT: DRUGS AND MURDER.'	Even now, all over the city, there are vigilante groups. Private citizens are arming themselves not only with clubs and knives but with shotguns and pistols.

VIDEO	AUDIO
134. 'ADDICT'S VICTIMS TURN VIGILANTE.'	It's happening everywhere – on the upper east side of Manhattan . . . in Brooklyn and the Bronx . . . in Little Italy . . . even in China-town.
135. 'STUDENT PUSHERS CALLED HARDENED.'	Contrary to popular belief, the Mafia is *not* involved in narcotics any more. It's a business almost entirely in the hands of the blacks,
136. 'PROBERS LABEL CITY DRUG WAR "FARCE"; POLICE, DA, COURTS AND SCHOOLS PANNED.'	the Puerto Ricans, the Mexicans, the Cubans . . . and the police. That's right. The men making the biggest profits in narcotics in this city today are not the Mafia, but the New York City Police Department. And I'm going to prove that statement in just a minute, when we get to P for police.
137. 'N – NEIGHBOUR-HOODS.'	N is also for the Neighbourhoods.
138. 'NEIGHBOURHOODS: MURDER STREET IN BROOKLYN QUIET IN AREA OF CHANGE.'	The neighborhoods were once the heart and soul of this city. How many remember the good old days . . . free dish nights at the movies . . . summer card parties
139. 'IN BROWNSVILLE, LOOTING IS CONDITION OF LIFE.'	on the roofs or in the yards with lanterns and laughter . . . when you were friends with your neighbours. And when your chil-
140. 'UNREST VEXES YOUTH IN A TORN CHINA-TOWN.'	dren got married, there was once a time when they were glad to move back to the old neighbour-hood to be near mom and pop.
141. 'RISING CRIME STIRS FEAR ON LOWER EAST SIDE.'	Now terror stalks the streets. No one is safe in his home, let alone outside.

VIDEO	AUDIO
142. 'NEIGHBOURHOODS: DERELICTS PLAGUING PENN STATION AREA.'	Quiet, decent communities have been turned into slums ... havens for narcotics addicts ... criminals ... Our children are being beaten and robbed on the way to school.
143. 'NEIGBOURHOODS: LAURELTON IN QUEENS WAS ONCE "IDEAL".'	Worst of all, when something goes wrong in the neighbourhood, there's no one to complain to. Garbage piles up in the streets ...
144. 'ARVERNE: THE SAME OLD RUBBLE.'	pot holes appear, the street lamp goes out. When you call City Hall, all you get is a runaround.
145. 'P – POLICE.'	P is for Police.
146. 'WORK OF POLICE PUT AT 50% OF POTENTIAL.'	The overriding issue in this city is not dirty streets ... it's not too-high real estate taxes ... it's not the poor or transportation or pollution.
147. 'FALSE CITY REPORTS ON CRIME SUSPECTED.'	
148. 'STUDY SCORES CITY'S POLICE AND COURTS AS INEFFICIENT.'	The main issue is Crime – Crime in our homes, Crime in our parks, Crime in the streets, Crime in our playgrounds and schools.
149. 'POLICE SCANDALS SPREADING: OFFICIALS BELIEVE MUCH CORRUPTION STILL UNCOVERED.'	The New York City police are the highest paid in the world; a rookie starts at more than ten thousand a year, and the average policeman makes over seventeen thousand a year – plus benefits. And he can retire at half pay in just twenty years.
150. 'GRAFT PAID TO POLICE HERE SAID TO RUN INTO MILLIONS.'	Yet, our police sleep on the job. They falsify crime reports in order to look like they're doing a better job than they are.
151. 'POLICE SAID TO GET ROOMS AND MEALS FREE FROM HOTELS.'	Furthermore, our police are corrupt. They are extorting money at the rate of tens of millions of dollars a year.

VIDEO

152. 'CROOKED COP: HARLEM TAKE RAN 70-G A MONTH.'

153. 'CITY'S 424 PLAINCLOTHESMEN GET $4 MILLION A YEAR GRAFT.'

154. 'MAFIA BOOK LISTS 10 COPS.'

155. '8 POLICE ACCUSED OF TAKING GRAFT FROM RACKETEERS.'

156. 'MORE POLICE TIED TO GAMBLING CASE.'

157. '24 POLICE INDICTED IN A BRIBERY CASE.'

158. 'GAMBLING BRIBES TO POLICE ALLEGED IN EVERY DIVISION.'

159. 'PAYOFFS COST BUILDERS $75 MILLION A YEAR COPS, AGENCIES SPLIT KITTY.'

160. 'GRAFT STUDY FINDS IN ACTION BY POLICE IN 72 DRUG CASES.'

161. '8 POLICEMEN INDICTED FOR STEALING ADDICTS' MONEY.'

AUDIO

This corruption takes the form of anything from a free cup of coffee or use of a hotel room, on up to huge payoffs amounting to tens of thousands of dollars per man.

It has been estimated that the city's 424 plainclothesmen receive over four million dollars a year in bribes and payoffs. That's more than $35,000 a year *each* – if every one of them were on the take.

Where does the money come from? From gamblers . . . from the construction industry . . . from prostitutes . . . from storekeepers.

And if this wasn't bad enough, the New York City Police Department is deep into the business of heroin and other narcotics.

They extort money from addicts . . . they demand payoffs from pushers . . . they push heroin themselves, making millions of dollars a year in profits from children . . . and poor people in the slums . . . and from turning nice middle class children into addicts, and forcing them into a life of crime.

These are not isolated examples, either. The fact is the average cop on the beat is taking home an extra fifty dollars a week. I'm not saying this is true of every cop. You've got to figure that half the force is in jobs such as the Tactical Patrol Force and the Safety Division where there are no pickings.

VIDEO	AUDIO
162. '15 COPS, PROSECUTOR FACE DOPE-FIX CHARGES.'	But the rest of them – probably ten thousand cops – or one in every four – is a thief, a gangster, an extortionist, a common criminal.
163. 'EVIDENCE OF $25,000 PAYOFFS BY NARCOTICS DEALERS CITED BY HEAD OF STRIKE FORCE.'	I mentioned earlier the Organization that is behind my candidacy makes ninety-five per cent of its money from gambling and money-lending. A miniscule part of our income is from narcotics and extortion.
164. '330 LBS OF SEIZED HEROIN – WORTH $70 MILLION – FOUND STOLEN FROM POLICE DEPT.'	I say a major part of the Police Department's income is from narcotics and extortion.
165. 'HOW DEEP ARE THE POLICE INTO HEROIN TRAFFIC? THE ANSWER IS "VERY DEEP".'	I further accuse the New York City Police Department of being the largest single dealer of illicit heroin and narcotics in the world; and what makes it so truly appalling is they have all the power of the courts and the Establishment on their side.
166. 'THE PUSHER-COP: THE INSTITUTIONALIZING OF POLICE CORRUPTION.'	
	Who respects the law today? Nobody. And we have absolutely no reason to.
167. 'R – REAL ESTATE.'	R is for Real Estate.
	The United Nations building and the grounds around it are valued at $100 million. There is no real estate tax paid on that property.
168. 'NYC REAL ESTATE ASSESSED AT $80 BILLION: MORE THAN ⅓ EXEMPT FROM PROPERTY TAXES.'	Nor is there real estate tax paid on any of the more than 100 foreign embassies in New York, amounting to another $100 million worth of real estate.

VIDEO	AUDIO
169. 'COUNCIL APPROVES $6.223 REALTY TAX: 39.7c RISE IS VOTED.'	In fact, one-third of all real estate in this city is tax exempt, including the Chrysler Building and the World Trade Centre.
	Instead, the real estate tax that is lost from these properties is made up by you – the small homeowners from Brooklyn, the Bronx, and Queens, and by higher rents from tenants.
	Given the tax structure of this city, a person who owns property is crippled.
	The UN is the responsibility of the whole nation. Yet your congressmen in Washington are too interested in foreign policy to do something for the small homeowners of the city.
170. 'S – STATE OF NEW YORK.'	S is for the State of New York.
171. 'STATE'S INFLUENCE HERE: BIG AND GETTING BIGGER.'	New York City is under the complete control of the State. The State retains the right to control such details of city government as the power to decide what taxes the city may impose . . . how many hours a policeman may work . . . what the bridge tolls will be . . . even the cost of a dog license.
172. 'US AND ALBANY SHORT-CHANGE CITY PANEL REPORTS.'	
173. 'GOVERNOR ASKS NEW TAXES OF $1.1 BILLION FOR "CRISIS"; REFUSES MORE AID TO CITY.'	This situation has not changed since 1905, when George Washington Plunkitt, a Tammany Hall politician, said, 'We don't own our streets or our docks or our waterfront or anything else. The Republican Legislature and the Governor run the whole shootin' match.'
174. 'WHAT CAN WE DO TO STOP ALBANY MILKING US DRY?'	

VIDEO	AUDIO
175. 'CITY SAYS IT LOST $250 MILLION AID BECAUSE OF STATE.'	That was 1905. It's true today. New York sends a dollar to Albany and gets back forty-three cents.
176. '$70-MILLION WASTE IN CITY CONTRACTS LAID TO STATE LAW.'	Last year, the state provided $182 in aid for each public school student in the city; each student in any other part of the state received $301.
177. '$525-MILLION PACT ON TAXES FOR CITY HITS INSTANT SNAG.'	Yet our legislators in Albany – as in Congress – cannot agree on anything. Goodman votes different from Ohrenstein; Olivieri and and Batista seldom vote the same way.
178. 'BRIDGE TOLL BILLS BEATEN IN ALBANY: FARE HELD PERILLED.'	And the city is suffering terribly because of it.
179. 'LEGISLATORS VOTE ADDITIONAL FUNDS – FOR THEMSELVES.'	In fact, the only thing that Albany legislators agreed on was to vote themselves a raise.
180. 'T – TRANSPORTATION.'	T is for transportation.
181. 'RUSH-HOUR TRAINS LATE AT LEAST 4TH OF TIME.'	A city is useless if people can't get from one place to another quickly . . . easily . . . safely . . . inexpensively.
182. 'HOLDUPS INCREASING SHARPLY AT SUBWAY CHANGE BOOTHS.'	Five million New Yorkers ride the subway on an average work day. There are delays . . . there is filth . . . there is graffiti . . . there is crime . . . there is danger.
183. 'SUBWAY COLLISIONS AND DERAILMENTS UP 50%.'	Equipment in our subways is old and out of date. There are over a thousand cars more than thirty-five years old.

VIDEO

AUDIO

184. 'LINDSAY VS. ROCKE-
FELLER AND UP GOES
THE FARE.'

As the fare continues to creep
up, the number of riders decreases,
so deficits get worse every
year.

Now all the metropolitan New
York mass transit lines are on the
brink of financial disaster. The
Transit Authority faces an operating deficit of at least $150
million a year. The Long Island
Railroad will lose $80 million;
the Penn Central New Haven line
faces a loss of $15 million.

185. 'TRANSIT RIDERS
DROPPED 2.5% AFTER
FARE RISE.'

186. 'TRANSIT: THE INK
GETS REDDER.'

Crack-ups . . . delayed trains . . .
begrimed windows . . . broken
lights . . . incorrect signs . . .
tattered advertising posters . . .
what can be done. Is it impossible
to have mass transit work in New
York?

187. 'SUBWAY ROULETTE:
THE GAME GETS DAN-
GEROUS.'

For once we have a villain. A real
enemy of the people. That enemy
is the Port Authority.

The citizens of New York and
New Jersey, acting through their
respective legislatures, created the
Port Authority in 1921 to 'co-
ordinate the building of a
balanced transportation system
to meet the needs of the bur-
geoning port and metropolitan
area around it.'

188. 'HOW THE PORT AUTH-
ORITY IS STRANGLING
NEW YORK.'

Instead, the Port Authority has
betrayed the people. It has
created a massive *imbalance* in
ground transportation that is
strangling New York. It has all
but totally ignored the com-
muter railroads. It has preferred
to grow huge – and profitable –
by catering to motorists.

VIDEO

AUDIO

How profitable is the Port Authority? Last year it had revenues of $224 million and cleared $91 million after paying operating expenses and debt interest. That's a 39% gross profit.

189. 'PORT AUTHORITY AMONG CITY'S BIGGEST LANDLORDS.'

Instead of doing what it was supposed to do – coordinating a balanced transportation system – the Port Authority spent one billion dollars for the World Trade Center, two 110-story skyscrapers that have nothing to do with transportation.

190. 'ESTIMATED $4-MILLION TAX REVENUES LOST FROM TRADE CENTRE SAYS BEAME'S OFFICE.'

Not only that, but these two buildings are tax free; they pay no real estate taxes to the city, because they are owned by the Port Authority. As a result, the small homeowners of Brooklyn, the Bronx, and Queens, not only have terrible transportation in the city, but also pay higher real estate taxes.

There are very few organizations in this country that make a thirty-nine percent profit. If you want to find gangsters . . . thugs . . . Shylocks . . . and thieves in this city, don't look to the Organization that's behind my candidacy.

Look at the Port Authority first.

191. 'U – UNIONS.'

U is for Unions.

192. 'SUBWAYS AND BUSES HELD UP BY STRIKE: LINDSAY APPEALS FOR A CURB ON TRAVEL.'

Labour has a stranglehold on New York City. Everytime there is a strike called, some vital area of the city is tied up; we all suffer.

VIDEO	AUDIO
193. 'STRIKE CRIPPLES SCHOOLS: NO SETTLEMENT IN SIGHT.'	With a transit strike, you can't get to work; with a school strike, thousands of women don't dare go to work and leave the kids home alone.
194. 'STRIKE AT DRAWBRIDGES IN CITY CAUSES MASSIVE TRAFFIC JAMS.'	With an elevator strike, the old and infirm can't get in and out of their buildings.
195. 'FIREMEN CONTINUE JOB ACTION.'	When the police or firemen go on strike, our lives are in danger.
196. 'POLICE DEFY APPEALS TO RETURN.'	So long as there are professional politicians running this town, we will be at the mercy of the union bosses, and the city will continue to be unlivable and ungovernable.
197. 'SANITATION STRIKE CONTINUES GARBAGE PILE-UP A HEALTH HAZARD, SAYS U.S. OFFICIAL.'	V is for violence.
198. 'V – VIOLENCE.'	There are an estimated two million illegal guns in the city of New York.
199. 'THE CITY AS BATTLEFIELD: A GLOBAL CONCERN.'	Guns come into the city at the rate of about 100,000 a year.
200. 'SNIPING, FIREBOMBINGS LIKELY IN MANY CITIES SOME AUTHORITIES SAY.'	The constitution of the United States declares that the people have the 'right to keep and bear arms'. But the constitution was written for a basically agricultural society; it was authored by a group of gentlemen farmers from Virginia.
201. 'HOMICIDE RATE RISES 42% IN FIRST PART OF YEAR HERE.'	The fact is, there is no place for guns in our cities today.
202. 'PANEL SEES CRIME TURNING THE CITIES INTO ARMED CAMPS.'	Even though we have lost four Presidents, countless national leaders, and millions of loved ones over the years, Congress still refuses to pass any kind of firm controls on the sale of guns and ammunition.
203. 'MILITANTS STOCKPILE ILLEGAL GUNS ALL ACROSS THE US'	

VIDEO	AUDIO

204. 'SALES OF GUNS BOOM-ING AGAIN.'

Again we see how our congres-sional delegation is made up of yellow-bellied cowards who haven't got the guts to stand up to the gun lobby, just as they

205. 'GUN LOBBY HAILS TYDINGS' DEFEAT.'

won't stand up to the highway lobby, the oil lobby, the farm lobby, the defence lobby, or any other lobby.

206. 'U.S. PANEL URGES HAND-GUN SEIZURE TO CURB VIOLENCE.'

The result is we can look for more crime . . . more violence . . . more danger in the coming months and years.

207. 'W – WELFARE.'

W is for welfare.

208. 'RECORD $2.9 BILLION ASKED FOR CITY'S AID TO POOR.'

One quarter of our city budget goes to the Human Resources Administration. New York City gives away more in welfare pay-ments than the entire budget for the states of Colorado and Florida *combined*.

209. 'SPIRALING WELFARE COSTS: NO END IS IN SIGHT HERE.'

One out of every six New Yorkers is on welfare.

Every family of five in New York City is paying for a sixth person – somebody who won't go out and

210. 'WELFARE IS A CAN-CER.'

get a job and earn his own way. You're paying for the children of women who keep getting pregnant and don't know who the father is.

211. 'CITY RELIEF LEAK PUT AT $700-MILLION A YEAR.'

Welfare is strangling us.

People come from all over the country to get our high benefits. And by law, we have to put them on the dole roll. Thirty per cent are ineligible, bilking the city out of $700 million a year.

VIDEO

212. 'CITY REPORTS WEL-
FARE FRAUDS BY
250,000.'

213. 'SUGARMAN SAYS
WELFARE FRAUDS ARE
NOT HORRENDOUS
CRIMES.'

AUDIO

Most people don't realize welfare
is a double burden. Not only does
the city send out almost a million
and a half welfare checks every two
weeks, but these leaches have to
be provided with city services –
police, fire, sanitation – for which
they contribute no taxes in return.

Welfare in New York is like
asking Alaska to pay the largest
share of the National Defence
budget, because it happens to
border on the Soviet Union.
It's like asking Florida to pay a
larger share of Social Security
because our older citizens retire
there.

Welfare is a national problem.
And until our do-nothing congressmen and professional politicians get off their collective duffs
and get the needed legislation, it's
going to get worse . . . and worse
. . . until each family of three is
paying for a fourth . . . and then
each couple is paying for a third
. . . and so ad infinitum.

With that, the 'New York ABC's' ended. When the lights came
back on in the studio, the candidate calmly let the screen up to
reveal the skyline of Manhattan. With a gesture to the great city
below, Page reminded the viewers that behind every one of those
hundreds of headlines was a story detailing some area of graft,
corruption, inefficiency, egotism, decay, malfeasance and misfeasance unmatched perhaps anywhere in American history.
Every department, every layer, every bureau, every facet of city
government was involved, bringing about what appeared to be
the total breakdown of the city.

It was H. L. Mencken who wrote thirty years ago: 'Politicians as
a class radiate a powerful odour. Their business is almost as firmly

grounded on false pretences as that of the quack doctor or the shyster lawyer . . . The typical politician does far better in politics than he could have done at anything else.'

This was true then; it's just as true today.

The candidate slowly returned to his pedestal chair and eased himself into it. During the time he wasn't on screen Vin, the make-up man, had bathed his face and forehead with a handkerchief soaked in witch-hazel (being careful not to smudge the make-up). Thus he came back on the air looking cool and refreshed.

So when my Organization saw what the professional politicians were doing to the city, it was decided to run a candidate – *a non-politician* – for mayor.

Now in this situation, any man who runs for mayor has good cause to examine his motives, if he's interested in attacking the problem on the old basis. To wit, running for mayor in such a way that he could be elected: making the old deals in the old ways, coming into power with an administration and a bureaucracy and a set of municipal unions who are all waterlogged themselves, all corrupt themselves, all full of crime themselves.

We chose the other path – a completely independent candidacy, wholly outside the established system.

It is true we had a campaign chest of ten million dollars. The *New York Times* expressed shock not only at the amount, but the sources from which it came.

Ten million dollars is not much to spend on an election. When Carter Burden ran for the City Council in 1969, he spent $260,000. That amount projected over a city-wide election – thirty-nine council-manic districts – would equal exactly $10 million.

When Andrew Stein ran for the State Assembly on Manhattan's east side, his father, Jerry Finklestein, spent $250,000; projected over sixty-eight assembly districts, that equals $17 million.

Nor are the sources of this ten million dollars so shocking when you consider the Kennedys, whose initial fortune was made in various illicit wheelings and dealings, and the Rockefellers, whose grandfather was one of the notorious robber barons of the nineteenth century. The Kennedys and Rockefellers have spent millions of these ill-gotten fortunes on American politics; the *New York Times* endorsed them; and the country has benefited enormously from their participation in politics

Page asserted that the money spent on his campaign had already produced tangible benefits to the city. For example, there was CERF, the Citizens Emergency Relief Fund, bringing instant cash to any deserving family who has suffered a fire or flood. To date, the campaign had given away $22,500 to needy families since the programme was implemented.

The Page campaign also established the Overdose Hotline, a 24-hour counselling service to help dispense information on drugs and drug-related problems. So far, the city's Health Services Administration had credited the new OD Hotline with saving fourteen lives since it had been started three months ago.

Some 68 neighbourhood headquarters had been opened throughout the city. It was Page's intention to keep these storefronts open after election, to be used as neighbourhood centres for the community. They would be staffed with paid workers and volunteers to assist citizens coming there for advice or help. Lawyers also would be available for the first time in a decade to *all* the people of the city, ensuring them of someone in their own neighbourhood to hear and act on their problems, instead of layer on layer of little grey bureaucrats buried deep in the Municipal Building downtown who don't even answer their phones, let alone give any help.

On top of that, Page told his audience that his campaign had established a meaningful dialogue with the voters. Much of the $10 million was being spent invisibly, going into computer letters, polls, phone calls, and neighbourhood headquarters. His organization was reaching the voters, finding out their needs, their problems, their hopes and fears, with a view to finding out what precisely was wrong with the city and where the priorities lay.

There are those who will say my organization will loot and plunder and sack the city in the course of my administration as mayor.

To them, I say this: you have the watchful eyes of a diligent and hardworking press.

You have your elected watchdogs in the city council and the district attorneys who are free to investigate every facet of city government, from the office of the mayor right on down to the lowest file clerk. If any malfeasance or misfeasance is found, the following may happen:

One. The mayor may be removed from office by the governor upon charges and after service upon him of a copy of the charges and an opportunity to be heard in his defense. Pending the preparation and disposition of charges, the governor may suspend the mayor for a period of not exceeding thirty days. That's a direct quote from your City Charter.

Two. Anyone in government is subject to the laws of the nation, the state, and the city. There is no immunity for the men in power. There is less, for the white hot light of publicity is constantly focused on elected officials. And if wrong-doing is discerned, they can be impeached, prosecuted, and if convicted, jailed. One has but to look at the unhappy records of James Marcus, Supreme Court Justice Seymour Thaler, Carmine De Sapio, to see this is true.

Three and lastly, there is an election every four years. This means that you, the citizens, have the opportunity to decide; you can vote out the old and vote in the new. So theoretically, you are completely protected from unscrupulous men in government. In actuality, you have had years and years and years of the most unscrupulous, corrupt, inefficient government imaginable.

Right now, New York City is a smoking ruin.

The camera dollied in until the candidate's face was filling the entire television screen. He looked directly at the viewer, talking earnestly. Each pore on his face was visible; even the tiniest movement of his mouth could be discerned. His eyes were unblinking. A liar and a crook simply could not withstand that kind of scrutiny without showing it.

What my candidacy offers you is one last chance to save this city – to get the government out of the hands of the clubhouse hacks, the hangers-on, the palm greasers, the bosses, the union chiefs, the corruptors, and the corruptees – and put it into the hands of the most efficient Organization the world has ever known.

To be sure this is a radical idea. But throughout American history, what is right for this country has been called radical by those who have a stake in preserving wrong.

As mayor, I can guarantee you there will be no more crime, because we are crime.

There will be no more narcotics problem, because we know who controls narcotics, and it's to everybody's interest to break the back of the drug problem once and for all.

There will be no more police corruption, because we are the corruptors. We know who the dishonest cops are, and we'll get rid of them.

There'll be no more housing and building problems, because we are already in the construction business, and it is to our benefit to get laws passed which permit building to go on without having to pay city inspectors and the cop on the beat millions of dollars a year.

There'll be no more shoddy justice in our courts, because we're the Organization that has bribed the judges and obstructed justice; we're the only ones who can force the crooked judges to resign from the bench.

Labour unions will never again get a strangle hold on New York City, because we understand labour and have been dealing with it for years.

There'll be no more transportation strikes to paralyze the city. No more teacher strikes to disrupt the education of our children. No more public utility strikes or building strikes or police and fire strikes to make this city a living hell for you, the citizens, and a haven for the junkies, the burglarers, the muggers, and the rapists. Why? Because we have ways of keeping people from going on strike! . . .

And never again will the New York congressional delegation be divided on an issue. Because if the congressmen don't fall in line and get us the federal money we need and the proper legislation for our cities, my Organization will put up the money to elect candidates who will.

The camera dollied back, and Page arose from his chair to amble over to where his daughters were seated. Both girls looked directly at the camera.

So I am here before you tonight to offer a clear choice. You can, in this election, give the city back to the professional politicians and be assured of getting more of the same.

Or you can vote for change. You can put to work the most efficient Organization in the world. And if the city isn't cleaner, and the streets aren't safer, and the subways aren't running better, and the air isn't purer, and the police and building inspectors are still shaking you down for the same hundreds of millions of dollars a year, then vote us out of office in four years.

The camera panned into a medium shot of the candidate, so that he alone was on screen again.

But right now I say to you, give me a chance, and I will give New York a chance. Believe me when I tell you, it's the only chance you have.

For in the words of my favorite poet, Rudyard Kipling:

> I'd not give way for an Emperor,
> I'd hold my road for a King –
> To the Triple Crown I would not bow down –
> But this . . . is a different thing.

I'll not fight with the Powers of Air,
Sentry, pass him through!
Drawbridge let fall, 'tis the Lord of us all,
The Dreamer whose dreams come true!

Thank you all. Good-night, and God bless you.

Chapter 28

The speech ran exactly one hour, which meant there was only time for Chancellor and Cronkite to sign off without comment before regular programming was resumed. Back in the studio, all the brilliant lights were killed, and it suddenly seemed very dark. Page slumped into a chair, exhausted from the heat of the lights and the emotional strain. The first to reach the candidate was Jack Leokum who patted him on the back and rubbed his neck like a prizefighter's second. 'You were great, Dev. Just great!'

'Did it go okay?'

'Great. Just great.'

Mark arrived on the scene, followed by Bobby DeStefano who shook his hand. 'It was good, Dev. Real good.'

'What next?' the candidate wanted to know.

'We go upstairs to meet with the press.'

'Not now. I couldn't handle it.'

'Just come with me, boy,' Bobby snapped. 'I'm going to do the talking to those bastards.'

Leokum and Mark helped Page to his feet. They threaded their way out of the studio, stepping over cables and dodging around cameras. As the candidate drew near the door, several technicians and cameramen came up to shake his hand and wish him luck. Others steered clear of him. Here was the first indication of how the final week of campaigning would polarize the city.

They took an elevator to the eighth floor and emerged into the crowded hallway where they were surrounded by the press. Astonished at seeing the candidate in their midst, they began shouting questions. There was a crush around Page as he made his way toward the studio. Cameras were snapping as portable strobe lights were flashed and the motion-picture crews jostled for position. The questions kept coming, but Page, tired now, pushed silently by.

At length they reached the great grey studio where the press had watched the speech on the giant overhead-projection screen. Mark and Bobby ordered everyone to take seats. There was a general milling around, but finally the room was quiet, with Bobby DeStefano, Mark Altschul, and the candidate standing in front of the reporters under the big white screen. Jack Leokum remained over to one side.

Bobby stepped forward. There was no public address system, so he had to shout. His announcement was brief and to the point. When the campaign first started, he said he had been told by Mark Altschul, who was with the Lindsay administration, that every reporter in room 9 of City Hall was on the payroll of the county leader of the Manhattan Democratic Committee. So he had decided it would be a good idea if the campaign sent a little cash gratuity to the people covering and writing about the Devereaux Page effort. The first mailing went out in July – ten envelopes, each containing $100 cash. Nobody said anything. The following week, twelve envelopes went out – $1200, and still no comment. Week after week the number grew until at this point there were sixty members of the press on the campaign payroll. Many of the reporters in the studio were among them. Much of the money went to the newswriters and editors who actually determined the placement and length of the stories.

Suddenly the young Mafioso produced a little round black film case – a single Mickey Mouse ear – and held it up for all to see.

Out of the sixty people on our payroll, we've got film of ten of you going to your mail boxes, finding an envelope from the campaign, opening it, and putting the money in your pocket.

The hidden camera was a Bolex, equipped with an Angenieux zoom lens system, so it is possible to read the campaign corner card on the envelope, actually see the two fifty-dollar bills being taken out, and of course, recognize who the person is.

I'm not saying now who these ten people are. It's enough to say there's at least one from each of the major papers and local television stations. There is one Negro and one woman. That's all I'll say.

There was absolute silence in the studio, except for the rustling of three score very uncomfortable people shifting their weight from one buttock to the other. The candidate and Mark Altschul could not watch. To them, the exposure of weakness in another human being was embarrassing; Bobby throve on it, like a wild animal sniffing blood and going in for the kill.

Now I don't mind you guys reporting the news fairly. I don't mind good objective reporting and criticism. That's your job. But I'm goddamn sick of the sanctimonious tone of moral outrage in your newsstories and editorial pages.

We've been good to you people. Since we opened the press suite at the Commodore six months ago, you people have guzzled forty cases of booze, sixty-nine cases of beer, and run up a bill at the Commodore of $33,000 which the campaign has paid.

We've given you good copy. We've given you cooperation. We've wined you. We've dined you. Even got you girls. And we've given you cash.

He shook the film can in his hand so the reel inside rattled.

Now, all I'm saying to you is this. You cut out this moral indignation bullshit and give us fair straight coverage for the rest of the campaign, or I'll release not only this film, but a list of the names of everybody on the pad, and even those of you who are not. It'll blow the lid off the whole fucking New York City press corps.

Now, if you've got any questions to ask the candidate, he's available for a few minutes.

There were no questions at that time.

Ten minutes later as he emerged from the revolving door of the RCA Building on to 50th Street, Page found a crowd of several hundred people waiting to catch a glimpse of him. There were no reporters hounding him with their endless questions and blinding lights. Here were only the people – his people – and they began to cheer when they saw him; the sound of their voices seemed to wash away the fatigue. As he felt the first handshake and then another and another, a broad grin began to spread across his face. Soon he was deep into the assembled throng, kissing the women on the cheek, clasping hands, touching faces; this contact with raw humanity again produced the old magic. 'I love you all,' he said over and over again as he moved among them. 'Everything's going to be all right in this city, because you're beautiful, and I love you.'

The Devereaux Page Alphabet Speech became a classic of its kind, ranking with the Checkers Speech and Ted Kennedy's apologia to the nation following the Chappaquiddick incident. But there was a difference. All three men had been caught with their hands in the cookie jar. Of Kennedy's speech, written by Ted Sorensen, one can only think of Dalton Trumbo's letter to his son from jail in which he wrote: 'Let the lie be delivered full-face, eye-to-eye, and without scratching the scalp. But let it contain one fundamental element of creative ingenuity – one and no more – to convince the listener of the improbability you have inserted; its mere existence places the stamp of truth on everything you have said.' Kennedy took the least imaginative approach, and he didn't pull it off.

The Checkers Speech was more successful. Nixon, too, delivered the lie full-face without scratching the scalp, saying, in effect, 'Yes, my hand was in the cookie jar, but without that cookie, I would have starved to death; and anyone who would permit a 100 per cent American boy like me to starve is a scoundrel of the first order.'

Page, on the other hand, quite frankly admitted his hand was in the jar, and said he found the cookies so rotten that he should be given the bakery to manage.

The effect of the Page television appearance was like an electric jolt to the city. Somehow the myriad stories of corruption, graft, inefficiency, and wastage seemed less offensive when they had appeared one-by-one over the years. But the piling them one atop the other for a solid hour rocked the already shaken city on its heels. The Alphabet of Horrors speech was just that, and apparently it worked. According to the Neilson rating, Page drew 83 per cent of the television audience in the city (27 per cent of the country), and early results from the polls indicated a massive leap in the percentages in his favour.

When the poll results were released the following Tuesday, the news media were astounded by the public's almost eager acceptance of underworld involvement. No doubt the Watergate scandal was still fresh in people's minds; this kind of thing always went on in politics.

And for all the outrage on the part of the press, it was these very papers and broadcasters who had fed for years on the Mafia, giving lurid headline coverage to the shootings, the gang wars, the investigations, the rackets, and to the dapper mobsters themselves. The critics and reviewers had thrown garlands at such movies as *The Godfather*, *Bonnie and Clyde*, *Little Caesar*, *Key Largo*, and such books as *The Valachi Papers*, *My Life in the Mafia*, *Honour Thy Father* and John Kobler's brilliant *Capone*. The fact was, crime stories sold papers. Books and movies about the Mafia made lots of money. Now in this week before the election, the media boys were trying to have their cake and eat it too. And it didn't quite wash with the electorate.

The story quite literally wiped out all other news as far as the voters were concerned. There was only one issue now: should the city be given back to the politicians for more of the same, or given over to the Mafia who promised to make some dramatic changes for the better?

A quick check the following morning indicated that all but one of his 68 storefront headquarters had been reopened, and new volunteers, furious at the current administration, were showing up by the thousands all over the city, insisting they be allowed to work for the candidate. The Commodore staff returned, Berman, Loomis, Klein, and the Chinese, Jimmy Lee. Also very much on hand was the campaign lawyer, Sol Rosen, short, with thinning hair, a paunch he covered up with natty double-breasted suits, and rimless granny glasses. He looked like anyone's dippy Uncle Harry, but he had an incisive mind, and an encyclopedic knowledge of the law; above all, he remained cool under the most intense pressure.

Early Monday morning the first truckload of a new piece of campaign literature was delivered to the Commodore. Titled *New York ABC's*, here was Dev Page's Alphabet Speech reproduced in full; not only were the headlines he had used included, but the full stories that went with the headlines as well. The document was the size of a tabloid newspaper and printed on newsprint; it ran 256 pages, with the candidate's speech running down half the right hand page in 24-point type, and the various news stories reproduced to the left of it, just as they appeared in their original form in daily newspapers or magazines. At the very top corner of each page were running heads: A is for Aged, or B is for Building and Construction; and each new subject was introduced with a massive letter of the alphabet, nearly half the page size, with the subject it stood for.

Subtitled *The Alphabet of Horrors*, the publication was just that, a hodgepodge of typestyles used by the different newspapers and magazines, a truly ugly printing job with some of the stories layed out slightly askew and with occasional blotches of black ink. But it was all there – a huge, lurid compendium of corruption, graft, official sinning, inefficiency, extortion, and profiteering that was causing New York City to lay strangled and dying, the victim of greedy politicians in City Hall and do-nothing congressmen and legislators in Washington and Albany. Taken separately and spaced out over a period of three or four years, each individual story would cause the reader to cluck and shake his head. All wrapped up in this crude, sensational, scissors-and-paste style, documented by the actual news stories themselves the thing seemed actually to vibrate in the hand and produce a sick feeling in the pit of the stomach. Also included were many stories not mentioned on the television show – Lucian K. Truscott's brilliant series on the Municipal Loan Scandals from the *Village Voice;* Jack Newfield's exposés on the judiciary, including his deliciously scandalous piece for *New York* entitled 'The Ten Worst Judges in New York,' which was reprinted complete with all the correspondence from readers, pro and con, that appeared after the article was published; and much, much more.

New York ABC's were coming off the presses of the *Bergen Record* at the rate of 50,000 an hour, so by Tuesday morning, there were close to two million in print, and for the rest of the week, campaign volunteers trudged through the streets of the city, up and down the front stoops of houses and stairwells in the endless high-rise buildings ringing doorbells and thrusting the publication into the hands of whomever came to the door. If there was no answer, it was left on the doormat outside.

There was no stopping Bobby DeStefano now. He pulled out all the stops in one wild last-ditch attempt to win the mayoralty for his candidate. The media department under Lou Klein was told to call the time salesman from every New York radio and television station and buy up all unsold commercial time for the next week. Already Johnny DiSantis and Leokum were at Armand's studio editing the tape of Page's Alphabet Speech so that each letter of the alphabet became a separate TV spot, running from as little as 15 seconds – A for Aging – to a full minute – H is for Health and Hospitals. At the end of each commercial came an announcer's voice-over saying, 'Vote Tuesday for Devereaux Page, the Citizen Candidate. Remember we're the only Organization that can change things.'

And so, the media blitz was on. Instead of $10 million, the campaign would eventually end up costing $12 million – one more million for printing the *Alphabet of Horrors* tabloid, another $600,000 for the incredible amounts of television and radio time, and a good $400,000 to put on a huge Election Eve rally at Madison Square Garden.

The morning after the speech, city and federal marshals fanned out through the five boroughs to issue subpoenas to the entire campaign staff and the candidate, ordering them to appear before the New York County Grand Jury, and federal grand juries in New York and Trenton, New Jersey. Many were returnable the next day at 10.00 AM. With the election just a week away, a series of grand jury appearances could well quash momentum by tying up both the candidate and the staff for many hours every day.

Actually, the grand jury appearances did not have much effect on the campaign. The reason was simple. Everyone including the candidate took the Fifth Amendment, refusing to answer every question put to them on the grounds of possible self-incrimination. If the government was going to build up a case of conspiracy, they would have to look for incriminating testimony from sources other than the principals. Thus the grand jury proceedings took only a few hours out of each person's time.

Devereaux Page himself now desperately wanted the mayoralty. He had known the city was in bad shape, but until they had thrown together the Alphabet Speech, piling case histories of decay and corruption on top of each other, no one really had seen how sick the situation was. Not the voters, not the candidate, not even Mark Altschul who was the instigator of the whole plan in the first place. It was as though the Alphabet Speech had become a kind of Apostles' Creed; the deeper they got into it, the more firmly they began to believe in what they were doing.

By Election Day, the entire Page organization – from the lowest volunteer in the most remote storefront in the west Bronx, right on up to the Commodore headquarters staff and the candidate himself – were filled with a kind of missionary zeal.

Chapter 29

Each morning of that last week, Page was out of bed at dawn to charge off to the hinterlands of Queens or the Bronx or Brooklyn to snag voters at key subway or bus stops on their way to work and exhort them to vote him into office. The pace was killing, with twenty-five and thirty appearances a day. And the complexion of the campaign had changed. No longer did the candidate and his entourage move through the city in sleek white automobiles. Instead, they rattled around on flatbed trucks with huge signs on the sides proclaiming DEVEREAUX PAGE – THE CITIZEN CANDIDATE. Page himself rode in a caravan of three of these trucks from morning till night, criss-rossing the city. Usually inch the final weeks of campaigning, candidates hire sound trucks to prowl the streets blaring their message to the voters. Both Bobby and Mark agreed that sound trucks, with their harsh blasts of noise and garbled messages, created more ill will than anything else. So with the Page campaign, the first thing to be heard was music from a live band on the lead truck. A dozen banjo players from the Red Onion nightclub heralded Page's arrival everywhere; they wore red-and-white striped shirts with garters on the sleeves, and boater hats; and the crisp autumn air was shattered by the Tumpa-tumpa-tumpa-tumpa-tump of their banjos.

Then came the truck bearing the candidate with a huge sign plastered on the side panels proclaiming: MEET DEVEREAUX PAGE! On the candidate's truck was a loudspeaker system, so if there was a crowd, the caravan could stop and the candidate say a few words. Riding on the following trucks were campaign aides, many of them pretty girls, waving banners and balloons and distributing buttons, bumper stickers, and, of course, copies of *New York ABC*'s. It was one wild final week of campaigning, of trying to get out into the teeming masses of voters all over the city.

The caravan of trucks went up one street and down another, band playing, banners flying, the candidate standing on the second truck waving and smiling.

And the crowds came round. They were curious to see this man who had behind him the legendary secret Organization that had suddenly surfaced and was offering a New Day for the city of New York. As the trucks pulled up to the main hall of a neighbourhood, shoppers and pedestrians would gather around to listen to the music and stare at the candidate. They were hesitant crowds at first, but once the music stopped and Page began to speak, the electricity flowed. He would begin with a low-key, self-depreciating series of remarks that would cause a ripple of laughter, or, if it was a humourless audience, at least put them at ease. He was one of them, he was saying, just an ordinary man who puts his pants on one leg at a time just like everybody else, flesh and blood, of the people.

Then, like a crack of thunder he would begin his peroration, holding a copy of the *New York ABC's* over his head; here was Billy Graham with a Bible, and he would slam into city government and the rooking it had been giving the people of New York all these years. Opening the big tabloid seemingly at random, he would pick a subject, point out some of the headlines and quote from his own text. Under Jack Leokum, Page had become a master orator, able to mobilize resentment against all politicians, no matter whether they were in or out of office. By the time he finished, he was bobbing and weaving like a prizefighter, shaking his fists and crying for revenge against those who had done the city wrong. After one final exhortation to the people to get out and 'vote some decency into city government!', he would leap off the truck amidst cheers and applause to roughhouse his way through the assembled throng, shaking hands, signing autographs, tousling hair, until he had them jumping up and down with excitement, women and children screaming for a chance to touch him. The pure vitality and physicality of the man in their midst seemed to send shockwaves to the outer fringes of the crowd. It was the old politics again, a combination of Huey Long, (a splendid orator who hated to be touched by people), and Robert Kennedy who, at the end of his trail, throve on the searing, thumping assaults on his person by a horny mob. It was as though Page's audience was a woman that could be sweet-talked with words until she was wet with anticipation, at which point words were no longer valid, and he had to thrust himself into the midst of her in one wild final orgiastic love-in. That last week, his campaign became like a circus hitched to a tornado. The electorate was a giant cunt, and Devereaux Page had at last found the button!

It had been an astounding campaign. From nowhere, a figure had come forward to win all those rowdy truck drivers, embittered cabbies, boisterous construction workers and hard hats, the women who spend Saturday in curlers and dream of going on 'Let's Make a Deal' – neighbourhood bound, fearful of going out at night because of crime in the streets, angry at the drop in property values and the incursion of 'the coloured' into nearby blocks. Like the Italian-American Civil Rights League, Page's candidacy provided a vehicle of outrage for these people of the boroughs, with low incomes, causing them to live in anxious suspension above poverty but well below affluence, whose earnings were being shrunk even further by inflation, who had grown bitterly resentful of the tens of millions of dollars a week being doled out in welfare payments to blacks and Puerto Ricans, whom they felt, didn't know what it was to do an honest day's work. And Page's performance was all the more remarkable, for he was an upper-class WASP with no experience in politics. Yet he had stepped into a leadership vacuum that had long existed among New York's low-income white working classes, filled only by such little rotund buffoons as Assemblyman Vito Batista and former Comptroller Mario Procaccino.

There had been a halt in momentum when the *New York Times* exposé came out, but Page, with a single television appearance, had turned the tables on the Establishment, heaping scorn and abuse on those in power, and battering it home with a brilliantly documented barrage of facts, figures, news stories which was suddenly made available in printed form to every voter in the city. Now in this final week, Page was repeating in twentieth century New York what the Honoured Society has been pulling in Sicily since the seventeenth century. With the help of Joe Colombo and *The Godfather*, and hard evidence of the most corrupt administration since Jimmy Walker, if not that of Boss

William Marcy Tweed, Page was convincing hundreds of thousands of honest men and women that whoever defames the
Honoured Society also defames them. Not only was he heating up
the city, he was taking it to fever pitch; the polls were shooting
upward in his favour like hot thermometers. He avoided Manhattan now, where the rich limousine-liberals were too well
insulated from the grotesqueries of big city living – their children
were in private schools, the streets were cleaned daily, and
weekend retreats in the country allowed them to 'get away from
it all.' Page's constituency was out there where it counted: in
Brooklyn, which if split off from New York would be the third
largest city in America; in the Bronx, itself larger than all of
Baltimore; and in Queens, with its two million population that
made it a bigger city than Detroit. These were his people, and
he was socking it to them. If events failed to occur naturally, the
candidate produced them by cracking the whip of his oratory
until he had created a frenzy of outrage in his listeners; suddenly
the atmosphere was charged, and a sense of danger pervaded
the air around him.

In Manhattan the liberal press was screaming for his head in
their editorials; at the same time the campaign was running full-
page ads in those very papers. All the city's television and radio
stations were running his commercials – excerpts from the
Alphabet Speech, pounding home again and again the facts, the
underpinnings of rot and decay in every corner of government.
Nobody was reading the papers much these days; instead, the
electorate was deep into the *New York ABC*'s, trying to understand the issues and see where their government had failed them
with welfare, housing, hospitals, the police, and the whole
unheavenly host of horrors Page had uncorked. It was truly a
modern-day Pandora's box, and the deeper you dug into it, the
more self-evident it became that in spite of his questionable backing, the only hope for the city was the election of Devereaux
Page. As the final days before the election approached, all the
polls – Louis Harris, Oliver Quayle, the *News*, and even the *Times*
which has been known to withhold news if they thought it might
help the candidate of its choice – agreed Page would lose Manhattan and Staten Island, but would win big in Brooklyn, the
Bronx and Queens. Devereaux Page was the next mayor apparent.

Chapter 30

That last morning of the campaign, Devereaux Page awoke at six and took Gelsey and Johnna for one of their dawn horseback rides in Central Park. By seven-thirty, the orange sun was high enough to reflect off the skyscraper windows, causing certain of them to glitter like jewels. It was to be a magnificent day. There was the snap of autumn in the air, and Page repeatedly brought his animal to a full standstill and inhaled the full, fresh fragrant morning, after which he would stand in the stirrups and drink in the spectacle of the skyline. Once Johnna piped up, 'Why do you keep doing that, Daddy?'

'Doing what, darling?'

'Stopping the horse and breathing in like that?'

Page seemed suddenly distant, as though he were playing some far-off scene in his mind. 'I just love this life so. I mean being here on earth in this great city and having you girls with me. That's all.'

'Do you think you'll be mayor, daddy?'

'The polls all seem to think so. But I don't know.' He shook his head. 'I just don't know.' He gave the horse a savage dig with his heel, and the animal took off at a dead run, kicking up black dirt behind as he went, while the candidate savoured the wind full in his face.

At eleven, Page left for the Waldorf where, with Jack Leokum, he rehearsed the big speech he was to give that night at the Election Eve rally; later, he took the girls for a ride in Central Park in one of the old horse-drawn carriages, and thence to Rumplemeyer's ice cream parlour for hot chocolate and sodas. On leaving, Johnna asked, 'Daddy, when you're mayor, where will we live?'

'I'll show you,' he said, and when they were in the campaign car, he ordered Jimmy the Dwarf, his wheel man for seven months now, to take them to 88th Street and the East River.

Up to Fiorello La-Guardia's time, the mayor resided in his own home, distinguished officially only by a pair of green police lanterns hung outside the door; but since then, the city had supplied its chief executive with a splendid 18th century mansion set inside Carl Schurz Park on a green lawn rolling down to the riverbank. The candidate and his daughters stood outside the black wrought-iron fence staring like ordinary tourists at the classic white house that was to be their home when Page took office January first.

On Election Eve, as the last of the city's 6871 voting machines were being readied in the polling places, the final rally was held. Tickets had been delivered to all the neighbourhood headquarters two days previously with instructions that everybody who came should bring a sign, drawn on cardboard, and tacked to a pole. Printed signs that looked like they came from official sources were meaningless; crude, hand-made ones added authenticity; so there were sign-making parties at every headquarters in the city. When the crowds arrived at Madison Square Garden, they found billboards and a marquee proclaiming:

Dev Page Is Having
A Little Party
For His Friends

At 7.00 PM, the audience was admitted, each member being given a box dinner, a small bottle of chianti wine and a Florentine silver keepsake – for the women a charm, for the men either a key ring or a tie tack. By 8.00 the Garden was filled with noisily happy campaign workers, their friends and family. The overflow was shunted to the Felt Forum where they could watch the proceedings upstairs on a giant movie screen. The arena of the Garden was covered with dirt in preparation for the National Horse Show which was opening the following night. Hanging from the ceiling were nets of coloured balloons – some 12,000 of them blown up by union men at 35¢ each – waiting to be tripped after Page made the final rousing speech of the evening.

There was a marching band specially flown over from Loreto, Italy, and a contingent from Pisa who marched in brightly coloured 12th century costumes usually worn only for the

Gioco del Ponte, the local game held in June. There were many other events from Italy, including a ball game from Florence in 16th century costume, and the entire Taormina Fete with Sicilian costumes and floats; and one spectacular display which brought tears to half the audience when the lights were turned off and the Night Festival of the *Rificolone,* with its hundreds of lanterns, was reproduced. During the festivities, some 20,000 splits of Italian champagne were given out, along with beer and more chianti for any who wanted it, so the evening was punctuated continually with the festive pop of champagne corks. Bobby DeStefano made a short speech and was greeted with wild enthusiasm; it was his first time in any kind of public lime-light, and he obviously loved it.

Although not scheduled to speak until after 10.00 PM, Page was in his dressing room under the stands at 8-30. It was a non-descript room, with grey walls and green carpeting. A dressing table and mirror ran the length of the room, and there were wall lockers to one side. Throughout the evening, various members of the campaign team stopped in to greet him and wish him well. But essentially his last hours were spent alone with his thoughts. The girls were upstairs watching the pageant and listening to the speeches from box seats.

At one point Mark Altschul came into the dressing room to find the candidate alone with his head in his hands in front of the mirror. 'Are you all right, Dev?' There was concern in his voice.

'I wish to hell I didn't have to go out there,' Page replied looking up. 'I just wish I didn't.' He sat cracking his ankles in castanet-like accompaniment. 'There were so many things I wanted to do.'

'There's twenty-three thousand screaming fans and six thousand more watching on the big screen in the Felt Forum,' Mark reassured him. 'There are bands, parades, champagne. It's a helluva a show. You'll love it!'

Page shook his head and looked at his campaign manager. There was a kind of haunted look in the candidate's blue eyes. His sandy hair was flecked with grey; the deep crow's feet at the corners of his eyes and the newly-etched lines in his forehead around his mouth made him look not five years older, but ten. His hands were grotesquely swollen and tender from the endless contact with the public. 'Do you know what my father used to say? "All I want out of life is money enough to be a sucker and pay my own way." I grew up on that. Now here I am, supposedly the next mayor of New York City. How'd it happen? How?'

'You pulled the plug on the Establishment, and the people responded.'

'I pulled the plug on the Establishment, and now I'm going down with the ship.'

'What do you mean by that?'

'I don't know. I don't know what I mean any more.' He put his head back in his hands. 'God, I'm tired.'

'Don't conk out on me now. You've got a speech to give.'

'I'll give it. The crowd always turns me on. Don't worry about that.'

They sat in silence. At length Page asked, 'Can I have a vacation?'

'What?'

'Can I have some time off after tomorrow? I'd like to get away somewhere with Gelsey and Johnna. Maybe we'll go to the Caribbean or the South of France. For a while I would just like to sit in the shade with a glass of wine in my hand, watching the people dance.'

'Sure you can have some time off. You deserve it.'

There was a knock on the door, and Bobby DeStefano burst in. 'Whatta crowd! They're loving it!'

Page smiled wanly.

'How do you feel, Dev?' the young Mafioso wanted to know.

'I'm okay. Tired as hell, but okay.'

'I got a great entrance figured out for you for tonight,' Bobby enthused. 'You're going to ride out there on horseback!'

'What?'

'The Horse Show opens here tomorrow night. They got 300 horses here, and I fixed it up with a broad that you can borrow one to ride into the arena.'

Mark winced. 'Are you sure, Bobby?'

'It's a hell of an entrance! Here comes the next Mayor of New York like a knight on a white charger to save the city! Actually it's a grey charger. But what a gimmick!'

Mark thought it through and agreed. 'Come on, Dev,' Bobby urged, 'come on up and take a look at the horses.'

Exhausted as he was, Page felt a surge of new energy – the man with a weakness for horses never wearies of inspecting them. He and Mark followed Bobby out of the dressing room to a cordoned-off section of the exposition rotunda where the horses were stabled. The smell of horseflesh, hay and manure filled their nostrils, and Page's mind cast back over his years as president of the Horse Show Association. If it hadn't been for this campaign, he would be presiding over the festivities during the coming week – the various events of the hunters, the jumpers, the equitation, dressage, as well as the endless round of luncheons, dinner parties, and, of course, the great ball, to be held at the Americana Hotel on the final evening. Several of the exhibitors came up to greet the former president, and were obviously taken aback by how he had aged. Page, completely at home among the great animals, walked along the aisles, his hands clasped behind his back, enjoying a brief excursion into his past.

'Guess what horse I got for you?' Bobby said excitedly. 'Cotton Colonel. Biggest fucking horse you ever saw. Seventeen feet high, the owner told me.'

'You mean seventeen *hands* high.'

'Yeah, maybe that's it.'

'How'd you get it?'

'Met this dame from Greenwich. Tyner her name is. She was in the lobby of the Garden and we got talking. She said with your background in the Horse Show, you oughtta ride out on a horse. I asked her where could I get a horse, and she took me down here and offered to let us use Cotton Colonel. It's a fantastic idea!' Bobby looked at the candidate. 'Don't you think it's a great idea?'

Page shrugged. 'If you say so, Bobby.'

At 10.00, the Garden roustabout crew put up a series of fences around the arena, and the Foxfield Full Cries were introduced – a group from the Foxfield School of Equitation in California who would be performing at the Horse Show later in the week. Bobby had arranged for their appearance. Nine girls, ranging in age from twelve to twenty, wearing riding habits and black velvet hats, galloped out on horseback, and, with no bridles or saddles, and without touching the animals with their hands, put on a spectacular exhibition of bareback riding and jumping. At first, the 22,000 spectators were silent, and the only sound was that of the horses' hoofs on the dirt. But soon the applause built, until toward the end of the performance, the audience was on its feet cheering.

Page was standing by one of the Eighth Avenue entrances to the arena of Madison Square Garden. Towering over him was Cotton Colonel, a magnificent grey gelding, combed and curried to perfection.

'I'm going to get horsehair all over my blue suit,' Page said.

'Nobody'll notice,' Bobby said.

'How do you feel, Mr Page?' P.J. wanted to know.

'I'm okay, I guess. I just wish I could see Gelsey and Johnna one more time.'

'What the hell do you mean by that?' Bobby snapped.

Page patted the horse on the neck and swung himself into the saddle. The great beast danced slightly and then calmed down, realizing the man aboard knew what he was about. Page looked down at Bobby, Mark and P.J., and took a deep breath. He seemed distant. Out in the arena, the crowd was momentarily silent. The only sound was the *tlot-tlot-tlot* of the horses' hoofs on the dirt flooring of the Garden. Page spoke.

> And how can man die better
> Than facing fearful odds
> For the ashes of his fathers,
> And the temples of his gods?

'Is that more Kipling?' Bobby called up to him.

'Macaulay,' Page replied absently.

With that the Garden erupted with cheers and applause; the great doors swung open, and the Foxfield Full Cries cantered smartly out past Page and the small knot of campaign aides below him. The doors swung shut. Outside, the garden grounds crew was clearing the arena floor of the hurdles from the preceding act. Moments later, the vast auditorium went dark and a single blinding spotlight fell on the door through which Page was to enter. The announcer's voice boomed over the loudspeakers announcing the candidate.

The doors opened. Page shivered in the saddle and then gave Cotton Colonel a sharp dig with his heels and cantered out.

Bobby had been right. It was a spectacular entrance. With only a single white hot spotlight on him, Devereaux Page charged into the arena to be greeted by a riotous ovation of shouts and applause that seemed to split the air and rock the very walls to their foundation. He was Roy Rogers, the Lone Ranger, and the US Cavalry all rolled into one, riding forth to save the wounded, bleeding city from its fate. Page was wearing his blue striped suit with the wide lapels and nipped in at the waist, a white shirt, and his orange-and-black Princeton tie. From his highly polished black shoes to his wind-blown hair, he was a presence. He cantered once around the ring, and the lights of the Garden gradually came up. On the 31st Street side, about 2000 overhead balloons were released; each balloon had been filled with a single drop of water so that instead of drifting aimlessly about, they plummeted straight down. Cotton Colonel, with Page astride him, was standing in the centre of the ring now. There seemed to be confusion at the speaker's platform. Bobby DeStefano was grappling for the microphone shouting that no more balloons were to be released; they were supposed to come down *after* Page's speech, not now. At that point, the balloons began falling into the crowd who held up cigarettes and hat pins, causing them to *pop-pop-pop* with a dull, Chinese-firecracker sound. All at once amidst the sound of breaking balloons came the first sickening *crack* of a high-powered rifle. The first slug caught Page in the belly; he looked momentarily confused and stared down at his stomach, almost as though he had noticed a button was missing from his shirt. Just as the red stain of blood became visible against the dark blue of his suit, there was a second shot, another gut-wrenching *crack* which caught him in the chest sending him spinning off his mount and into the dirt, his left foot twisted in the stirrup. The big grey horse suddenly reared up and panicked and began prancing in fear at the strange weight pulling at him and the balloons coming at him from the ceiling. People were screaming now. Many ducked for cover, scrunching down behind their seats. Others gaped in open-mouthed horror, as the horse started running madly back and forth trying to shake loose the bloody figure caught by the foot.

The sniper fired a third shot which missed, sending a spray of dirt from the floor into the doomed man. Page was clawing weakly at the ground trying to get loose, but his ankle was in the stirrup. The animal began to run, dragging the mortally wounded candidate around the arena, leaving a trail of blood. The sniper fired again, and missed. None dared jump into the ring to try to save the dying man. Panic had set in on the audience. Many rushed for the already clogged exits, clamouring, pushing, trampling each other in blind terror. Into this throng of frightened humanity the sniper must have melted, making good his escape.

There were no more shots. Finally, out of the shrieking, howling, fear-ridden mob several men leaped into the arena and grabbed the horse, bringing him to a halt. Page lay on the ground face up, terror in his eyes, blood spurting from his chest. The first of the campaign team to reach him was Mark Altschul who pulled out a handkerchief and tried to stuff it in the wound to stop the massive spurts of blood. 'You're going to be all right, Dev,' he cried. 'You can't die. You're a noble human being!'

Page's lips went into a desperate little half grin. 'Oh, Mark,' he choked weakly, 'that sounds like a quotation.' He went suddenly limp and died.

The *Empress of Nassau* sailed from Pier 37 at 8.00 PM with 327 passengers. Two hours later she was forty miles south of Sandy Hook. From the bridge, First Officer Alissandro Pegnataro noticed a series of bright flashes from the distant Jersey shore; they reminded him of World War II and how three-inch guns looked when fired from several miles away. He focused his 10×50 Zeiss binoculars on shore. There were several more eruptions. Four seconds later he heard the muted reports. He shrugged and ordered the helmsman to steer a course of one-six-zero. Then he entered the course change and noted the explosions ashore in the ship's log.

On shore, the entire compound was afire. The force of the explosions had blown off two sides of the big house. Old Joseph DeStefano, patriarch of the family, almost managed to escape in one of the rope slings he had first installed forty years before, and had since replaced regularly every year, because of his paranoid terror of fire. But he was quite feeble now, and apparently slipped out of the harness, landing headfirst on the flagstone court below. All the servants were trapped on the third floor and either died of smoke inhalation or were roasted alive. The charred corpse of Guillamo, the DeStefano butler for twenty-five years, was found in his closet where he had fled to escape the heat.

Mia DeStefano leaped from her bedroom window into a hedge just before her own house and her father's went up in a raging inferno. There were more explosions. The pool house was blown apart, with great flaming timbers hurled into the air, some landing in the pool with a smoking, angry hiss. Suddenly the air was alive with the hysterical cries of horses. Mia catapulted herself out of the hedge where she had lain trembling and sprinted around behind the burning stucco mansion to find the little red wood stable turned into a holocaust, the five great animals trapped within, kicking and wildly whinnying. Molly Pitcher, the big mare, momentarily stuck her head through an open window, and white-eyed with terror, cried out piteously in the night before turning away, her long brown mane in flames. Still the building burned, the orange flames licking at the sky. The shrieking of the animals did not stop. Mia ran toward the stable, but was repelled by the heat. At last there was silence from within; only the vicious crackling of the fires could be heard. The smell of roasting horseflesh was mingled with that of the smoke. Mia stood, transfixed; she was silhouetted against the dancing firelight that was everywhere in the compound. A shot was fired, and the bullet caught Mia in the shoulder, toppling her into a low hedge. She remembered seeing the sky overhead; the stars were like cut glass. And then she lost consciousness.

Bobby DeStefano had planned to return to the compound immediately after Devereaux Page's speech at the Madison Square Garden rally. Accordingly, the little Bell Jet-ranger helicopter was awaiting him on the pad at the West Side Heliport at 30th Street. The moment he heard the assassin's first shot crack out over the popping of balloons, he realized he might be in mortal danger. There was no way of knowing then who had let out the contract nor who the murderer was. Others may have infiltrated the huge ampitheatre and were lying in wait for him. So at the sound of the shots, he and P.J. rushed from the speaker's platform and down into a stairwell that led into the subterranean halls and catacombs of the Garden. Pistols drawn, P.J. and Bobby moved catlike through the long concrete corridors lined with pipes and multicoloured electrical cables of red, yellow and blue, even on tiptoes, the sound of their feet echoed eerily down the empty tunnels. Each new junction was approached with extreme caution; P.J. edging up to the corner, his pistol next to his cheek ready to be punched forth, its muzzle blazing fire and death. He would peek around the corner and then motion Bobby to follow. The hallways seemed endless. They had no destination beyond trying to get as far from the scene of the shooting as possible and thence to the heliport, where the aircraft would return them to the safety of the compound. There Bobby would be in control of the communications network in his basement – a battery of telephones and radio equipment that could keep him in constant touch with operatives in any part of the world.

They came to an exit, and after cautiously proceeding up the concrete stairwell, pushed open a door to find themselves on 34th Street between 7th and 8th Avenues, directly across from Paddy's Clam House. A taxi came by; they hailed it and climbed inside. Not until they were halfway to the heliport did they at last relax a bit and slip their weapons into their coat pockets. They sat well back in the cab away from the windows so that their profiles would not be visible. P.J. was on the left; normally he always rode on Bobby's right; but when the stakes are life or death, the rules of protocol are supplanted by those of survival.

They came around the corner of 34th Street and the River and drove under the ominous black structure that was the West Side Highway. At 30th Street, the helicopter was waiting for them, red lights blinking under the cockpit and on top of the rotor, and the blinding white strobe flashing on the tail. The taxi squealed to a halt near the landing pad. P.J. peeled off a five-dollar bill and told the driver to keep the change. After a cursory glance, the two men alighted from the car and started to sprint for the safety of the small craft. They had almost reached it when a half dozen figures emerged from the shadows. The two fugitives turned to run, but it was too late. The air was alive with the ear-splitting sound of automatic weapons as they spat their white hot bullets, some of them tracers, into their targets, crunching bone, burning muscle, shredding vital organs. Even after P.J. and Bobby had fallen under the hail of fire, the bullets kept coming as the assassins walked slowly up to the two stilled bodies, squeezing off rounds. At length the shooting stopped. One of the men pulled a flashlight from his pocket and shone it on the victims. P.J. was splayed on his back, his face horribly contorted and bright red blood streaming from the corners of his gaping mouth; his mutilated skull was torn open by the barrage of fire-power, the grey brains spilling onto the concrete of the apron. The light was then shone on Bobby, who lay face down. Two of the men rolled him over. Half the young Boss's head was shot away, but clearly identifiable was the bent nose and high cheek bones. 'It's him all right,' muttered one of the men.

'Yeah,' was the grunted response. 'Let's get the fuck out of here.'

They waved to the helicopter pilot who jumped down from the cockpit and ran to join the others. A flashlight signal brought a black limousine from the far curb, where it had been inconspicuously parked in the shadows, to where they were standing over the two corpses. When it stopped, they all piled in and sped off into the night. On the pad, the helicopter waited, its lights still flashing.

The details of the Devereaux Page funeral were kept secret for obvious reasons. Only about thirty people showed up at St John's of Lattingtown Episcopal Church in Locust Valley for the service. Virtually no one from the campaign attended; the threat of reprisals made it inadvisable. As a result, there were a few old friends from the horse show circuit, along with Peggy and Stu French, Ray Kahn, and the man from the Fiduciary Trust; two cousins came from Boston, and, of course, Gelsey and Johnna, wearing black dresses and veils. They came down the aisle of the little stone church and took seats in the second pew right next to their father's coffin of polished rosewood with bronze handles and covered with a blanket of white carnations. Both had cried for two straight days and nights, but were now composed, red-eyed and numb with fatigue. Page was to be buried next to Kay, although neither of the two would have wanted to rest side-by-side for eternity.

The minister, a young man with blonde hair and rimless spectacles, appeared and everyone rose. The service began; it was virtually identical to the one held for Kay, short, literate, as only the *Book of Common Prayer* can be. It was punctuated with a single hymn which the organist played and the little congregation sang haltingly. It was Devereaux Page's favourite – Number 47:

> God of our fathers, known of old,
>   Lord of our far-flung battle-line,
> Beneath whose awful Hand we hold
>   Dominion over palm and pine –
> Lord God of Hosts, be with us yet,
> Lest we forget – lest we forget!
>
> The tumult and the shouting dies;
>   The Captains and the Kings depart:
> Still stands Thine ancient sacrifice,
>   An humble and a contrite heart.
> Lord God of Hosts, be with us yet,
> Lest we forget – lest we forget!
>
> Far-called, our navies melt away;
>   On dune and headland sinks the fire;
> Lo, all our pomp of yesterday
>   Is one with Nineveh and Tyre!
> Judge of Nations, spare us yet,
> Lest we forget – lest we forget!
>
> If, drunk with sight of power, we loose
>   Wild tongues that have not Thee in awe,
> Such boastings as the Gentiles use,
>   Or lesser breeds without, the Law –
> Lord God of Hosts, be with us yet,
> Lest we forget – lest we forget!
>
> For heathen heart that puts her trust
>   In reeking tube and iron shard,
> All valient dust that builds on dust,
>   And guarding, calls not Thee to guard,
> For frantic boast and foolish word –
> Thy mercy on Thy People, Lord!
>   Amen

NEL BESTSELLERS

Crime

T017 095	LORD PETER VIEWS THE BODY	*Dorothy L. Sayers*	40p
T026 663	THE DOCUMENTS IN THE CASE	*Dorothy L. Sayers*	50p
T021 548	GAUDY NIGHT	*Dorothy L. Sayers*	60p
T023 923	STRONG POISON	*Dorothy L. Sayers*	45p
T026 671	FIVE RED HERRINGS	*Dorothy L. Sayers*	50p
T025 462	MURDER MUST ADVERTISE	*Dorothy L. Sayers*	50p

Fiction

T018 520	HATTER'S CASTLE	*A. J. Cronin*	75p
T027 228	THE SPANISH GARDENER	*A. J. Cronin*	45p
T013 936	THE JUDAS TREE	*A. J. Cronin*	50p
T015 386	THE NORTHERN LIGHT	*A. J. Cronin*	50p
T026 213	THE CITADEL	*A. J. Cronin*	80p
T027 112	BEYOND THIS PLACE	*A. J. Cronin*	60p
T016 609	KEYS OF THE KINGDOM	*A. J. Cronin*	50p
T029 158	THE STARS LOOK DOWN	*A. J. Cronin*	£1.00
T022 021	THREE LOVES	*A. J. Cronin*	90p
T001 288	THE TROUBLE WITH LAZY ETHEL	*Ernest K. Gann*	30p
T003 922	IN THE COMPANY OF EAGLES	*Ernest K. Gann*	30p
T022 536	THE HARRAD EXPERIMENT	*Robert H. Rimmer*	50p
T022 994	THE DREAM MERCHANTS	*Harold Robbins*	95p
T023 303	THE PIRATE	*Harold Robbins*	95p
T022 986	THE CARPETBAGGERS	*Harold Robbins*	£1.00
T007 503	WHERE LOVE HAS GONE	*Harold Robbins*	90p
T023 958	THE ADVENTURERS	*Harold Robbins*	£1.00
T025 241	THE INHERITORS	*Harold Robbins*	90p
T025 276	STILETTO	*Harold Robbins*	50p
T025 268	NEVER LEAVE ME	*Harold Robbins*	50p
T025 292	NEVER LOVE A STRANGER	*Harold Robbins*	90p
T022 226	A STONE FOR DANNY FISHER	*Harold Robbins*	80p
T025 284	79 PARK AVENUE	*Harold Robbins*	75p
T027 945	THE BETSY	*Harold Robbins*	90p
T020 894	RICH MAN, POOR MAN	*Irwin Shaw*	90p
T017 532	EVENING IN BYZANTIUM	*Irwin Shaw*	60p
T021 025	THE MAN	*Irving Wallace*	90p
T020 916	THE PRIZE	*Irving Wallace*	£1.00
T027 082	THE PLOT	*Irving Wallace*	£1.00

Historical

T022 196	KNIGHT WITH ARMOUR	*Alfred Duggan*	50p
T022 250	THE LADY FOR RANSOM	*Alfred Duggan*	50p
T017 958	FOUNDING FATHERS	*Alfred Duggan*	50p
T022 625	LEOPARDS AND LILIES	*Alfred Duggan*	60p
T023 079	LORD GEOFFREY'S FANCY	*Alfred Duggan*	60p
T024 903	THE KING OF ATHELNEY	*Alfred Duggan*	60p
T020 169	FOX 9: CUT AND THRUST	*Adam Hardy*	30p
T021 300	FOX 10: BOARDERS AWAY	*Adam Hardy*	35p
T023 125	FOX 11: FIRESHIP	*Adam Hardy*	35p
T024 946	FOX 12: BLOOD BEACH	*Adam Hardy*	35p

Science Fiction

T016 900	STRANGER IN A STRANGE LAND	*Robert Heinlein*	75p
T020 797	STAR BEAST	*Robert Heinlein*	35p
T017 451	I WILL FEAR NO EVIL	*Robert Heinlein*	80p
T026 817	THE HEAVEN MAKERS	*Frank Herbert*	35p
T027 279	DUNE	*Frank Herbert*	90p
T022 854	DUNE MESSIAH	*Frank Herbert*	60p
T023 974	THE GREEN BRAIN	*Frank Herbert*	35p
T012 859	QUEST FOR THE FUTURE	*A. E. Van Vogt*	35p
T015 270	THE WEAPON MAKERS	*A. E. Van Vogt*	30p
T023 265	EMPIRE OF THE ATOM	*A. E. Van Vogt*	40p
T027 473	THE FAR OUT WORLDS OF A. E. VAN VOGT		
		A. E. Van Vogt	50p

NEL BESTSELLERS